Also by the author:

The God in Flight

Published by Lethe Press
lethepressbooks.com

ISBN: 978-1-59021-718-4

Guilty Parties

Tales of Infatuation and Menace

Laura Argiri

LETHE PRESS

In memory of Monroe Engel.
Ave atque vale.

Contents

Milltown

Purple

Tansy's been whipped once this week for sneaking out of the Baptist church and sneaking in with the Catholics, who have prettier windows. Mam went wild on her for that. Now Tansy's sweating, and her whipped legs sting. Tansy's lying in wait. She read about *lying in wait* in a story, an English story in a book at school, about a highwayman. That's an English robber who, naturally, robbed people on the roads. He jumped out from behind walls and bushes with a thing called a cudgel. The story didn't say what a cudgel looks like, and Tansy hasn't got one, so she'll make do with what she's got.

Tansy crouches in the bushes by the dye ditch. Stifling shade, only May but oppressive at three in the afternoon. *Oppressive* is also an English story word, for *hot*. Gravel digs into her shins.

This patch of scrub woods has no name. A path cuts through it, an easy way from her house on Gin Street to the grammar school. The mill's dye ditch also runs through these woods. The dye ditch has a wild reek; sometimes even the air blowing over it burns her nose, but it runs in glorious colors, rivers of church-glass. When it froze back near Christmas, it didn't smell and was the prettiest thing in town, in Tansy's opinion, far better than the Christmas tree the Baptists put up. While the freeze lasted, Tansy came here often to look at the frozen rainbow in the sharp winter sun.

Today the dye ditch runs purple. Purple is a church color as well as her favorite one. Maybe they've been making clothes for Lent, or saints.

Tansy lies in wait for Johnny because he killed her cat. He left Snowflake where Tansy would find her. Tansy tried to wake Snowflake up, but the dead cat flopped like he'd broken every bone in her, and her long white fur was sopping with blood, still warm when Tansy found her. There was blood from her pretty pink mouth, her nose.

Why? Maybe because Tansy won the spelling bee, as she wins most prize things at school. Or because she gave Johnny a bloody nose when he tried to kiss her on Valentine's Day and kept trying to put his hands on her on the sly, and the last time he tried, she bit him. She's eight, too young to want any truck with boys, even nice ones. It's on account of something about boys that people call her sister Clary a slut now, though Clary seems just the same to Tansy.

Once Tansy finished crying, she'd found a trowel and buried her cat, wrapped up in one of Mam's lace dresser scarves that Mam hasn't discovered missing yet. Anyone would be right if they guessed she didn't tell Mam about Snowflake; if she had, Mam might have quarreled with Johnny's mother, maybe screamed herself into one of her sick headaches, and that would've made Papa mad. "Cassie making a spectacle of herself one more time," he'd say, and get drunk and mean. Or, more likely, Mam would have just said, "That cat was a nuisance," and kept crocheting. That would have hurt worse than just burying the cat here in the woods and crying in the dark under the porch. Mam never cares if she's hurtful.

Mam's family used to have a plantation before the War, which means Mam is a lady. Mam sews dresses and underclothing for her daughters and cooks but won't otherwise do housework. Tansy and her sisters straighten and clean, wash the floors and dishes, and chop the stovewood. The cooking is Mam's one concession to the real lives they live. A black laundress washes the clothes she makes. Mam does the dressmaking because she enjoys it, and she's smart at it. She brings in money that way. She can make any dress from seeing a picture of it, and she can embroider and crochet and make lace. As Cassie's youngest, Tansy wears Clary and Annie's hand-me-downs, but Mam makes a few new dresses for Tansy because of her looks. Clary and Annie are ordinary girls; Tansy's a pretty one. When Mam's in a fine mood, ***beautiful.*** She wants people to notice Tansy. She always sends Tansy to church in a clean and ironed dress, her white-gold hair well-brushed and tied back with ribbons. Above her green eyes, her pale brows are darkened with a burnt match.

"Damn," Tansy tells the gravel and the dye ditch. Then she almost puts off what she has planned because of one of those dresses that Mam made for her. Mam put her in it because today had been poem-recitation day at school. Just cotton but ladylike and pretty: cream with dainty mauve flowers, with a lace frill at the neck and rows of tucking down her flat little chest. Mam had braided her hair and tied her plaits up with mauve ribbon to match and said that none of the rich people in the big houses had a child half as pretty.

After today, this dress won't ever be the same.

Tansy decides *it cannot be helped,* also storybook words. She needs to strike while she's this mad, this brave. At least she's not wearing stockings and shoes to ruin too, since it's warm enough to go barefoot.

In her right hand is a perfect rock, a rock that fits her grip. It has a smooth side for her palm, and the sharp side's for Johnny. Johnny walks this way home. He's in fifth grade, so he's not let out until three, and he might linger with the other boys and play stickball, but he'll come. All she has to do is wait.

He comes loping past, heading for the planks that make the dye ditch's bridge. He's got an apple and a little knife, peeling it. Tansy connects the knife and her poor red cat. She spits a little on her right palm to make it stick and gets a perfect grip on her rock.

She means to make it sudden, and she does. Like her cat... Snow was a good mouser. She'd hunker down, very still, then spring and catch rabbits, squirrels, big rats. Tansy waits until Johnny's on the shaky plank bridge over the dye ditch, and then...

Tansy leaps on Johnny's back, and down they both go, splash, in the purple! Her thin tight legs hold him down, and she leans on his neck with her left hand before he knows who's got him, much less why. She beats on his head with her rock: one, two, three, four! And more, and others! She holds his head down. Bubbles come up through the purple murk.

The air over the dye scalds her throat. Of all the mill's colors, the sumptuous purple smells worst. And the dye stings her whipped legs so... that might be the reason she lets him up. She might not have stopped otherwise. Maybe not until his head was pulped like her cat.

She climbs out and lets him crawl up into the dirt. Blood's coming from both ears and his nose. He's gulping and heaving and bawling; he's swallowed some, he wants to spit it up, he's heaving up both red and purple.

He looks at her with terror. Not even at a hanging has she seen anyone so scared!

And the two of them are purple! They'll both get whipped for ruining their clothes, maybe whipped double for fighting. Her eyes and lungs and nostrils feel like she's sucked down fire. Everywhere she's got even a scratch, she glows molten with purple pain.

He doesn't ask why, but she tells him. "You know damn well what that's for!" She takes a step toward him, and he cringes back. He's blubbering, his hands go up to shield his face, and it smells like he shat his britches... "This'll be worth it," Tansy thinks, "even when Mam gets hold of me."

She clutches her rock in her good right hand in case he gets ideas. She thinks she'll keep this rock. If she ever comes up against any other boy with ideas, that one can get a dose of her rock too. Not like it's going to wear out.

She watches him crawl away and somehow get his feet under him and limp off home. She picks up his knife, which is now her knife. That could come in handy too.

That boy's going to be purple where her rock got him even when that dye washes off. He's not going to tell anyone a little mill girl in the third grade did this to him.

A little purple girl! She's purple too, even her hair! And her legs feel so hot that she thinks of that girl some king set on fire for wearing britches, seeing angels, and leading an army like a man.

Silver

Under the moon and the silken dry wind, Tyrell fell asleep on the slope between Bolton Street and the road. That Friday night's liquor came from a strong batch: smoke that poured, kind fire. The moon was so full and bright that it made Milltown pretty, like snow did. He wouldn't have stayed asleep long in May because it would've gotten too cold, or in July because the wet heat would have descended along with the mosquitoes. In June, though, he flopped on the grass and was gone.

He woke all cool and silvered, and there she was in the road—the kid. Walking in her sleep.

He knew her family—Perrins, mill folks. Chase Perrin was an ugly drunk; Cassie Perrin put on airs. Cassie, who claimed her family used to own a plantation back in the day, sat on the Perrin porch crocheting and made her daughters do all the housework but the washing. Momma said that Cassie hadn't fallen as far as she claimed.

"Miss Cass's folks," said Tyrell's mother, "maybe they had a farm, and a few hogs, and a field hand or two before the war. Or maybe they ain't never even had that. Folks tell these stories often enough, they start believing 'em."

Tyrell's mother was underpaid for washing the sweat and grime out of white people's clothes and the blood out of their women's drawers. She did the Perrins' laundry. If you washed people's clothes, you knew their smells and everything else about them. One of those things Momma knew was that Clary, the middle Perrin sister, had become a woman at the young age of eleven. Momma seemed to think that made Clary a tramp there and then, and Clary had gone on pretty soon to prove her right.

Tyrell wondered if the white people had any notion how the laundresses talked. The grown white people were fair game, but Tyrell hated nasty talk about the children. Black or white, children were helpless. Slandering children was godless. "Clary couldn't help bleeding," Tyrell had thought. "Ain't like a girl can help something like that."

And Tansy Perrin, too young to be a tramp, could not help being a sleepwalker, and here she was, alone in the road in a thin white nightgown, her long straight hair a silver-blonde flag down her back. Tyrell had seen her downtown, barefoot in the summer, in a wash-faded dress that his mother's hands had ironed. She was cleaner than most of the mill children and carried herself with straight-backed assurance, as if she saw no defeat in the road before her. Her hair would have made her different anyway; those silvery-white blondes were rare. Her face was pretty too, its small features so fine, its wide eyes startlingly green.

Tyrell had the impulse to lift Tansy off her feet and carry her gently to her own doorstep on Gin Street. Before setting her down, he'd look at her face up close and feel her hair on his bare arm. He'd never have that chance again. If she grew into a good woman, a girl with Tansy's looks would marry above her beginnings, maybe a factory line boss or store clerk rather than a mill man. If she went bad and worked at a cathouse, Tyrell would never get his hands on such a choice white whore even for a whole week's wages.

Then he came awake as if he'd never had the 'shine. *Never mind about touching her, she better not even see you. If she wakes up and you scare her,* his brain said, *you're one dead black man. You won't have to lay a finger on her to get strung up.* On the other hand, if she came to any harm wandering around, and that would be easy—roaming dogs, roaming men—he'd be in the crosshairs that way too, a drunk black man out under the midnight moon. Tyrell's mother had told him often, since he turned twelve, that white people imagined all black men lived and breathed to put their hands on white women and stick their peckers in them, even tramps. Momma had things to say about Tansy too: "Hoo-eee! That one's gonna make trouble whether she wants to or not! When that one's old enough, every color of man's gonna want to get his hands on her."

Tyrell's eyes agreed this was true. As the kid meandered in the road, Tyrell thought that yes, when she was five years older, her twig legs would be flower stems and every man under a hundred and forty would wonder if the floss between them was as pale as the hair of her head. The mystery of prettiness... the soles of her bare feet were probably tough as his boots, but the feet themselves were somehow pretty, and even now, so were the thin mosquito-bitten legs. She was pretty from the crown of her head to her dirty toes.

This was exactly how he should never think, even about grown white women. *I didn't think that,* he told the moon. But the moon was the mistress of all mischief by and for women, not anyone's friend.

At a distance of about half a block, he followed Tansy Perrin. They went past the rental houses on Hillsdale Street, to Main Street and the town's one bar. Tansy smacked the glass of its door. Tyrell had seen her do just that by daylight and yell inside: "Papa! Mam says come out of there now!" *That's trash for you,* Tyrell had thought, *sending a little girl to holler a worthless man out of a barroom.* Then Tansy turned; in her dream, Chase Perrin either came out of the bar or didn't, and she turned toward Gin Street and home, perhaps with the dream-Chase weaving and cursing in her wake. Tyrell slunk into the shadows so she wouldn't see him if she woke. If she did, she'd shriek the moon down.

It was the slowest time he remembered, the slowest he ever would know, hiding from that little girl while watching her home. He could hear every pebble that turned beneath his feet. An owl called, and Tansy paused, not too far from her parents' house, as if she felt someone around—when she turned and seemed to look around her, when she seemed wide awake, when she froze. Then she seemed to decide to be asleep—that if she was asleep, she wouldn't have seen him and maybe he wouldn't have seen her. He understood that cringing hope: *maybe if this, then not that, and not worse.* But she'd lost her indirection, and when she neared her doorstep, with the screen door flapping open just as she'd left it, she darted indoors.

Tyrell didn't sleep any more that night; he prayed that nothing would happen. And nothing did, not the next day or the next or after, and the leaden fear that had settled on him finally lifted. And finally he'd wonder, "But what'll she ever think of that, or say? I just watched her safe home, and nothing happened."

Cottage Industry

Snow is rare here, fragile as a wedding dress. I love snow—I've lived in places with the long white winters this place lacks—but here we don't get much. Looking out into the tangerine light of this January sunset over our silent street, I realize what else we lack: that *scunch* of feet on snow that lets you know someone's approaching. Fair warning—I like that too.

LaLoma and her mother and sister usually did approach on foot, from the nearby bus stop. They'd be on the front porch ringing the bell before we could retreat to the back of the house and pull the curtains and pretend no one was home. I hated that about them. When they did turn up, we stopped whatever we were doing and fed them their next meal, and Grandma found out what else they needed and gave it to them. They had aborted many of our shopping trips and treks to the park, blighted many a Saturday, and that was reason enough for me to dread them. Were they poor, I wondered, and that was why we had to feed them? Back then you could still see hunger in the slums and the sticks down here: slack-faced people whose joints seemed large under their pasty skin. But LaLoma and her mother and sister were tall and fat, LaLoma especially. Her mighty thighs seemed like weapons, her whole body a bouncy battering ram. She was always radish-red in the face, as if perpetually furious above her big smiles. She was ruddy when she turned up that winter afternoon, chap-cheeked and underdressed: just a jacket over her shirt and tight Capri pants, big bare calves, sneakers and socks.

"Got to let her in, she's family," Grandma said, as I scowled.

I'd put in my eight hours at school and meant not to spend the rest of my waking hours bored. I wanted to sprawl by the fire, read, and sink deep into my own head. I wanted to listen to *Swan Lake* on Grandma's new record player; I wanted to dream of tremendous winters in the Russia of my imagination, sledding and skating and sequined nights of snow, ballerinas swept up after their curtain calls into the czar's sleigh. LaLoma would linger until supper, after supper, until she got what she wanted and the day was worn down to a numb nub. After LaLoma finally slouched off to catch the last cross-town bus, Grandma would be withdrawn and grim.

"But I don't like her," I whined.

"I don't either, but what can we do? They're our blood," said Grandma, and worked her way upright to hobble to the door. Grandma was a cutting, unrelenting snob about some modes of misbehavior, despite her hardscrabble beginnings, and she encouraged me to be the same. She used the harshest terms: *worse than a low-down dirty dog. Tramp, lowlife, trash, slut.* Along with her contempt for her disreputable kin, though, was an unhappy loyalty. When they shambled up her porch steps, her expression did not say *Welcome.* It said *What fresh hell...?* But she opened her door.

"Why did her mom name her LaLoma?" I persisted.

"It's a trashy name, all right," Grandma admitted. Trashiness and avoiding the slightest hint of it were hot concerns for us Milltown strivers. According to Grandma, trashy names usually involved some ignorant attempt at fanciness: all those LaWandas and LaRhondas and LaVernes and LaRues named in the optimistic postwar years by mothers who wanted to raise starlets. "June Louise never did know much," my grandmother allowed reluctantly. June Louise was Grandma's sister, the one who'd conceived and birthed and named the thunderous LaLoma.

I wasted my breath a little more: "LaLoma's mean." When I was younger, LaLoma had liked to point out violent deeds and the characters doing them on TV and tell me, "I'll make them come get you!" She'd smile. I knew TV show events weren't real, on one hand, but I also knew her threat was a cruel, mean-minded tease. Normal grownups didn't go out of their way to scare children who weren't even bothering them. That one wanted to make a fraidy-cat out of me and make me scared of a television set.

"She's ignorant, I never said she wasn't. They all are. Now go put some cookies on a plate," said Grandma. When she had let LaLoma in and herded us all to the kitchen, she put the coffee on.

"So, what is it now?" she asked our guest.

"Does it have to be anything?" LaLoma shrugged and took two cookies. "Just wanted to drop in on my Auntie Sue Marie. I'm going to see someone on Vale Street, and you're on the way. You still got that crochet bedspread I like? Can I have that after you're dead?"

"I'm feeling just fine," Grandma assured her, and chunked wood into her woodstove. The hungry winter fire seized it.

"I said when you're dead."

"I'm not going anywhere anytime soon—I'm not the one running around outside half-naked and begging God to give me pneumonia. It's not even thirty degrees out there. Haven't you got some long pants to wear?"

LaLoma shrugged. "I'm not cold. Hot-blooded, that's me."

Maybe boiling blood explained why she was always so red. Her flaming face and blonde hair clashed. The blonde was real, sunny honey. That hair didn't seem to belong to her. It seemed that she ought to have gotten it some lying, sneaky way, but Grandma had confirmed that nothing from a bottle was involved. "That hair's Loma's little bit of good luck," Grandma had said. "Just about all the good luck she ever had."

Maybe her natural insulation kept LaLoma warm; she was even fatter than when last seen. I hated to be in the same room with LaLoma's fat, which looked contagious. The sight made me feel that something was expanding sneakily under my skin. I knew about periods and tits and the big butts of grown women, which they crammed into strangling girdles. I would have sold my small queasy soul to attain adult height and power without all those adult afflictions if only I'd known how to make the deal. It seemed like you could catch them, blood and bags of jouncing fat fore and aft, just from being in the room with that woman and her sweat. Now that I was taking ballet lessons, I knew how important it was not to be like that!

LaLoma probably knew I hated her, if not exactly why.

For my part, I knew that LaLoma's mother, June Louise, had once defrauded her own sister, my Grandma, by altering a check for a loan of fifty dollars. That sounds small, a scanty week's groceries for a little household, in 2015. In 1960, though, fifty dollars was a substantial sum. June Louise had made it even more substantial by changing $50.00 to $150.00. June Louise might not have known much, but she knew how to commit fraud, and she knew that my grandmother wouldn't turn her in for it.

"You gotta put up with 'em, they're family," was all Grandma would say.

Now LaLoma's eyes were on me—like her hair, eyes I thought she shouldn't have had, pool-blue and gold-lashed. If she hadn't always looked like she was thinking about doing something hateful, I'd have admired her eyes. Was she mad at herself for the flopping tits, the curved jelly gut? She never tried to hide any of it.

"You still stuck up, Lizzie?"

"Yeah." *Stuck up* was LaLoma's term for people who did not like to be teased, called names, poked, pawed, or tickled. "And no one calls me *Lizzie*," I thought. If I'd said that aloud, LaLoma would have battened on my name and crowed—*Dizzylizziebusytizzy, stuck up!*

"Want to go for a walk with me? I'll buy you a treat."

"There's no place around here that sells stuff for kids," I said.

"Go on," urged Grandma, the treacherous thing, probably wanting a tot of something alcoholic to enjoy alone. To celebrate not being hit up for a handout yet, perhaps, or get numb for when she did get hit up. "Take a little walk with Loma. It won't hurt you any."

So I did.

It was not a long walk, barely three minutes. Right before twilight, the evening light had caramelized on the horizon, and it was far colder than when I came in after school. Lamplight, whiskey-gold, bloomed in some of the little windows. Our shoes, small loafers and big sneakers, made sneaky, gritty sounds on the sidewalk.

There was no one around to see me poke the enemy with a pointed stick, so I did. "It's nasty how you come over here and tell Grandma the stuff you want when she's dead."

"Well, how's she gonna know if I don't say nothing?"

"You sound like you're going to be glad when she's dead. And I won't let you take her stuff." Without Grandma to urge me in the direction of charity and niceness, I didn't go there.

"You ain't gonna be able to not let me."

"Will too. I'll change the locks." That was what people did when a thief had gotten their keys, a fun fact from television. "She only lets you in because you're related, and she says you're pitiful." Grandma meant *pathetic*, a notion I couldn't connect with LaLoma. For a fourth grader, *scary* and *pathetic* have no overlap. "She says we have to put up with you. But when I'm grown, I won't."

That was sass, and something more than sass. It should have made LaLoma hostile. The wheedling tone she took instead puzzled me. "Don't be mean," she coaxed me. "This is my friend Sadie we're going to see. Be sweet and I'll buy you something."

I was about to point out that the Dixie Drug was the only store anywhere near here, and not all that near, and that it closed at five, and that LaLoma's normal reason for visiting was getting some of Grandma's ready cash, not spending her own. But we were already at Sadie's place.

Sadie's house was small, like all the houses on Vale Street. Its tiny yard had the draggled grass and dead flowers we have here instead of snow, plus a concrete baby angel—one of those cheap yard-statues that go with genteel poverty. When we entered, though, there wasn't the camphorated reek that went up your nose when you opened most front doors in our neighborhood, Milltown. That was the mill smell, liniment—people who worked in the Erwin mill and basted themselves with liniment to tamp down the pain from continuous repetitive motion at the roaring machines. Inside, Sadie's home looked more prosperous than I'd have guessed. Her front room was warm and very neat, without scattered newspapers. Her couch and chair were rose velour. The ash trays were empty and clean, as if Sadie expected company. A frilly pink lamp and a curtain of rainbow beads over one door were the only memorable features. There were no Jesus pictures; most living rooms in our neighborhood had several. There were friendly winter smells of wood smoke and oil heat and an undertone of country ham and biscuits.

"Sadie, this is Lizzie," LaLoma told her friend, an unremarkable old woman in a flowery house dress and a cardigan. I'd seen that old lady in the grocery store.

"Elizabeth," I said. Grandma had told me mine was a refined name, a name for a lady, after a saint in the Bible.

"Here, take off your coat," said Sadie.

"It's okay. I'm not staying long." I didn't know why I was here in the first place, but I had no plan to linger.

"You'll catch a cold if you sit in a hot room in a coat," urged Sadie, and somehow I was shrugging out of my coat. She looked me up and down as if she found something fascinating about my clothing: red pullover, sweater tights for cold weather, scratchy skirt of gray wool. My hair was ordinary brown, but it was lush then, almost long enough to sit on. Sadie admired the only striking part of me and said she could tell someone took good care of it.

"It's Grandma," I said. "Grandma Sue Marie does that. She shampoos it every week and puts Avon conditioner on it."

Sadie's expression changed, as if something I'd said was a surprise, though not a good one. However, she smiled—"Oh, you're Sue Marie's grandbaby! Didn't know you right off. You've grown. I buy my Avon from your grandma," said Sadie. Then she offered me a honey bun and joined LaLoma in the kitchen. They spoke in secret voices, but the little house kept the sound close and clear. My skin felt strange, as if someone had seen me naked. I thought I heard, "old Clarence that runs the dry-cleaning shop" and "what he really likes" and "five hundred, and you can gimme twenty-five percent," from LaLoma.

"How old is that kid?" asked Sadie, impatient—perhaps disgusted.

"Twelve," LaLoma said quickly. "Lizzie's twelve."

"Nine," I told them. "And it's Elizabeth."

"Okay, so she's tall for her age!" LaLoma seemed to find something important in the ritual query about kids' ages. Sadie hadn't bothered with the other half of it, about where I went to school.

Sadie crossed her arms over her breasts and shook her head. "Nine! And she's Sue Marie Swain's granddaughter, and Sue Marie's right there on Swallow Street, and I've told you time and time again about not shitting where you eat. Sometimes I don't know what goes through that fat head of yours!"

LaLoma protested in a hiss of whispers. Her chins quivered.

The old girl still shook her head. "Nine! I wouldn't touch her with a ten-foot pole. Too young!"

LaLoma weighed in yet again. She wanted something badly, but Sadie was having none of it.

"You need money? Make some yourself. Not like you ain't got what it takes. The men love those big fat tits. I'll fix it up for you." Then came a fervent warning: "But don't you ever mess me up with Sue Marie, girl. If you ever get Sue Marie on my tail, that's the last day you'll work here, and that's a promise. I know Sue Marie from school—it took a fool to tangle with Sue Marie, even then. I remember when Tansy Perrin called June Louise a whore. That wasn't right—your poor mama didn't sell her honeypie, she let 'em have it for free. June Louise never did have any business sense. But Sue Marie wasn't letting anyone insult her big sister. Sue Marie wasn't as big as a skeeter, but she scratched up Tansy's face and yanked out a handful of Tansy's pretty yellow hair from the front, where it showed. Served Tansy right. Even back then, Tansy prissed around with her nose in the air. But Tansy comes from mill people too, and that man she married ain't right in the head. Looks like a movie star, but that fella's got shit for brains. And if you don't have shit for brains too, you'll keep your hands off Sue Marie's granddaughter and not take her to any house like this one. Or they'll have to wash what's left of you off the floor with a hose when Sue Marie gets done with you."

"Aunt Sue Marie puts up with all Ma's shit." A sullen, defeated protest.

"Sue Marie's sorry for your mama. But I bet she ain't all that sorry for you, girl. Call me when you're ready to work, and don't bring kids like that one around here."

LaLoma wouldn't let the topic go. "Well, what kind you got in mind?"

"The kind with mamas like yours!" Sadie told her, and I did hear disgust then. "Ain't you got any sense? Sue Marie's got custody of that kid, she ain't letting that crazy daughter of hers raise her grandbaby, and she don't let that kid run loose like you and your sister did. She prob'ly makes her do her homework first thing after school. I heard she's sending her to dancing school. She has plans for that little girl. Look for the ones nobody's got plans for. You ought to know 'em when you see 'em. Now take Elizabeth straight back to Sue Marie's."

LaLoma took me straight back. "Sadie says you're not pretty, not good for anything," she told me on the way.

That wasn't what I'd heard, though I didn't argue. Now I know what there was to fear. Then I just felt fear, a cool, bright knife, and knew it for an accurate emotion. I thought it was stupid of Grandma to let LaLoma into her house, and that her crass nagging for that coverlet after Grandma was dead was the least of it.

Grandma brightened when I trailed in alone. "Did she go on home, then? Good. You can take off that skirt and hang it up so it don't wrinkle, then practice while I cook supper. Turn your feet out like Miss Rose told you. Hold your stomach in tight."

I wanted to say that the visit had been scary but could not have explained why or even formed my questions in my head, and Grandma had small patience with vagueness. I took off my scratchy skirt and hung it up, put on my soft ballet slippers, and moved one of the kitchen chairs into the hall to use as my barre. I put on my practice record, and slow Chopin mingled with the kitchen clash and sizzle. I gripped the back of the chair, turned my feet out as far as they'd go, and started my pliés. A couple of years later, Grandma would hire a man to nail up an old stair railing for a barre.

*

Grandma's dead now, and Sadie is too. Like most houses around here, Sadie's house has been redone, its history gentrified out of sight. It has blonde bamboo floors, ceiling fans, clever compact cabinets, and a Bosch washer and dryer. The walls are painted in postmodern designer colors: Sky, Clay, Ice. The realtor's flyer, designed to make people feel brilliant for overspending, details it all in luscious language. The home stagers put in lamps and left them on at night while the house was for sale. People passing saw sweet amber light in the new windows and pooled on the new flowerbeds, the April-green turf. If you lingered in the twilight, you couldn't resist imagining yourself in there, sovereign of all that compact slicked-up deliciousness. That four-room house sold for $243,000. The new owner surely doesn't know that an old lady once ran a cottage-industry whorehouse there, behind a door veiled in twinkly beads. Yet I have to give Sadie credit for equal attention to the importance of appearances. Viewed from the sidewalk back then, her house had appeared as sad and respectably poor as any other on the block. Nothing about its outside would have interested anyone, even a paranoid vice cop.

Rather than getting lamed at the mill like most of Milltown, Sadie had put her skills and the assets of others to work in less wearing ways. She probably got quietly, modestly rich and made sure that no one ever suspected as much. Nothing about that scenario would trouble me if Sadie's pocket prostitution venture had involved only consenting adults, but it hadn't. LaLoma brought little girls to Sadie, some disgusting man paid Sadie $500.00 for the chance to rape a child, and LaLoma got her cut. She and Sadie had been so easy with the topic that I have no doubt—what might have happened to me there had happened there many times to other kids, slightly older and not as lucky.

I go by that sleek, freshly Pottery-Barned little house often. Sometimes the owners' daughter is playing, safe behind the gated white picket fence. I remember what I escaped. The media's full of it now: pedophiles, child trafficking. That buzz started when Madeleine McCann evaporated from a resort in Portugal. And right here in Milltown, back when the Beatles still sang over the radio, how many times did LaLoma collect her finder's fee for a little girl Sadie didn't consider too young? While Sadie and LaLoma did their specialty business, I had been watching television, or playing in my fantasy snow in the Russia of my imagination, or yawning through my homework half a block away. What would my fierce Grandma Sue Marie have done if she'd known what her niece got up to with her neighbor? Would that information have trumped pity and blood and made Grandma call the police?

Now Grandma's house is mine, and it's gentrified too, with all the conveniences between its vanilla-cream walls, and pretty birch flooring, and a real barre. I guess I'm gentrified along with it, as Grandma Sue Marie planned; I teach ballet at Rose's Studio of Dance. We teach all levels, from pre-dance and creative movement on Monday afternoons through pointe on Fridays. This is my niche. I have nice proportions but bad feet, the kind that the rehearsal schedule of a professional ballet company would shred, though Gaynor-Minden pointe shoes with hard shanks make Fridays easier on me. I am safe from the mill-future Grandma feared for me as well as from dirtier dangers than any she imagined.

I can imagine LaLoma jeering: *You were s'posed to be hot shit, Lizzie, why're you teaching in that dumb hick town dance school?*

If LaLoma ever turned up here, I'd have questions for her too. I'd ask her how many little girls she'd found for Sadie to rent out to the local pervs. That may be one reason the overheated troll doesn't appear to claim that bedspread. There's also that I'd rip her a new hole to monetize if she set her feet on my porch, though I have no idea if she's still in town. Someone like LaLoma could be anywhere—dead, or still selling her crotch, or in jail somewhere under another name.

English Basement and Two Tansys

I did not say *look, little stupid, we could be hauled into court, we could lose our jobs at the damn mill, you could have lost our house for us, our house that I work from dawn to dusk to pay the mortgage on, our car, everything I work for so that people don't look at us like we're white trash, everything I slave to provide for us. We might've had to move in with my sister and that worthless drunk she married. What I hope for you would have already been over. Not just hard, impossible. The worst could have happened, the very worst.*

No, I didn't say that. I took Claudette, already blubbering, by the shoulders. "Now, you be quiet," I told her. "You're not going to say that, hear? You're not going to say anything about it to anyone, ever. Do you understand what Mama's saying to you?"

"But what if—"

"I said *not ever.* If anyone asks you, you don't understand what they're saying. So you don't say anything. Because you don't know anything." *Just look stupid,* I think. *You do that just fine.*

"But—"

"Do you remember when Sadie called you across the street, and I'd told you time and time again that you don't cross the street without me, not ever, but Sadie called you and you went right into the road like you never heard a word of what I said?"

Claudette gulps and nods. I don't believe in hitting children. That time Claudette crossed the road was the only time I ever used my hands on her. She was just two and a half, too little to have good sense, but I needed to teach her, and teach her for good. So I cut a switch and took her by her dress tail and whipped her all the way home, slow. I meant for every step to sting. She screamed every inch of the way, but by the time I had her at our steps, she'd given up and stopped pulling, stopped trying to run; she'd broken and was just letting me whip her. When I had her safe in the house, I went back to Sadie's. I let Sadie know that if she ever called my baby across that street again, Sadie could expect to get the next whipping, and I'd beat the skin off those fat legs of hers. I cried over the streaks on my baby's skin that night, but I had to teach her. She learned not to cross the road, not to go anywhere without me. When I'd caught my breath, I thought how strange that had been. When my Mam took a switch to me, I jigged and kicked and yelled my pretty head off. If Mam was going to whip me, at least I made hard work of it! One time I bit her and drew blood and got whipped double. Point is, though, I didn't just stand there and take it. When Mam was in her coffin right here in this room, I could see the scar from my teeth in her arm.

Claudette's eight now. I am not threatening her with a whipping this time. It's beyond her to imagine how much worse than a whipping this could be if anyone finds out.

And when I think of what I went through to get this child! I didn't want a man messing up my house, but I wanted a child, so I had to marry. Claudette's father isn't the sharpest knife. I picked him because he was a handsome looker and I knew he'd never hit me. He's sweet and has no get-up-and-go, a harmless man but not smart. With men, far as I've seen, *harmless* is as good as it ever gets. She's not as smart as she'd be if I'd picked her a smarter father. But I didn't want the risk of a smarter man, smart enough to be angry about the life we'd have to lead and what we wouldn't have unless we were careful every minute and never made a mistake. A smart man like that might know enough to be furious with the Erwin family that owns the mill we work at and with the government that wants us poor and low. A smart man with a temper might beat on me since he couldn't get at the Erwins or the government. Or take to drink. I didn't want a man smart enough to see how far the unfairness really goes and turn into an ugly drunk. He's a sweet man, my husband, but there's this look he's got, peaceful and dumb like a cow. I have both him and Claudette to think for, and I do it.

"Do you know that Mama wasn't supposed to have babies?" I ask next. Claudette shakes her head. "Well, I wasn't. The doctors all said I shouldn't, but I wanted you. It was dangerous for me. They had to break a bone in my belly and take you out, and you had broken ribs, but I got both of us out alive. You wouldn't be in this world except for me, and Mama might have died." When they cracked that bone, I thought I had died. Later on, lying flat on that hospital bed while it grew back, I wished I had. "I risked everything for you," I tell Claudette. "And we had to pay the hospital a lot of money." So much that I had to scrimp for five years before I could make a down payment on a house and get a mortgage. We had to rent while I was paying off that hospital for Claudette. "Now you need to do just what Mama says, every time. Now what are you going to say if anyone asks you?"

She just shakes her head.

"That's right. And there's nothing to say, because nothing happened anyhow. And you're never going to do anything stupid again. If anybody tries to fight with you, you tell Mama, and Mama will settle their hash, but you don't fight back. And you're going to do exactly what Mama says, everything, every time, from here on out."

She nods. She doesn't say a word.

"That's good. Now stop crying. Forget about it. No, there's nothing you've got to forget, because nothing happened. Nothing you know anything about. Go play."

*

"There were some little girls who slipped away from the class on the play-yard at recess, and the teacher wasn't watching them, and that little Millie Jarvis fell down a wall to the basement and hurt her head," I tell my husband, Claude, when he asks. "I told Claudette she's got to always stay with her class, not listen to some bad little girl who wants to slip away and do something stupid. Claudette's a good girl, she understands." Either not interested or not wanting to be, my husband nods, and that's the end of that, at least as far as anything said out loud in this house. It's like we take what we know about that little girl and tie it to a big rock and throw it in the deep ocean. It goes down, under the waves, where the long dark is.

Little Millie never woke up to say how she fell off that wall. Her brain bled and drowned in blood, and she died. She never knew anything. We can do worse than to die in our sleep, in our innocence. People talk about the death and the funeral all over Southdown, but not here.

There's one close call when a busybody from the other church, the Methodist one, asks my girl if it's true, if she really did it. My child gapes like a fish on a hook, and I nearly grab her by the upper arm, but that won't look right; I stop myself and take Claudette by her hand and give the bitch the old shit-eye. She's a swag-bellied thing with a big brooch of glass grapes pinned over one of her old floppy dinners. Her name's Carrie Holloway Jenks, and I know her people, the ones she got away from by marrying the garden store manager. Those Holloways, they're trash. As far as anyone knows, they're white, and that's all you can say for them. They aren't even clean.

I ask Carrie, "What kind of a sewer have you got for a mind? Claudette was on the playground with the rest of her little class, that's all. And those other little girls were off playing somewhere they hadn't ought to have gone. Claudette knows better than that." By now, that's true. Claudette's lip quivers, but she hasn't said a word. Carrie all of a sudden looks like she's trying to hold in some bad gas.

It's a shame, isn't it, about people like that Carrie, who get their hands on money by flopping on their backs and opening their legs? That's something I haven't done. But when you don't have money, you end up either doing that or doing some meanness, and I've done my meanness, laying down the law with my weak daughter. I didn't send her to school until she was seven. I told people I kept her home an extra year because she was sickly. Really, I thought that if she started when she was a little older than the other children, she'd have an advantage. And when it came time for her to go to school, I told her that school was her job and she was going to have to make straight As and never misbehave; she'd have to always be perfect in school, even if people weren't nice to her. Because of where we come from, because we only had what we earned at the mill, some of them wouldn't be nice. That wasn't always true about us.

"Your people didn't always to have to work in the mill," I told her. "We used to have a big house in Sampson County, a plantation, and slaves. We lost it all in Abe Lincoln's war." *And my mother ended up marrying my papa instead of someone with land and money, I think to myself, and raised mill hands instead of ladies.* And the best I could do was to marry Claude, even though I was a beautiful girl. I could've found a rich man who'd buy me presents and knock me up, but not one who'd marry me. Made-up stories are the only places rich men marry beautiful girls from families like mine.

"I couldn't finish school because I had to work," I told Claudette. "But you're going to finish school. And when you finish school, you're going to college. You know the college. We go past it when we go downtown to the movies. Well, you're going there. Just like you would if we'd kept our plantation. But you're going to have to get a scholarship, so you have to make straight As and always act right in school. And when you finish college, you're going to be a schoolteacher. Everybody respects a schoolteacher. You'll get good pay, and you won't marry some lowlife because you'll be able to take care of yourself, and you're going to help Mama when she's old."

I don't tell her the other reason she's going to need a good job: She's not going to marry money. She's not pretty. I don't know why not, her father's a handsome man, and I was a looker in my day, not like my sisters. My oldest sister is a fool, beaten down by a worthless drunk and sucked white by his passel of brats. My other sister is a little roundheels slut. They look exactly like what they are, too. I don't look related to them, praise Jesus. I am a natural blonde with green eyes and pretty flapper legs, and I've never let any man but my husband touch me. In my pictures with my sisters, they're like dirty old nickels, but I have the silver shine of a new dime. If Claudette had either my looks or my gumption, there'd be more for me to work with; I could get her farther up in this wicked world with a lot less pain. But she's a little ball of biscuit dough, with nothing to say for herself. She has dark eyes, pale magnolia skin, and thick dark hair. The eyes, the skin, the hair, they're all pretty, but beauty isn't arithmetic, and Claudette's parts don't add up to beauty. It's a waste making smart clothes for that child. They all hang like potato sacks, and no matter how smart her clothes are, she acts like she'd like to disappear. I think she would like to disappear. In a crowd of happy children, she almost does disappear. I'd say that her light's gone out if there'd ever been any light. But whatever happened in the schoolyard won't happen again.

See, I know what got into her that day at school, that mean nervy courage that weak people who're scared of everything get once or twice in their lives. The other little girls were teasing her, probably daring her to climb up on that wall, and she wouldn't. I bet she was remembering her whipping. And then that mouthy little Millie climbed up and stood up there on the wall. She probably stuck her fingers in her jug ears and nah-nah-nahed at Claudette and called her a fraidy-cat. Then, well… these timid weak people, they get sick and tired of being picked on, and for a few seconds, they're not going to take it anymore. *That* got into Claudette. They get mad enough to be brave for two seconds, and then they lash out. They're more dangerous when they break than strong people ever are. They'll do bad things, stupid things, and then be stunned at themselves. I'm sure there are plenty of men like that who've walked up the gallows steps, and they still couldn't believe they did the things they were getting hung for.

Well, it's 1981 now, and they don't hang murderers here anymore, and Claudette's old, and I'm older, and most everything's all spilled water now, isn't it? I'm eighty. I have a bad leg with an ulcer from the sugar diabetes. I've learned how small the reward for doing right really is. You know there's no way anyone would ever run a country if everybody knew that? We'd be cutting the heads off our politicians like the Frenchmen did with their king. It'd be a damn good idea to cut off the heads of some of that trash, if you ask me, and their peters too. I'd stick their heads up on fence posts for the buzzards. And why do I think a nasty thing like that? I'll tell you.

First, do you have any notion how forty years in that mill felt? No ma'am, you don't, not unless you've been there. After you've worked there a few days, there's this pain that settles into your bones. It stays with you, the pain. Somehow it's both sharp and dull. You take aspirin and rub down with liniment before you go to bed, and you still wake up feeling like you're two hundred years old. Though sometimes I'd wake up before the alarm, and for a few minutes the pain stayed asleep. It just made me sick when I woke all the way up and the pain came back. To ease the pain, you baste your damn self with liniment until you smell like the mill, even in church. Go into any house where mill people live, and that's the first thing you smell, liniment. Menthol. It hits you in the face at the door.

When I was awake, I hardly ever sat still. If I sat still, either it hurt worse or I noticed it more. If I kept moving, it wasn't so bad, or I told myself that. Mill people got so used to pain that the really bad things, like the cancer or the sugar diabetes, would creep up on them. The mill pain was worse than whatever you'd feel from the thing that'd kill you. By the time you retire, the mill ruins you. (*I want to write,* my granddaughter said. Write about what? What's there to write about? There's nothing but this. Work, and pain, and people who're no damn good.)

When I retired from the mill, they gave me a certificate saying that I'd worked there forty years, and a watch. And that watch!—Do you know that miserable thing wasn't even gold? That trinket turned on a light, a bright one, in my head. I saw what I had: Claudette, a grown woman with the face of a half-bright child, and Claude, who was already wetting his pants and forgetting where he was and what he was there for, losing the little sense he ever had, and a cheap watch that didn't even come from a real jewelry shop. Now that I know what the reward for hard work is, I don't care what anybody says. I just plain don't care. I just keep seeing how far I can go.

Here's one way—I make Claudette drive me to all three of the grocery stores every Saturday to get the brands I want. I get the coffee from the Piggly Wiggly, the Ann Page Cherry Delite pudding mix from the A&P, the meat from Kroger, and the fresh produce from Cottingham's, everything that tastes good, and then we go to McDonalds. If I forget something at one store, I make Claudette go back. I watch the mileage on the car, but she never gives it a look or argues back. It's amazing how far I broke her, amazing that one person can break another person that far. I hate that it had to be that far, but I didn't have a choice. Of course there's an answer to "How can you break a person that far?" And the answer is that really you can't, unless that person's already part-way broken. There are people that the Germans couldn't even break in those camps Hitler built to kill off Jews. Those Germans beat the hide off them, the ones they didn't kill at the get-go, and starved them on rotten potatoes, and made them work twenty hours a day. But some of those people got liberated by the Americans and came over here and opened stores and restaurants and did fine. Hitler couldn't break them. I broke Claudette with a few hard words.

Am I sorry? Well, I really need someone who'll mind me with no backtalk, now that I'm too wobbly to drive. Now, at least, I can get all the brands I want and have a long outing. It's almost as if I can do everything I ever did, maybe better since I don't have to pay for the gas and the car insurance. Claudette's no use to herself, so she might as well be some use to me. So I guess I'm not sorry. I let my diabetes go to the devil too. I'm not sorry about that either. I could be taking shots and eating lettuce all day, and I'd bet anyone a shiny red apple that the same damn thing would happen. Only while it was happening, I'd be eating salad and putting saccharin in my coffee.

Monster, they call that actress, that Joan Crawford who beats her bleating little girl with the coat hanger in the new movie. Maybe I'm a monster too. Maybe a woman has to be a bit of a monster to haul a daughter and husband like mine and herself out of the white trash category and buy a house for them and pay it off. So maybe I'm a monster, but we are not white trash! And for damn sure, I'm a diabetic, but I still make Claudette buy me Little Debbie raisin cakes and Kraft caramels. None of it stays on me, I've got no butt or belly, I just pee the sugar away. I like my food sweet. I like feeling the sugar grains in my coffee between my teeth. I lick out the white cream from the raisin cakes. There aren't many real pleasures, but sugar is a real one. It's only a problem when my granddaughter visits because she won't buy me my cookies or anything else sweet, and she'll tell Claudette she ought not to do it either. Claudette gets tearful when she's got two people telling her what to do and it isn't the same thing.

My granddaughter's name is Tansy, after me. Young Tansy's not pretty like me, but I know her eyes: green like mine, and not the eyes of a person you could break with a scolding. I never took a switch to Tansy. She'd have kicked my shins bloody if I'd tried, probably put her teeth in my arm too, same as I did Mam. Tansy's like me that way, she's just never had to show it. But she likes how I am. She used to love for me to tell her about when I was eight and Johnny Dawkins killed my cat, and I jumped Johnny and pushed him into the dye ditch that runs from the mill to Virgie Street. I had a real good rock, a perfect rock, a comfortable fit in my little hand but big enough to knock tarnation out of Johnny Dawkins. When I got done with that boy, he had a bloody nose and two black eyes and was bawling out of both of them. He was pouring blood from a gash in his chin. I whopped him good. Since he was wet from the dye ditch, I couldn't tell whether I made him mess his britches, but Young Tansy would say I *beat the shit out of him.* Then, when he got home, his mama near about killed him for ruining his clothes in the dye ditch. Johnny Dawkins got his comeuppance.

Claudette's never been easy with Tansy. Claudette's lip quivers when Tansy's eyes look at her certain ways. She complains that she doesn't see much of Tansy, now that Tansy's grown. I don't know why she whines, since she doesn't enjoy it when the girl does visit. Some parts I don't enjoy either. Young Tansy cleans the house up righteously when she's here, just like I taught her, but I don't get my Little Debbie cakes, just stuff she cooks, and I don't like her cooking—she has these modern ideas about sugar and salt and grease. She learned Yankee cooking up there. It almost makes me feel sorry for Yankees. Almost. But she doesn't come home all that much. Young Tansy can't stand but only so much of Claudette.

In my head I use some of that bad language Young Tansy learned at that fancy Yankee college. I bet she and Claudette would both have a conniption fit if I said it out loud! Someday I just might! Just to see their faces! It feels good even just thinking about saying it—no wonder people like to cuss. I swish my coffee and feel the sugar grains between my teeth and eat my cookies. I look at the pair of them, Claudette and Tansy, and I think: "Fuck it all. And fuck you too if you get in my way."

I'm going to keep right on doing what I want.

*

I'm Tansy Two/Tansy Too, named for my late grandmother, Old Tansy. I wish I looked more like her. If you saw Dakota Fanning in *Hound Dog*—grubby, scrawny, at ease in squalor, but glinting through the filth—you can imagine my grandmother in her few early photographs, amidst her pellagra-dazed kin. At least I have her green eyes and some of her hard edges. When Claudette looks at me, the green eyes are all she sees of her mother. That's not enough.

I am supposed to be a writer. I have been one. *A once-has-been,* someone called me on his website. My last three years have been spent taking care of my parents, mostly Claudette. Before that—messes and houses! I cleared out and sold one house that my parents trashed, that one at a fire-sale price because the damage had gone so far. A blue-chip developer bought it and rehabbed it, probably at astronomical cost, into generic elegance. I cleared out and sold another house, the one my parents had been living in through the last phase of their nominal independence, at a good market price, a couple of weeks before real estate crashed in our part of the Upper South. I reconfigured my house to accommodate my parents and moved them in with me. Cleaning out houses, selling houses, housework and eldercare are what I've been doing instead of writing. The house I call my house used to be Old Tansy's, and she passed it straight to me rather than to my mother. She'd seen what Claudette and Dad did to houses, for one, and she probably thought I'd never been able to buy a house on my own, which actually didn't turn out to be true.

When I was sixteen and first decided that I was going to be a writer, Old Tansy said, "Why d'you want to do a thing like that? I mean, what good is it?" It was an honest question; she wanted to know.

I said, "There's some secret we need to know. I want to find it out. I want to know the secret." (Why life is so sad, so uphill, so unfair, and so often turns out so badly.)

My grandmother shrugged: "Well, I sure don't know it." Then she moved on to practical matters: "You sure writing pays enough so you can eat?" Of course I thought so, but she had her doubts. She never depended on luck. Old Tansy left her house to me, and now her declining daughter, my mother Claudette, inhabits it with me. Claudette has the master bedroom that her parents used to have, and I have the one that used to be Claudette's. If she were to fall, I could get to her in seconds; I can hear her if she calls. I can hear her cry. Her tears have been a river through my life; I was four when I first woke to hear her wailing in her bed. She wouldn't tell me why and wouldn't get up, just told me not to go out of the house. She spent the day in bed, alternatively sleeping and weeping. She got up at dusk, in time to dress and throw together a supper for my father. This began to happen often, until I got used to whole days alone with the ticking clock and dripping tap; she's just lucky that I wasn't the kind of kid who'd sample the bottles under the sink or wander off. If I got really lonely or scared, I'd watch the clock until 2:30, when the first shift at the mill let out, then call Old Tansy and ask her to come and get me.

Depression runs in our family, the serious and recalcitrant kind that yields only to the noble SSRIs, and this was long before they existed. Now that they do exist, they still don't do Claudette any good. She's supposed to be on Zoloft but won't take it. The best mood meds in the world don't fix an unthrifty serotonin/dopamine cycle for someone who hides them in her pillowcase.

Claudette's depression used to be a kind of contentless, slow-bleeding grief, and she never could say why she stayed in bed and wept. Now she can. For several years now, there has been this thread, this theme (I am looking for a word that answers, "What are you crying about?") in my mother's crying spells. As Claudette began sliding down the greased slope to the afterworld in old age, more and more often she was crying about specific events. Whether they were real, imagined, or something between those poles, I did not know.

From what she's said, something happened one day at recess at school, the elementary school she attended and I attended later. Architecture was involved; what happened could not have happened without a particular architectural feature. This school was a stately brick and granite structure with big windows to ventilate the basement in those pre-AC years. There was a concrete-lined air well around each of those basement windows, and at ground level there was a brick wall around the well. The wall, about waist-high to a grownup, was meant to keep people from falling down the air well. A kid climbed up on the wall and fell—not onto the ground, but inward, down to the hard concrete outside the basement window. From wall to ground would have hurt: three feet down to the mud and gravel of the schoolyard, a scare, bruises and scrapes and some howling. The kids who'd been watching and daring the little asshole to climb up on the wall would have scattered before the teachers rushed up to soothe the victim and thrash the instigators. Inward, down the air well, was a long fall onto concrete and stone, with certainty of serious damage or death.

In this story, the story behind Claudette's wild crying spells, the kid falls inward, down the shaft, onto the concrete and rock. The kid breaks her head. This was 1936, in a little town with a tiny little hospital. With a skull fracture, the kind you'd get from that long fall, you would have been a goner. Comatose, this kid hung on for a while and then died. Some neighbor terrified Claudette by asking her if she pushed the kid.

For quite a while, I didn't believe any part of this story. See, I learned (late in my life and even later in my mother's life) that my mother is a liar, and a good one. Perhaps the best liars come across flushed and fragile, hesitant, like Claudette. She told stories to deceive and to do damage, and also stories for drama's sweet sake. Asked for a reason she was crying, she was capable of compounding a colorful one. Knowing her for a fabulist, I shrugged this story off. I never tried to find out the facts, since there might not be any. And, quite actively, I want not to know Claudette's secrets. I don't want them in my head.

I only just learned the term for that subfloor ventilation feature involved in her story; it's called an English basement. You find these in old buildings: vertical rows of windows, and ground-level air shafts down to the basement windows. I remember the window that was involved; my first year at that school, I had looked over its wall and down with no special interest. Leaves and blowdown twigs and compost dredged under the basement window below. Wet, it had a pong.

Looking once was enough for me; I felt no temptation to climb up and balance on the wall. My coordination is wonky, and I've always been conscious of my awkwardness when moving through space and hazard. It wouldn't have occurred to me to get up on that wall. I did my bit not to be in places where accidents were likely. Without ever looking for that kind of trouble at that school, I have bad memories of a young teacher there who tried with obsessive fervor to make me learn to skip rope: an idiotic/sadistic humiliation over a skill that seemed entirely useless unless you enjoyed it. I encountered one of my limits: I simply couldn't skip rope. Forced to jump the rope, I landed on my ass or twisted my ankles or bloodied my knees, depending on which way I fell. I learned about limits and about class.

That teacher—we called her Miss Winnie—taught me about class and what it means, or meant, in the Upper South. I suppose I should be thankful, since my parents wouldn't. Both from ambitious poor families, they found the topic dirtier than sex and just as unmentionable. Miss Winnie was fresh from my mother's college, and my class was the first group of children she taught. Really, she was too young to recognize her impulse toward whimsical torment as cruelty or contempt.

Young Miss Winnie wanted to be generous too, so she invited her whole class to a kind of picnic affair at her parents' house across town at year's end. Theirs was the second-largest and finest home I'd ever been in. Our little two-story brick house was nothing to it. Miss Winnie came from money. I guess hers was as old as money gets in Southdown, which isn't very old by, say, Boston standards. Even though my father was a college teacher and my mother was a librarian, we were educated proles of no wealth. Miss Winnie knew this. The knowledge had freed her to torment me in a way that she would not have tormented a child who came from money or, at the other end of the economic arc, a child with a mean redneck father who would have slashed her tires or poisoned her poodle. At the year-end party, after nine months of tormenting me with the skipping rope, Miss Winnie showed us her house. I could not have put my understanding into words, but when I saw her bedroom with its white rugs and white voile canopy and the ruffled white voile fluttering at the windows when the AC ran, I understood. These furnishings were like nothing in my house. They belonged to a different class of people, and these people could hold me in contempt and be "nice" to me at the same time. They could do it with fine manners and seeming generosity. They were doing it right that minute.

In my mind's eye, under a summer sun of steel, I saw that mill where my grandmother had worked off her mortgage and brought home irregular and defective sheets to sew into our curtains and my dresses. The mill could and would be held against me. The understanding marked my beginning as who I am now: a very educated prole with a sharp tongue and a dour appreciation of revenge. I thought of the teacher's white voile bedspread when I went to college in a town where some of the money is really old, as in *it landed there in 1638*. The snobs there are in a whole other league, and the decorative taste is bleeding-edge. I saw bright, stark Marimekko comforters in the shop windows. I thought how the people who owned the Marimekkos would have found Miss Winnie's white voile dowdy and old-lady-fied beyond polite words. The idea pleased me. So did remembering that I had never gratified the nasty little country-club snob by learning to skip rope.

There's a smell behind my current revelation: I call it *reasty*, a made-up word that encompasses *yeasty* but avoids any association with the sweetness of rising dough. It's yeastlike but evil, fungal and nasty; it's the piss of my mother's present old-age incontinence. It's a hot yellow smell, like vinegar except not clean.

It's grief too. Grief makes a stink. My mother's had her share of grief. She has a serious psychiatric diagnosis which makes the loss of her loved ones worse for her than for most. It is something called *symbiotic psychosis*, a diagnosis that adults don't normally get, but the Ferrier University Medical Center shrink was sure enough of it to stick his neck out and pin it on Claudette. Someone who has it doesn't realize that she is one person and her mother is another. Normal people realize this a few months after they are born: *I am me, and Mom is Mom.* For Claudette it was *Mom is Mom,* and *Mom is omnipotent, and I am part of Mom and have no power but Mom's power.*

Claudette's mom is Old Tansy, who died twenty years ago, full of years and diabetic neuropathy. Claudette's position with Old Tansy was untenable in life: Claudette never had a gambler's chance of defying Old Tansy's voracious will. Claudette's position became even more untenable after Old Tansy died. Claudette never really had a soul of her own, but the soul she shared, the soul that powered her on a fraction of its inconsiderate vigor, was gone from this plane of existence. Claudette was finally on her own power, only she had no power. An irony that anyone, even a cruel person, would find cruel; I do. Claudette's expression after Old Tansy died was just like that on a crusader in some medieval fantasy film I remember from childhood, the second after a Saracen cut his knightly guts out and they sloshed at his feet. He fell down dead. Claudette survived, destroyed.

First she tried to put her husband in her mother's place. "Mama... Cartwright," Claudette would say. Now that Dad is dead, it's "Mama... Cartwright... Tansy." Sometimes she called my father *Mama*. *Mama* is really her shorthand for "Soul Source/Person in Power Who Takes Care of Me." That was spooky. Now she says, "Mama... Tansy," sometimes without knowing that she's doing it. Sometimes she just calls me *Mama*. She never really existed for herself, and we never existed for her. At our very best, we were substitute sources of light, heat, and physical support, auxiliary power supplies.

So picture this: Dad has been dead three months, and Claudette's center does not hold. Her center is an unsealed basement from a Lovecraft story, and monsters that have bred down there for decades are rising from the spidery dark. The English basement story, which had been floating to the surface at bad moments for years, takes on frequency and heat.

A bully who would push another kid to a fatal fall would look for someone like Little Claudette, weak and meek, to blame it on. If this story had any truth in it, I'd thought, the real culprit probably beat feet and hid until the bell rang. Meanwhile, the teacher would have advanced on the stammering Claudette, who wouldn't have had the sense to run. I imagine

Claudette at eight, fattish in one of the chic outfits my grandmother made for her, standing at the scene of the crime with her raisin eyes guilty and her mouth hanging open. In any conflict, Claudette has never known that there was anywhere to go but into a corner.

Now the affair of the English basement is an obsession, undeterred by the Zoloft Claudette won't take, and she asks me, "Did I have my arms out like I meant to push her? Did I startle her and make her fall?" I wasn't there, I say; that was 1936! She is barmy enough to think I could have been a witness, or that I can exercise some kind of omnipotent judgment on events that happened decades before I was born. Then again, I don't really exist; whoever takes care of her is Mama, her despotic and omnipotent god. I am the human left standing, doing eldercare, so I stand in the god's shoes. A god is supposed to know.

I used to want to defend Claudette, and she seemed to need it often. While she worked at the library, she was prime meat for every old bitch in Serials and Cataloging. One of those librarians, one Ruth Anna Mae Spurgeon, was so hateful that when she retired, the department collected money and bought her a bag of horse manure as a farewell present. It was supposed to nourish her hybrid teas, but really! Her colleagues could've gotten her a gift certificate at the garden store, but that horseshit made a statement! Claudette, Miss Spurgeon's most frequent victim, bemoaned the manure. For my part, Ruth Anna Mae's retirement was welcome; I enjoyed *not* hearing, every few weeks, about some fresh run-in between my mother and the old hyena. I wondered why my father did nothing to shy off Ruth Anna Mae and those other she-beasts at the library. This is, after all, my dad, Cartwright, that we're talking about—a hunting man known to have numerous firearms, a bad temper, and good aim. One phone call from him would have had those desiccated virgins piddling their beds from fear. He said nothing, though. Perhaps he was applying private knowledge, imagining Claudette's neediness and indecision transferred to the work setting, and the legitimate annoyance of these women, bitches that some of them were. Dad had to have some strong, considered reason for not defending his pitiful wife—like considering her behavior indefensible.

I used to think that pushing someone to her death was totally out of character for my mother, and I told her so as often as she needed to hear it. Did it really matter what she thought, at this juncture, so long as she was at peace? Never mind *happy*; she was never happy. *At peace* was as good as it ever got with her.

I had moved my parents in with me because Claudette was getting more and more immobile and staying upstairs, and it was only a matter of time until Dad fell down those steep stairs while carrying and fetching for her. Okay, I'd bought a single-story house near mine and moved them into it. That was Plan A. Plan B started when both of them had come down with the flu, and I came to check on them and found myself tearing out a hall carpet full of drippy shit. The house was like one of those places in a reality TV show about hoarders: crammed, cluttered, smelly, greasy, and foul. If you needed any of the things people usually need, like the scissors, the aspirin, or the salt, they were unfindable, and there was no clean place to sit down. After the initial mighty effort to get the place decent, I did the housework and laundry there. On a very good week, by my count, maintenance required three hours a day for six days of the week and five to seven on the other day.

This went on for a year, two years. You aren't called upon to like me for this. Just do the math and see that those hours add up to a big chunk out of anyone's time and energy. I have an autoimmune problem and don't have as much energy as most people. Lucky for me, I found a doctor who would prescribe me some pharmaceutical speed, which was cheap and gave me the stamina I had to have. I don't think I could have managed otherwise. Methylphenidate doesn't just give you energy, it also makes you superficial: breezy, chatty, and optimistic in situations that warrant no optimism.

Any reasonable person might guess that this scenario could not extend forever. I could not keep up the mortgage on that house and be increasingly full-time household help and nurse. Even chemically enhanced, I could feel the tipping point approach. Why not a nursing home? Well, Dad didn't need one, and Claudette thought people got raped in nursing homes. She had long ago made me promise that I'd never put her in one. I did suspect that if there were some nursing home staff member who was desperate and unfastidious enough to rape octogenarians, he'd pick Claudette out of the whole lineup. More likely, though, she'd press the call button forty times a night, and grizzle and whine until someone lost it and smacked her.

On to Plan C. I once had a client who said, "I don't like it when you make a Plan B and Plan C because I might not get my Plan A." Better than ending up with nothing, I thought, which happens a lot to people who don't have fallbacks. At any rate, I made a Plan C. I decided to reconfigure my house, which used to be Old Tansy's, and move my parents in there. Both of them come from long-lived families, and the situation we had could have lasted a very long time. I was getting my head around the long time: ten years, maybe fifteen. We needed a scenario that was at least endurable for that long. I thought that if Claudette were lifted from the private slum she inevitably created around herself, she might be less unhappy; I knew that Dad needed to retire from any and all caregiving. One night my phone rang, and no one spoke, but I heard some heavy breathing I recognized as his. I raced over there and found him trying to get Claudette off the living room floor. She hadn't fainted; she had seated herself on the deep sofa and hadn't been able to get up. Then she wallowed down on the floor to try to pull herself up with her hands and couldn't do that either. Dad got down there and tried to get her up, couldn't, and then couldn't get up himself. I went down there and called the EMTs to get them up off the floor. Dad weighed two hundred pounds, Claudette weighed about a hundred and sixty—each way more than me and way more than I can lift. I needed to have them where I could hear them if they fell. It was time, I told them, to consolidate our households. I thought

I knew what I was inviting over my threshold: a very sick old woman with several co-morbid diagnoses, a mentally ill and difficult old woman, and a relatively healthy man in his nineties. At that point, I had no idea of Claudette's willingness and ability to deceive. I thought all her noise about Christianity meant that she wouldn't do certain things.

Do you want to know about the lie she told? It met the criteria for a black lie: conscious, deliberate, told for damage and personal gain. If Claudette's lie had been a chess move, it would have been a brilliant one. I had two nearby close friends, a couple; the lie concerned behavior toward my mother from one of them. If the behavior really had occurred, it would have been extremely inappropriate, and my response to it would not have been out of line. The result of my hot response was alienation from both those friends and isolation with my mother in her bell jar. Her lie put me on her team; it sent me into the ring to defend her. It gave her seventeen months alone with me. All seventeen of those months, every day, I had that early-morning experience of waking and for about sixty seconds imagining everything was fine, then remembering it wasn't. Repetition never made that hurt any less. I wonder if this short, repetitive delusion happens to people as they are dying. Do they wake up with the years stretched before them like miles of clean pavement, then realize that there's no more sidewalk, just pain and a clock? I suppose that one day I'll find out.

When my two friends and I were too tired to fight any more, when I found out about Claudette's lie, I think I said, "Well, the wretched old bitch." I had a sense of parts knitting up, of light coming into perfect refraction. There seemed little more to say. My lifelong worry about whether or not Claudette really was a good person underneath it all went suddenly quiet, like that object at complete rest that is supposed to be somewhere beyond the universe. My enemy was in my house; I knew so. Life with her would be considerably simpler now that I knew what she was. I did not owe her love. Shelter, food, laundry service, and cleanliness were all I owed her. I put on the mask of someone who didn't know what I knew and resumed the process of providing services. But I did not know the truth entire.

Now it is early December. If you are, say, a talented young ballet student, maybe you've auditioned for the local *Nutcracker* and you're rehearsing your part. If you're a musician or singer, maybe you're rehearsing the local production of *Messiah*. The solo soprano part of *Messiah* in 1957 was Claudette's high mark and one of her good memories. Maybe you're just looking forward to seeing your kid or husband or wife in one of the Christmas performances. Or perhaps you're just happily shopping, looking forward to the family Christmas. Up to our nostrils in our tacky gothic misery, we're not doing any of that. Here you have a failing, despairing old woman and a writer who doesn't write, gnawing the bones of our exhaustion. Am I a failure? I have had one book published by a major publisher, with good reviews, and no more. There has been too much else for me to do. Most of it has been stuff I'm not good at, stuff that takes a long time, like pulling up shit-ridden carpet and then pulling out the nails that secured it to the hardwood below.

Claudette thinks I'm a failure. I tell her, "Well, maybe that works out okay for you. It means I'm available, here, not in Hollywood. Whatever I am, I can do this, and I will. That's something." That something isn't love, and she knows it. However, a lot of people my age who claim to love their parents dump them in nursing homes. Love doesn't mean everything. Sometimes it doesn't mean anything.

And her candid observation takes my squeamishness and dislike and distrust of her a crucial degree further. She tells me that she is "disappointed in me." The reason: I have failed to sell the house that she used to inhabit, the house that she pigged up from one end to the other and crammed with crap, within two weeks. Never mind the three months of hard labor to clear and repair and paint the place, never mind a real estate market on the verge of collapse, Claudette is disappointed!

I hate her so much then that I wonder if this is what mass murderers feel before they click off the safety of their automatics and start spraying the crowd. Claudette doesn't retract her comment when the house sells, which happens just ten days later. I don't retract my hatred either. The house is sold in August; Dad dies in September. With no demilitarized zone left to us, no third person as a buffer, Claudette and I soldier on. Soon enough, we're near Christmas and the end of this year's calendar.

Christmas makes me want to cut my throat even in a good year. I don't feel the urge as much as usual this year, which would seem ironic, but I have steeled myself not to feel my grief for Dad so I can carry on. Even when I am running alone at night after putting Claudette to bed, I cannot feel grief or anything much. What pleases me is how light I am! When I wear something thin and tight, you can see my ribs through the fabric like a ballet dancer's through her leotard. The bathtub hurts me when I sit down in it, but I want to get thinner. I have some jeans in kids' sizes, and some of these need a belt to stay up. I don't even have to starve myself to do it, what with all the work and how disgusting food seems. Old Tansy was right, I'm a sorry cook. The experts on eating disorders are right too: People like to get thin because that is something they can control and it feels like an accomplishment. I also like it because, the thinner I get, the better I can see Old Tansy's elegant skull beneath my skin, and her proportions. The twenty-seven pounds between 145 and 118 blurred the truth: underneath, I really do look like Old Tansy. She was shorter, her bone structure was more delicate, but yes, get me thin enough and I do look like her. My legs have become her wiry boyish legs. I can even wear the clothes she left. Some of them hang loose. I remember her brisk, can't-sit-still buzzing around the house and yard—I move like that now.

By December 15, I put up the tree with its pink lights and arty ornaments for Claudette. There is no snow outside, only naked brown ground. Tonight there's a cold, cottony fog. Weather for criminals, I think. Weather you could disappear right into if you wore a light gray coat, not a black one like mine. I've always wondered about the logistics of successful crime, the kind that works so well that nobody ever hears about it, or maybe even knows it happened. How do people do these things—murder? Steal?—and not get caught? By calculation or by seizing one perfect instant of someone else's inattention? Or by one hard push in plain sight, so unexpected that it's also unbelievable?

Claudette is not going to be here forever, as I keep telling myself. The discount-shopping, bowl-scraping, pinching and grinding recession ways I keep house are probably here for the duration, but she's not. I feel sorry for her. It's got to be hard for her, being taken care of by someone who doesn't love her, who is coldly, exactingly doing a duty. People want to be taken care of from love, only love. But being taken care of out of duty beats the hell out of not being taken care of at all, though, or being abused. It might even be easier to lash out at someone you love, if that person is constantly, despairingly mean to you, because love makes a tender spot and meanness stings the soft spot sore. I know Claudette wore Dad down to this same grim pity I feel now. Being in this house with Claudette weakens me, as if I lived in the hot zone around Chernobyl. Who would have dreamed it was possible to be so tired as I am now?

Even so, I do think about what I might want to do when Claudette has finally gone where she can find Mama. Sell this house, my house that used to be my grandmother's house, and everything in it, and go somewhere else, start all over again, and set myself up in a place with no history and everything in it as purposeful, keen, and literal as a nail? Stay, fix this house up, mend the plaster, cover the old dark floors in silky blonde wood, bring the bathrooms into the twenty-first century? I imagine the outside painted the clean white of ice, the interior cream-dipped, a warm white like melted vanilla ice cream. I imagine my house pretty, convenient, with no sorrowful mysteries and no drawers with ancient sharp objects to jab fingers in search of the aspirin or the stamps. Cleared out and fixed up, this would be a beautiful house. And even more beautiful with us all gone from it. This house, bought so dearly, deserves better people than us.

I imagine my untidy, sorrowing family erased from this house. Oh, how I would like to erase us: our unhappiness, our messiness, our lack of grace and congruence and our failed creativity and weirdness and how laughable we must have been to people who actually knew what to do with themselves in this life, the secrets we kept and the secrets we never knew. I want to unremember the lives we lived and invent the lives we lacked. (In some books, like *The Hotel New Hampshire,* weird, chaotic people have charm; is that ever true in real life? Or is that why the books are written—to repackage chaotic lives as good stories? Because the truth makes no sense? Or such a terrible sense that we should hide it, because knowing it would paralyze hope?)

But fuck the truth, fuck the secret. I just want to wake up rested, with bright, clear vision, dreading nothing.

When Claudette has passed on, there will be decisions, and I need that clear head to make them. Selling the house as is, fixing the house... and there's also the option of doing nothing at all, nestling into failure like an old rat in its burrow, letting the house fall down on me if that's what it wants to do, while I watch my old VHS films and read my old books, or new ones from the library. Maybe failures who can handle their failure lead secret, quite comfortable lives. How would I do that? Settle into a soft and cozy despair, warm as an ancient feather comforter. Let the wallpaper come off in lacy scallops, a tier or two a year, let the plaster crack and the floors sag and the down quilt spit tiny feathers through its pores until it is soft and thin as skin. Let the yard grow green and jungly and re-read my Plath. Sweet least resistance! When it is all over with Claudette, will I have the energy to lift my hand?

This is the mood on which Claudette's latest outcry falls: "Tansy! Did I do it? Tansy, answer me, did I push her?" She is crying again, again. She has wet the bed too. Reasty. Her rising yellow smell. She has pills to help her not wet the bed so much but has added them to her list of medicines she won't take. The continence pills change the color of her urine, and she thinks that will damage her; she feels that she has the right to be depressed. She claims her sovereign rights to be piss-soaked and depressed. She cries out my name again. "I said, did I do it?"

It is her recent lie that moves me from where I have been, and the edged terror in her eternal question. I remember the summer and being worked to the outer edges of my energy as I got her ex-house ready for the market, when it had not yet sold, and Claudette saying, "Tansy, you disappoint me." I remember being called a failure when I least needed to hear that, true or not. Three factors, three barbed vertices. One is the lie, two is the smug venom of "You disappoint me," and three is the frantic repetition of "Did I do it?"

A nasty person who heard, "I said, did I do it?" in this moment would say, "Hell, yes, bitch, you pushed her. That was you."

I don't say anything, but my head is very suddenly clear. Clear as ice, as vodka, as water from some spring in far Siberia, some place so pure and remote that they've never heard of Jesus, or Prozac, or Hewlett-Packard. Clear, sharp, and cold. I have been poured back into my empty self like that clear liquid. I am all here.

You did it, I say in my head. *Yes, you did.*

Family Tree

As I sit here two doors down from you, I think that that if they had a big drafty loft over the old post office downtown, I'd go live there. I have an abiding love for headroom and uninterrupted, echoing spaces. If I did live in a loft over the P.O., it would have a few pieces of very good minimalist furniture, maybe just a few clear glass dishes. I once had an apartment I loved, bigger than I really needed, but I relished the scope it gave to my solitude. My possessions were few, and I used one of the spare rooms to store all the stuff I didn't use daily. That apartment always looked neat, clean and white as a fresh ice cube. I was calmer there than anywhere else I've lived, before or since, in the seemliness, the clarity of that temporary home. A mess, if it occurs in such a place, is minimal and the work of a few minutes to clean up. I wish I were there right now. Or, failing that, in a big clean attic above some P.O. or one of those empty spaces in the second story above a mall.

Even at the beginning of this story, free to lay it aside at any minute, I am spent. Why? You. I will not call you *Mama,* as you tell me over and over you wish I would. You are the wall that sense hits, like those dummies head-firsting into a wall with a numb bang in some simulated car crash. Among other very young writers at college, I was told time and time again that I just had to write about you—this on the basis of very occasional, conservatively-chosen anecdotes of your weirdness confided to a few friends. But I didn't. Why not? Well, for one, we'd all been told to write about "what you understand." But I didn't understand you, I just happened to know you. And you still don't make sense to me, and any story I tell should make sense to me before it tries to make sense to anyone else. You don't even fit into that genre of *That's Just Whut We're Like Down Hyah* that an editor friend of mine learned to dread with such fervor while trying to run a "southern" literary magazine. He named that genre after reading about ninety pounds of unsolicited manuscripts on The Southern Way, with its connotations of charm, sugar, azaleas, and ruining one's hands to save the plantation. The Southern Way is the preservationist's way. That means it isn't yours.

What do I mean by that? I mean you don't save things; you ruin them. If someone did save Tara, restored it perfectly, garlanded it with lilacs and azaleas, then shoved it onto the Historical Register and handed you the deed and the keys, you'd have it looking like Cold Comfort Farm within the month. You'd have cat litter pans in Scarlett's white bedroom and three-day-old spoiled bacon reposing on a greasy paper towel on the stove. The heavy old Napoleonic silver would be blackened and pitted after being run through the dishwasher, which would have a cat food can lid stuck in its outflow valve. You would be in Miss Ellen's chaste four-poster, talking on the phone to one of your fellow hypochondriacs about your intestines.

There is for me some supernal irony in your insistence on dirt and clutter and biological candor. I remember myself in my malleable years, inevitably enjoined to *hush! be quiet! don't say that!* and being nagged about how careless I was. *Be careful! Be nice!*—your mouth pursed like the opening of a tight drawstring bag, as if trying to hold it in, to hold the whole world in. These late days, you're letting everything out. Now you recline fretfully for most of every day, plucking at your sweatshirt, in your bed full of cat hair—murmuring of cats, pharmaceuticals, and shit, either theirs or your own.

By the way, I know exactly how I sound. In our town, a man was recently convicted of first-degree murder on the slenderest grounds. I followed the trial and thought often: *Save me from a jury of my supposed peers.* He was, by most people's standards, an unsympathetic defendant—wealthy, intellectual, and cocky. And he was better-looking than I am; I should be careful. I would make an unsympathetic defendant myself. I am the bad daughter, doing my duty without love. Increasingly I think of what it would be like to drop my duty on its ass and tell it to fuck itself, and I wonder if I could stand my bad conscience. Lately I can't help thinking that I might be able to, the same way people stand chronic minor illnesses that are annoying but can be relied upon not to kill them. You can thank yourself for this creeping realization. I don't blame the tree.

The tree is perhaps the only innocent party in this story. In one way or another, the rest of us are guilty parties. The tree was in the wrong place at the wrong time: in your front yard and the path of a lightning bolt. It was older than your house and, unlike that house, beautiful. And you (who are terrified of the muggers and junkies supposedly infesting all cities north of Southdown, NC, but tend to ignore dangers actually present) stood at the metal screen door watching that lightning storm. In a thin cotton nightgown, pressing your seventy-year-old chin and tits to the cool metal. Your eyes wide and black, no doubt, with that fear and fascination that is all your own. And what happened next? Well, the lightning struck the tree, not you, but you *felt weird* after seeing the strike at such close range. I happened to be working very late on the night of the storm, so it was Dad who took you to the ER. After he'd finally gotten you checked in, it was past midnight and he, never a night person, was already tired, so I said I'd go sit with you and bring you home.

When I get there, I thread my way through the usual Saturday-night-ER chest pains, drug freakouts, and knife cuts. I find you placidly relishing the Valium drip and blood pressure monitoring accorded hypochondriacs and hysterics. "Oh, honey, you're finally here," you say, beatific. You love the ER. It has good drugs. I should ask, "So, what do they say?" You wait for me to, then answer me unasked: "They say I'll be fine."

"What do they say is the matter with you?"

You beam. "They say I've experienced a Lightning Splash," you announce.

Oh, fuckfire, I think, a *term*. You love terms. Diabetic neuropathy, viral encephalopathy, leptospirosis, Spotted Fever, Mad Cow Disease... Lightning Splash. Now that you've got a name for it, we'll be hearing about it for the next two decades every time someone tries to open a window. *A Lightning Splash*, you repeat, as if it's a luscious sweet drink.

An hour later, around 3 AM, I ferried you home in a cab driven by a polite dark foreigner. An Arabic book lay on the front passenger seat, as you kept remembering for months, telephoning twice a day to ask me if you should have reported him to the police as a 911 terrorist.

"He's probably a Divinity School student studying the Koran," I said repeatedly. "I don't think al-Qaeda terrorists have to moonlight as cab drivers in Southdown, North Carolina. I think people on the al-Qaeda payroll have a nice cash flow and a nice apartment and are probably there right now watching *The Sopranos*. If you call the cops on that cab driver, I won't ever sit with you in an ER again."

We're old dealers in threats and consequences, you and I.

So, time passes. Your house, for a long time the ugliest on the block and crumbling by the month, gets untenable for you as your bad leg gets worse and your mobility diminishes. At Cold Comfort Farm, as I call it, you are virtually trapped upstairs, and Dad runs up and down them bringing you meals and books and the mail and doing all the housework. And, as maintained by my father, Cold Comfort has a special intransigence; it's a house that fights back at every turn when a person tries to clear, clean, cook, or just flush a toilet without incident. People have broken their hips and started down that slippery slope to the undertaker's slab in environments far less challenging than old Cold Comfort.

The house next door to Cold Comfort, immaculately maintained for the past fifty years, goes on the market later that summer, and I buy it for you and Dad because it is all on a single level and in good shape. I have no savings left after that and feel a shuddery void that I keep expecting to fill up with some warm sense of Doing the Right Thing. Meanwhile I clear out the old house, unheated and cold as a witch's tit in November and December; I rent a dumpster and fill it with as much crap as I can haul out, evenings and weekends spent chucking mateless shoes and plastic flowers and dead philodendrons and other languishing plants into the dumpster. This is the only paragraph of the house-buying chapter that feels anywhere near as good as it should feel. It's fun to clear the crap out, strip the house naked. Packed trash bags land with a *whump*, loose hard objects with a pleasing, empty, echoing bang.

Maybe I should explain. To the person without your compulsion, hoarding seems a vice, and a dreary one—messier than heroin, more like putting out cigarettes on your forearms or making yourself throw up. Like burns, it's nasty and hard to eradicate. And the hoarding itch runs down our thin family line but halts, *slam bang*, at the wall of my different temperament. I'm not nice and possibly not even good, but I do have a drive for clarity, and hoarding offends me. When Gram's house came to me, it was packed to the ceilings with stuff crammed arbitrarily into boxes: old satin ribbons, old letters, half-eaten and ossified chocolates in ancient boxes, socks full of silver change, and too much real jewelry and handmade lace for me to just toss the lot. The packrat packs out of insecurity about the future, but after a while the junk takes over. Then you might as well own nothing, since you can't find anything you own, and you don't even own your space. Your stuff owns it. And if the Bomb gets dropped, there's more to fall on your head.

The out-of-control packrat discards the future for an impacted, impassable past and makes the present moment always and forever less than it could be. The ultimate waste, even if this life isn't the only one we get.

I have never found a pattern in your acquisitions: the precious and the worthless get equal abuse. I could open your long Victorian bookcase right now. I can remember the day you bought it, when I was in sixth grade, and you had it moved into the living room... one of many purchases that meant something at the time, but never proved anything in the long term. If I open it now, I find an 1858 prayer book underneath a pile of stained Avon sales brochures from 1987. I find a 1934 Shirley Temple doll in its original package, ruined by melted drippings from the chocolate Easter eggs you brought back from dinner with your late adored mother at the Cracker Barrel. Moving you to a new house weeded some of the mess out, that's all. The new house doesn't look like a sane person's house; it's just not an egregious firetrap like the old one. If I had imagined you in cool, calm, inviting spaces, I was a fool beating off to a magazine dream. Is that dream the remnant of love, the need for control, or some fond foolish notion of order? Perhaps all of those. At any rate, linked by blood and nothing else, you and I are doomed to offend and affront each other. You find me unfeeling, and I find you disgusting. This tangent on hoarding would seem off-topic but that it is something that makes sense. It is something that may explain this grim relationship, even to a loving mother or daughter. (At work, for several years in the pre-texting era, I could hear half of my friend Molly's phone conversations; she and her mother were close in a way that seemed to oppress neither, and Molly always said good-bye with, "I love you, Mama." And I was both envious and squeamish.)

But, to return to the saga of the empty house and the tree, Dad finds down-on-their-luck tenants, Good Ol' Boys, to inhabit Cold Comfort Farm, with its now-lightning-blasted gothic oak in front. Dad proceeds to play Lord of the Manor in an unbecoming way and tells people that he owns half the block, but this fanciful lie is the least of several evils. I ignore it. This September, there's a hurricane that no one can ignore, a storm that tears some of those neglected limbs down and leaves others dangling precariously, and the GOBs start to agitate: Now that it might fall on their heads, the oak must go. I urge you to get on the phone and find someone to remove the tree. Rather amazingly, you find someone who will do it for $3,200. This scenario is so much better than it could be that I don't worry enough.

Dad is flying back to his childhood home in Arkansas—the template, I think, for Cold Comfort. He is going to stay two weeks; he needs a break from you and the big cooked breakfasts-in-bed that you require every morning. But everything is in order for the tree's removal in his absence.

That week while Dad is afield, you note that one tenant, the middle one of the GOBs, let's call him GOB2, seems to be yelling much of the time. I walk by and hear him: a flat, loud, mush-mouthed rant, so I can't get the words. He looks "funny," you say. This is an example of what I call your eleven-year-old-responses. You think about sex like an eleven-year-old, with too much logic and no desire at all, and you think in the same way about the other adult pleasures/releases. Actually, sometimes the eleven-year-old stuff is amusing; a couple of Thanksgivings earlier, the morning after Dad and his bud Victor had killed a bottle of Dickel, you called me at 6 AM to report that Dad was "shuffling" and "slurring" and you thought he'd had "a series of small strokes." I came up the block to look into his flinching eyes. A snapshot taken of him at that moment would have looked perfect under the dictionary definition for *hangover*, but that point you'd missed. I suggested that he was just tired and to offer him aspirin, let him go back to sleep, and make him some coffee when he woke. Then, I predicted, he would stop "shuffling" and "slurring." Anyhow, it doesn't occur to you that GOB2 is on a bender, so I gently suggest that GOB2 may be drunk. "Don't pay him any attention," I say. "Call me if you feel threatened. Seems he's on a bender, that's all."

You say, "Well, he's been on it three days, then. Why does he do that?"

History, misery, I don't know. He could probably tell me why he does what he does, but you can't tell me why you do what you do. Why should you expect the same from that near-stranger?

The oak is sheared of its many arms over three days. It is mid-autumn, a greengold, honey-struck season in these parts. The two sycamores that guard each end of my block are lashing their brilliant bones in the chilling winds. Unlike them, the oak will be denied its final beauty in November, its round gold lucency at sunset. That has always been its season and hour of holy beauty. I am sad about the oak, which isn't the first one to suffer here. Across from me there lives a woman whom most of us on this block hate—some for other good reasons, but I have a special feeling for trees and hate her because of a tree she maimed, a month after she bought the house and moved in with her back issues of Martha Stewart. It's an oak that might have been standing, already a big tree, when the first Europeans arrived in these parts. I can imagine them, their English flesh pinkened by the mighty heat of our sun, cooling their stinging faces in its shade. That oak is a golden icon of my childhood and a survivor of all the historic hurricanes, a cathedral of a tree. Because it shed leaves on her roof, that woman had half of its limbs lopped off. Now, when I sit on my porch, I look at the mutilated half-tree and am glared at by a huge, too-bright swath of sky that used to filter through the leaves as slow, syrupy, ambered light.

I try to keep the Cold Comfort oak a strict matter of business since, as an actual safety issue, the tree must go. Furtively, at work, I spend a couple of hours on the phone getting the phone company to come move the phone lines at the times when you need them moved. I try not to look down the block. The Cold Comfort oak is the neighborhood's only buffer from the flayed and staring ugliness of the house, its four teary front eyes. It's a resigned battered child, grubby and perpetually sniveling.

You and Dad have been no blessing to this neighborhood, which is small and kind and tolerant, perhaps too tolerant. Our last one suffered from us too. Across town where we lived when I was small, we had the smallest and worst house on the block, and after we moved, Dad would neither sell the house we left behind nor maintain it. He seemed intent on conveying his contempt to his former neighbors by forcing an eyesore on them, even after the original neighbors had moved and the people he was offending were pure strangers and the city fined him quarterly for the weed-wild yard, the dangling tree limbs.

This is the pushy and hostile thing in Dad, the desire to create some meaningful ugliness and make people pay attention to it. To his way of thinking, everyone who grew up more comfortably than he did, and that's most people, deserves to have Meaningful Ugly foisted upon them—every house nicer than his first home, and that's most houses, deserves to be defaced. Attila was the Scourge of God, but Dad's content to be just the Scourge of Houses: He neglects them, gouges them, paints windows shut, lets drips drip and rots rot on. He buys hideous pink paint at closeouts and slops it all over interior walls, lets it bleed and dry deathlessly onto window glass. He piles backyards with empty plastic milk and juice jugs, builds little shacks to put the jugs in. He erects little structures of barbed wire.

When we moved into the house that is now Cold Comfort, I was nine. I was thrilled with this house that had an upstairs, windows looking into trees, a yard clear of junk. I remember how I played in the clear, clean back yard of the new house those first years, mainly climbing the trees and reveling in the remoteness of everything seen from the heights. But I felt defeated when your habits caught up with us: the house started showing wear, the spaces filled up, the yard burgeoned with Dad's scavenged crap instead of grass. I thought we had something bad in us that would follow us like a nasty tail. What we had, though, was your packrat panic and Dad's appalling hostility.

As a child, I thought of you as the victim and Dad as the aggressor, the person who imposed this nastiness on us females. As a young adult, I reframed you as the spider and him as the bumbling prey, dozing complacently in your squalid silks. Where I am now, I see that you finish one another's work. It is the kind of relationship known in math and logic—see, there is logic here, though dark logic—as complementary.

In the here and now, I get a hysterical morning message to call you after the work on the tree is three-fourths done; I get out of the bathtub and put clothes on and get there as fast as I can. What I learn: that GOB2 has told you the electric company will take down the tree for free, which is roughly as likely as interest-free loans from Central Carolina Bank. Rather than shrug off this obvious fiction, I learn, you have paid off and sent off the tree surgeon and his cherrypicker. The tree surgeon has $3,200 for a job he hasn't finished. You haven't had the electric company verify the idea that they remove trees for free, as the electric company isn't even in its corporate offices yet, but you've just accepted it verbatim from a tenant who's been beer-boiled and ranting for three days.

You have some clue that this was a bad move; you are in a state of tearful defiance, saying: "I know you don't think I have any sense," as if to block me at the pass.

"You haven't," I say. Your jaw screws tight, your little puckery rubbery rose of a mouth draws in on itself; you look like a toddler who's trying hard to shit her pants in some highly public venue. I don't think toddlers are cute, I think they are ghastly. Their puffy, drooly faces remind me of yours. I can feel the fury with those brawny mamas who lift their tough beach-burned arms to belt their brats right there in the Wal-Mart. I bet it feels grand to give that nasty fat-cheeked creature that's fouling its pants for the hell of it, or howling like an air-raid siren for sugar or plastic junk, the proverbial *something to cry about.* What trumpets of rage must bray in the brain in advance of the shame! Smacking your jaws now would probably send my blood pressure up to 300 over 300, and I'd thump heavily to earth, dead on impact, but feeling the delight in my teeth and toenails even as I flared out.

I make my voice neutral and put a stone Buddha look on my face. I say, "Who do you expect to put up with this kind of thing for the next twenty years?" I don't stay to talk further, I can't. Yes, this is a nasty story from a nasty person. Or a deep dip from the vinegar vat, the acid after the last of wine or love.

As we all find out, surprise!—the electric company does not take down trees that are not a clear and present danger to its lines. Now the tree is no danger to anything except the aesthetic sense and the aligned entity known as Property Values. But that's not all there is to the tree.

Just what is the tree at this stage? It is a towering limbless stalk, maimed, doomed, and hideous. It is a jagged spike against the sky.

I knock hard on Cold Comfort's door, raise GOB2 from his sweaty slumber, and point to that limbless monument to madness. And I say, "All you had to do to get that out of here was keep your mouth shut, and you apparently couldn't even do that, so don't come complaining to me because you have to look at that thing there." *You're on your own, guy,* I think, and yes, I know how I look.

The next day, you are murmuring tremulously about what Dad will think. What's happened? You went to sleep crazy and have wakened sane.

I can deal with crazy, and I can deal with sane, I have my modes for each, but any flip-flop this fast disorients me. Pick one and stick with it, I want to say. Pick *crazy* and do the thing up big. Mess around with propane torches. Fish up one of Dad's many firearms and point it at me, please, and threaten to blow my brains onto the wall behind me. For that scenario, the law and the medical establishment provide a script. What's the phrase, *posing imminent danger to self or others?*

I travel frequently as part of my job, and I have to leave before Dad gets back. I expect, when Dad arrives, to hear him yell about the tree. I'll be in Montchapelle and might not even need the telephone to hear him yell in Southdown. Dad rather relishes ugliness, but he intensely dislikes spending money even if it does get results. He has just spent a shitload of money. The results must be regarded as, at best, partial.

I don't hear anything, though. When he comes back, Dad acts as if he hasn't seen the limbless remains, though it would take Helen Keller not to. Is it because Dad's eighty-five, and his visit to his relatives was tiring—they're old too, but very active, always running off to bowling alleys and the early breakfast buffet at Denny's and rodeos and turkey-shoots—that he hasn't thought of it yet? Or has he deduced the obvious? And said to himself, *I can't stand any more*, and simply decided that he sees nothing? (Worse, has he noticed that this place got exponentially uglier in a fortnight with no effort on his part, and it's even more of an affront to the eye than it was when he got into the airport shuttle? And does that make him, in some unfathomable way, happy?)

So... arrival at Rope's End, I wondered, or is Dad looking on the bright side and viewing this totem as his personal store of firewood? In some manner, you and he and the GOBs have settled in with the situation. When I pass the tree at night, walking the dog, the oak looks like one of these doleful obelisks they've put up on some concentration camp sites, sculptures formed to reach up at the sky in a silent, static, unending wail. I think: *You two so-helpless, I-just-can't-do-no-better types run a concentration camp for trees and houses.*

And that's the end of the story, if it is a story. It is entirely unbeautiful and unredemptive and makes no sense. It is not a tale told by an idiot, but a tale told by a hissing bitch, an unsympathetic defendant.

You wonder if I love you at all, and what I will do with your stuff when you're gone. You have this sneaking suspicion that I won't treasure it. I suppose I will divide it between sale, trash, and charity in color-coded garbage bags. But in some way I will get rid of it, all of it. I will incinerate the scrapbooks, the photo albums. Will I enjoy that? Oh, I'll enjoy it. I will scrub the house until the bones of my hands burn. I'll enjoy that too. I will have that wooden spike removed. I will forget you.

Snakehouse

If you want to know why I done it, I mean the shit that got me my personal minute on CNN, don't follow the money... there ain't none... follow whatever leads to the girl. Every tribulation is a road that leads back to some bitch. This one, people call her Sha... rhymes with *day*... but she's got one of them long fake African names. She's fine, she's smart, she's *too* smart, she looks like a little black panther in them funny clothes she wears. She goes for thin white skirts that, like, drift around her so you can't see no leg, and little white shirts that let you see just the littlest bit of belly skin, and ain't no belly under it because this girl is tight. I say like a panther because she is one very black, very narrow girl. She moves like silk in the wind. Big hooded goldbrown eyes, lashes that look a inch long. I kept telling her she ought to get some good pictures of herself naked, so she can look at them when she's in the rest home and remember how fine she was at twenty-two. I said I'd bring my camera over, but she said *get out of here.*

Then I ast her what that name of hers meant, and she snapped at me.

"I got no clue, Rodney," she said. "It's some foolishness of my mama's, and that fool can't find her ass with both hands." I don't know why, but Sha don't respect her mama. One time Sha tole me, "I hate it when we"—she meant black people, she sure didn't mean me and her—"give our kids these made-up names that're supposed to sound African but don't mean nothing, or names that mean something but the mama don't know it. They ought to go on Google and find their kid a real name, you know? My son is Nathaniel Turner Judd, and that's for Nat Turner."

"That his daddy?"

Then Sha gives me this look. "You're so ignorant. Isn't it boring being so ignorant? Nat Turner led a slave revolt and burned down half of Virginia. In 1840 or something. He scared the shit out of those people before they caught him and hung him."

She has her a attitude, Sha does. She didn't go to college because of this baby she's got, but she did finish high school, and she really remembers stuff from there. I don't remember nothing from it but a few fights and them old walls I stared at. And you can tell Sha knows she's smarter than most people, with college or without it. And yeah, that fine bitch is smarter than me, but she was not smart enough to turn twenty without no baby. And take it from me, babies are bad fucking shit. Me being where I am is that damn baby's fault. She's different about that baby than other girls I know who got a baby when they didn't mean to. She cares about that baby. She don't give him no Kool-Aid or let him eat no lunch meat. Sodium nitrates gives you cancer, she says. Saturated fats gives you the high blood. She gives him weenies made out of soy beans and expensive orange juice without no sugar. That kind with the pulp that just about makes me gag, she makes him drink that stuff. She don't never smack him, but she thinks I did. Didn't think she could hear all the way from the kitchen. He wouldn't hand me the TV remote, kept stickin it in his mouth, so maybe I did pop his butt, and the little bastard yells, and Sha's telling me to get out and not come back. Said she'd call 911 if I wasn't out that door before she counted three, and that was one and two, and her brother would be in touch with me if I came around again. I don't want no beef with her brother. He's ice-black like her, ice-cool, about 6' 6." The last fool that crossed him's still in the rehab, learning to count and walk again.

When I'd cooled from getting throwed out, when I'd thought about what happened, I was shame. I thought about a million generations of little kids getting belted by their mamas' boyfriends that wish them kids didn't exist, the kids growing up waiting till they can belt someone who can't fight back. Hate's like some STD you get from your parents, like syphilis. You see those ads in the bus about getting checked for syphilis, though?—I say that's wrong. Little kids that read that ad, they gonna think their mama got VD. Anyway, I don't pretend I got right on my side here. Sha was not having no man hittin on her kid. She done the right thing. Me, I know I'm wrong, but that don't keep me from being mad.

I kept both ears open to hear if she was spreadin her stuff around, but she wasn't. She took care of that kid and worked, and her job, it's the kind of job that gives work a bad name. Before she throwed me out, I come to take her out for lunch, picked her up where she works and run into her boss, and he was this old white fucker with this beard like Santa Claus and these hippie beads around his neck. I ast her did he look down her shirt, she said no, he was way past that, but she'd rather have him look down her shirt than interrupt her forty times a day, then fuck up the computer so she'd have to fix it. Well, I knew her job took it out of her, I would not want to be dealing with no mess after eight, ten, twelve hours on that computer typing shit for that old white Alzheimers fucker.

I thought, *I'll go away and come back not ignorant. I'll come back as a man Sha can respect.* I got a job at Ferrier University because after you work there two years, you can take classes free, get your education. I started cleaning rat cages, then I moved up to snakes and lizards. They got this Komodo dragon that can take your hand off. Animals there sort of like Sha, they ain't none of 'em tame, you better respect 'em.

Them ones with scales kinda spooked me at first, then I got interested. The rats ate rat food from a bag, but the snakes ate stuff we had to fix by hand. Just like Sha's baby name after that slave revolt dude, them snakes only eat quality food, but for a snake that means crickets and mice and rats. Them rats all fat and happy in clean warm cages didn't know what was coming to them. *Prey*, the supervisor calls the animals they raise to feed to the snakes. Herpetology is the right name for the science of snakes. I learned the words that have to do with snakes. I learned them metric measurements I missed in high school. They ain't hard when you got a use for them.

Down at the university, they got this Burmese python name Baby Love that shits and pisses like a horse, and he's three hundred pounds and one dangerous fucker. They got a albino python name Blanche Du Boys, but she ain't really white. She's this pretty neon yellow. The pythons ain't poison, they squeeze things to death. But, are you ready for weird? I like the ones that bite. I like the ones that're poison. You gotta respect them things even when they still wet out of the egg. They born poison and they just get more poison. And some of them are sneaky fuckers, like some dealer that dresses like a bum and drives a used car but runs all the crack in his town. The Australian Brown snake is just a boring-looking brown snake but the most poisonous in the world. But lots of snakes are pretty like jewelry. The African Green Mamba's green like leaves in April that kind of glow in the light when the sun's about to go down. And when the Green Mamba stretches its jaws to strike, the inside of its mouth is the prettiest... most awesome... blue. The coral snake has wicked hot pink bands. The sea snakes move prettier than any woman, even Sha. A few months on that job, and I was different about snakes.

That spring I'm near the place Sha works, not stalking her if that's what you're thinking, just walking to the bus stop—I'm passing a vacant lot that'd just been cleared and I see this little baby copperhead on the sidewalk. I knew what kind she was, brown and tawny gold like Sha's Gucci bag she's so proud of, sticking out her tongue and hissing, little Pretty Baby Death. I found a piece of cardboard in somebody's recycling box and threw her back in the grass.

That made me think about how baby snakes, even the mean-ass biting kind, are... well... portable. They weigh only a couple of grams when they're hatched. The person keeping the records could write down the wrong number of eggs and then take the extra baby home. That's how I got my first Green Mamba. By then I knew how to make her a habitat, and I had it all ready, and plenty of the right food. I had a container to take her home in and keep her warm—she hatched in the middle of winter. Had this container under my coat while I slid over the ice after this big crazy snowstorm and waited for the bus, and of course it was late because of the snow. I hugged her little container and hoped that it let in enough of the warm air under my jacket and listened for her little shifting noises. Named that snake Delilah. Fed her exactly like we fed the Mambas at work, and she grew big and bad.

I think right about then something changed, my *focus* I think they call it. I'd been working that job so I could get a education, so I could impress

Sha. Then I was working it so I could be around snakes, then so I could get snakes, the kind I wanted. Only way you could get the snakes I wanted was to go where they live and catch them, or through a place like the university. They wouldn't have sold me no poison, lethal snakes. But I was the best damn animal care technician the university had, see, because I needed them to trust me. I boned up on spelling so I could keep the records right. I got a raise and a new place to rent, a little house in a neighborhood where there wasn't no crime and people minded their business but talked to each other too. Good enough folks, they'd've been glad to hang with me, they wanted me to know they weren't prejudice, maybe they was chafed because I didn't want to hang with them, but I kept to myself because I had my own shit to do. My place had this big, warm basement where I could build snake habitats, and it had a deep back yard like all the houses on the block. It gave me privacy. I had two real good years in that house.

At work I was careful, I timed what I did and did not write down the wrong number of eggs or hatchling snakes more often than every three months, and nobody caught me. If they had, it would've just looked like a human error. I got another Green Mamba, Samson, and a Black Mamba I named Tina Turner. Got me a Coral Snake, a Blue Cobra, a Australian Brown I called Bad LeRoy Brown, like LeRoy Brown in the song, because he had him a attitude, it didn't matter none to him that I fed him, he still wanted to put his teeth in me. Maybe he was pissed to be in a snake habitat in Southdown, North Carolina, not in Australia all wild and free and biting Australians and kangaroos and them retarded-looking koala bears. I put Samson and Delilah in the same habitat for a while and played some mood music for them so they'd mate. If I had not had to be so secret, I could of sublet the rest of the house, cause I moved a big chair and my CD player down to the basement and that's where I stayed most of the time off work. I didn't bring the TV down there because I'd rather watch the snakes. Getting into them like I did gave me a focus, but it got my ass where it is today too.

You want to know what else got me where I am? The weather! The weather in this state is fucked! This is supposed to be the south, but in the winter it can snow ten, twelve, twenty inches. They ain't got no plows to get the snow off the roads like they got up north, so the whole damn place shuts down when it snows. I've walked two miles over snow and ice to take care of my snakes at Ferrier, and two miles back to take care of my snakes at home when it snowed like that. *Dedication*, my boss said. We get ice storms that knock the power out and paralyze the whole damn state. I had me a kerosene heater at home for when the lines went down, and the university has a backup generator, so their snakes don't die. My kind of snakes, they hate the cold weather. And it can get wicked cold here, but it can get wicked hot too.

I'd had my little snake condo complex in my basement for two years and everything was okay, hot or cold, until the early part of that August. That was a dry summer, man, and most of the time it was pleasant after dark. But then the heat ratcheted up during the day so high that it did not even cool off much at night. Only 20% humidity and a hundred and six degrees, not natural southeast weather. My basement was usually just right for tropical snakes, but that weather made it too hot. And if I had put a air condition down there, that would've made them too cold. So you can see the fix I was in. I ended up standing this big old box fan at the top of the stairs to send just a little fresh breeze down and running a lot of orange drop cords and little fans to keep the air moving in the basement. Couldn't have the cool air too direct or close, or it might hurt my snakes. I'd put a bed in the basement, and I usually slept there, but that was such a hot night I went upstairs to enjoy the AC myself. It worked out okay the first night, so I just kept running them fans. Didn't know my nice little house got its wires installed round about 1940 and nobody'd done much to them ever since.

So, hot like Phoenix two, three, four days. Old folks without no air condition getting heat stroke and dying, having heart attacks. The town made this temporary law that you couldn't water grass or flowers, so the woman next door, she'd sneak out at night to water her lilacs. Round about 3 AM I'd hear her water hose, and I could've looked out and seen her in her pajamas, but I wasn't that interested after the first time. Them PJs covered everything she had like a old potato sack. Tyrone Carter went on vacation, so I had to take double shifts for a few days. Meant I had to leave the fans on for sixteen hours at a time. When I came home, I'd turn them off for a hour in case the wires was hot.

I was late getting home that night. I got off from my double shift at eleven and stopped at the bar, then I stopped by the grocery, and the bus was late. So I sat there with ice cream melting in my bag in the hot, hot night, and finally the bus comes. I don't have no car because snakes are expensive to keep up even if you get them for free. I could afford a place of my own and snakes, or a place of my own and a car. Not both.

I heard the sirens when I got off the bus two blocks away, so I started walking faster. Then I turned the corner onto my street, with my ice cream melting and a bottle of ice tea slopping in my Kroger bag. Then I saw it: the whole block full of fire trucks and cop cars, the police barriers... and my place burning. The big hose pouring chemical foam into those flames. Orange light like Hell in the Bible all over everything. Everybody on the block out on their porches in their PJs, staring. Kids barefoot in the street like it's fireworks on the Fourth of July.

I dropped my groceries. I couldn't get through the police barriers, so I slipped through the backyards, got my ankle bit by a damn dog, but I kept down low in the shadows and shrubs and made it to my backyard. Only luck I had was them firemen was so busy in front that I could get in the back.

The way the fire started, the wires that overheated was in the front part of the house, where the line comes in from the big power pole. So the front of the house was burning up while the basement was just smoky. I smashed the basement window in and wiggled through.

They say I did not take no precautions, but it's a lie. I had me some snake-handling gloves and a big sack made of this woven metal material they can't bite through. I got Delilah and Samson and their latest eggs into my bag, and I got a bunch of the others in there before I started coughing on the smoke. I zipped the bag up and undid the lids on the other habitats to give my other snakes a fighting chance—I propped up a bookcase board like a ramp from the floor to the window—and I got my bag and my ass up through that basement window again. Cut my chest and back pretty bad on the glass. Tried to leave by the back way, but some cop saw me—"You the occupant?"

It ain't my fault that they made me put the bag down and some kid fucked with it. When they'd finished asking their questions, the bag was unzipped and my snakes had done headed for the brush. And I seen Delilah's newest babies had hatched and headed for the tall grass like their instinct tells them to do. Snakes don't need no personal safety instructions.

So I'm arrested for felony endangerment, and I'm also arrested for possession of illegal animals or some shit, and my stuff is all burned up, and I got nowhere to go but my mama's after I make bail, and I have to go to the damn University Hospital ER and get sewn up while I still have insurance before the university folks fire me. They didn't lose no time doing that. I got a court date in December. I ain't bothered with no lawyer yet.

But it's not like I ain't got no satisfaction. Them people on my block was jumping out of their skin about my snakes. The police put fliers on every door telling them not to go out in their yards after dark or barefoot. Now them people are wearing big old hiking boots in this stinking hot weather when they walk their dumb yellow Lab dogs. Bet they're gonna still be calling 109 Meadow Street the Snakehouse, even when the landlord tears down the black shell and builds a new rental place. They're gonna stay nervous about the high grass. And it's still August. Animal Control says my snakes gonna die when the temperature goes below sixty degrees, but that ain't gonna be for a while. This is one wicked summer. Could be October before it's down to sixty. Them people gonna spend eight, ten, twelve weeks shitting their britches over my snakes. For all they know, ol' bad LeRoy's curled up in the honeysuckle, just waiting to taste yuppie ankle meat. Ain't like I didn't make no impression on them people.

The Animal Control tried to catch my snakes, but my snakes are smart, and only a few got caught. Animal Control in Southdown, North Carolina, ain't trained to catch no smart, fierce, poison African snakes. And animals do what the scientists at the university call *adapt*. And evolve. My snakes were very healthy, I made sure they were. Maybe they'll evolve and adapt and survive even when it gets cold. Keep them people's lives exciting.

I did get a call from Sha at my mama's: "Rodney, was that you with those snakes? How come you get a good job and then you steal snakes? You eat up with the dumb ass for sure. You do that to get my attention or something?"

I got one more satisfaction then. I said, "This ain't about you, girl."

Maybe it started out that way, but now it ain't.

The Longfords

Well,

I know how this ends, but where to begin? I was not doing well, but with my mother's divorce festering like gangrene through my teens, I'd have looked insensitive if I'd bounced around, flourishing. Just so I wasn't doing badly, in some way that was a personal nuisance, nobody fretted over me. We were all drifting, drifting was the norm—just so we avoided freefall.

My brother Carey, our superstar—even Carey drifted. Back then he slept with a movable feast of fair, gawky, loose-limbed, and slightly younger boys who always seemed to have colds, and with Sophie. Sophie was the constant, and the part I least understood. In the glittering, guttering seventies, we were all thin and cocaine-burned. That is, except for Sophie, who had a butt and a belly and preferred chocolate to the best blow money could buy. What Carey wanted with Sophie was a subject in the realm of those real and at least somewhat adult emotions that I meant to postpone indefinitely—he loved her. My take on that was, "Yuck, love!" as if it were lice, which also became an issue during this time, with Kwell popping up on the shelves of CVS and Brooks Drug stores in even blue-chip urb-burbs like ours. Drifting people end up in dirty beds and get lice. Not that Carey's boys ever gave him lice. And Sophie took Carey's boys easily in stride; she called them all "Drippy Noses." After a while, though not when they were around to hear him, Carey called them Drippy Noses too. Sophie was smart without seeming that way pointedly; with that little not-even-unkind phrase, she managed to make the boys somehow less important, both to herself and to Carey.

When Sophie came into our lives, she and Carey were teenagers. Late teenagers, but teenagers still. I was a kid. As a kid, I got used to Sophie at the family Thanksgiving, Sophie at the family Christmas. During the time I am talking about, we all were post-adolescents, trying to grow up in a down economy. My mother had finally proceeded with her divorce, exorcising my dad from our house like that demon Pazuzu from Linda Blair. My father had plenty in common with Pazuzu—the garbagemouth, the spewing, self-renewing rage. Even the same expression. Dad was one of those bipolar people who like their highs so much that they won't take their drugs, even if that means they are furious and hysterical about 80% of the time and the rest of the known world hates their guts. We needed to exorcise him, but the strain of doing it left us one shell-shocked sample of postmodern gentility, way poorer than we looked, living in a house that was a holdover from an earlier, wealthier life.

In that post-adolescent season, I began my special social life. I grew a tad hostile toward Sophie and the Noses, all of them, because they complicated my social life. Privacy was definitely an issue, since our house only looks big and there's just one bathroom on each floor. I'd staked out the living room for my social life. Well, to cut to the chase, my close girlfriends were Helen Sloane, Darci Marsh, and Aviva Ullstein. We'd taken ballet together since age six, and we were very body-worried. If you remember the clothes back then, you know that they began as comfortable things like jeans, then they got tight. Or they were soft but clingy: those silky, petal-thin Quiana tops. None of these clothes left you anywhere to hide. The jeans either hugged your hipbones and squeezed you out above the waistband or rose to your waist and gnawed you there. Nothing reflected worse on a person than flesh squeezed out above the low or high waistbands of those silly jeans, size five or size three—sizes one and zero hadn't been invented yet. Take it from me, though, the threes and fives were tiny. However, Helly, Darci, Viv, and I had a tactic. We did not eat all week. Oh, we consumed rice cakes and salad and Tab; we ate blueberries, strawberries, kiwi berries. Negligible-calorie food. Oh, and popcorn, saltless, butterless, like hot Styrofoam. We stuffed our spasming, raving little guts with popcorn. In winter we had spells of shakes and shivers as our metabolisms faltered in the cold.

During the week, we did uppers: all the cocaine we could afford, the occasional touch of meth. Our pictures from that time show us hipless as whippets, our hair full and windblown the first couple of years and then punky and short, our eyes dilated and dark. Our pictures show us in little tees tucked into crotch-slicing, low-riding jeans. The tees show our nipples, wicked candies. You probably think we were screwing our brains out, but we weren't, at least any more than necessary to acquire a modest steady stream of blow. We had jobs where such connections were easy, and my job was the most glamorous of all—I tended bar in an S&M-themed club. I worked in tiny little clothes of rubber or leather, sometimes in costumes I made from materials like Saran Wrap or black garbage bag plastic or duct tape, which made me sweat off gallons of waterweight. Watching me in action, it would've been easy to imagine my sex life as comprehensive and perverse. The fact that it was me in that place, *that* was perverse—under my bondage pants, I was tighter than Credit Suisse.

I didn't fight much with Carey, but we did have one fight about him and Sophie coming to the club. I didn't want them there, they didn't belong, you could tell that before they opened their mouths, and Carey likes to talk. He was already in a snit; he thought the upstairs bathroom smelled sour even though it looked clean. He'd snarked about the outfit I wore to work that night too, and my high chances of getting harassed on the subway if I looked like a little jailbait whore who catered to perverts, and advised me not to whine to him if some creep groped me. At the club, some friend of mine asked my brother if he studied Postmodernism, since this is a town where people think a question like that's an icebreaker. And Carey said, "I don't need to study Postmodernism, I live with Postmodernism. Postmodernism is a shaky fake. Postmodernism is a numb little virgin in a hooker's clothes." Since remarks like that impress people here, my friend was impressed and asked Carey what he did. Carey informed my friend that he studied dead languages, his girlfriend studied baroque music, and that tonight they were slumming, thank you very much! When I got home that night, I told Carey to stay out of the club and out of my business, an outburst of the kind that passes for incivility in our house. He arched his fair brows at me and asked, "And what business would that be, Zo?"

Helly, Darci, Viv, and I did have business, and it wasn't business I meant to discuss with Carey.

Every Saturday night, one of us rented a video, always a loud one. *Excaliber* worked great: very loud, with some real heat in the fuck scenes if we raised our eyes to notice them. And after we'd finished our Saturday night shifts, we convened in my living room, closed the door, started the film, and unpacked the food. We brought Doritos and gloppy dips, that thick and not too sweet New York cheesecake, jars of fudge sauce, and chocolate-and-peanut-butter ice cream. We brought bakery cakes an inch deep in buttercream. Or canned cake frosting that we ate with spoons. We mixed Margaritas or Bellinis or other sweet, sticky girl drinks in the blender and washed the solids down with them. That was the first course.

We brought ipecac syrup, which was the second course.

And we brought ketamine or other serious downs for the third.

"Zoe and her friends are in the living room doing club drugs," was how Carey put it when, for instance, telling someone they couldn't watch our TV on Saturday night. But he and Sophie were decent about never knocking on the closed living room door, and we were decent about using the upstairs bathroom to yark, rather than the downstairs one where Carey kept his shaving stuff. Ma was comatose on several of the paralyzing tranqs available for depressives pre-Prozac, and she was a sound sleeper, which solved one obvious problem. We alternated duty cleaning the bathroom before crashing in my room, usually around four in the morning. We did not eat all week, and then Saturday night we ate all we wanted, yarked, and crashed. Carey would be at a concert or movie with either Sophie or one of the Noses. They all liked to eat supper out, late, then come home for the horizontal bop. Occasionally, during a trip to the kitchen to heat stuff or get ice, I'd meet Sophie in her flowery Lanz nightgown on the way to the bathroom, probably to wash Carey's secretions out, or one of the Noses in Carey's bathrobe. I couldn't imagine how Carey could put his dick into someone aslosh in Chinese or Thai or Indian food, whose breath was a steam of indulgence. The idea nearly made me yark without ipecac.

I couldn't see the point in Carey's social life. At that point in my life, I'd never felt a thing down there. I thought maybe I'd been born without the G-spot that was all the buzz. Truth was, my body was busy with hunger and with the mild chronic electrolyte imbalance produced by sweating under impermeable materials. My head was busy with horror.

None of the explanations for my condition has ever satisfied me. Yes, I read magazine stories that were written to make women desperate about their bodies, but I'd swear that my terror was chemical. My mother never said a bad word to me about my body, and neither did anyone else, though such comments would have come naturally to my dad. Carey didn't tease me. Carey didn't think I was very bright and could be relentless in not taking me seriously, but he'd have never let anyone hurt me or purposely hurt me himself.

The real divide between Carey and me does not have anything to do with brightness, though, but with dark. As a child, Carey was not afraid of anything. As a man, he continued to live in the light, cheerful, entitled, pleased with good dinners and good weather and male or female skin against his own. As a child, I was afraid of everything. This did not end with being a child.

When you are a child, if you have my kind of terror, you're forced to live with it, and it just gets ground-in. In fact, the worst thing about childhood is that you're stuck with what it gives you, even if it is unendurable. Lash out or act out, and an unenlightened parent will beat your ass; the enlightened kind will haul you off to a shrink, who'll give you a kindly lecture. Either way, while you're a kid, you're stuck. Drugs may be bad, but it's worse to be snagged on those spikes of mood and have to stay there. As a kid, what can you do about yourself? Maybe you do sports, as I did, not because you love sports—it's a family myth that I do—but because the motion stills that pulse of low panic. I only felt better running up and down the hills of our suburb. I only felt better in constant motion, dancing. I only felt better driving fast enough that all the neon blurred, and on the kind of drugs that narrowed my vision and drove my metabolism like a piston. I needed to move faster than something that coursed through me like wolves. When you're finally a teenager, you can buy drugs, and that was what I did about myself, and what many others do. And drugs are certainly not *the* answer, but they're *an* answer, which is better than *no* answer. And they're usually better than the panic itself. If you're female, that panic probably attaches itself to your body. The women's magazines suggest that to you, the clothes suggest it, but don't be too quick to say magazines and clothes are to blame. The body is just the most obvious hook on which to hang that horror, it's something that's your own, and it feels like the cage you're in. You don't know that the cage is the whole world, the only world you can be sure of, and not exactly a cage, and that you have to find some way of settling into it as something other than a prisoner on punishment.

You are probably thinking that my near-and-dear should have staged an "intervention." The truth was, my dad was out of the picture, and he'd hammered my mother down until all she could do was make herself breathe, take a shower every day, and occasionally eat. "Intervene in what?" my brother would've said. He had plenty to do already. The further truth was,

I had a job and earned my way and paid my contribution to the household, obeyed the traffic laws, and voted. No one, unless they were closer to me than I wanted them, would have called me dysfunctional. The only hint I got that anyone might think so came when I overheard Carey snarking at Sophie for telling me I was looking good. I'd just come back from a couple of weeks in Acapulco. I love me some Mexican food, so I'd been eating. My hungry body had packed on five pounds. My pants were tight, but I did look fine, cat-sleek and tanned.

"If you compliment her, she'll starve her dumb ass until her ribs stick out again! And then she looks like something out of Belsen, and she worries Ma!" hissed Carey. And I expected... I don't know what I expected... Sophie to say something condescending, or to defend herself against Carey's carping. What she said was, "I'm not going to treat your sister as if she's a crazy person." And Carey said, "You know perfectly well that Zoe's always been a mess. I think Dad molested her, or if he didn't succeed all the way, he gave it the old college try." And Sophie, sparkier than you'd think, just says, "Well, she's your sister. I'm not going to treat her like some insane child."

I'd had no idea she had any respect for me.

Despite Carey's little line about club drugs, I'd never done ecstasy until that night. Good cocaine was my thing. E was supposed to induce empathy, no draw for me. Helly contributed some E to the chemical candy-pantry that night, though, and the first thing I noticed was it didn't affect me the way it was supposed to. I didn't feel like joining the emotional sloshfest that the other three were enjoying. They had *Bambi* playing and were bawling over it. I mean, sitting in a row on the couch and clutching one another and bawling right out loud! It was gross! The second effect of E was this horrible, horrible thirst. It was winter and cold, but I went to the kitchen faucet and drank and drank, the coldest water the tap had to give. I don't ordinarily drink tap water. Chlorine and dioxin and DDT and all, though, I sucked it down. Then, my whole body tight with water, I wove around, trying to clean up. Helly and Darci had crashed in the living room, and Viv was on my bed. I got rid of the mess and drank down the last ipecac in the bottle. I felt too hot and still thirsty, so I had some more water and stood at the laundry room window. A green shooting star fell down into the icy city night. The ipecac started to work, and I wasn't going to make the bathroom, so I made for the kitchen sink and hung over it.

To say that nothing happened, that would be wrong. Two things happened, in two opposite directions. Every muscle I had below my armpits seized, trying to help me throw up what I had inside, but my throat locked. My stomach tried to punch its way up my gullet, and my throat fought back. The water was too cold, it had caused some kind of spasm. I couldn't throw up, and my breath came through a pinhole that felt like it would soon be no hole at all. God, the pain!

Holding onto the sink, praying to breathe, I heard Carey's door open, and Carey saying, "...and cranberry juice!" And here comes Sophie, in her usual Victorian nightgown and Carey's bathrobe, a joint property between herself, Carey, and the Noses. Teeth clenched against the chill, she made a beeline for the cabinet where the glasses are, then saw me. I'd sort of slid down, as if all of a sudden my legs had turned to tapioca, and the lamplight of the kitchen was going far and dim.

"Chrissake, Zo!" says Sophie. She thinks I'm choking; I am choking, though not for the usual reason. Sophie knows the Heimlich maneuver. She's down with me, wrestling me around, so I end up with my ass in her lap, her hands under my ribs over the tight drum of my stomach. Everything blacks when she puts the pressure on, but, oh, glory, my throat unlocks and I'm not going to die tonight. I yark all over my shirt, my jeans, her ruffly sleeve. I yark quarts and quarts. Our kitchen floor tilts a little, so it flows downhill.

"It's nothing," I snuffle, when I can.

"Nothing, my fat fanny," says Sophie. She doesn't let go of me; I'm still in her lap. We both breathe hard. Then she tries again. "Zo, I've known you since you were little. If you want to talk about it to me, you can. If you don't want to talk to me, I'll find you someone."

"Nothing," I say. "There's nothing to talk about. No *it*." I wriggle away and try to stand up. I slip back into my own puke.

"I know you and those three little druggie sluts spend every Saturday night throwing up," she says. "I know you scrub down that upstairs bathroom like an operating room after you four have done your thing, but that's a lot of puke, and that smell clings. Doing this for months on end isn't *nothing*."

"Sophie!" called Carey, aggrieved.

"Please," I had to say.

"I won't tell anybody if you'll promise me to stop doing this. If you won't, I'll go tell Carey we're taking you to the ER right now. I'll make him get up and get dressed and drive us."

"That's blackmail," I said.

"Yes, but it's the only mail you're going to get tonight. You want to answer me, or you want me to go get your brother? You know the look he's going to have on his face when he gets an eyeful of this."

Actually, I did know. He'd laugh first. Then he'd be righteously mad. Then he wouldn't shut up about tonight for months on end. "Okay, okay," I whined. I wanted Sophie to let go of me. She felt too warm, like flesh. "I'll stop. I won't do it again."

"You know I'll know if you do. I'm here all the time."

"Yes," I agreed, "you're here all the time."

"Now we're going to stand up very slowly, and you're going to find me something to sleep in." Sophie flicked something off her sleeve into the spreading slime: *splat*. "What the fuck is this, Zo, bean dip? And Skittles?"

"Right," I said.

"Well, they smell really bad together."

"Sooooophie!" yelled Carey again. And Sophie called back to him, "I'm coming, hon. I've got to clean up, I spilled something." She got to her feet and slowly, gently pulled me up.

Well,

*

I didn't stage my own intervention because of Sophie, but because I woke up before the other three. For once I hadn't gone to sleep on heavy downs after our weekly orgy, so I woke up clearer than I was used to, and in a fierce amount and kind of pain: my abs, my neck, my scoured throat. I retched blood and got a look at Viv on the bed beside me, looking like the Vampire Lestat had been at her. She'd drooled all over my suede and bunny fur pillow, too. I looked at myself in the mirror. My hair was sweated flat to my head, and I had this crazed, shocked look, as if some crazy cop had zapped me with a taser between my shoulder blades or right at the sensitive base of my spine.

Realizations can get you when you're weak, and that one got through to me. It told me this situation was a high cliff. Telling myself I could always jump later if I had to, I stepped back. I started begging out of Saturday nights. I said that I had to work/had a date/was seeing someone/would be out of town. And I decided to live as if I were not afraid. I decided to have meals, to have sex, to have relationships if I could. None of this felt good at first. I thought a zillion times: *This is too much, too warm, too close.* I was not gracious about it, but I did make myself stand it, as you make yourself hold still while a nurse draws blood. The people I'm sorry for are two good men who shared apartments and beds with me during the chapter entitled *Zoe Forces Herself to Live a Real Life.* They were both kind men who tried to deliver for someone who was young, and young for her age, and needy—someone who shrugged or slapped their comfort off more times than she accepted it. In this way I traveled through a cold, hard decade, one long economic slump in my part of the world. I remember how Sophie wore all black for a few years because it matched and washed in one load and was mourning. Carey's grand plans and her grand plans were stalled; here they were, unknowns, much the same as when they were new little graduates. We all felt that some fine, dangerous future had withdrawn from us the instant before we could fling ourselves on its blades. Some of us wore mourning; everyone who had a brain mourned. I made myself accept what happiness that was left to us, though, because I'd seen the consequences of saying no to it. I made myself stay open to any other form of happiness that might stray within my reach.

*

Segue now to the family Thanksgiving a few years forward. Ma is exhausted from the cooking, and I'm in the kitchen, scraping plates. I have just moved back home, away from the second of those good men. I overhear Carey, *sotto voce* to Sophie and my cousins: "Oh, I don't know why we're beating around the bush—Zoe's having a scare. Zoe's probably pregnant. And we're going to have to do something about it, because this kind of situation is just why God made abortions. Can you imagine Zoe with a child?"

If I had slung the greasy turkey platter at him, I'd have been within my rights.

"She's better than she used to be," said our cousin Nadia.

"But still!" said Nadia's brother Jake.

"Does Zo still have that club job?" Nadia wished to know.

"Yes, at least it's full time. She tends bar," Carey told them. In our family, you are not supposed to be twentysomething and tending bar.

I took a long look at the turkey platter, got Carey well in my sights, then decided not. I was having a scare—I should have been scared, just like I should have been mad at Carey, in the next room talking about me as if I weren't there. But the weather in me had changed since the start of what ought to have been a scare. I was strangely calm. Strangely happy. It felt so good that I'd put off calling the clinic to schedule a scrape. And I didn't need to, because I miscarried just after Christmas. I'm sure my brother gave me no credit for what went on between my ears and in my heart then: adult grief. And a sense of injustice for someone else—carrying the baby even that little while had chilled the bad electricities in me. I'd felt calm for the first time since I was virtually a baby myself. And, doing something that good for me, that baby still died while it was just a little curved fish inside me.

But I remembered the calm—like this! Suppose you've grown up in some really nasty place... well, I've never been to any nasty place, but I've seen pictures of Mississippi, and it sounds nasty in Faulkner. Anyhow, some nasty place where it's flat, where it's hot about nine months of the year, and the sky is soggy gray or gunmetal blue, and you can't see the stars at night for the mosquitoes. And suppose, after knowing nothing but this nasty place, you get to go to Maine or Vermont in the winter and see those pure, sheer pink sunsets when it clears after a long snow, and the long pink or mustard-gold light of sunset. Even if you have to go back to your nasty place, you're happier and calmer because you know something else really does exist. And I knew that calm existed somewhere, like snow. I'd had calm pumped through my body with my blood, all warm with pregnancy hormones.

For a couple of years, I stayed in my holding pattern. Give me credit where it's due, this means that on no Saturday night did I purchase a controlled substance... or a pound can of Almond Roca that I'd eat in thirty minutes. I kept my job and ate healthy food two times a day and worked out five times a week, but no more. I'd make a point of buying a pound can of Almond Roca and making it last a week. This sounds small, but for naturally unhappy people, moderation and rationality take real concentration. Real commitment. And, oh, did I mention that Sophie and Carey got married? The Noses attended the wedding, then drifted away in several directions and sent Christmas cards in December. That's Sophie, patient. She waited Carey and the Drippy Noses out.

I did not get married until later. Back then, marriage would've been too close, too hot, too real for me, but I did ease into a relationship. It would be strange if I hadn't. The truth is, I've always been eye candy. The damage in me didn't show. I worked to fix what I could and keep the rest invisible. Every time a conflict surfaced between my new man Harvey and me, I told myself *this doesn't have to be a fight. We're grownups, and there are ways we can solve this. I don't have to be scared of a fight. I won't die if there is a fight, but there doesn't have to be.* In some way, Harvey picked up how terrified I am of fights, even though once I'm in one, I'm a totally dirty fighter and ashamed of nothing I say or do, at least not till later. It was like Harvey was saying, "C'mon, Zo, we'll work it out, here's what I give, what do you give?" I've heard a lot of talk in my day, but never any that made better sense than that. Bit by bit by bit, Harvey and I were able to work out our conflicts. It was like getting the rocks out of a field, but fields in this part of the world just keep churning out more rocks. We got rid of our rocks. We moved in together. First we had a household, then a home.

I am the most obvious case, but we've all gotten better. Carey's bad allergies have cooled down. Sophie used to have terrible headaches, and every few months Carey would have to drive her to the ER for a morphine shot, or, later, after it was invented, Imitrex. Those're the only times I ever saw Sophie look as bad as I've seen myself look, weak and heaving. Sophie doesn't say anything about headaches now. The other day I asked her if she still had them, and she said no. Furthermore, she said it seemed unreal that she'd ever had ER-level headaches. She knows she did, but it's stopped being a threat, stopped being important.

Maybe it just takes a very long time to settle into this plane of existence, to get used to living in the body and do it well.

My Harvey is a quiet man, easy in his own skin. People in my family talk too much for me. It's always been on my nerves, all that glittering, bantering talk. I'm not good at it. But I'm perfectly good at other things.

When we found out that I'd started Harvey's baby, we didn't get rid of it. This time, since I'd been eating well for years, I was able to go the distance. And calm settled into me like a winter sunset nine months long. Having the baby hurt, though not as much as when my throat locked and I might've choked except for my sister-in-law, who's never mentioned that night again. In fact, that episode put all fear and all pain in perspective for me: death at kiss-distance. Death that hurt. *Not-that-bad, not-that-bad, not-that-bad* was my mantra during the pushing phase, and it wasn't that bad: I could speak, curse, breathe. I didn't resent that having the baby hurt, because her nine-months inside me altered me for the better—permanently, as far as I can see. There are ways we can go wrong, something skewed and short-circuited in the control panels of soul and body. I went wrong, and my daughter put me right. Calm is not just possible, I know. Calm is available. I can have it. And, raising her well, I can do exactly what I'd say God put me on earth to do, at least if I believed in God. I can raise her as if there really were a kind, noticing God who doesn't mean for us to live in pain.

My daughter's name is Emilie, meaning *eager.* I wish there were a name that means *Zoe's cure and calm and salvation,* but there isn't, so I picked a solid, sensible name, not a trendy name like my old pal Darci's. A silly name like that is cheap like a fad, and fads don't last and mean nothing in the first place. At least I came into the world with meaning: *Zoe* means *life.*

"How's Zo?" I heard Sophie ask, right outside the birthing room door while they were cleaning Emilie up. And my ob-gyn said, "Doing well." And I am, still.

Is it trite to make this kind of promise? I do, anyway. This may be the age of reduced expectations, but where Emilie's concerned, mine will be higher than what I've known. Emilie is not going to grow up in a house where she can have a social life involving multicourse dinners of street drugs and junk food and ipecac. So long as she lives in this house, I'll know when she comes in at night, and in what shape. And she'll know that what she lives in is not a cage. Some way I'll balance those two agendas. And I'll be the first to know if ever she's not well.

Sophie and Boots

I have a very handsome husband. Carey was worshipped as a boy at Exeter and Harvard, and for cause. Carey looks like F. Scott Fitzgerald before the gilded novelist dissolved with "a paper bang at the last party given by the rich." Carey is not a cold man, but he has that boreal gloss, that pale and pure physical glamour belonging to F. Scott and a few other blessed blonds. A Renaissance light shines on him, even in the dark. I am not impressive until you hear me sing. That some people begrudge me my husband and my marriage should probably not surprise me.

We met when we were just kids. In a student production of Gluck's *Orfeo* at Dunster House, Carey played the harpsichord continuo. I, a nineteen-year-old whose mezzo voice matured very early, sang the lead. I don't mean for a second that I sang it as it should be sung; Janet Baker and Maureen Forrester did that. To give credit due, though, for a nineteen-year-old, I sang it well. It's still my favorite role. As Carey has a beautiful face, I have a beautiful voice. Carey followed my voice home.

We took to each other immediately and learned about each other very fast. With true proletarian squeamishness, I learned about all the sex Carey had with worshipful other boys at Exeter. Then I settled to the task of making myself more worthwhile than the holdovers, his six or eight epicene sidekicks. For some reason, all of Carey's catamites had outrageous allergies, perpetual colds, and noses that seemed perpetually a-snivel, so I called them the Drippy Noses. I have not waited out this assortment of lanky, loose-limbed, Claritin-popping snot spigots in vain.

One of the pieces at our wedding was the march from *Judas Maccabaeus*, with its mighty thundering obbligato played on a Flenthrop organ–"See, the Conquering Hero Comes." And in my head, I saw that hymn as a tribute not to Carey, but to me, Sophie, for being able to offer something the Noses could not—and I don't just mean tits. Most people would've said the odds of sex and class were stacked severely against me. I've found my marriage worth every tiresome, awkward, or self-doubting minute leading up to it—worth the effort it takes to deal with the past and its Pandora-possibilities of dissolution, even. Well, anyway, in that moment I gave myself credit. And in the matter of Carey, I don't back down easily.

So my confrontive first response to Boots will make sense. It took place in a school, like much of our mutual life. Here is the timeframe: Carey and I turned twenty-one in our last undergrad term and suffered through our last reading period and exams; we graduated; we married. Compared with anything else we'd done over those four years, getting married was easy. Because we were so young and our parents loved us feverishly and were so proud of our little résumés, they paid for the wedding and did the hard work of putting the wedding on. All we had to do was put on our wedding clothes and say our lines. Then they sent us to England for an old-fashioned honeymoon. By late June, we were back in the States and headed for graduate work—Carey in languages and linguistics, and a cram course in Russian for me, Sophie, so I could sing in it. The setting was a highly competitive graduate school with a famous summer program; you've probably heard of it. Going there, I stepped further into Carey's world; the dean, Amy Tilden, was an old friend of his family. I do not come from people who are old friends with prominent, powerful administrators whose ancestors came over on the Mayflower.

The summer program features one odd anachronism. There are male dorms and female dorms and no married-student quarters; everyone lives like an undergrad. Most everybody has a roommate. Mine was a big blonde girl, a Victorianist. Carey's roommate Boots was from a "good" family down south, whatever southerners mean by that. Usually it's a combination of old money, bad genes, manic depression, and nicknames like *Boots*. Some of those people may not mind being called things like *Boots* because their parents name them much worse things, like *Pinckney* or *Ingersol*. Boots isn't gay—if he were, what follows would not be as spooky as it is. I am used to gay guys drooling after Carey. That happens every day of the week. Another pertinent detail: Boots had gone to Exeter with Carey. Carey says that some of the boys there called him something way less flattering than *Boots*.

So we're settling in. We've set up my half of my room, and we're putting Carey's stuff in his half of his room. Then Boots opens the door, recognizes Carey, and falls on Carey's neck. Shaking out the quilt on the chaste single bed, I thought, "Well, here's more of this *formosam pastor Corydon* shit." Frankly, what I'd heard of screwing around at prep school sounded so furtive and perilous that it was hard to believe anyone found it worthwhile. Now, if the staff catches kids fucking, they just talk to them, and no doubt the "talks" are excruciating, but back in Carey's day, the consequences were far-reaching, life-altering, dire.

Boots had the lingering, hungering gaze of the misunderstood, the famished-for-understanding. The hot, intimate reek of desperate loneliness, a huge turn-off for someone like Carey. Carey makes the introduction: "Boots, my wife, Sophie Lyon-Longford." And Boots says unconvincingly that he's pleased to meet me. He asks, "Do you write or something?"

Or something, meaning anything I might do is inconsequential. I say, "I sing." Boots, no hypocrite, doesn't even ask what kind of music.

Anyway, Boots moves into a dorm room with my new husband, and then the weird times roll. Boots's nondescript clothes get discarded in favor of pastel oxford shirts and seersucker or khaki pants like Carey wears in the summer, and bucks. Boots manifests with pale cotton sweaters tied around his neck the way Carey ties them. Boots gets a watch like the one Carey wears. And Boots changes all his courses and takes the same ones that Carey had chosen that summer term. Boots wants to study with Carey; he wants Carey to help him with his work.

Does that sound weird? It is. A person normally arrives at a graduate school like this one with focused academic interests. People don't normally change such interests. They certainly do not put those interests on the shelf to follow an academic program chosen by someone they never knew well and haven't talked to in years. Even more unlikely was the act of shelving a normal graduate literature program in favor of Carey's program for that summer, which included Manx and Cornish. Carey has a passion for languages and an astounding memory, but it's his golden sense of himself that allowed him to choose a specialty like dead Brythonic and Goidelic languages in a prostrate and groaning economy, in a family that had lost most of its money, in a region where the competition for academic positions is unrelenting. Passion, talent, and self-certainty are the only reasons to choose such a specialty, and I was quite sure Boots did not have these reasons. And, lacking those reasons, Cornish and Manx, which are no longer spoken in Cornwall, the Isle of Mann, or anywhere else, are useless as stone boats.

A couple of weeks into that summer term, Carey and I didn't know whether to be amused or unnerved.

"Every chance he gets, when I'm out of the room, he gets my laundry out of my laundry bag and washes it, and I come and find it clean, *ironed* for Christ's sake, even my boxer shorts, back in the drawers," Carey had told me. "I keep telling him not to, and he keeps acting like he doesn't hear. He does this icky thing of putting what he calls *our laundry* together to wash it. He threw away the Tide he brought and now he uses Ivory Snow, like we do. He threw out his deodorant and his shaving stuff and got the same kinds I use. He's also started referring to his stereo as *our stereo*. And I want you to come have a look at what he's done to the room."

"Was he one of the ones that you, you know... at school?"

"No, Sophie! I had a couple of little affairs, okay? Worthwhile experiences, you know? Not with him! He was a sad little waif with bad skin."

"Well, while you've been here, has he ever, you know—?"

"No," said Carey, with an emphatic shake of his fair head. "It wouldn't be half so weird if he did. I know the script for that. It's more like he... well, remember that headcase we met in Waitfield, the one who kept saying he was a big opera critic? And you kept telling him you'd never read a single review he'd written? The one you said looked like he was dressing up as Roman Polanski? He wore these white jeans and those pink silk knit polo shirts, all of it so tight over that nasty little gut he had sticking out in front?"

I remembered him well—a perv, a creep. "Yeah, I heard he got arrested later. He collected all those dogs and was violating the health code bigtime, having an unlicensed kennel, animal cruelty, necrophilia, he had frozen dead dogs in his freezer."

"Well, Boots seems to be costuming himself like that freak did, only he's dressing up as me. And it isn't Halloween."

The nearest holiday, in fact, was the fourth of July. On the afternoon of the fourth, Carey and I were going to pick strawberries at a farm about thirty miles away from the school and savor a little private time. Coupletime and strawberries grown in this slow-warming northern earth, strawberries dead-ripe and fragrant, sweet and sour. I came to Carey's room early so we could chat while he dressed. Clean shorts and a polo shirt on his bed suggested that he was in the shower, so I checked out the room. We'd brought summer-weight comforters with blue chambray covers. Our other one was on my dorm bed. The second bed in Carey's room now had an identical comforter. The other desk had acquired an identical banker's lamp with a green shade and a Wind Machine mini-fan like Carey's, and an I. L. Bean travel alarm clock, same model, also blue, and Manx and Cornish dictionaries and grammars. I had the compulsion to look in the drawers, and guess what I found? Identical boxer shorts in identical folded stacks, identical tees, identical button-downs identically folded.

I had on a summery white dress, low in front and back, and I swear I could feel Boots's stare right between my shoulder blades, a fingerpoke from a feverish hand.

"What're you doing in there?"

"Oh," I said, "is this your dresser? It looks just like Carey's."

"No, that's Carey's, but what're you doing in our drawers in the first place, Sophie?"

Boots made my name sound ugly. The way he looked at me made me feel frumpy too. Not at all like a happy girl in a pretty white peasant dress, with French-braided, just-washed hair sweet with the green-tea and grass esters of a rich shampoo, with a string of blue sea glass beads around her neck. I recalled a city crone in the Star Market, an old girl who looked about 140, with a broad Slavic face and tits down to her navel under her ratty house dress, slamming cut-rate hams into her cart. *Sophie.* Still, I turned to face Boots. I somehow didn't dare not to. He was wearing what I seemed to remember on Carey that morning at breakfast: chinos, mint-green button-down, topsiders. This all happened before colored contacts, or I'm sure he'd have had some, as near as possible to the slate blue of Carey's eyes. His gaze this time was not the liquid hunger I'd seen in him already. Rather, it had a flatness, an intentness, an intention… at once violent and still.

"If it's Carey's, then it isn't yours," I pointed out; this was no time to overlook the obvious. "And since it's Carey's, that means you don't have an issue here. Maybe I want one of my husband's sweaters to keep my arms warm this evening, or a stick of his gum to chew while I wait for him, but whatever—it's nothing to do with you."

"You've no business riffling through our clothing," Boots huffed. That was a Careyism, a bit of stolen speech; at the beginning of term, Boots would have said, "You've got no business in our stuff!" like most Americans.

'What's this *our* shit?" I couldn't resist asking. "There's yours, and I haven't touched it, and there's his. This stuff is his, and he doesn't mind me borrowing it. If there's an *our* here, it's between Carey and me. People can go in one another's drawers when they're married."

"I'd have done something about that if I'd known," he said next, and then I knew where I was—that spongy, quicksand sensation. *Uh-oh, alone with a psycho.*

How sudden all this was! I heard a tooting band as the little town's Fourth of July parade turned off its Elm Street and headed down its Main Street. Life without fear, a stone's throw away.

"You weren't one of Carey's special friends when you were in school. And you didn't know me two weeks ago," I said, riveted, as Boots crossed toward me and with total deliberation clamped his fingers around my wrist and removed my hand from Carey's sweater drawer. As if he meant to strangle my hand, his fingers ground the little bones of my wrist against each other.

"You've just got to learn to leave Carey alone," Boots pronounced. I was too astonished to struggle, though he was hurting me, and that was what Carey saw when he returned from his shower—with his boxers already on under his big terry bathrobe. That was so not-Carey; he normally strolls from the shower robeless in summer, and in a Japanese robe of heavy, creamy silk when it's cold. The terry robe was a graceless novelty purchased early this term at the Ames store in town, after the five minutes or so that it had taken Carey to discern that lolling and lounging in his Japanese robe in front of Boots might be a bad, bad idea. Carey paused to take in the spectacle of Boots and Sophie apparently arm-wrestling over his dresser.

"What's this shit?" Carey wished to know. And Boots went righteously eye-to-eye with Carey.

"I'm just telling Sophie," said Boots, "that she has to learn to leave you alone."

I watched Carey contain himself. His face takes on a porcelain immobility when he's thinking hard. I wondered what he'd come up with, and I steeled myself to play along with it.

"Okay, guy, she's a fast learner. Let go, okay? I'll handle this." A non-Careyism, a bit of phony machismo. Something Tom Cruise would say in a film.

Finally Boots did. Under his grip, my flesh had gone from pain to numbness and now made the transit back as my wrist bones decompressed. The nerves he'd ground between them flamed and flared. The red imprint of his hand was on my arm. "I'll explain to Sophie about all that," said Carey. He gave Boots a between-us-guys nod.

Finally Boots backed away from me, and the buzzing potential for violence might have subsided by a half-tone. Carey strode lightly between me and Boots and plucked up his shorts. With his body in front of mine, he stepped into them, not bothering with any further clothing; he let the robe drop from him, then casually took my hand and led me out. Later I thought that was really his first act as my husband; since our marriage, he'd done nothing else with me that he had not done before. In March we'd been grown-up kids who stopped by the newsstand every day for chocolate, as we'd done almost since the first time Carey followed me home. After we got back from England, we'd been married grown-up kids who stopped by that same newsstand every day for chocolate. Nothing had really changed. Now something did change, right in the present tense, but with no time to think it through.

"Sophie, don't run. You go down first," Carey whispered as we approached the stairwell.

I counted at full value those fifteen or so seconds that it took Carey to follow me down, praying, yes, praying that the door of that dorm room above wouldn't open. It was amazing how afraid I could be of a man who, to my best knowledge, had no weapon but his rage. I may not ever get rid of the image of the dark old stairs and the big milky-glass skylight in the ceiling above them, and the mild diffuse light that filtered through on the old green walls. So civilized, so remote a place to find danger. Some housemother's irritable small dog is the most danger you'd normally find there.

Barefoot, Carey led me outside and away.

We did not go strawberrying. Just as we were, with Carey shirtless and shoeless, we proceeded straight to the administrative building and Dean Tilden's office, and Carey told our tale. Upset as I was, I was also impressed with his demeanor: equal-to-equal, dispassionate, all business. "He's a freak. I need him out of there, Amy," he said. Then he showed her my hand, the wrenched wrist: "Look, the psycho hurt her. In the morning there'll be a huge bruise."

The dean called Boots in and moved him to a single room by that evening. The Boots mess was cleaned up in the most laconic New England ruling-class way, with no hesitation and no discussion. I couldn't help thinking that if I, another outsider, had been the mess, I'd have been cleaned up just as summarily. The single room really was a good idea, as Carey observed; buying another wardrobe to match another roommate would have made for a prohibitively expensive summer for Boots. Perhaps Dean Tilden told Boots not to speak to us, or perhaps he had enough sense to keep clear of Carey after that. In any event, Boots went all cowed and furtive. The cafeteria offered bag lunches for everyone who wanted them, and he always got one; at breakfast and dinner, he sat alone and inhaled his meal and looked neither right nor left as he strode out. He didn't speak another word to either of us that summer. I'm told that he spoke as little as possible to anyone. He acted like someone who'd disgraced himself in some way that everyone knew.

Still, the scare and the brazier heat of hate that had come off him had driven a wedge into me. Sometimes, in my single bed at night, I imagined him having his say to me, telling me that I was frumpy even at my young age, that I'd overreached in every possible way, that I'd never succeed in opera, that my husband was really gay and would get tired of pretending otherwise, that my marriage would dissolve and I'd end up divorced and pathetic. And that weepy disgrace was what I deserved for interrupting this fated connection of comrades. Whatever message from the interior that had told Boots that he and Carey belonged together, comrades forever, must have seemed terribly authentic to Boots. Insanity probably does sound authentic because it's you talking to yourself.

And, whatever Boots was in my mind, in his own mind he was surely righteous and wronged and probably unforgiving. Also, he had sprained my wrist and squeezed a deep, dirty-looking blue bruise there, and for a solid week, whenever I'd let that hand stay still or get cool, or whenever my thoughts failed to distract me from it, it hurt. Its dull but fierce throb disturbed my nights so I could lie awake in a kid's bed, across the room from a stranger, and wonder what Boots was doing or thinking in his single. We heard he switched back to the Milton and Spenser courses he'd dropped. We heard he did poorly in the Milton and Spenser courses, and I felt a little bad about that. Low grades in such a place are impossible to live down. In August the term ended, and everybody went home. For us that was our first apartment in Cambridge, the linguistics department at Harvard for Carey, and, for me, my music and my singing coach, Alecto Argyris. My career.

*

What I put on the occupation line of forms: *operatic contralto.* Not someone you'll ever hear as Carmen or Azucena or any of the other sluts and old mamas of the high Romantic mezzo repertoire, but a baroque and classical specialist. Gluck's *Orfeo* is still my favorite role, the one most totally comfortable to me. If you perform the role, you have a pseudo-classical costume with draping to minimize your female curves, and you get to be the romantic hero who loses the girl and gets her back. It's very cool. It doesn't matter if the costume doesn't do a complete job of concealing your curves, by the way, because mezzos and contraltos are not known for spare, boyish builds. Opera singers in general aren't. I am big enough that every bulimic bitch in my dorm at college wondered how I got Carey, but slim by operatic contralto standards. I'd never given that more than a passing thought until after Boots. And I resent being made to think of it now.

Nearly a decade after we married, I finally got pregnant. An impending *Orfeo* production in Boston was postponed until the next year so I could sing the lead; they did *Moise in Egitto* instead. And we spent that year in a faculty apartment at Carey's prep school, where he was guest-teaching languages and history.

For a month or two, I mourned my sidelined condition; then I worried about getting through the rest of those nine months. By mid-pregnancy I wondered if I'd fit into my *Orfeo* costume ever again. I don't know how anyone has the breath to sing opera when pregnant enough to look pregnant, though Marilyn Horne once sang Arsace in *Semiramide* when she was far along. Did some costume designer actually manage to transform a short, chunky, pregnant coloratura mezzo into an Assyrian stripling? And how did she carry on? I couldn't have done it. I'd been ordered off work at month two, been painfully bored by month three, and by month four, I didn't have the energy to practice. By month five, a flight of stairs was a challenge. I might have resented being stuck at Carey's school at first, but by month six, I was pleased to be within a few steps of a bed or chair at all times, and it was a big bonus to have cafeteria food so that cooking and cleaning up were non-issues.

My son will never have a sib because pregnancy is perilous for me. I had gestational diabetes and blood pressure that stayed high despite aggressive treatment and spiked sky-high if I got upset. At month eight, I was as big as a Shetland pony and troubled with a sense of physical disorientation because of the pressure on my pelvic bones. It messed with my sense of balance and made me afraid of falling. I remember how conscious I was of hard surfaces and slippery marble or tile floors and sharp angles; the school was full of balconies and stairs. Architecturally, boarding schools are made for teenagers, creatures who take stairs two at a time and bounce when they fall—all those stairs! Oh, I had a keen sense of myself as a vulnerable person, someone who couldn't run and mustn't fall. And I was alone in a faculty apartment in the otherwise-empty dorm. But that's actually Act II. Let me handle Act I before we go there.

We lived on the third floor of one of the ancient student houses. By month 8.5, I'd been forbidden the stairs except for the most strictly necessary purposes, fire drills and doctor appointments. Carey brought meals for both of us upstairs on trays from the dining hall. Or, when he had dining hall duty—an onerous innovation to deal with the anorexia epidemic, checking students off a list to see that they come to meals—he'd send a student with a tray for me. I'd just taken delivery of my lunch, eaten it, and licked the last mayonnaise, the only salty item that my careful husband had chosen for me, from a plate that had held tuna salad.

Then I established myself in my armchair, an ottoman under my legs. I looked out at the campus through a spit of sleet and thought about what I'd do when the kid finally came out. I'm a fiend for salt, and I planned to celebrate the baby's arrival with guacamole and a big bag of corn chips. Other salty, crunchy treats were in my plans. However, because the blood pressure spikes alarmed me, I was pretty good about salt avoidance and rest. I was supposed to rest for at least an hour after lunch, and I settled in to do just that. When my cat, Nicola, woke up from her morning nap to lick the dishes, I beckoned her up, and she settled her light weight on the arc of my belly. I focused on her purr, matched my breathing to hers.

When someone tapped on the door, I was annoyed but not afraid. On this campus thick with the offspring of the rich and famous, security is thorough. "All right, all right," I said as the knocking got louder, and I began the work of getting vertical. As I got to my feet, I heard this *swoosh* of blood in the vessels in front of my ears, a human plumbing sound that filled me with low terror every time I heard it—I couldn't help wondering if the force of my blood through its highways was breaking little vessels in my eyes, weakening big vessels in my brain, preparing me for some blowout stroke at eighty. Making my whole circulatory system leak like the ancient plumbing of London, which bleeds shit and fresh water equally beneath the highest and lowest of London streets.

I hobbled to the door and opened it, as I say, without worry. Raw, stale stairwell air came in. I didn't immediately recognize the nondescript man there, neat in a storm coat. He didn't say hello, just looked intently into my eyes.

"Hello... I don't think we've met. Perhaps you've got the wrong apartment—did Officer di Felitto give you directions?" Officer di Felitto manned the guardshack, where campus police officers registered all visitors to campus before admitting them and directing them to the guest parking area. As the man didn't answer my question, I said, "Who're you visiting?"

"I'm here to see Carey Longford."

"Well, you're in the right place. I'm Sophie Lyon-Longford. And you are—?"

But then I realized who he was, and he said, "I know who you are," as if he had just bitten into something spoiled.

Enormous as I was, Boots shoved by me into the apartment, and before I could say anything at all, he said, "I've had optimal luck thus far. Officer Friendly at the front gate must've been taking a piss when I drove up. And I met up with a kid cutting class who held the door for me in return for a fiver." He gave me a lightless smile. He said, "Say, you don't look so great."

"I'm not so great," I said, then mentally kicked my own tail for giving him any information. "What's your business with Carey?"

"Unfinished business," he pronounced. He scanned the apartment, probably looking for the telephone. "Well, aren't you going to offer me coffee?"

"No. I don't have any. We don't drink it." That was the truth. "I remember... the last time we spoke. Maybe you better tell me what you came for. Carey's teaching now, and I'm not really up to seeing people." I wasn't even what my mother would call dressed, wearing leggings with a stretch panel in front and a stretched-out t-neck under this big wool sweater I'd found in a thrift shop. I'd accessorized with double layers of wool socks this ice-raw day, and ratty sheepskin slippers. Boots was blocking my way to the phone. My blood went *swoosh* in my head.

He grimaced, as if from headache. "I've stayed away," he said, "a long time."

Why say *stayed away*, I thought, as if we were some compass point, when there was never a reason for you to be here? But it might be dangerous to think in terms of things I'd call reasons. Some electrochemical short in Boots's head had sparked bright and hard like a camera flash and imprinted us on his brain: Carey as his fated soulmate, Sophie as the impediment. The honors seminar that Carey was teaching at the time lasted ninety minutes. By my watch, Carey was thirty minutes into it. A lot of harm could be accomplished in an hour. *Swoosh.* God knows what my blood pressure was—180/100? Worse? Battering my baby's veins and mine?

"It was unfortunate," I said. "I mean, the last time we spoke. I think you felt... hurt. And I was frightened. Carey was frightened too."

"Carey knows he doesn't need to be frightened of me," said Boots. He didn't say that I should know the same. If this happened now, I'd have a cell phone in my pocket and be able to speed-dial 911, probably, before he could stop me. There were two phones in that apartment. One was in the bedroom, the other in the kitchen.

"I suppose you think you've won."

"I beg your pardon?"

Boots curled his lip. "Getting yourself knocked up. Women always think they've got a lock on a man when they get themselves knocked up. First there's the ring, then the damn belly."

"I don't think people in happy marriages think of it that way," I ventured. Certainly I wouldn't tell this hostile intruder how much we wanted the baby. We knew he was a boy, and he already had his name, Wolff Neill Lyon-Longford. Wolff is Carey's mother's maiden surname, and it would let me call him Wolfie, as in *Amadeus.*

I put one hand to my lower back, which was spasming in response to the adrenaline flush in my blood. Nick, concerned, pressed up against my ankles. The sight of my cat agitated Boots further.

"Oh, don't tell me you've got a cat to give Carey's baby toxoplasmosis!"

"Nick doesn't have toxoplasmosis, and neither do I," I said.

"Cats are filthy fucking beasts that all carry germs. It's just like you to have a filthy cat."

"Carey cleans the litter box, not that it's any concern of yours."

"I might have known," sneered Boots.

"There's no reason you should know anything about us," I ventured. "If you really have business with Carey, you need to go to the main office in the admin building, tell Ms. Flagler there to page him for you, and wait for him there."

"Here's fine."

"No, it isn't. I don't feel well, I'm not up to company, and I'd like you to leave."

"You do look sick," he allowed. "Tough shit, you've got no business burdening him with brats. And I won't go anywhere until I want to go. I've been thrown out once, I let them throw me out, I've stayed away, but they had no right, and now I'm back. I've found out about you, you see. I only guessed that summer that you got me thrown out, but now I know."

"What do you know?" my voice asked, before my head could tell it not to.

"That you're Miss Nothing from Nowhere, for one thing—you come from Baltimore. Probably some slum in Baltimore. It's a sad day when Harvard has to take people like you to make itself look broadminded. All sorts of people go on stage, so maybe you belong there. But you never belonged at Harvard, you didn't belong at Middlebury, and you don't belong here!"

(I talked back in my head: *My father is a university professor in Baltimore, the first person in his family to go to college, true, but he has a Ph.D. from Ferrier. He graduated summa, which is more than you ever did. And Carey said you were a sad little waif. That was all the thought he ever gave you before you sprained my wrist.*)

"If Carey was going to hook up with a woman, it ought to have been Caroline Kennedy, not you. She was in our class. Both ways, she was in our class. He should've gotten someone with the money and connections to help him," added Boots.

(Carey knew Caroline and couldn't have cared less. He had his chance at Caroline if she'd been what he wanted!)

"He's forgotten it, what we had at school. That bond of brothers." Boots sighed at the pity of it all. "We didn't let those frumpy, geeky girls at school into our circle. They were the wrong sort. The school only had them because of pressure. From liberals and media lowlife, for it to go coed and let in riffraff with high IQs. You too, you're the wrong sort, but you've done something to Carey's head so he doesn't know it."

At that point, I did speak. "It sounds like you've been thinking about this a lot."

"*Stalker*, they called it. I didn't stalk him. I waited for him!"

I'd been counting the minutes until Carey came back and wondering how I could keep up this patter for fifty-five more. Then I wanted someone else to come first. It had been nearly a decade since that summer term and the incident in that dorm room with its twin comforters and desks. Since then, we'd grown into marriage and gotten our MFA degrees; Carey had earned a Ph.D. and written a book; I'd made my American debut, conceived a son, and had a contract waiting for me after the baby. What had Boots been doing in all that time? He'd been thinking about us. What else had he had time to do?

"How about your career?" I asked, as if this were an ordinary conversation. "Is it satisfying?" (Do you sit in the boardroom and brood about Carey and hate me? Which company's boardroom? Because I think the HR people there ought to know what a sicko they've got on staff.) My blood went *swoosh* in my head.

"It's a career. It pays the mortgage. Do you think that if you keep me talking, I won't hurt you?"

So hurting me was an option, as my nerve endings already knew. What did he have in his pocket under the big coat? *Swoosh* again. He might not even need to shoot me to do Wolfie and me in. He could just drag me out to the landing and shove me down all those stairs. Or scare me into a stroke. But what if Carey walks into this, and Boots does have a gun? If I keep him talking, maybe someone else will come first.

So I kept Boots talking. I let him strafe me with words. I kept wondering whether he knew my real secrets, which involved sex with my cousin in his car as often as we could manage, at a pretty young age, and a certain final on which I hadn't cheated but had come prepared to do so if necessary. Flunking exams at Harvard is not an option; you cannot live that down. Whatever anyone thought of my family, I would not ever have failed them that way. Boots didn't mention this. Boots wasn't, it seemed, an actual fly on the wall. He didn't know how Declan and I had gone at it in Declan's Camaro and had no intimations of my academic insecurities. He didn't know how, at thirteen, in the throes of depression, I'd once eaten half a Morton's apple pie, five minutes of piggery that felt dirtier than all the sex I'd ever had since then. Or how I'd hated my high school with such fervor that once, late Friday afternoon after a really shitty week, I turned on all the faucets in the girls' bathroom and hoped they'd run all weekend and shoot the water bill up to high hell. I could have just smashed the mirrors in there, no one was around to know, but that was too-violent vandalism for a girl who already meant to sing opera and be a civilized person. My blood beat in my ears, and I kept Boots talking, spewing about my unworthiness. Perhaps his rage would burn out before he hurt me and before Carey came home.

Meanwhile, I remembered everything that ever made me ashamed.

Boots kept standing between me and the door, between me and both phones, and I could feel his long anger like the wavery air off an overheating stove. I remembered how, at long intervals over the early years of my marriage, the phone would ring a single time very late at night. Not often, not more than once on those nights, but it had happened every single place we'd ever spent time. Cambridge. Dubrovnik. Oxford. Rome.

"And now you're in a fix, aren't you? No one's coming, you can't get to the phone and call Officer Friendly to throw me out, and maybe I wouldn't let him, because maybe he doesn't have a gun, not in a place like this. And you're afraid I'll hurt Carey, though I wouldn't, and you're afraid I'll hurt you. An awkward position, right? But awkward positions are your usual ones, aren't they? You were awkward then. Not at all in Carey's league. I could tell you'd be a cow before long, and now you are one. What can you do?"

I wasn't consequential enough for such bitter hatred, I thought. Never even mind whether I deserved it! But my voice spoke without permission and said, "I can sing." Whatever was true or ever will be, that was true too.

That got his attention. What would he say next? Nothing, it turned out, because of the noise that distracted us both. *Splap!*

A snowball had hit the window. Probably a student who'd forgotten his key, wanting to be let in.

Boots turned from me and looked down onto the quad. Another ball of wet snow hit the glass, and a voice pealed out, "Soooophie!"

Down there, in the soggy snow of the quadrangle, was my sister-in-law, Zoe, with her three stair-step children—Emilie, Rosalie, and Coralie. Zo was in her usual black leathers, but the kids wore princess-pink coats and pink rubber boots, and they were holding hands in an obedient string behind Mom, wading through the slippery slop toward the door of our building.

"Sophie! Carey!" yelled Zo. "Are you dead up there? Come let us in!"

"It's Carey's sister," I said. Boots let me open the window and lean out. Zo and the kids made an eye-grabbing sight, and he paused to stare at her, and she saw him—as if there really was a God who didn't want this man to hurt Wolfie and me after all.

"Hi, who're you?" Zo yelled up at Boots. "Sophie, who's he?"

"This is Boots!" I yelled. "Remember Boots? He's come to see Carey!" I prayed that the silly sobriquet rang an alarm in her head. She'd been a distracted, self-involved teenager when Scary Boots was fresh news. *Please, Zo,* I thought, *don't blank on the name. Remember!* "Could you and the kids stop by the office and tell them to page Carey and tell them it's Boots? Carey's teaching, but he'll dismiss them early to see Boots!"

Zoe had gone very still, listening. She probably tightened her hand on Emilie's. She called up to me, "Sure thing, hon! Be right there!"

"Wait, Zo," I yelled. "There's a phone in the library. The front desk. They can ring his beeper. I bet they've got some new books to show the girls!" I meant that Zoe should leave the girls with the librarians until it was safe again here.

"Yeah!" Zoe called up to me. "We'll do that. See you soon!"

Boots was not alarmed. He was, I noted, distracted. He was fixing on Zoe in her black biker jacket and skin-tight leather pants. In black leather or anything else, my sister-in-law is one fine female. His expression didn't match the disapproval he felt compelled to express, but he did express it, and for a minute it derailed him from me.

"What's Carey's sister doing dressed up like some biker's slut? I remember Zoe before she had tits. She'd come to Parents Day here with his folks. Who'd have thought she'd grow up like that? I bet those little brats have three different daddies."

"She's into punk." With three daughters born in lawful wedlock.

"I heard she hooked up with some guy who runs some pizza shop or something."

"Right," I said, as if I agreed, as if this were a normal conversation. Zoe's husband was the heir to Papa Tony's. In other words, a national chain of pizza shops. Which isn't patrician, true, but had put Carey's family back on a patrician money basis and helped them keep their big house in Boston.

Boots watched Zoe all the way out of sight, then re-fixed his eyes on me, this time three feet away instead of eight. "But you admit it?" he asked. "You entrapped him? You made him think he needed a cow life with a cow and babies. You made him leave me behind."

They'll come in a minute, I told myself. *Zo will go to the library desk and have them call 911. They'll be here really soon. Say what you need to say. Say anything.*

"Yes," I said. "Everything. It's all true. I admit everything."

"And you're everything I knew you were."

"I'm sure I am," I said, feeling that oceanic rush in my ears, and my stomach lurching. *Whatever you need to hear so you don't hurt us, I am it or I did it. I'm guilty, guilty, guilty as charged.*

We are never all that we might be, but we're usually lucky enough not to know anyone who lives to corner us and flog us bloody with our omissions and commissions, our small shoddy consolations.

I let him talk five more minutes, then ten—so many licks of the whip. It would take Zoe at least five minutes, with the girls in tow, to get to the library. A minute to explain to the librarian, then the 911 call. The campus cops would call the town cops in on this one. I visualized the town police station, which was five minutes away in normal traffic, eight or ten in flying slop. I made myself see and hear a police cruiser, tires hissing over gritty ice, splashing mucky slush. I made myself see the officers' guns and nightsticks and their powerful, practiced hands, and I told myself that they would have experience dealing with dangerous people. (Though this was Exeter, not Boston—what kind of danger did cops confront in Exeter? Small-town dealers, fights in the pool hall? Shoplifters?)

Finally the door slammed open: three large policemen, Carey and Zoe behind them.

"It's he!" said Carey. Even in the heat of this moment, he doesn't say "It's him!" like some ordinary American. "What're you doing here, you freak? Sophie, did he threaten you?"

"And you," I said.

Carey yanked Boots away from me. "You get away from her!" he spat, and I saw the change in Boots's face. From anger to devastation. Shock. Despair!

Officer di Felitto stepped between them and got hold of Boots, and the other two cops closed on each side of him. "Come along, sir, you're not an authorized visitor. You're trespassing on Academy property. You're under arrest."

They cuffed him. As they were hauling him out, my voice spoke again without permission: "Boots!"

"What?" (Not, in front of the police officers, *What, you fucking cow?)*

"Boots, I can sing," I said. "That's what I can do." I took breath and sang the first few bars of the aria I loved and sang best: *"Che faro senza Eurydice? Dove andrò senza il mio bene? Che faro, dove andrò senza il mil ben?"* A call of lyrical anguish from spouse to spouse. I don't think I've ever sounded better. Maybe it was all the adrenaline.

It would have been elegant, perhaps made all this more forgivable, if Boots had said, "Yes, you can sing." But it was one of the town police officers, the one with the Italian name on his nameplate and the Boston accent, who said it—"Yeah, sweetheart, you sure can sing! Did this stalker freak say you can't sing? You sing great. He's fulla shit. We're gonna get him outta here." Maybe that cop and his Italian family had opera albums and sat around the radio Saturdays, listening to the Met broadcasts. Then he turned his attention to Boots, who'd been making inchoate attempts at interruption. "So, it's like this. Ms. Longford-Taglieri here says you're a fucking stalker, and you bothered these people back when they were kids in school, and now you're trespassing on campus, you didn't register at the guard shack, and then you parked in the faculty lot and entered this dorm unlawfully, and then you came in here and threatened the lady. You come along nice or we'll split your head for you. You got the right to a lawyer when we get to the stationhouse, and you got the right to remain silent, and if you're smart, you'll keep your mouth shut and come along."

Boots kept his mouth shut and went along. Down below, the officers hauled him through the evil mix of sleet and freezing rain and put him in the cruiser. The Exeter cops didn't get all that many chances to use their siren in town, so they turned it on full-blast and blazed their way toward the stationhouse, their red lights bloodying the snow. I could imagine the kids gawping from every classroom window, their frantic imaginings over that night's supper.

If this were some TV show, I'd have gone into labor right then and there. I did feel dizzy. Carey got the school doctor to come and check my blood pressure, which was scary, and give me a shot to bring it down. I lay on the sofa while the shot took effect. The doctor stayed and re-checked it until it was down to somewhat-normal. Zoe had left the kids with the librarian and went back to collect them after the doctor took his leave; we all tried not to get them scared. "There was a crazy man here bugging Sophie, but everything's fine now," Zo explained. "That's why I had you wait with the library ladies. The policemen came and got him and put him in jail."

"It's okay," said sweet Emilie, the oldest. "They had books about koala bears and kangaroos."

"And crocodiles," said Rosalie. "That's what they've got in Australia, man-eating crocs."

"Will they beat that man up like on TV?" asked Coralie, the youngest and feistiest of the three.

"I think they might, babe," said their mother. "They were really upset with him for bothering Sophie."

"I'd like to see them beat him up," said Coralie.

"I know you would," Zo sighed. "Haven't you got Skittles in your pocket? I remember you had Skittles. Now's a good time to be quiet and eat those sweet things. Give Em and Rose some."

"Zoe, thank you," I said.

"Welcome, Soph. Now chill out and let that godawful blood pressure go down before it comes straight out the top of your head. Wolfie needs to go full term."

My blood pressure went down, and Wolfie went full term. And by summer, I was back, my baby weight lost, full-steam into my real life. *Orfeo* in Boston, and my Eurydice was Alecto Argyris; I'd become a colleague to my mentor, which anyone would say is a real step up. Alecto is a glamourpuss even without makeup and, unlike most opera singers, tiny. She looks like a size-two version of Maria Callas and is loyal to anyone she likes, fairly terrifying to anyone else.

During the break at the first rehearsal, Alecto complained of my absence and explained that of her Russian husband. "Ah, Sophie, you don't know what you did by putting off the *Orfeo*. I ended up with Yuri in that college town in North Carolina—opera workshops for those howlers down there. You've never seen such a hot, brain-dead, smelly hole in all your life. I was so chafed with you then! But it all turned out. You know I'd already had it with Yuri? And it was the last straw when he dragged me to North Carolina. Yuri, he's been no good for a long time now. And I met this big sweet young man who played piano for Yuri's workshops. Just nineteen and so sweet! So I'm a cradle robber now, and I have a new lover and an accompanist." She called the hulking teenager over: "Alex, over here, love. Alex, this is my Orfeo, Sophie Lyon-Longford. I taught Sophie to sing. You listen, hear what good work I did."

After Alex made his manners, Alecto said, almost diffidently, "We heard about the stalker." She put her hand on my arm in this weirdly gentle way, like you'd do with someone in a hospital bed. "You'll tell me about it later? You're all right?"

Am I? I still wake up sometimes from dreams, saying, "I didn't!" or "I'm not!" Sometimes I wake up crying as I say it. In my sleep, I don't suffer that conversation the way I did in waking life, being silent to be safe.

I was right to be silent, though, right to be afraid. The police found the handgun, new and freshly oiled and evil, in the pocket of Boots's big coat, plus two extra clips of ammunition. Enough to spray a crowd, not just make point-blank short work of Wolfie, Carey, Nicola, and me. And how much intent had he brought there with it? If you really want to kill someone, after all, why stand around criticizing her? The forensics people said later that the gun had never been fired, and he had its instructions manual in his pocket with it. Somehow, packing that little booklet along with his spandy-new gun was pathetic—like Boots was somehow miscast as a stalker, in a role and a place where he never should have been—as unequipped to be a stalker as we were to deal with one. Still, how much skill does it take to fire a gun? As for intent, half a second's worth will do. You don't have to think about it for a decade, though he probably had.

I wonder what Boots thought would happen. I mean, when he put that gun in his pocket and headed out into the sleet. Did he have some wild Technicolor happily-ever-after in mind? Carey falling on his neck, cold as Cathy fresh off the moor? Carey sobbing that he'd learned his lesson? Or, if Carey wouldn't cooperate, did Boots expect to force Carey into his car with that gun and go—where? Or to take us both as hostages and have a long, red-headlined standoff with the cops? I can imagine that one: the academy on lockdown and a circle of cop cars down below, SWAT team en route by helicopter, lights flashing bloody carmine and antifreeze-blue, hazard barriers holding back the hordes of reporters. Later, if we got out alive, trashy tabloid gossip we'd never live down. Carey would have never gotten another decent teaching position as long as he lived; no school with any reputation to protect would risk such publicity. That gun clarified only one of the options.

In Boots's condo they found a big plastic box full of newspaper and magazine articles mentioning Carey and me, and all sorts of pictures, and some diaries that were all about us. They found graduation programs with our names circled in thick red ink. He'd spent a decade assembling those souvenirs. Something had made him wake up and decide that his stalled story needed an ending, some ending, that very day. Despite bad roads and wild weather, he'd set out to make that end.

I have had standing ovations at Covent Garden and, for Christ's sweet sake, La Scala! But still, in my dreams, I argue with Boots about my personal worth. And sometimes, when I'm awake, alone and uneasy, I find myself protesting his accusations of the evils I haven't done and the depravity that would have never occurred to me on my own: ***I didn't, I'm not!*** I wonder how long I'll do that.

Boots has a plea deal he'll respect if he has any sense: a suspended sentence, probation, and surveillance. A restraining order. No further prosecution unless he makes any contact, even the slightest, with Carey or me. We have three locks on every door to our place and check them very often. I have a cell phone now, of course, and I carry my cell phone everywhere but onto the stage. I can speed-dial 911 in my sleep. Am I all right? A person who could shrug off that kind of experience wouldn't be all right. Shrugging it off would show you didn't have good sense. The forensics officer told us that people like Boots don't forget.

"I'll tell you about it," I told Alecto. "We'll do lunch and I'll tell you. It's over. I think it's over." As over as stalker stories ever get, at least. "I'm all right. I think I am."

Ancestry

For Your Dreams

"Well, I wish he worked for me," Kris said as she brought the new client up on the screen. Bryce saw why: twenty-three at most, totally hot. A young man in loose white painter's pants and white sweatshirt. He sat in the insectile revolving chair, two thousand dollars worth of angled chrome, and started jigging it in quarter-circles with one restless foot. Then some tiny noise made him look straight into the monitor: olive skin, dark sleek hair cut close, black-lashed eyes of Caribbean blue—not cosmetic contacts, just glorious genes. He wasn't big—maybe five-nine, maybe a hundred and fifty sinewy pounds. Every part of him was tight and fine.

Bryce was far more used to seeing aging Beautiful People with their Versace clothing unmercifully tight on their nipped, tucked, and liposucked bods. Their eyes brimmed with entitlement and predatory despair. Their skins were soft and bright with designer collagens at night, papery-dry by morning. Part of the training at Kris's was keeping your hands away from their hair so you wouldn't dislodge anything. Also, the feet: Don't touch, don't look. The feet on both sexes usually got gross long before the bod needed urgent work, though Bryce thought the women's feet were the nastiest, with all those knobs and calluses from high heels. Yet another rule was pretending to be dead asleep when they got up to reconstitute themselves.

"Dancer," Bryce guessed. "Why does he need us?"

Kris just smiled.

Kris's card read *Kristine's for Your Dreams. Wish Fulfillment.* That could mean sex, of course. It could also include other recreational experiences, tailored to the client's desires, in a setting of unparalleled comfort, opulence, safety, and privacy. Unparalleled expense, too; a night there would run you twenty thousand at the least. There were rules: no drugs from outside, no diseases. But Kris also guaranteed that your experience would be as personally scripted as you liked, within the limits (no hospital-level damage, no juveniles who actually were juveniles, though Kris had twentysomethings who looked fourteen). Once all the specifics had been worked out and agreed upon, in the hour before the encounter began, the client and entertainer met in the establishment's medical office to have their blood drawn for the instant STD test. As per the contract, all sheets and towels and toiletries were incinerated the morning after. The pleasure rooms were wiped down for prints and checked with blacklights for trace amounts of human juices. Nobody could prove that you had been here.

Kris's entertainers were contractually guaranteed for health, for conversational and sensual skills, and for flawless looks. If she didn't have someone flawless according to your definition of that word, she'd find someone, do a health and background check as thorough as the CIA's, and plunge the newcomer into intensive training. Kris's people were contractually guaranteed to please all night long. And after the night was over, if client and courtesan met in public, the client could rely on the courtesan to show no flicker of recognition—that was contractually guaranteed too. That obscenely high up-front fee, cash only, bought complete safety along with the obvious. Oscar winners, Palme d'Or winners, fabulously wealthy old rock stars, and American presidents had long figured on Kristine's VIP list. It stood to reason that Kristine's would flourish when all those Boomer demigods started looking like pickled prunes.

"He says he has something to get out of his system… that's how he put it," said Kris. "Someone he loves, who loves him, who isn't available." She reached for the bowl of jellybeans, selected a pink guava one, and continued. "A top's top, that's what he wants." Kris was a roundish short woman who looked like she'd been a Brownie Scout, a really cute kid. She had. When she set out the scripts for these encounters, she did so with the cheerful, sensual precision of a happy caterer laying a flawless wedding table.

Bryce: "That's who I'm supposed to be for him, this top's top of his."

"Right. He wants someone forceful and dominant, he wants to be held down and tacked down… forcefully. 'I want it to feel like rape with love, I want it to be like he's wanted me for years and now he's got me,' he said. He said, 'I want to feel need, hunger, anger.'"

"Oh, puke, poetry," Bryce thought.

"One of those complex types." Kris shrugged.

And Bryce thought, "God, I hate this therapy-type shit. If I'd wanted to be a therapist, I'd have gone to therapy school or something." Bryce had managed to avoid college, much less graduate programs in psychology. Bryce was a big, extravagantly endowed twenty-four-year-old: a heavy-boned, buff six-four. He figured in the work of a couple of world-famous photographers, stretched on black beaches or sprawled on volcanic stone. Because of his size, he was usually the one called upon to deliver the rough stuff, or as rough as it ever got at Kristine's. Kris's was known for blondes; a surprising number of clients wanted nothing more than a bottle of very cold white wine and a genuine platinum blond, or a bed full of them. Bryce had some experience as the biggest blond at some of those blond parties; they could be a lot of fun. Once a white-blond kid, he was an ash-blond adult with extraordinary eyes. They were a pale and lustrous golden brown, unusual in a true blond. The clients who chose Bryce generally weren't heavy into conversation. That was cool with Bryce.

"You can stop your tanning pills," said Kris. "He wants you pale. Oh, and contacts. He wants you with blue-green eyes, he said. He said *very light eyes, just slightly more green than blue*. For the sheets, he said celadon. Or pastel teal. The guy knows his colors."

"Picky dude, huh? How about clothes?" asked Bryce, sure that someone so picky about eyes and sheets would have ideas about clothing too.

"Oh, he was very clear about that. Nothing faggy, he says. He was funny, actually. He said, 'That's my department.' On you he wants stupid-normal stuff, khakis, button-down. I'll take care of the costume," said Kris, who knew that Bryce wouldn't be caught dead in an outfit like that and certainly wouldn't know where to buy it. "He can afford us as often as he wants us, he comes from serious money, he's one extremely desirable repeat customer," Kris said, watching to see her point went home. Bryce cocked one eyebrow to show it had. "Well, I think we've covered all the bases, any questions?"

Bryce guessed not. Weird, he thought. Psychological bullshit. He didn't say so. He commanded premium fees at Kris's; the fees went up when any serious weirdness was involved, and the tips could be astounding. Screenwriters worked sixty-hour weeks for that kind of money. Hell, poor slobs of migrants worked six months for that kind of money, getting up at dawn to pick stuff in muddy fields. And Bryce needed the job for the down payment on a Merce he had his eye on.

"Oh, and he says he's bringing his bodyguard," said Kris, an afterthought. Bryce barely nodded to that; many clients brought bodyguards along despite the security at Kristine's. He had learned to do his job under the cold eyes of bodyguards of both sexes, often with Glock semiautomatic pistols in their holsters. He watched the client grind out his half-smoked cig onscreen. That was one of the ways you recognized dancers, cigarettes. Between cancer and carbs, some dancers found cancer the lesser evil.

By the day of the job, Bryce had been off his tanning pills a week and felt raw and naked without his tan. His hair had been lightened with lemon juice and a touch of peroxide until it was as light as it had been when he was five. He had on the preppie clothes and wore green-blue special-order cosmetic contact lenses when he finally met the client in the clinic at Kris's. The contacts had Bryce mildly miffed. "I have fabulous eyes," he thought. "He'd like my eyes the way they are."

"I'm Forest," said the client. Another rule at Kristine's: first names only. "You're Bryce. Cool name."

"My mom couldn't make up her mind between Bryan and Bruce." This was not strictly true—it wasn't even slightly true—he'd invented the name and the history for it. Kris encouraged invented names and histories.

"Pleased to meet you, looking forward." And he shook Bryce's hand and looked Bryce up and down with the candid eye of a practiced horse-dealer. His glance paused at the fly in regulation fashion. Nothing surprising in that, though Forest would have already seen Bryce in the altogether on video during the precontractual arrangements. Still, usually, a man hiring another man to fuck him would glance at that man's fly with a split-second shudder—a pleasurable shudder, but a shudder still. What Bryce thought of as ***a bottom's look.*** What wasn't usual was Forest's sparkly cheer, as if assured that his needs would be met. He might look at a powerful car he planned to buy in the same way. "That's a lot of onions," Bryce's old mother used to say when someone had gall. And this guy had a lot of onions.

Then Bryce was aware of Forest staring up into his eyes, this time with true concentration. An assessing look, checking out the extent of the illusion.

"Contacts," Forest said aloud, but to himself. "That's okay. That's near enough." As Bryce wondered, "Near enough to what?" Forest stretched out his arm to the waiting technician, who drew a vial of his blood and a vial of Bryce's and ran the panel under their eyes. Both tested out clean. Kris led the way to the pleasure chambers and showed their guest the amenities. Bryce took note of the spread that had been prepared: the usual giant grapes and yellow Rainier cherries, slivers of smoked salmon and cheeses, crisp little flatbread discs and champagne, but some odder items too: vodka and Guylien's chocolate shells and, no shit, those cheesecake slices that came two to a package, plain and chocolate-marble, in chain grocery stores. No clients at Kristine's ate that kind of crap. Perks for the bodyguard, maybe. There were also the pharmaceuticals that had been requested, X and GHB and coke.

Forest didn't touch any food. Apparently he meant to do his drugs bareback. He opened a blue bottle of filtered water and thoughtfully selected two tabs of X. He swallowed them and looked pleasantly at Bryce. "This'll blur the boundaries. After it hits, you'll look just the way I want you to. I'm going for a nice cool shower. Perhaps you'll join me in a minute."

"Yeah." Bryce's mouth felt full of feathers. What if, after keeping his dick up all night for fifty-year-olds, he couldn't deliver for this beautiful man younger than himself? He heard the shower jets go on and, safely alone, started getting psyched. He opened a bottle of water and considered the drugs. He'd decided on X and a tiny hit of coke when he heard an undisguised heavy step behind him, and hands bigger than his own pinned his wrists behind his back.

"No dope," a voice said into his left ear. "That's for him if he wants it. One of the things we're paying for is someone not fucked up on drugs. You aren't doing him under the influence."

"I'm afraid I can't without a little ..." Bryce faltered. He could hear the shower running, he knew that no one standing under it could hear much of anything, so he felt safe speaking. "I mean, he's not my usual... he's too... he's stunning. I'm not used to that." He swallowed hard. "You the bodyguard?"

"That'll do for your purposes," said the guy, his grip tight and mean.

"Well, you can let go, then. Getting manhandled by clients' staff isn't in my contract."

Bryce felt the guy's fingers pressing into the little hollow places on the outsides of his wrists, just a nasty little testosterone display before he let go.

The guy slumped into the deep slouchy sofa and looked Bryce up and down. He had pale eyes in which the pupils seemed very black, very defined. He looked at Bryce as if Bryce were some germbucket from some escort service that advertised in the back of cheap weeklies.

Scary handsomeness, Bryce thought. Astounding legs, like those Vikings might have had under their chainmail and furs. And a blazing pallor and silver-blond hair clipped close and muscles and bone structure like some Nazi god. He could make a mint working at Kris's.

"Let's review the rules," said the bodyguard levelly. "I sit here in the next room with both ears open. He likes pain, but not too damn much of it, and force, but only the illusion of it. You ram into him like you just can't wait, okay? Like you can't help yourself. And tie him up if he says to. But he's dancing next week, so now's not the time for wear and tear."

"I thought he was, like, a dancer or skater or something," said Bryce.

"My point is, he can't afford any sprains or pulled muscles or bruises or anything like that. So you're careful, okay? Because if you hurt him so it really hurts or do him any damage, I'll come in there and put you right in the fucking hospital, you got it?"

"This is Kristine's, not some cruddy amateur B&D den where people get hurt," said Bryce, offended. Then stuttered, "Sorry." The bodyguard raised his eyebrows faintly and gave him a look that said *don't apologize, don't explain, change the behavior.* He definitely didn't act like an employee, and it occurred to Bryce that perhaps he wasn't one. More weirdness, Bryce thought with irritation. Twinkletoes in there's brought his lover, who likes to watch?

Bryce tried to put the situation back on a businesslike basis. That seemed the safe tactic. "What's his safe word?" he asked.

"It's *Winslow.* Better not make him need it," said the guy, with one of the most unreassuring smiles Bryce had ever seen.

"You don't have a gun," Bryce said, really just thinking out loud.

"I don't need one." The bodyguard helped himself to vodka, yet another thing normal bodyguards didn't do. "He's taking his shower now. He'll like it if you interrupt him. Push him up against the wall and fuck him standing up."

"Yeah, coach, right away," Bryce thought, but he didn't say it. He kept that thought to himself.

The pleasure suite shower was not just a shower, but a whole blue-glass-tiled room of adjustable waterfalls and hard rain. Forest in his seamless tan stood under one of them, his back to the door. Bryce had thought he couldn't, not with that white wolf posted on the sofa, but he found himself ready, willing, and able, the fear that had slid itself into him only goading him on. He took his shirt off and stepped out of his shoes and stepped under the spray with Forest, who gave a gasp of scripted surprise when Bryce grabbed his wrists and forced his arms up and pushed him up against the tiles. Bryce pressed the metal of his zipper up against his cleft. Using what he'd just learned, he dug his thumbs into Forest's wrists, just enough to elicit a gasp that really was a gasp.

*

"Yes, you're like him," Forest murmured. "Thank you."

"Welcome," Bryce muttered. Ever since the clock started running on this session, he had been taken aback by both Forest's sense of command and by his politeness.

"I like to be held while I sleep. Is that all right?"

"Sure it is." Bryce accepted Forest's dark head on his shoulder. Bryce had a telegraphic thought, so telegraphic that he had to parse it out later: *used to/expecting affection.* His body, faster than his head, accommodated; his thighs relaxed to let Forest settle his left leg between them. No wonder, thought Bryce. Gorgeous, sweet, genuinely lovable, of course he should be used to being cuddled after the fuck. The question was, why should he need Kris's for that, or anything?

"Mmmm," Forest purred, and kissed him good night at the base of his throat. The kiss had a warm flick of tongue at its center, sweet as a cherry in chocolate. The tongue tasted him and his sweat. That would've gotten Bryce going again if his guest had not already worked him to the point of a stony numb ache in the balls. "I'm not going to have a working nerve in my dick in the morning," Bryce thought. "And he's going to be too sore to move. I'll have to call Kris and get him some Percocet or those Tylenols with codeine."

Bryce made himself stay awake for the time when Forest would get too warm in that skin-to-skin clench and roll onto his back; Bryce wanted to look at him. He fought exhaustion until he could.

I don't know him, Bryce told himself in skittery panic—*and we don't fall in love with clients here.* But no one here or ever had ever eaten him alive, grazed Bryce's shoulder with his teeth and clutched him in with his insides like that. What else was there? Bryce wondered: "Can I even fake it with someone else? I'm no top's top, I'm like a horse. Horses are big and strong, but people own them. He could own me if he wanted to."

For the first time, Bryce wondered why anyone thought that shoving your dick into someone else meant you had power over him. Letting Bryce pound him like a piston, that man had taken Bryce entirely under his control. Power was by no means the crude and obvious push-button people thought it was. Bryce bit his tongue on a question forbidden above all others by Kris's Rules: *Will I see you again?*

At the crack of noon, the bodyguard rose. He'd apparently found it too hot in the outer room and stripped to his skivvies. He bent down over the disordered bed, as no one else's bodyguard would have done, and shook Forest awake with one hand; he had a cigarette in the other.

"Hey, you trash."

Forest blinked. "Hey, you thug."

"C'mon, sit up, get up, rise and whine."

Forest tried. "OhhhhhmyGod." Eyelids at half-mast, he noticed the cigarette and, with surprising energy, smacked at the hand holding it. "Get *out* of my cigarettes, you don't smoke!"

"Knock it off. Come on. Plane leaves at two, and we need a bath before we get on it. That sofa in there's covered with some kind of fake silk. Made me sweat all night." The bodyguard hauled him familiarly up to a sitting position. "And if you're sore, well, you paid up the wazoo to get that way." The bodyguard's hostile mood seemed to have passed in the night. "I guess that was worth our while, huh?—enough party that you wake up just barely able to walk."

"That's a vast exaggeration," said Forest. "Help me get vertical."

With eyes open just barely, covertly open, Bryce saw them exchange a stare.

"Fine," Forest said, as if the other man had asked, "How are you?" But he had not. "Just fine." And he gave the guy a brisk little pat on the cheek. Bryce counted the hanging beats of silence, then finally the bodyguard spoke: "Okay." And Bryce heard Forest: "Let's wash."

They withdrew into the shower room for a while and emerged enlivened, opening their duffel for a change of clothing. Forest turned on music and got dressed to "Higher Love." Bryce pretended to sleep and watched covertly through his blond lashes. The so-called bodyguard, slower, got into his loose shorts and pastel-teal Oxford shirt and sliced himself a thick wedge of cheese from last night's staling lovefeast. He chewed soberly while Forest danced the way he probably did alone at home, for himself. Bryce could imagine him, as awake the minute he opened his eyes as he'd be all day, bopping around his kitchen while his java perked and his protein smoothie whirled in the blender. *And we rise, we rise, we rise!* sang the singer, whoever he was. Forest, coming up out of his jeans like a bouquet of flowers, bounded around the furniture and stretched his arms up in slow delighted arcs to the music. Bryce felt the bodyguard's boreal eyes, as if he suspected unauthorized enjoyment on the part of their rental, so Bryce made himself shut his eyes all the way, like a good boy waiting for Santa.

On the way out, one of them slipped something under Bryce's pillow. When the door had closed after them, he got up, discovering little blue bruises at the hollows of both wrists and an envelope—a stunning tip. Bryce went and bought the Merce.

*

Kris did not encourage her entertainers to know one another. Many of them had worked for her for years without meeting. Engagements and baby showers were rare among this crew, and no company Christmas parties or birthday lunches encouraged alliances between staff. Cody arriving early for a client consultation a couple of years later, and Bryce leaving late after one, was how Bryce and Cody met.

(Bryce had not managed to get Forest out of his head. In fact, when he needed a mental picture to perform to, the fantasy-Forest did duty, and talked his incredibly effective dirty-talk into Bryce's ear.)

The real Forest had a surname; it was *von Grauling.* A perfunctory walk through the periodicals at Barnes & Nobles and a copy of *Dance Magazine* had informed Bryce about Forest's career. Though he couldn't get into ballet, Bryce had acquired a couple of Forest's *Swan Lake* posters and hung them in his condo.

Now, having found this astonishing lookalike, Bryce made it his business to get a phone number. Cody had the ballet build, the golden skin, the dark hair, the bluegreen eyes and sunlit sensuality. He hadn't actually been a dancer, but a gymnast—"I never was that great," he told Bryce, shrugging. He liked Kris's better than coaching prep school gymnastics.

Kris had never had staff move in together, and she disapproved of that too, but they did move in together after a couple of months. Bryce still wore the contacts; Cody liked them, and Bryce had found that clients responded to that sea-ice gaze in a way that they never had to his natural golden eyes.

*

Well into the relationship, Bryce and Cody ordinarily watched TV before going to sleep, and that's what they were doing—and consuming avocado-flavored protein chips and Diet Sprite. One downside of looking good enough to earn the down payment on a Mercedes in one night of sex: no Coke, no dip, no Doritos, not ever.

Cody was a talker, ready with running commentary on anything on TV. Drowsing, Bryce didn't notice at first that Cody had gone quiet. Then Cody's hand took him by the arm, its grip urgent and businesslike.

"What?"

"Look! I know him! I've done him... or, I mean, he did me."

"So?" Between them, they'd done/been done by a lot of people, male and female, whom they'd seen on TV before or after.

On the screen was a singer, a temporary god in the center of an ice cathedral of thick white strobes. He might have been any big white man at that distance. But Bryce recognized the silvered rich tones and a song that he'd heard on the radio, "Pillar of Light." Bryce remembered it because the guy, unlike many rock singers, really did have a voice. He was like that fat guy Meat Loaf back in ol' Dad's day—God, could that man sing! Most of the time, the engineers had to digitalize the hell out of those guys before they sounded like anything.

"That's from Berlin," said Cody, which would explain why the guy was singing in a foreign language. "That's him! I know him!"

When the song was finished, the camera zoomed in. Easy to see that its lens loved the singer, knew his all his good angles. The lens preened on his profile, the power of his shoulders, lingered loverlike on his spooky eyes and took a bath in them—green, with just enough cobalt flecks rimming the pupils to cast an illusion of blue.

"These damn contacts, they're supposed to make me look like I have that kind of weird eyes," Bryce thought. Then the wide-spaced throbbing dots in the California and Wyoming, the Kansas and Florida and Alabama of Bryce's mind grew pulsing neon lines and connected, a wide-area network in the sizzle of synthesis.

"Hell… that's the *man* I was supposed to look like. That's the spooky bodyguard. That's who he's turned out to be. When he pinned my hands and gave me my marching orders, he was really young. Twenty or something, he was a real mean boy, but real young too. And Forest von Grauling pays someone who looks like his own bodyguard to do him? I don't get it. Why pay both of us?"

A stupid voice in his head, like some lovelorn teenager, told Bryce, "You were nothing to that pretty dancer. Just another prop to fill out a scenario." Why the hell didn't he just get his kicks with his own damn security staff? Make them multitask. But even as he considered these details, Bryce felt sure there was more to know.

"That guy, he's huge in Europe and he's climbing the charts in the States," said Cody, strangely breathless. "They like him so much in Germany they have fucking *riots* after his concerts and, like, set stuff on fire and smash out windows. Against oppression or fascism or something. He has a German last name. And he comes from a family with a shitload of money."

"People who turn up at Kris's do," Bryce thought. So?

"So when did he do you?" he asked Cody, trying not to sound too interested. He was trying to make a timeline here. He'd done Forest six years ago. Two years ago he'd hooked up with Cody.

"I'd just turned twenty-three," said Cody, looking away, cigarette trembling in his hand. "So it was five years ago. I'd just started with Kris then. March. I was a wedding present from, get this, the woman this singer guy was about to marry. What he got instead of a regular bachelor party with a hooker. Farewell to being bi, I reckon. You know these jet-set type people, they're immoral." He gave a nervous shrug. "Well, that was disturbing to think about, and he was disturbing too."

"Disturbing, like, how?" Bryce drew Cody's answer in like a skittish fish on a trout line.

Cody drew his shoulders up tight, then exhaled, went loose, and told it like a secret. "He brought me an armload of roses," Cody said. "He made love to me like I was a woman. I mean, as if he knew me. As if he adored me. As if he cared. The way he talked to me, it was filth and it was sweet. When I'm having problems looking excited at work, you know, I remember the stuff he said to me that night. He took a handful of the rose petals and scattered them over me. I mean, talk about romantic, I was crazy-jealous of that woman he was going to marry, even though she arranged the whole gig. It took me about five minutes to hope that the next time she got on a plane, it would crash and burn, no survivors. He fucked me senseless and I'd have paid him to go on if he'd tried to stop. I went all soppy, he'd let me have some of the drugs he'd ordered. Not the usual club stuff, but some really major barbiturates. He was, I dunno, protective! He wouldn't let me have a whole cap, he opened one and shook out most of it and let me have the rest, and he was right because it was wicked strong. My mood went all wonky and, search me why, I cried and he comforted me. Can you believe it?"

Actually, Bryce found that a stretch. Most of these people would complain if your fingernails weren't filed perfectly smooth. Weep on them, and Kris would refund their money, fire your sorry ass, and make it hard to get employed at a lesser establishment. End of work.

"So, did he turn nasty later, or something?"

"No, but get this. There I am crying, I didn't know why, but after he'd wiped my eyes, he asked me what that was all about. I couldn't say. I didn't know, okay? Just that something intense was going on. So I go to sleep, and then I wake up later. And I saw he'd eaten those horse tranquilizers like M&Ms and washed them down with vodka, he ought to've been out like a light. But it was like all those pills did was shake something loose in him. He was crying his eyes out. I touched him and he, like, let me hold him."

"Damn straight, that's fucking weird," Bryce agreed, his throat tightening. Cody could be over-the-top sensitive, catching the spill of others' moods and feeling their pain as if it had something to do with him. He got upset over SPCA ads about people being mean to animals. Bryce could imagine him catching some powerful sorrow like a cold.

"What'd he do? Did he tell you why?"

"He cried until he had the hiccups, and then he said, 'Someone I love has AIDS.'"

Bryce had had the test numerous times between then and now, and with his own eyes he'd seen Forest test clean, so he didn't panic about HIV. If Forest had it, he'd gotten it after his night at Kristine's. Bryce worked out the rest of the scenario, though. What if the big guy had Kris handpick Cody for looking like Forest? All I have to find out now is that they've got the same last name and they've both been to Kris's for an imitation brother to...

"I hope it doesn't weird you out, but I couldn't get him out of my head. It bothered me. I wanted to know why he acted like that. And I wanted more of him. It was like being a teenager and crushing on someone you can't have. You look like him. That's why I liked you so much right away. You don't mind that, do you?" said Cody, anxious.

Bryce figured he couldn't afford to mind it. He forced a smile. "No. Why would I mind? What's the guy's name? We could get his albums. He sure can sing."

Cody paused and concentrated. "One of these first names like a last name. Winslow. Of course he didn't tell me the other one." Gesturing toward the screen—"Listen, maybe they'll say it."

They did. "Winslow von Grauling."

*

Five years further down the line, in the nacreous prelude to a seaside twilight very far north, a little girl raced down a beach with a uniformed woman sprinting after her. The place was a Baltic Sea island called Sylt, and it was too cold for Cody's comfort and Bryce's even in July. They were in sweatpants and heavy cotton sweaters, and their bare feet felt blue, and they wished they'd opted for Hatteras or Rehoboth even though they could afford European vacations. They had their own business now, a casting agency for movie extras.

The kid slid to a halt in the salt-white sand before the two shivering Californians. She was tanned, long-legged, and very slender: healthy-looking, but every rib showed. In that European way that made Bryce uncomfortable, she was wearing a tiny bikini bottom but no top. It didn't matter that she was at least five years away from needing a bra; she was way too female and way too naked under this open cold sky. At Kris's, Bryce had done women for money, but women braless or naked outside unsettled him somehow. The little girl had binoculars hanging by a leather strap around her neck, dangling too far down to protect her modesty. "Hey, do you speak English?" said this kid.

"Yeah," Bryce admitted.

She had the kind of white hair Bryce had had at her age. Some of it clung around her narrow face in tarnished-silver tendrils—that strange color that the very blondest hair goes when wet.

The nanny or whatever skidded to a halt right behind her. "Edda, don't bother the gentlemen."

"I'm not bothering them, Nan, I'm being friendly. Look, it *is* like I saw with my binoculars. If you wanted guys to play my daddy and my uncle in a movie, you could just hire them. Hi, my name's Edda, and that's my Nan," the kid told Bryce and Cody chattily. "Actually she's my bodyguard, but she takes care of me and puts me to bed when my folks travel, and we're close, so I say she's my Nan." She beamed up at the nanny/bodyguard. "Nan, don't they look just like Daddy and my uncle?"

Nan had a shoulder holster under her blue uniform blazer. Her ninety-percent-naked charge must have a very wealthy, very paranoid daddy, Bryce figured.

"It's remarkable," admitted Nan. "But we're over the property line and your dad won't like that. He wants us to stay on our own beach."

"Come see Daddy," the kid entreated them. "I'll make him sign an autograph for you." They must have hesitated visibly. She added: "He's Winslow von Grauling, and most people want his autograph." It was true, most people did. He was Mick Jagger big, David Bowie big. He was in *Vanity Fair* and *Spin* and *People* and *Mainline* all the time.

Bryce, always up for a little danger, stood up first, following the kid and her warder up the beach. Fuck it if it made the guy uncomfortable. Someone with some sexual thing for his own brother deserved a little social discomfort. Besides, Bryce had never gotten payback for that wrist-wrenching stuff back at Kris's.

"Aren't you cold, hon?" Cody asked the kiddie as they padded up the beach. Skinny as she was, her golden skin wasn't goosepimpled like theirs.

"Oh, I'm used to it. That's our house up there. We come here a lot. When we go to the beach in South Carolina, it's so warm it feels like bathwater. Only dirty, fishy bathwater. Here it's real clean." She half-turned to them, smiling, innocent, her eyes right between pale green and pale blue. What did you call that color? Pastel teal?

As they approached the silverblond man sprawled in a canvas chair, the two men saw that the moment wasn't a good one. A woman wearing nothing but her hair had been leading a toddler through the surf, but quickly she positioned the naked baby where she ought to have had her bikini bra. With the baby's head over her shoulder, the woman retreated into the swift blue water, which had to be goddamn cold.

"Daddy, look at them, I found them on the beach, they look just like you and Uncle Forest," said the kid, breathlessly pleased.

The large man lifted his gaze slowly from the tablet on one thigh, a wafer in a titanium case. He wasn't as young as when Bryce first encountered him and had a gut on him under his Yale sweatshirt, but his icy charisma was magnified tenfold.

He considered them, then said kindly to the kid, "Hot damn, Eddalein, they do."

"I thought you might like to see them."

"Well, that was nice of you, baby," said Winslow. He fished up a ribbon of lime Lycra from a canvas bag. "Here, put your top on."

"Mommy says I don't need it."

"Put it on," said Winslow, not liking their eyes anywhere near his daughter's nonexistent tits. She wriggled into the little thing. Then he addressed the bodyguard/nanny person. "You and Edda head on back to the cottage. It's getting near her bedtime."

"Oh, Daddy, it isn't!"

As though uninterrupted, Winslow proceeded, "A hot bath and supper, with soup *and* milk, and then right between those nice flannel sheets on your bed."

"Oh, Daddy."

"I'll come soon and sing that song that you like, the funny one about the fish, but only if you go with Nan now. So give me back my spyglasses so I can keep an eye on Mommy and Belle, and head on home with Nan."

All three men watched the bodyguard and child make their way toward the house in the dunes. Strange—nothing fancy, just an old boxy cottage. The kid turned and gave the strangers a bright little wave.

Once she and Nan were out of earshot, Winslow said, "I thought there was something in that contract about no social recognition."

"There is, but we got socially recognized," Bryce told him. "Not the other way around."

"We didn't want to hurt your kiddie's feelings," Cody added.

Winslow maintained a few hanging beats of silence, then said, "I appreciate that." He hadn't moved. Despite the weight he'd put on, he still had fabulous legs and still had that Viking raider look. Bryce remembered all kinds of things about him, even that his peremptory hands were beautifully shaped.

"We would never..." faltered Cody. "I mean, we thought... it was great... it was an honor to meet you then, and Bryce here... he enjoyed meeting your brother. We're sorry about... Anyhow, we'd never... you know."

"Okay." In really quite a reasonable and civil tone.

"How is he?" Bryce's mouth said, without Bryce's permission. "Your brother?"

Then there was the plummeting chill Bryce remembered from having his wrists pinned. Winslow's sea-ice eyes filled even as the rest of his face immobilized.

"Well, he's sick," he said. "Read the magazines, the gossip sites. Whatever." Before either of them could conjure a reply, he contained whatever had welled up in him and added: "This is a private beach, and my wife would like to swim without a suit and come out of the water without being looked at by men she doesn't know. And if she got close enough to see you well, she might find you... disturbing to look at. I know I do. So, if you don't mind."

"No," said Cody, hand on Bryce's wrist as he started back in the direction they'd come. "No, of course not. Sorry."

Want

"Araminta, isn't it? What a pretty name. Please come in," Eric von Grauling said, answering his young neighbor's ring on his doorbell.

"It's after the ancestress who made our family fortune," Minta told him, looking collected despite the flutter in her gut. She was inexperienced at being up to no good. The necessary demure-and-mature social front and the novel conditions of malice and forethought, taken together, amounted to complex choreography. And, even though her business here was with Eric's teen sons and even though Eric was old, probably forty, he was a glamorous man. In her sensitive state, she found his looks distracting. All the von Grauling males had astounding eyes… she yanked her focus firmly back to the family-tree palaver.

"How did she make her fortune?" asked Eric, regarding the girl with the warm adult approval and courteous interest she was used to. And she picked up the dance of adult conversation, which she had mastered passably at almost-sixteen. "Oh… a laudanum factory. And cotton. Indigo. Phosphates. Slavery. I came to see… I wondered… if Winslow can go to Lakewood with me. For ice cream."

"Sure, after he finishes practicing. It'll get his mind off that mess at school. We're all still pretty upset about it." Luckily, Eric sounded upset for Winslow rather than with him. She could hear Winslow's piano a few rooms away.

"I'm glad you don't mind. I mean, I thought you might've grounded him after the fight," Minta said, and self-scolded: *You're babbling. See, you don't know how to act natural misbehaving.*

But Eric shook his head. "No, no, no. I know it's Forest's doing. Our boys've grown up in a very protected, privileged situation… well, not that Dogwood Downs isn't nice. But if these messes at the school continue, Melanie and I think she might stay on and finish her year teaching at Ferrier and let me take the boys home and put them back in their school there, because I'm not going to stand for… just because Forest doesn't get the social dynamic here."

"What's it like, your home place in West Virginia?" She'd heard they were obscenely rich and that the money was new. Maybe that was true and this sweet man wasn't used to it yet? An old-money person wouldn't have been so forthcoming. An old-money person would have had the maid bring her a lemonade and left her to wait. This man talked to her almost as if she were an adult at a drinks party. Too nice to be old-money-rich, she thought.

"Well, Haliburton's a tiny little town with a tiny little school," he began, shrugging. "My wife's family owns the only industry there, and most of the property, and Forest, he's always played the best kid roles in the little theatre productions, he was Franz in the ballet studio's *Nutcracker* there every year until he got too big." Eric gestured toward a row of photos of his elder son in ballet costumes. "And that's partly because he deserves it, but partly because of who we are. And the homefolks are used to him. He probably could show up at school in a tutu there without too much flack. But if he acts natural here, his kind of natural, he's going to stir up all that rich white trash at the school, and Winslow's going to catch damage fending them off. We call Forest *Trees* sometimes because he's a stickler about little things... can't see the forest for the trees... well, in this situation, Forest can't see either the forest *or* the trees. Or the wolves, for that matter. I guess it's my fault Forest doesn't know we can't just do what we want all the time."

"Forest is about to ride the old learning curve," thought Minta. She said, "Cornell and Yale Wasserman and the Incagnoli boys are wolfish." Her parents didn't allow her to say *white trash,* but it sounded right for upperclassmen who fought thirteen-year-olds.

"And you've hit it off with Winslow," Eric said. "That's super, sometimes he isn't easy, he can be uncommunicative, he was so late to talk that we worried he was autistic." The heat and emphasis of this statement confirmed a personal fact Winslow had shared with Minta: *I'm my Daddy's favorite even when I'm bad.*

"I like Winslow's silences," Minta ventured. "And I like what he has to say, once he gets ready to say it."

Eric beamed approval at her approval, then turned the same look on Winslow when his younger son appeared, his left cheek a bruised plum, with a vicious gouge from Yale Wasserman's class ring. "Already bigger than his dad," Minta noted to herself, seeing Winslow and Eric together. And you could tell Winslow's current bulk was just the beginning. Despite that pudgy teddy-bear look Winslow had when he slouched, he was going to be six-four or more, with great lumbering heavy-boned strength. His hair was so blond that it was almost white, and his eyes were a pale and startling blue-green, the color of broken safety glass. He was a work in progress now, an overgrown teenager, but his appearance already had extraordinary effects on Minta. When he grew up, she thought, he would be spectacular.

"Hey, sport," Eric greeted him. "You're in luck, here's the fabulous Miss Tattnall wanting you to go get ice cream with her."

Perhaps reluctant to show his damage off his home premises, Winslow volunteered that they had ice cream in the freezer. "We could take it up in the tree house," he ventured.

"Your young lady friend wants to go to Lakewood, so go get your bike," Eric urged. "My treat." He handed Winslow a ten.

Winslow did what Minta wanted. From their first meeting, he'd looked at her as if she were diamonds and gold. At the ice cream shop, they ordered a vanilla malt—another thing she knew about Winslow was that he didn't like complicated flavors. He actually liked kid junk food like coconut snowballs and Twinkies. Ordinarily he loved vanilla malts, but soon he pushed the glass in her direction and in his telegraphic style explained: "Hurts. My tooth. Too cold. You have it." So she did, and he watched her drink it, concentrating on her in that way he had, as if listening to light. Once the glass was empty, she led him into Wendy's Beauty Supply.

Winslow took a vaguely alarmed look at the ranks of conditioner and shampoo and wrinkled his nose at the aggressive sweet reek. "What're we doing here?" he ventured. The clerk there wondered too and looked curiously at the two of them, butter-blonde girl and blonder boy, pondering shades of brown hair tint.

Minta explained what they were doing there. Dedicated from day one to Goals, to Achievement, to Maturity or at least to adultlike behavior, this would be the first time in her life she'd gotten down and dirty with a peer or planned a vendetta. For what she had in mind, they needed hair dye. "Féria's supposed to be the best brand," she noted. "Though I hear Garnier's good too. Which shade do you think is Forest? Rosewood? Walnut? Expresso?"

Winslow had not protested any detail of her plan. Getting down to logistics, he noted, "Well, we need one that'll cover blue."

Actually, *electric teal* was what Forest called the shade in question. Forest had a coif that he described as "asymmetric," or "chromatic," or both, though other people had other words for it. His straight brown hair came down just below his earlobe on the left side, but all the way to his collarbone on the right. A vivid stripe of fluorescent blue was dyed into it on the long side. When the von Graulings first arrived in Dogwood Downs, Forest had revealed that he'd gone to New York with his mom and paid someone there $200 to do this to him. The peer-powers-that-were at Dogwood Downs Country Day School might have forgiven Forest his ballet dancing, his clogs, and his clothes, which seemed chosen to inflame any local pederast past endurance. Minta wondered where he got them. Did Victoria's Secret have a department for teen boys? Unforgiven and unforgivable, though, was that hairstyle with its manic turquoise streak. Surely as God made both lice and lilacs, the bullyboys of Dogwood Downs Country Day School would make Winslow's life a misery until someone did something about Forest's hair.

Winslow chose Teakwood Brown, and Minta paid for it.

"You can say I did the whole thing," she told Winslow, who probably wouldn't have finked on her under torture. Once back at his house, in the brothers' bathroom, they opened the box and read the directions.

"You wouldn't do this to your brother," Winslow murmured.

"My brother doesn't get me into fights so I get hurt," Minta returned smartly, and the boy put his large hand up to the thunderous blue of the bruise. "Now," she asked him, "have you got any sharp scissors?"

Winslow fetched kitchen shears. "These cut melon rind. It won't hurt him, will it?"

"Not if we don't get it in his eyes."

They hunkered down in Winslow's walk-in closet and awaited Forest's return from ballet class. "This is like a surprise party, only different," Winslow observed. Yes, it would be different, Minta thought, and inhaled him in the warm closed space: the vanilla on his breath, Ivory Snow and fresh starch from his clothes. His sweet skin, implausibly soft over those muscles—the skin of his arms felt like a baby's.

Finally they heard the appropriate noises: Melanie von Grauling's Saab purring up the drive, the front door's exuberant slam. And Forest scampered upstairs and into the huge sunny blue-for-boys room, with its white fur rugs and its two desks and two beds with comforters done in pale blue pinpoint Oxford cloth, its Bowie and Nureyev posters.

Forest finished his bottle of mango juice, turned on the ceiling fan, and shucked his clothes. He dawdled a moment, probably just liking the air on his hot skin, then headed for the shower. And Minta and Winslow slipped out of the closet. Winslow turned on some music, an ancient Meat Loaf album at the highest volume he dared: a sound screen. It would just seem that he'd come in and decided to play music. Not that Forest had time to ponder, for Winslow jumped him from behind, pinning his arms. Seventy pounds and six inches is a size difference that makes struggle almost meaningless, but Forest struggled anyway.

"Sorry, Trees, we're gonna do it," said Winslow, perhaps an unfortunate choice of words since Minta had just taken up the scissors. Forest kicked wildly; Winslow hugged harder.

"Hold still or you'll get cut," Minta told Forest. "I won't mean to, but I might if you thrash."

"What the fuck do you mean, get cut—"

"Oh, nothing permanent. Just your hair," Minta said, and tried not to smile. To Winslow, she said, "Now, hold him so he can't shake his head." Winslow bearhugged his brother in one big arm and got an unambiguous grip on Forest's right ear with his other hand. Forest began to understand his situation.

"Winslow, did you put her up to this?—I'll tell Daddy—he'll ground you till you're forty! Minta, I'll tell your folks, and you won't have to worry about getting into every school in the Ivy League because they'll kill you dead and donate you to science!"

"More like they'll only talk to me for strictly necessary reasons," Minta thought, "a month or so. And everything they say'll be in the imperative mode." That had happened after an unprecedented lapse on her part, a B in sixth-grade French. "No eye contact, and the temperature around them'll fall to about -15. Oh, well, you take what you want. And pay for it."

When Forest tried to yell, she stuffed a washcloth in his mouth—a big plushy one that amply filled it. His muffled grunts were drowned out by emotive lyrics about a motorcycle crash. The kitchen shears were very sharp. They snicked efficiently; brown and blue tufts drifted around Forest's bare feet. Minta chopped out as much Day-Glo blue as she could without leaving an obvious bald patch. She cut the rest brutally short—it would stay that way a while!

Winslow contemplated him worriedly: "It's not his style."

"That's the whole idea. His style is what's getting your teeth knocked loose and your face messed up."

This process was somewhere between chemistry and cooking. The dye directions instructed her, next, to snip off the tip of a squeeze bottle full of syrupy white liquid, take the cap off, empty a little poisonous-looking vial into it, screw the cap back on, seal the snipped tip with her gloved finger, and mix thoroughly. She did, and slathered Forest's head with Féria's Teakwood Brown. The dye pervaded the closed space with its wild reek.

Winslow sniffed and coughed. "Yuck! Looks like Hershey's syrup. Smells like cat pee." For Winslow, quite the descriptive mouthful. He had to like you a lot before he ventured much beyond *yes* or *no*. Minta had spent a good bit of this warm autumn encouraging Winslow to communicate in words of more than one syllable.

Before they could rinse the dye off, they had to wait twenty minutes—through one song about date rape, and another about adultery. Minta had to keep blotting the dye so it wouldn't drip into Forest's turquoise eyes and blind him, which was not part of the plan. Angry heat rose off his skin and made her more aware of his nakedness than she wanted to be. She tried to look over Forest's shoulder and out the little high window, green-gold with September sun through an oak, away from Forest's tan lines and rageful gaze.

"I'm sorry he's naked," Winslow muttered, abashed.

"That's okay, I don't care about his dick. I care about making him stop provoking every Neanderthal at school and making you take the heat."

At nineteen minutes, Minta turned the shower on so it would run warm, and at twenty she signaled Winslow to let Forest go. He jerked the gag out of his mouth and flung it at her, hot with his spit. Minta ignored this gesture and held out the special shampoo that had come with the dye: "Here, we're done, now you can wash it off." Forest smacked it out of her hand with his left and would have slammed her into the wall with his right, but Winslow intercepted him and shouldered him into the shower.

"Don't hit girls," pronounced Winslow. "Me if you want to. Not her."

If looks could kill, they'd both have been carrion. Forest gave them one more smoking glare and stepped under the spray. They sat on the end of Winslow's bed and awaited developments. Once showered, Forest wasted no time taking Winslow up on his invitation.

"This is for you," Forest said. He marched over to his sibling and slapped him on the left cheek, getting his whole wiry arm into it. Winslow didn't drop his eyes, make a retaliatory move, or even stir. His expression was the same mute, regretful obduracy that Minta had seen in horses' eyes when they were refusing to go in some direction that spooked them. And they'd just keep refusing, even if you used your crop.

Forest plucked something from a drawer and stepped into it, then turned back to them. "Before I shop you two," said Forest, "you want to tell me what that was all about? I mean, I'll still shop you, but I'm interested. Weird shit naturally happens around my kid brother, but it's a new one when I walk into my own room and get lynched by some sub-deb in Dogwood Downs, North Carolina."

"So shop me," Minta shot back. "Your dad likes me. He thinks I'm a nice, mature young lady, and he'll listen to me. I'll tell him that you carry on at school so Winslow has to fight people to keep them from killing your slatty ass dead. And you let him get hurt, not because of stuff you can't help, but so you can walk around with blue hair and those stupid shirts that show your navel, because you think everybody ought to want a piece of you. You tease those stupid jocks who probably do want a piece of you, but they don't *want* to want a piece of you, and so they go after you to tear you up, and Winslow goes after them so they can't, and he gets hurt. And I warned you last week that if you didn't lighten up, something was going to blow."

"Define *lighten up*," Forest said, his arch hands on his hips, his blue silk thong underwear. He hadn't bothered with the rest of his clothes yet.

"Wear chinos and a button-down shirt and some regular shoes! Like my brother!"

"Then I might not ever link up with anyone I'd like," Forest protested. "I mean, your brother's clueless."

"Well, he doesn't get me into fights! Believe me, Forest, it's better if you don't link up with anyone now. You can date when you're in college."

But Forest wasn't buying that. "This is the twenty-first century, girl! Why should you be allowed to date, and I can't?"

"I'm *not* allowed to date! And let's keep this thing on-topic, it's not fair to make Winslow fight for you. He's only thirteen!"

"But he's big for thirteen," Forest pointed out superfluously. "Hell, he'd be big for twenty. And he wins. Jacob Incagnoli's going to have to have his nose job redone after Winslow's left hook."

Minta put this argument back where it belonged. "I'll tell Eric that you get off on provoking those dufuses. Your dad's a sweet man, he just thinks you're dense, he'd be shocked if he found out what I could tell him—that you like stirring the shit and watching when the situation blows up. You get off on it. And you let Winslow get hurt for you, and I'm not going to stand for it."

This silenced Forest for a second or three. Then a visible light came on in Forest's head, and a grin spread from one reddened ear to the next. "You really... I thought you were just putting up with Baby Bro here. Like, sorry for him. But you... amazing! You like him!" At this revelation, Forest's mood did a pivot. "OHMYGOD. Miss 2400 SAT, Altruism Award, Twenty Tennis Trophies, National Merit Scholar, graduating-early, sure-to-bevaledictorian... and an eighth grader! OHMYGOD! This is better than shopping you. Wait till this gets out, they'll forget about me and I can kick back and watch the crucifixion... OHMYGOD!" Then he surveyed himself in the mirror. "Jeez, Minta. It's a good thing you aren't a real hairdresser."

"So go see a real hairdresser," Minta managed to say. "And blab anything you want. You will anyway." Forest grinned again: He would. He wriggled briskly into jeans and one of his slutty little jerseys, grabbed his mobile, and sauntered out.

The tensile strength seemed to go out of Winslow's body as his head tried to process everything coming at him. "Come here," Minta told him, and he said, "What?"

"You've heard the expression *take what you want and then pay for it*?" said Minta, who could feel her pulse... where it belonged, and also further down, where she didn't usually feel it.

"No, not really. I haven't heard that one." He stepped nearer, though, and she put her hand on his just-slapped cheek.

"Well... we've just heard how we'll pay for it. So let's have what we want. You have to come close for that."

No Apology

Manon Geoffrey Robillard and her son William were spending the spring at Belle Rêve with her widowed sister-in-law, Araminta. The young widow was a Tattnall from Charleston and should have known what was what. She was supposed to be in mourning for Manon's brother Rémy, who had finally poisoned his liver with brandy. He had fallen in fits and died, eyes yellow and rolling. Since the funeral, Manon noted, Rémy's portrait had disappeared from the front parlor, and a new portrait of Araminta and her three-year-old Peter occupied the frame. Many of the other frames now had Araminta's paintings and drawings in them. She chose the oddest subjects—feathers, an untidy heap of jewelry, a crow, a broken brandy glass, her black butler. Her pastime would have been a scandal in a place with enough white gentry to notice it in the first place, or be scandalized in the second. She had drawn Manon's portrait, but Manon didn't care for it. It looked exactly like her.

The weather was sweet still in spring of 1858. The year's heat had not arrived; it just murmured its threat between noon and three. Mornings and evenings were still fresh, the grass was almost violently green, and all the tender, fragrant plants rushed to bloom ahead of the hot half of the calendar. The air was candied with lilacs and other flowering trees; the daffodils and tulips had already bloomed. The foxgloves and delphiniums and hollyhocks, the English-garden flowers that bloomed in June and July in the Northeast, were in their glory here. In a few days, the petals would fall like the litter of a wedding, opulent and early and over too soon.

In this fine weather, Araminta and her little boy and Manon's Willie were rollicking on the lawn. With their gauze nets, Peter and Willie bounded after a yellow butterfly. Scampering after them in her black dress, Araminta moved like a black butterfly, not a grieving widow. The wide hat shielding her face had a scarf of black silk gauze around it. After she tired of the sun and the game and turned the children over to Peter's nursemaid, she sauntered into the parlor to join Manon, who was drinking chocolate and embroidering. When Araminta took the hat off, Manon noted that it had a spray of satin roses, also black. In no way was it a proper mourning bonnet! Araminta's frock was wrong too—black cotton! It had short puffed sleeves and a broad sash, and it came down low, front and back. It bared the girl's pale arms, not thin but very shapely. It was a morning dress, not a mourning dress. Except for being black, it was a dress any happy young woman might wear in early April, here on the warm border of Georgia and Florida.

"Where are Rémy's pictures, Minta? I seem to recall different ones in these frames, and his portrait—"

"Oh, those. They're in the attic. You can have them if you want them."

"They're very valuable," Manon told her. "They've been in the family since—"

"Really, please take them," said the widowed bride. "I'll get one of my people to pack them up for you." She took up her sketchbook and began making notes in it.

Meanwhile, scrutinizing the black dress up close, Manon could tell that it had begun life as a blossomy print and been dyed black. Now it had the look of a rich floral jacquard. When Manon advised her that the fabric was too light and delicate for a mourning dress, Araminta said, "I had our winter clothes put away back in March. It gets very warm here. It's tolerable now, but it'll heat up good and proper before May. You'll see. Saluda is a much more pleasant place to spend the summer."

"It might do to wear at home if you have your seamstress set in long sleeves," advised Manon, ignoring that she had just been urged to go to Saluda.

"Why? It's comfortable like it is."

"Being comfortable is not the point. You're supposed to be in mourning for my brother." *And you don't exactly wear the face of devastation,* thought Manon.

"This dress is black. It could hardly be blacker. There's no law that says that because he's dead, I have to be hot. If I'm hot, I get the prickly heat, and he stays dead. And I'm *not* wearing one of those ridiculous black veils they show in *Godey's*. A veil could catch fire from a candle or a spark, and I'd like to see anyone look after a child with one of those black curtains over her head! If I went about like that, it would scare Baby Pete."

Manon had never heard Araminta raise her voice, and she didn't raise it then either. Manon often found her level statements offensive, which was inconvenient because they were logical. Perhaps that was why they were offensive. Manon imagined the girl's brain as some unwomanly, unnatural, coldly clicking machine, like a Colt revolver. She had never won an argument with Araminta. Actually, she'd never even had an argument with Araminta, who could cut off a contentious discussion with the neat skill of a duelist.

"Sometimes," ventured Manon, "the way you express yourself is shocking." She had made similar observations over the course of her visit, and not one yet had prompted a demure apology. This one didn't either.

"There's usually nobody here to be shocked," Araminta told her. "Only the overseer and Baby Pete and me, and our people, and none of them care. It's a very isolated place, Belle Rêve. I've found there are advantages, living in the country. A person... a landowner...can be a law unto herself."

"How about the vicar at Saint Andrew's?"

"Well, if he's shocked, he's got nothing to say about it. I doubt he cares. He's a practical man. He buried Rémy and knows Rémy's as dead as people ever get, and Belle Rêve's tithes keep that church alive."

That was an outrageous thing to say, even if it was true. "Not everything comes down to arithmetic!" cried Manon.

"Most things do. Speaking of arithmetic, I have to go review the accounts and the overseer's report now," said the girl. "Now I do all those things that Rémy did. Or should have done. Please excuse me." Her black-butterfly frock rustled as she got up and ascended the staircase to the plantation house's office.

Why wasn't she petrified of slave revolts, a lone girl running a plantation? Really, Manon reflected, her overseer was the only person between her and the rage of some new Nat Turner. Every single visit to this house, its isolation had fallen on Manon like the black Egyptian night of Exodus, "even darkness which might be felt." Araminta, Peter, and the overseer were the only white people living at the estate with the slaves. That overseer, one Jack Binks, was a rough and nasty article if Manon had ever seen one. She wondered how Araminta managed Binks.

Presently Binks came to the back porch; Manon heard him scraping his boots. Then he tiptoed in the back door, eyes down, shoulders hunched, hat clutched before him with both hands. Manon's nose itched at his stale smokehouse scent, hot male sweat and tobacco. "Pardon me, ma'am, sorry, ma'am, I wiped my feet real good," he said in Manon's direction as he scuttled stairward.

Manon wondered what prompted his fervid servility, then realized that he went in fear of that girl of nineteen. She wondered how Araminta had so daunted the brute. One of his strangler's hands could have gone around her throat.

When Manon inquired, Araminta told her. "Oh, I found out he'd been stealing. You know—I'd send him with a list to the general store in the village, and he'd keep the change. That and taking bacon from the smokehouse and money from Rémy's cash box. I made him tally up how much he'd stolen that way, and I set a penalty in addition to that. I'm docking his pay two dollars a month until it's all paid back, and when he started to grizzle about that, I told him I'd report the matter to the sheriff if he didn't give complete satisfaction, and the sheriff and I would start taking an interest in whatever made him so willing to work in this malarial fever-hole. Being nervous has brought out his hidden talents. Now that I lit a fire under him, he's really not bad at his job. And he knows that if he starts thieving again, I'll catch him."

"But how did you find out such a thing?"

"Arithmetic." Araminta shrugged and smiled. "One of those things it's good for—I went over the ledgers."

"And this had been going on, and Rémy could have...?"

"Rémy didn't."

When her older brother Rémy had married Araminta, a third of his age at fifteen, Manon had found the girl polite but unreadable. Like Queen Victoria, Araminta was petite but a bit too buxom to look delicate. She had grown since standing up at the altar of St. Michael's with Rémy and had perhaps reached five feet by now. To her cold poise, she'd added a stern edge, like that of some formidable older woman. Manon felt sorry for Rémy, who'd always been weak. She almost felt sorry for the smelly overseer too.

*

At three in the afternoon, the ladies had tea—cold, with sugar and lemon and ice, a luxurious novelty. Araminta had a passion for iced drinks, desserts, soups. One could develop such a yen in Charleston, where an icehouse sold ice cut from New England ponds at a high price. On her late husband's property, she'd found a limestone cave that stayed cold far into the year. During the brief winter, she had her house servants pour well water into shallow pans to freeze outside at night, and in the morning, one of them took the ice and stowed it deep in the cave. Gracious for once, Araminta had told Manon to have all the ice she liked—"It won't last much longer, so we might as well have it before it melts."

Manon's Willie, though two years older than Peter, seemed taken with his cousin and followed Peter's lead. Manon saw nothing of her sallow, gangling brother in Peter. He was a fair blonde child, blue-eyed, usually fearless and cheerful. Peter had recently made the transition from baby frocks to breeches and shirts, and he still had a cushiony baby look. He was not tongue-tied like her Willie and spoke better than many far-older children Manon knew, though Manon would not have suffered such sass from Willie. She'd once made some casual comment to Peter's nurse about his free speech, and the woman grinned and said, "Bless him, he talks right peart! He's real smart. Miss Minta, she means to send him north to school when he's grown!"

Peter took two macaroons off the tea tray and gave Willie one. "Willie and me are going to do you a play, Auntie," said Peter, sidling up to Manon's chair.

"How gay!" Manon told him, and patted his fair head. Araminta was right about the heat; by tea-time all was hot, and still, and redolent of pine resin from the timber-cutting. The thick languor of summer, a certain promise, would linger until the sun started down. In the distance, black women carried buckets of well water and sacks of fruit to the woodcutting crew. Belle Rêve was too far south to grow apples, but the estate had fig and pear and peach trees. The sacks probably contained pears, picked green so they would last, then stored in the house's deep cellar all winter. Araminta was a benevolent little despot to her slaves, who got an hour for the noon meal and a break in the afternoon and ended their day at five. *Spoiling those darkies*, Manon would have thought, except that those methods worked so well. Araminta was always civil with the slaves; they were never familiar with her. She'd achieved an accord with them that had eluded Rémy, who'd been inclined to drink with the men and fornicate with the women when in good humor and thrash them savagely when not. If only to herself, Manon admired her sister-in-law's handling of her human chattel; she realized that there really was much less danger of a revolt now than when her poor brother was master here. She watched the four women trudging through the sun-stunned meadows. She was sleepy and bored. Yes, a play would cheer her, though it would inevitably be silly.

"Muvver, may we borrow your ring?" Peter importuned Araminta, who slipped it off and gave it to him. Both children ran upstairs. What could he want with a ring? She soon learned.

When they reappeared, Willie had Rémy's tophat on and was holding it with one hand to keep it from slipping down over his face. He had his other arm out like a gallant gentleman, and Peter was holding onto it with coy enthusiasm. Not the way Araminta had set her hand on Rémy's arm at Saint Michael's. Also unlike her, Peter was grinning from one ear to the next. He had a lace curtain on his head and a rose behind one ear, and he had pulled one of Araminta's lacy chemises on over his shirt and breeches.

"Don't tread on that shimmy," Araminta told her son, but she smiled.

"Oh, Muvver, I won't. I wish Vicar was here. He could do the churchy bit."

"You can do a perfectly good play, just you and Cousin Willie," Araminta assured him.

"It's called 'Weddings,' Auntie," said Peter. "You'll have to be the vicar." When Manon didn't say a word, he continued, "Willie is the man, and his name is Lord Burleigh. He's a ristocrat. I'm the girl, and my name is Liza Lou. Liza Lou is from the country, but she's so pretty it don't matter. The king wanted to marry her, but she likes Lord Burleigh." Perhaps he mistook Manon's consternation for ignorance, for he patted her hand and said, "Your bit's easy. You pretend there's a little boy here who's carrying the ring, and you say, 'May we have the ring?" I'll give it to you. Then you say, 'Lord Burleigh, will you have this woman to be your awful wedded wife?' And then Willie says *yes*, and you ask me, and I say *yes*, then you say—"

"Peter, this isn't a suitable play," said Manon. "Your mother should have told you this kind of thing isn't nice."

Peter differed: "It is too a nice play!"

"It's against religion, and wicked! Boys don't marry boys! It's an abomination!"

"It's only just pretend!" whined Peter. "Pretend isn't wicked!" Her Willie, Manon noted, dared not protest. He knew better!

"Do a play about soldiers and a war, that'll be all right," Manon suggested, not wanting to scold him too sharply in front of his mother. "Wars, soldiers, horses, riding to hounds, and hunting foxes—or you could be the overseer and whip the darkies. Something suitable for boys."

"Muvver don't let him whip the darkies! She says it just makes them mean and they can't work! And I don't want to do a play about a dirty old war! I want to pretend something that's amusing!" protested Peter. He was passionate, unlike his mother. Standing with his little pink hands on his hips, he stared Manon down.

"Well, boys who act like girls with other boys and want to marry boys go to Hell," Manon informed Peter. "Do you know about Hell? *That's* not amusing. The flame never expires, and the damned cry for water but never get a drop, and the worms never die."

"Worms do too die if you cut 'em in half," said Peter, who could be factual. "They wiggle a while, but they're dead pretty soon."

Manon would have loved to smack the backtalking little beast but contented herself with a game attempt to scare him. "The worms in Hell don't die. They gnaw the dead souls."

Peter responded with the results of a recent experiment: "Worms burn up if you set 'em on fire. Willie and me tried it. They go all flat and greasy, and they're for sure dead."

"The worms in Hell are bigger than you, bigger than alligators, and you can't burn them up! In Hell, they torment the wicked for all eternity."

Peter seemed to consider that notion. His lip quivered. He looked at his mother, who'd been shocked into silence, then back to Manon. "Is Papa there? One time he hit Muvver. Vicar came to call and said he was wicked."

At that, Manon had gotten up so fast that she didn't properly know whether she really meant to slap Peter, but Araminta was up faster, between Manon and the children. She'd regained breath and voice. "Keep your claws to yourself and be quiet. No more about religion, and wickedness, and abominations, and worms, and alligators, and Hell. And no more raving rubbish about wars, we're probably going to have a war soon enough, and God help us!" She rang the bell hard, a painful jangle. When Peter's nursemaid appeared, she said, "Lucy, take the boys to the nursery and then bring them their supper there. I want them to stay in there with you and go straight to bed at seven." Peter opened his mouth to start roaring, but she stroked him quiet. As if he were still a baby, she picked him up and put him in Lucy's arms. "Lucy, take that curtain off his head when you get him upstairs. It's Malines lace. It's fragile. Peter, stop your fussing and give me back my diamond and go upstairs with Lucy and Willie. I'm not punishing you. I'll come up later. And tomorrow we'll draw some pictures and amuse ourselves."

More than glad to go, Willie was fully cooperative, but Peter had rallied enough to talk back. From the first landing, he actually dared to call down to Manon, "I'll pick out who I want to marry! You can't make me not do it! You're an old baggage!" He squirmed so energetically that Lucy had to put him down. Then he glowered down at Manon, puckered his lips, and made a disgusting noise. Lucy, stammering apologies, renewed her efforts to haul him up to the second floor.

"Peter, that'll do," said Araminta. "Mother has already said to go upstairs with Lucy." Manon had the fleeting thought that she really tolerated no nonsense from Peter. At least no nonsense that she didn't happen to enjoy.

"I'm going! I can't be more going than I am, Lucy's pulling me!" A parting shot to Manon: "You don't smell good like Muvver! You're mean to Willie! I bet you've *got* worms! Old bad baggage!"

"Where," Manon asked Araminta, "did he learn to say *baggage*?"

The girl shrugged. "It's a word in English. It can mean an objectionable person, or the trunk and portmanteau someone like that brings on a visit. I expect he heard it said." Before Manon could reckon she knew who'd said it, Araminta added, "You can thank yourself for the part about worms." She followed the boys and the nurse upstairs.

*

"Have they both been smacked for their shameful display?" was the first thing out of Manon when her young hostess returned.

"What shameful display? The only shameful display was yours. You got them both in an uproar with your ranting about Hell! They'll probably throw up before they have their naps. I'm sure Peter will. And it's bad for them, and nasty for Lucy to clean up!"

At that, Manon boiled and foamed over. "You have to be the most ignorant young woman I've ever met. Do you really not understand that you must break that child of those... proclivities before they take hold for the rest of his wretched life?"

"His life isn't wretched. I might not say the same for Willie. What proclivities?"

Manon had heard of such proclivities in a whispered story about someone else's son, expelled from the University of Mississippi for vices learned in Paris. Everyone who was anyone in Mobile had shunned his entire family once his disgrace became known. She wasn't about to let that happen to her boy! "When Willie had just started walking, he started carrying ragdolls around and coddling them like babies, and I broke him of that. He was switched until he screamed every time he was caught at it, and now he won't touch a doll. If you don't break Peter of... playing charades, and wearing ladies' clothes, and drawing pictures, and wanting to play weddings and be the bride... he might grow up to do unspeakable things. With other men. As men do in Paris, and London, and in the cities of the North."

Manon had never been north of Charleston. Except in drinks, she had never seen more than a thin scrim of ice floating in a gutter. But she felt on thin ice once those words left her lips. Araminta was giving her the most unwomanly look.

"What on earth is wrong with drawing pictures?" Araminta asked, as if worse idiocy had never been uttered. "Peter's already good at it! He's gifted! Like me. Only he's a boy, and he can achieve something with his talent if he wants to! Whatever are you running on about?"

"Sometimes a boy grows up and wants to be with a man the way a woman is with a man, and they like to wear women's clothes and draw pictures and act out plays. Or play the pianoforte."

Araminta thought that novel notion over for almost a minute by the mantel clock, then asked, "Well, I've never heard of it, but why shouldn't they? If that's what they want? Suppose he did form an attachment with some gentleman. They could settle here and live off timber and indigo and cotton, like me. It's not so very hard to run a plantation. If they wanted a child, they could get one out of the Orphan House in Charleston."

"It's filthy! Don't you know the church forbids it?"

"No—I've been to church all my life, and I've never once heard anything against dressing up for plays or drawing pictures or playing music, or gentlemen fancying gentlemen."

"You're horrifying," said Manon. "Did that blue-blooded mother of yours never instruct you about behavior, and morality, and duty to your husband, and marriage, and bringing up children?"

"No, she didn't, she had the consumption, she didn't have the strength to 'instruct' anyone. I've played the hand I was dealt, and your disgusting brother was one of those cards." With that, the opening pleasantries of this skirmish were over, and the cannon coughed out its first salvo: "Since we're already quarreling—I despised your brother! A fool and a drunk, and what surprise is that? You Geoffreys are degenerates with money, who've married your cousins and God only knows who else in Martinique, or Saint-Domingue, or wherever else you've been! And it's only up-jumped pushing nobodies like you, who have no manners and never had any, that carry on all the time about other people act. You keep poking at me to make me say I'm sorry for one thing or another—well, I'm sorry Peter's got your family's bad blood, *that's* what I'm sorry about! I'm sorry my father was so reckless with his money that he had to exchange me and my pedigree for the Geoffreys to pay off his mortgages! It's one step up from being sold on the block!" The girl, standing about as high as Queen Victoria, looked just as imperious. She was white with anger but plainly not faint with it, as if she found it an energizing emotion. "It nearly killed me to get Peter born. I was just sixteen! When Rémy first called at my father's house to wheedle him about courting me, I was still in short dresses! Men shouldn't make little girls have babies! You want to pitch a fit about abominations? Well, that's one! I'd never dreamt there was such pain! For a month after Peter came, I couldn't walk without feeling like my insides would fall out. Anyhow, I got Peter into this world, and now that he's here, I won't have you telling him something's wrong with him and making him a fraidy-cat like your poor Willie. Am I understood?"

"This is my brother's house," began Manon, feeling as if she might choke.

"No, not any more, it isn't! Dead people don't need houses. It's mine and Peter's now, and we're going to do as we like. You ought to leave tomorrow and go back to yours. Am I understood?

She could not have been better understood, by this time, if she had used the royal *we* instead of the first person singular. Manon went upstairs and began to pack. Her hands trembled; that chit of a girl had made her shake! One of the house servants knocked and handed her Rémy's discarded art collection, a neat roll of canvases tied with string.

*

At twilight, carrying a lamp, Araminta went barefoot into the nursery in her nightgown. Peter had thrown up as predicted, and Willie had cried monotonously until he finally fell asleep. Lucy, now asleep on the truckle bed, had cleaned up, but there was a sour lingering reek. The nurse was terrified of colds and chills and night air, so she'd closed three of the four broad windows. Araminta opened them as far as they'd go and hoped for a strong breeze. Every minute of coolness felt precious. If it wouldn't have meant leaving Peter unguarded while Manon was in this house, she'd have taken a lantern, had her pony saddled, and made her way to the cold-cave. Even after the last of the ice was gone, the limestone cavern was chilly. She went there often to get cool, to clear her mind. She'd tie up her pony and take off her dress and petticoat, which would have been torn and dirtied otherwise. Then she'd hang them on a branch, slip through the narrow opening into the dark, and sit on a flat rock until her whole skin felt tight and dry. Only she and two house servants knew about the cave; it was quite safe, what she did, though it would have given Manon apoplexy. It was calming, now, to think about the cave. For a few minutes, she let her mind go there. The sounds of children fretting in their sleep brought her back.

When she took the covers off the flush-faced little boys, Willie's stick legs brought tears to her eyes, though she wasn't a weeper. Neither child had eaten any supper. She hadn't either; she'd ordered a pitcher of cold tea, extravagantly iced, and sipped it until she felt better. The butler had served Manon alone at the formal dining table. She'd sent her sister-in-law a meal that would be repulsive in the stuffy dusk: fried chicken, fried cabbage, fried potatoes, biscuits, pie, and cheese. With any luck, the grease and heat would give her dyspepsia, but that likelihood didn't relieve Araminta's feelings. Probably nothing short of wearing the woman out with a horsewhip would, and that was illegal.

She took her sleeping son out of the bed and sat in the rocking chair to rock him and let him cool off in the piney air. "There's nothing wrong with you," she murmured to him. "You're fine and clever, and you've been paid for with pain." She tried never to think of how he'd begun, the iron and fire of the drunken man on and in her. And something had never gone back to the way it had been before this child was born; she was not flat and tight below the waist, as she'd been before. Peter's warm weight felt good, as if it pushed her loose parts back into place.

Willie's sad red-rimmed eyes opened.

"Are you all right now, Willie?"

"Yes'm, only Mama'll whip me when we get back to Mobile. For playing weddings. Cause I've been a bad boy."

"I think you're a good boy, Willie."

"Mama don't think so."

Peter had come awake too, and straight back to what had probably been the last thought in his head before he succumbed to this day's tempests.

He pressed his button nose into Araminta's shoulder and sniffed. "Auntie's stinky like medicine. But you're a tree with flowers." He was a barefaced little flatterer, but sometimes he said the sweetest things!

"Go back to sleep. I'll rock you." Araminta hadn't rocked him when he was newborn; he'd looked like a big pale frog. It had been hard to like him then. She'd kept remembering how it felt when the doctor pulled him out of her. Then, about a month old, he'd begun to grow fair hair like hers and give her big gummy grins when she bent over his cradle. Then he began to seem like her child, and she'd begun to feel that she really was his mother. Being a mother could be frightening, though running the plantation was complicated and she'd never been frightened of that. She quite liked running the plantation.

"Why does Auntie come here when she don't like us?" asked Peter.

"*I* like you," chimed sad Willie. "I couldn't come if she didn't."

"She ought to just send Willie and stay in Mobile," Peter reasoned. "Why don't she do that? And why don't Papa come back?"

"Willie's right. If Auntie didn't visit, we'd never see him. And we're fine with Papa gone. We've got the money and the house." *Mine,* Araminta thought, ***this estate and Rémy's money and all this place's crops are mine, and this boy's mine too.*** Then she noted Rémy's stovepipe hat, which had come up to the nursery with the two miserable little boys and was probably reminding Peter of Rémy. "Papa is dead from too much brandy, and dead people don't come back. We don't need to worry about dead people."

"But I want to see him," Peter persisted.

"Well, I don't."

"I mean, just to know he's not burning up."

"Nobody's burning up! Papa's just dead, that's all. And now you're all mine. You don't have a father now, and you aren't ever going to have another. It's nicer without. No one's going to come here and order us around and spend our money." Araminta bit her tongue on that theme. Speaking of ***suitable***, it wasn't. Children shouldn't hear grown people carrying on about money; money-talk was vulgar. And her late husband's casual handling of finances had been the least of his sins. She felt too emotional, heated, and Peter felt downright hot. If Manon had excited him into a fever, Araminta thought, she would settle with the harridan in no uncertain terms before packing her off to Mobile. She set Peter on his feet and fluffed out his nightshirt, sweat-stuck to his skin. "You're too warm. Stand up and get cool in that breeze."

Peter leaned his sleepy self against the chair. He took hold of her sleeve and held it to his cheek, as he liked to do when he was agitated, and pursued yet another difficult question: "Can you make Auntie go home and let us keep Willie? Auntie don't love him, and we do."

"No, I can't do that. If I said I could, that'd be a lie." Briefly, she considered saying that Auntie really did love Willie, but that was untrue too, as far as she could tell. "What would help you and Willie feel better? What would feel nice and help you forget all about that stupid uproar?" She wanted to give them something.

Willie seemed to be thinking it over. He probably was not offered treats very often. Finally he uttered: "I'm going to get whipped for it anyway when I get home, so can we please do our play?"

Araminta didn't lie to him that Manon would forget about whipping him; Manon would remember.

"Reckon I might as well do what I'm going to get whipped for anyhow," said Willie. Manon had him cowed, but he had a good head on his shoulders.

"You're clever, Willie. You think like a little lawyer. Yes, if you both go to sleep right after your play," said Araminta. ***They'll forget all about this,*** she thought, ***but if they didn't, what of it?*** Peter could do far worse than Cousin Willie. She thought of herself still here, old and gray and probably fat, at this estate with the grown-up Peter and Willie. A renowned portrait artist, she thought, and a laconic, well-trusted country lawyer, perhaps the Lowndes County judge. There'd be nothing to apologize for.

Peter snatched the lacy scarf off one of the little tables and put it on his head. "So I've got lace on my head like a real lady, and there's Papa's hat!" he crowed. Willie got out of bed and tried to make the hat stay on his head, and Peter moved on to ***dramatis personae.*** "So he's Lord Burleigh, and I'm Liza Lou, and can we borrow your ring, Muvver?"

"Yes, and I'll be the vicar."

Poetic Justice

Leighlah

"It was true, what I said," I kept telling myself. Then one morning I woke up knowing that not every truth needs to be told. A gun can go forever without being fired, but people have trouble keeping what they know under their tongues. Before that New Orleans levee broke during Hurricane Katrina, I bet some happy ass braved the rising flood in his motorboat and rammed the levee just to see if it was sound. And then maybe saw the packed earth of the levee plume out into the thrashing waves and sped away, well in advance of the wall of brown water that would crash through a few hours later and drown the seething, splintering slums.

Like cities, people age variously. Unpretty, unfashionable high school girls are often the striking women of their college class at forty-five. Ever see photographs of Maria Callas at seventeen, a greasy fat pudding, and at forty as Medea, sharp and fine as a drawn sword? But I didn't evolve that way. I am beaky now, though I thought of myself as exotic at eighteen. Never conventionally pretty, I'd found exoticism, signaled at my college by long dangling earrings, lots of eyeliner, and Indian cotton skirts aflame with cheap bright dye, a necessity. Twenty-fifth class reunions show how the conventionally pretty fade and lose definition. People put on weight or lose it, often obliterating the silhouette of new adulthood. Whoever you were at eighteen goes beneath the waves like Atlantis. You may turn into something rich and strange, though getting beaky or losing definition is a likelier scenario.

What you do *not* do is stay the same. My victim... I will call her Vic here, as if her name had been Victoria... she had stayed the same. No, that's not right: She'd reverted, and to a degree that the best plastic surgeons can't offer their clients. And I have a basis for that assertion because the alumni of my college can afford the best plastic surgeons. (Some of them *are* the best plastic surgeons, so we can even have the blub under our chins suctioned out by an old friend.) For convenient comparison, my twenty-fifth reunion's kick-off party provided a showcase of aesthetic surgery.

And, by contrast, among all those Botoxed necks and lifted faces, there was Vic as she'd looked at eighteen, with petal skin and a horsetail of hair. Put any teenager, at least one with clear skin, alone in a room of fortysomethings, and you will see what isn't obvious about the young among their peers: Anyone that age is beautiful.

While we were at college, I'd not admired Vic's looks. She wasn't thin, which we girls took as a requisite for beauty and almost for any claim to respect. She'd had a sort of old-fashioned healthy and demure air, like a contemporary Tess of the D'Urbervilles. She didn't fit any of the accepted personae at our college—exotic, punk, stoner, and prep were the major options. She'd had a bland maturity of manner that I found off-putting. It could morph into surprising sharpness, little nips of bitter wit, or into unguarded moments of skittishness. The skittishness, as things turned out, was the current that ran deep and long. And her unconcern with her looks could have meant either supreme confidence in them, or in some other strength—or the feeling that her surface wasn't worth tending. Maybe she arrived among us with a little extra social inexperience, struggled more to think of things to say at parties—only natural if a person had been the isolated genius of her provincial high school—but she didn't arrive radiating obvious fragility. That doesn't mean it wasn't there because emotional intelligence wasn't my forte then, and it isn't now either. But I know that real fragility is something you can't afford at our college. This is not a place to bring your little fissured psyche in the hope of healing.

"The thing Ah hate," said the southern classmate who'd buttonholed me by the champagne fountain, "is kids my son's age calling me *ma'am*." That one was a card-carrying member of the Lost Definition Camp in full, flouncy Laura Ashley. "*Ma'am* takes the shine right off my day," she repined, and stuffed something into her mouth. "And of course you can't ask them not to, because they're trying to be polite. But Ah do hate that *ma'am* stuff."

"No risk of that where I live," I told her. I'm based in Jersey, where we don't have an overcivility problem. I couldn't keep my eyes off Vic. No risk that anyone would call her *ma'am*.

"Coming through, coming through," chanted one of those plastic surgeons, silver-haired like Richard Gere. Like the actor, he had allowed himself to age well. Let's call him Dr. Silverman here. Dr. Silverman had a glass of white wine in each hand and was making his way to Vic's side. His interest was both professional and personal, I suspected. I could well assess the details of his aging because he'd lived across the hall from me senior year. Dr. Silverman's seasoned face projected his awe at this woman who'd come up unchanged from the drowned world. He listened to her as he never would have done at eighteen, wanting to keep her there, unable to believe his eyes. Maybe he'd never looked that way at the most beautiful woman whose clothes dropped at her feet for him.

(And beautiful Vic was: not thin but firm and shapely, and I would swear she was wearing a snug denim jumper she'd worn at eighteen, with a moss-and-mauve flowered blouse. And Frye boots, which, like denim, matched everything when we were at college. I tried to tell myself—maybe this was Vic's daughter, exactly resembling her? But what was a teenager doing at a reunion cocktail party? At college here? Why would Vic allow her daughter into this venomous social cauldron to meet people exactly like me?)

But it was Vic, and she'd seen me. And the moment came when she extended her hand... her firm, silky, perfectly eighteen-year-old-looking hand... and said "Hello," and spoke her name, though we all had nametags. At first I could not say my name, likewise adhering to me in its original ridiculous spelling. (I wonder, did my mother spell it that way like some good fairy with bad taste, trying to confer on me... what? Lightheartedness, the blessing of a not-too-serious life? A Leighlah should be ever-young, a flower child forever, running fleetly over wet green grass. It has not turned out that way.) But there was no getting away from the name bit: The reunion committee had had the bright idea of giving us nametags with first names only so we could break the conversational ice with past and current surnames. So *Leighlah* in hand-done italics was gummed to my lapel.

I couldn't get *Leighlah Kowalski* up my throat. "Leigh Vangelikos," I managed—I use the surname of my second ex. I tried to swallow. "I thought... there was a rumor that you... God, the way some people gossip, it's foul! What's your secret, though? You... you look amazing." I saw myself make some pathetic gesture toward her outfit. "And very Spirit of the Seventies."

"Yes," Vic said. (I wondered: *yes, I do look amazing* or *yes, the way some people gossip is foul*?) "So I thought I'd treat this gathering like a costume party, wear some of the clothes I wore here my first year, and come as my own ghost," she added reasonably. And very politely/lightly, as if there were no history between us. Her comment was somewhat like remarks I remembered Vic making as a girl; you could never tell whether they were metaphoric, elliptical, or symbolic. Literary bullshit, I'd thought back then.

"Did you marry? Is your hus... partner here?" I faltered, groping for happily-ever-after.

"Oh, no. I didn't marry. Or make a million, buy an island, or publish a book. Or even have an Olympic medalist child who scored a perfect SAT and financed a hospice with a lemonade stand. I'm our class fuck-up, back to be flippant." Was there the slightest sting behind her smile?

So the buzz about her suicide had been just a rumor. Every single month after I, the vicious gossip, first heard the suicide rumor, I dreaded getting my alumni magazine. But when it came, I had to open it before all the other mail; I had to skim past the announcements of hyphenated children's births and triumphs, their triple-named parents' dotcom fortunes and endowed chairs and gallant battles with cancer—it seems that nobody from our college raises a boring, nothing kid or dies a petulant, retching death. I had to go immediately to the back, to the obits, and check the deaths. That's when I'd be telling myself, "It was true, what I said," as if truth were the issue. Her death was never mentioned, but every time I took the magazine from the mailbox, my stomach would freeze until I had found her unnumbered among our dead. Surely my alumni magazine would not lead me astray by omission.

In midlife, I am not an immaculate saint... my admin, after a couple of happy-hour Bellinis, probably tells her pretty young friends exactly what I am. But I would not do to anyone now what I did to Vic when we were both young. If I heard someone talking drunk-talk or drug-talk, I would try not to listen, I would pretend not to hear, I would not take whatever was said seriously, surely I would not repeat it. At twenty-one, I had no idea that there was something for me in discretion, namely a cool conscience and the ability to take my alumni magazine from the mailbox without a twenty-point rise in blood pressure. Not to carry, in my pocket or purse or the blue hand of my sleep, a guilt that weighed about as much as my alabaster paperweight but was an entirely different kind of stone.

Also... while not precisely a failure, I haven't made a million, bought an island or even a lousy condo, or published a book. I've failed marriage three times. I'm a literary agent, good but not the best. Being a top-flight literary agent requires passion and talent I lack. Or simply the voltage and concentrated charm that a person cannot muster while carrying a stone. I look good enough on résumé paper that you might not be able to tell it, but when I knocked Vic off her track, I also fell off mine. God's fair, which doesn't mean kind.

If I'd kept my mouth shut... I have no idea what Vic's outcome might have been, but I know that I would not have heard rumors of her self-murder and felt guilt fill my body like a slow flow of liquid lead. Mistakes are not supposed to count full weight when you're dumb and young, but no yellow light winked a warning when I stepped out of Practice Lifeland into the Republic of Real Consequences.

But even a pathological person, you say, has a reason for doing a mean thing? Yes, and in my case, not even an interesting reason. My reason for not holding my peace was a young man, surprisingly coveted by young women at our college. I took a statistics course with him. Known for brilliance even here, he had a strange, unaccommodating beauty, like the guy who played the space alien in *The Man Who Fell to Earth*, and a personality to match. Mr. Fell's schizoid chill did not prevent young women from lusting after him, wanting to straddle his ice-white flanks and rub themselves like cats all over his lanky body. I knew at least five who desired nothing more than that. Perhaps I might have wanted the same. Pre-AIDS, the sexual climate at our college was all lush ambiguity, and ours was a campus full of beautiful, bisexual young men and women playing an ongoing game of movable beds. However, it was my impression that this young man only lusted after other young men, so I didn't let my fantasies flower or my crush uncrush like those Japanese paper buds you drop into water to blossom and pulse faintly when the surface is disturbed. Part of Leighlah has always been a desert, salty and flinty. I did not, and do not, bother with projects that won't pan out.

Anyway, it shocked us all when Vic began paying attention to Mr. Fell our junior year, and he began paying attention back. The unlikeliest of outcomes, they became inseparable. Mr. Fell came down to Earth, he warmed and smiled and made eye contact with people. He sat on the grass with Vic, once, with a childish chain of dandelions around his neck. Vic, always so outwardly composed, re-became a teenager with him. And a silly one, I'd thought, watching out my window as the two of them pelted each other with the winter's first snow. Whatever went on between them had unlocked silliness in her, also joy. If you looked closely, which I did as the term proceeded, you could see that it had unlocked need as well. You could read need in her pitched effort to please him. He must have stilled some long pain in her, perhaps woken a new one. *Fixing on him,* I thought later, as they sat together in the cafeteria. Getting enough of him to last her through the night. And he enjoyed her. Hell, maybe he loved her. But I could tell that she wore him out.

More casual observers noted that Vic had become looser, more outgoing. Though not so much as at the reunion party, where she circulated with a bantering ease she could never have managed when young. When I got through with her back in 1979, she had stopped looking young, or well, or pretty at all.

So, you're probably thinking, Leighlah, Leigh, Whoever, get to the point! And I will.

Then, as our senior year began, after a term of watching Vic and Mr. Fell to Earth, I went to a party in this very room. The party was given by a friend of Vic's, now an eminent plastic surgeon, then an exotic pre-med. I'll call her Ariel. The name was very popular immediately post-Plath, especially with mothers of Ariel's ethnic persuasion. This particular Lioness of God, for that's what it means, owned a leonine ego and big bouncy curves. Ariel was as even-by-local-standards-brilliant as Mr. Fell, and she didn't care if my friends and I thought she was fat. I used to wonder at Ariel, eating all the manicotti and tapioca she wanted. She never touched the salad and sour yogurt that most of us girls subsisted on, at least whenever anyone else was watching us eat.

At her party, Ariel had a pound of gypsy jewelry swinging from her neck and ears, her big breasts free under her peasant blouse, and her lover, Morgan, dancing attendance. Morgan, a househusband in training, was known for his cooking, which was probably why I drifted down to Ariel's party. I'd missed dinner; I'd smelled Morgan's Korean barbecue sauce simmering in the dorm kitchen. And Mr. Fell, whom Vic had coaxed into occasional sociability, might manifest. I wanted to look at him up close.

There were drugs at Ariel's party, though probably no more than at any other student party on the campus or in the city. Back then, most of us children of the seventies were willing to ingest anything short of Drāno at least once. Mr. Fell did not attend, but Vic did. Vic was not a girl who normally did drugs, but that night she'd definitely had something, and more of it than she could handle.

Yet again, I wondered... in annexing Mr. Fell, had she scored a coup that none of us could manage? How could she do that, that insipid girl—win a man who didn't like people as a species and, when he liked them, liked men, and for narrow and temporary purposes? Had she really gotten him to cross over, was she ahead of us all, or a fool for love? Hearing her voice play on, a rapturous contralto clarinet, I decided: fool for love. One who's had enough coke to loosen her brain, to loosen her tongue, to make this wet night a rain of jewels and that relationship way more than it is and her future a breathless revelation rising like a second sun. To her good friend Ariel, Vic was confiding her plans for next summer, plans which it sounded like she and Mr. Fell had in common. I sidled closer to hear. Apparently struck by Vic's manic edge, Ariel looked concerned. The Lioness had snubbed out the joint she and Vic had been passing back and forth. *Enough drugs for you, babe,* she was probably thinking. Barefoot, an anklet strung with little bells around one brown ankle, Ariel had gone so still that their tiny tinkle ceased. Ariel had beautiful feet, long and narrow. She liked to show them.

Noting my interest, Ariel put her hand on Vic's elbow and steered her a few feet away. "...crashing," I thought I heard Ariel say, and "... bitch." And "So where is he?"

"We both meant to come, but he had to work," responded Vic.

We, we, we, Vic kept saying, like the little pig crying all the way home. That first person plural was holy gold to her! But who is *we* with such a man? I wondered if he knew about this *we* Vic had woven around him and herself. I wondered what he'd think if he learned that Vic, like most females, was building a nest in her head even before she could rent a cheap apartment, buy a few sticks of furniture, and get a kitten from the pound. Even ordinary men, wholly heterosexual, are terrified by females' need for nests and things and people to put in them. So what would that man think of these breathless plans, that *we*? She was, no doubt, his first female. He'd probably panic at the spectacle: love that had broken its levee, need that had tugged free of reality like a helium balloon from a heedless little fist. A girl who saw everything as possible and platinum, and all her possibilities embraced him.

Oh, now I know that people really hate innocence, despite all this bogus nostalgia for what childhood used to be; I hated Vic's innocence, her shining face. I have seen rows of glasses on the lit shelves of stores and wished I could knock them down and hear them hit the tiles with that delicious sound of irremediable breakage; I wanted to knock her down. She was a fool and no one's future was platinum and there would be no blazing love triumphing over common sense and people's true natures, no! Not for me and certainly not for her! Probably not for anyone.

She could have discovered that without my input, soon enough, but I helped her.

I did nothing that night but listen and fill up on Korean barbecue. I don't think I consciously planned to do much more. When I took a seat by Mr. Fell in Advanced Resampling that Monday, his fair brow furled, and he moved as far away as his chair would let him. That seemed autopilot for him, so I didn't take it personally. I remember thinking that all his glamour was in his distance. At less than arm's length, he smelled of stale sheets and, I think, baby powder. The air close to him was sort of sourly sweet. Close up, in fact, he was depressing: chiseled face unshaven, pale hair greasy, fresh out of bed in the clothes he'd slept in. Possibly for the last two nights—this man didn't dress to impress. His sneakers were foul, and he'd been drawing on them in ballpoint. It looked like he'd also been doodling on his pants. Except for his hair and his bone structure, he was so nerdy that I wondered why I was bothering with him. I cleared my throat. "Hey, congrats," I said. "I heard you got that internship at CU. And that you and Vic are heading out to Denver this summer."

Mr. Fell frowned as if that didn't compute. "Yeah, I'm going to Denver. Not Vic."

"No? Well, she thinks so." His jaw twitched as if this was news to him, so I pressed on. "I think Vic misunderstands you. I think she has it all wrong about you." He didn't ask me to explain, but I did. I repeated what I'd heard. Perhaps I giggled and grinned. Perhaps I added bits.

When I'd exhausted my material, he said, "I see." He stared straight ahead and didn't take notes from the lecture. He didn't say *thank you.*

("You're mind-blind," my second husband sneered after a conflagration with a novelist to whom I'd administered some home truths about people who can't crank out a book per year. One of my regrettable episodes of blowing my cool with writers... that one blew his cool right back at me. That mid-list nothing, that nobody! He yelled at me! Right in my own office! And if I'd hoped for sympathy in the three-martini aftermath, that evening at home, I was out of luck. My second husband heard me out and scoffed, "Nobody ever says *thank you* for something like you gave him. Nobody's ever grateful for it. People hate you for that kind of 'favor,' don't you get it, Leigh? Of course you don't." And my second husband and I didn't last much longer.)

I don't know what I expected, but Mr. Fell and Vic were never seen together again after my revelation in Advanced Resampling. I have to imagine the scene between them; I don't have to imagine the aftermath.

The Hurricane Katrina "photo essays" brought that aftermath to the forefront for me—people who'd watched all they had and all they hoped for as it went beneath the waves. From Vic, I knew that expression. Have you ever seen someone perish alive with grief? She went silent. She seemed to lose all the adult or semi-adult defenses she had.

My timing was vile, too: the beginning of senior year, the worst time to lose your edge. Vic lost hers in a way apparent to all. There were rumors of her scanty class attendance, her tenuous grades. She walked like a shoplifter, or like someone who finds herself on wet ice with no traction. Worse, unconcealed grief was a magnet for more meanness. Some wag began drawing caricatures of her on the tables at the dorm's grille, including one witty and ugly one of her and Mr. Fell—I do have the decency not to describe it. There were reports of her furtively covering the nasty pictures with Liquid Paper late at night. And people actually sniped at her. Some talked to her in ways that we wouldn't have dared talk to the janitors or the cafeteria workers, who served us with expressions of patient and enduring contempt.

Take Dr. Silverman, just Pre-Med Silverman then. A guy sniping at a girl was exceptional, an expression of utter disdain. I don't think he'd have done it if she'd fallen to pieces over a straight guy; perhaps Mr. Fell's fagginess fueled Silverman's straight-guy rancor. At any rate, Silverman curled his lip at Vic over the salad bar and told her that she'd taken too many tomatoes. "Take them," she'd said. "Have them." She'd set her tray down and fled. Silverman gaped, then grinned. Then he laughed. Humor is one face of hostility, of course, but I wonder: Is horror also one of the emotions expressed through laughter? Our horror at someone our age who had taken on real grief, or just scary excess?

(People are supposed to shrug their early losses off, there's a hopeful postmodern expectation that they do. But how many don't? What if the Victorian novelists are right about early sorrow? And early collapse, and early death?)

Loyal Ariel came to meals with Vic, making me think of nineteenth-century nurse-companions shepherding their neurasthenics. Then there were the two girls who tried to buck the trend of their peers; they deserve a footnote for good intentions, if not for good results. They battened earnestly upon Vic whenever she showed up for a meal without Ariel, trying to befriend her, to make her talk. She dodged them by coming early to meals, when she came at all, and carrying something away in a napkin. Ultimately she wasn't seen in the cafeteria any more.

If I'd had ambitions, they went no further than petty torment. And I'd meant to be amused rather than what I was, which was scared. Who knew that malice could become such an uncontrollable animal? Or that someone could shrivel and expand at the same time? Vic put on a lot of sudden watery weight, as if grief turned to waxy flesh. Perhaps cheap fast food, in off-campus places where she wouldn't meet any of us, was the culprit. And by the time we all finished our senior year, she no longer even looked like a student, but like one of those sad ladies who worked in the cafeteria. Her college girl wardrobe must not have fit anymore, and she'd acquired some nondescript clothes like a cafeteria server might wear. She looked thirty and exhausted. I wondered what there was behind her eyes: a determination to last college out at any price in pain? To encapsulate shame and grief until the glass might be broken in some far private place?

In late April, our dorm had a "strawberry tea," which involved no tea: rather, bottles of cheap champagne and heaps of big California strawberries and cream. Through strawberry teas, the college tried to soften the end of term, when the high whine of tension on campus hurt the nerves like cicadas' noise and people overdosed. Mr. Fell appeared at the strawberry tea with a muscular theatre major, a guy with the dark, fulsome bloom of a soap opera star. Mr. Fell maintained a frisking liveliness that must have been a strain, hanging on the hunk's utterances like a little fishie on a hook. "That's a boy who's going to be on his knees before the night's out," I thought, as the gathering broke up and Mr. Fell scampered after that object of desire. I went back upstairs, tried to work, and gazed out into the green and blue gloom as people drifted back to their final papers. I thought of ***Brideshead Revisited***, which I'd read in a course: a book saturated with a drunken, plangent grief that hit like the scent of lilacs and was beautiful. The canopy glowed white over tables bearing the remains of the fruit and wine.

Once everyone was gone, I became aware of Vic slipping under its shelter to scoop up some leftovers before the cleaning crew came. A handful of reject berries, a bottle with a couple of inches of flat champagne?

The sight sent me to Ariel's door to say... I don't know what. Going there took some nerve because Ariel had always taken a dim view of me. Moreover, she was fully informed about my role in her friend's capsized condition and had cut me dead at every chance. I hadn't dared to crash another of her parties. Nor was my timing the best; Ariel's floor was covered with drifts of India-gauze clothing and coffee cups and Hershey chocolate wrappers and a scrawled-up typescript of something that was probably due in the morning.

"I need to talk to you," I'd ventured, though the Lioness's wrath was evident and daunting.

"No, you don't."

"You don't understand—"

"Try me," said Ariel. "I understand you're a hateful troublemaking cunt who can't mind her own business—how's that for understanding? See this?" She pointed to the floor and the typescript. "I'm behind with it, and the last thing I need is to worry, really worry, about what Vic might be doing to herself while I finish that paper. Which is going to matter in my life a year from now and five years from now, and so on. And I do have to worry, I've had to worry like this all year, and it's because of you, so yes, I do understand, but it's not like understanding's going to lead to rapport, or anything else cozy and uplifting."

She waited for me to go; in a moment, I thought, she'd slam the door. But I'd been fool enough to come there, and I got it with both barrels. "You think Vic needs your shit, Leighlah? You think she hasn't got enough shit in her life? Her family's hideous, they live to rub it into her how much this place costs and how she ought to have gone to the nice, cheap, perfectly good college right in their neighborhood and lived at home. They're after her on the phone all the time as if she's got something to hide, and thanks to you, now she does have something to hide. This year's been a train wreck for her, she'll be lucky not to flunk something, and this train wreck's going to matter in her life down the line. How do you think she's going to finance graduate school after this train wreck, if she even gets it together enough to do graduate school? God, I hope you come to some place in your life when you're trying not to drown, and someone pushes you under and laughs. Why couldn't you just let her be in love with the creep and let things work themselves out? Maybe you wanted your turn with him?"

"I know, I'm sorry, I didn't mean for it to be like this!" I mewled. "Ariel, I know you're mad at me, you're right to be, but I really, really need to talk." That 1970s therapized whine, a white flag that was supposed to suspend the most ardent hostilities, but Ariel wasn't buying it.

Ariel crossed her arms across her considerable tits. As she rendered it, this was no vulnerable, defensive pose. Her knuckles were white. She looked ready to hit me. Instead, she said, "Go talk to the shrinks at Student Health. You want absolution, they'll absolve you. They'll tell you you're perfectly okay. Or just misguided, or in transition, or something. That's what they get paid for."

"I didn't mean—"

"You meant it," said Ariel. "Now fuck off." And she did slam her door, hard, right in my face.

To give Ariel credit due, I'm sure I complicated her senior year immensely. I'm sure that Ariel did everything she could for Vic. And that, in the midst of Ariel's medical school applications and Vic's demolished condition, it wasn't enough.

Vic got her degree but did not take part in the graduation ceremonies. I wondered: Did a degree from a college like ours matter when you'd just barely squeaked through? Then, later, I heard the rumor of Vic's four years of sputtering, half-failed attempts at jobs and grad school followed by her death. And I thought that no, when you died at twenty-five, the crest on your degree didn't matter a damn bit.

And tonight I met up with her at our class reunion, among many incipient wrinklies, looking a dewy eighteen. The baby skin of her hand chilled mine. For the hour or so that she remained in the same room, I was giddy with sprung tension and the reorganizing sensation you must get when you learn that your lump is benign, your plea bargain is accepted, your charges are dropped. It's like all your molecules turn over! My little Iago moment had ruled my whole idea of myself. For most of my adult life, I'd considered myself a bad person, an accessory to a wrongful death, and each divorce and professional disappointment seemed only appropriate: another heaping helping of Leighlah's Just Desserts. And when I tried to talk myself out of it, my brain whispered the cold truth.

Feeling twitches and shivers in my midsection, I thought of getting a drink, but decided not. I wanted to experience my reprieve sober. Somewhere I heard that the solar plexus is a primitive brain, and that's where I felt the release, as if my stomach might fall out. I tightened my abs and imagined my own platinum horizon. And, beyond it, freedom to seek a sweeter life.

I talked to people, I'm sure, during the rest of the party, but I don't remember a word. The gathering seemed to revolve around Vic. Probably because a number of those people had acted bit parts in the play I scripted, they too were tingling with relief.

Ultimately the gathering lost its energy—not too late because there was a breakfast colloquy the next morning. Incipient wrinklies cannot stay up reminiscing until three in the morning and reconstitute themselves by nine. It was in the winding-down phase that Ariel, probably fresh from some crisis in the plastic surgery pavilion at Beth Zion, made her entrance. She'd probably just saved someone's face and sped home to throw her glad rags on, gun her Mercedes across town, and sail in, ablaze in scarlet silk. This was the familiar Ariel, larger than life and buoyant as a clipper ship, walking tall on high red fuck-me shoes. Ariel had gotten herself wine and crab puffs and was already talking shop with one of the other medicos when her eyes fixed on the denim dress in the midst of all this silk and challis and microfiber and linen. Perhaps she knew the dress before recognizing the pseudo-teen among us. Not bothering to excuse herself, Ariel shouldered her way through the bodies and tentatively set her hand on the denim shoulder.

Vic turned to face her. The color drained out of Ariel in a way I could see across the proverbial crowded room, even in the merciful mellow lights. Ariel dropped her drink.

Vic kissed her blanching cheek. "Sweetheart, you're late. I was looking forward to seeing you. I'm so sorry I've got to go when you've just come." She reached out to a tray of wineglasses, probably the last of the night, which a tired server was carrying among us. She handed Ariel another glass of wine and stroked Ariel's arm through its silk sleeve. She whispered something, her expression tender and fond as no eighteen-year-old's ever is: the tender-and-fond expression of a woman our age. What might that have been, I wonder? Was it *Thank you for sticking by me*? Was it *Sweetheart, it's okay*?

Scattering good-byes along the way, Vic moved toward the door. Ariel stared after her, then sank strengthlessly into the nearest chair. I reached out toward Vic as she neared the exit, meaning to say... I have no idea. She looked amused. "It's okay, Leighlah. You have your stone." Lightly touching her face: "I have this."

Probably with my jaw hanging down, I followed her out. I noticed she had no purse hanging on the shoulder of her denim jumper, no car keys in her hand. The late traffic roared hollowly on the thoroughfare. She was striding in that direction, though in no hurry. She was not afraid of me, not diving for solitude as for oxygen. Her walk was free, jaunty, as if she had shaken pain from her long ago. Car lights, edging out of the few precious on-street parking places, lanced the indigo air. I raised my hand, and she waved back: "Bye, Leighlah! Have a fabulous old age!"

Even a moth circling a streetlight has a shadow. She did not. Out there in the dark, the light shone through her hand.

Almost Fiction

I've Googled your name when something prompted me—one time it was a midlife couple, uncannily like us if we'd lived to grow up together, in Whole Foods. The guy was strikingly slim and dapper-dressed, with flaxen hair, fine features, and dark blue eyes. Yours were so dark that people assumed they were brown, then were startled at close range by your indigo gaze. They rarely looked long because it was discomforting, like looking at a burning light bulb filament. It radiated the same fire-staring unhappiness in Sylvia Plath's pictures, her overbright dark eyes. (You too were a harp tuned to darkness. You required the brightest days to see light. You were so thin you evoked envy in those cocaine-burned disco days. I don't know what most people like you look like when they reach midlife. There are few people like you in the first place, and I don't think many of them make it to fifty.)

This fifty-something man in the store was calm; his limpid gait and mildly bored expression suggested decades of minimal worry, and certainly none in the moment. The woman was forgettable, in clothes that suggested no vanity or interest in her own surface, and she was plainly in charge of the shopping, as I'd have been. He had most likely chosen or perhaps designed the arty wedding rings they wore. I think they loved each other and had worked the kinks and the radical inequities out of the love. They had made their peace. We did not live to make our peace. We did not stay together to draw each other out of the terrible narcissism of adolescents raised for Harvard like lobsters for five-star lobster rolls.

I tried not to stare. I knew it wasn't you. You died young. I survived, destroyed. Your obit said that you made a difference. That could be true.

If you have loved someone truly and that person has died, you don't stop wishing for some cosmic email to send the dead one notes about trivia that would have amused him. You might Google him to see what new details of his living time might have floated to its surface. I searched you today because of a sick joke you'd have laughed at: a garbage truck with a big stuffed yellow dog fastened onto the front bumper. This time I discovered something new. It's been a long time since I learned anything more than you'd told me. In our inseparable youth, you'd told me often how poor your family was, how cold your house was, and many a harrowing flourish. Your revelations about poverty had, or seemed to have, the intimacy of truth. On the listening end was a twenty-year-old, somewhat naïve, with a literary craving for drama, even angst, if it meant one had a real life. On the telling end, a twenty-year-old with an unruly literary flare, the ability to tell a story and make it hit bone. I was, I understood, to feel guilty about your misery.

Love is patient and kind and also credulous, and I was never invited to visit your family's home. Your mother, you said, would be ashamed for me to see it. I believed you. Certainly the clothes on your thin body suggested poverty. You'd go out in the cold, in the blowing snow, in sneakers and an unbuttoned coat, with no cap on your head. You said that the chill of your childhood house had made you stop feeling the weather. It was true that your skin was nearly always mildly hot to the touch. Now I wonder what drugs made you burn such a coal inside. I wonder if you chose those clothes at the only nearby thrift store, Keezer's, tingling with mischief and pleasant tension about the ruse you meant to work on the other 1,599 members of our college class.

I remember buying you things I couldn't afford because you supposedly couldn't afford them: a jaunty cap made in Greece, a silk shirt, ballet tickets. I worried about your survival, even then. Toys and trifles could not forestall the doom you projected.

And maybe I was prescient there. Your family isn't robust. They die young, even if not all as young as you. Not many make it to sixty-five. Your only surviving sibling has made a family website, perhaps hoping to get it all online before he strokes out. Your brother's photos of your parents show a cheerful, well-dressed young couple, and your mother has a fleecy, bouncy mane of beauty-shopped hair. If people are hungry, I think they skip the hairdresser, the dry-clean-only tailored clothes. And what that couple projects is not desperation but fresh young American hope. Their supposedly leaking, freezing house is larger than any I ever lived in and looks better-tended. Your family's business lasted for decades, which is not failure or bankruptcy. The tombstones over your dead parents and siblings are expensive, as I know now from buying tombstones for my own dead people. In the dark-blue eyes that look out of your family photographs, there is no vacuity or despair. I don't think a person can hide vacuity or despair, even in pictures. When I look at those pictures of the desperately poor in *Now Let Us Praise Famous Men,* I see the fatigue of hunger, the despair that expects no relief. I can almost smell the dirty feet.

So often I've wished I'd grown up in a Vermont mountain town, raised by sensible people, playing in the snow. If I had been brought up by laconic, unfanciful folks, I would have most likely ignored you: *He's full of shit.* But I was raised by high-strung people who loved stories, who were fiercely bored and ready to accept pain if no other excitement was forthcoming. You needed for people to believe you grew up starved and cold. Certainly you were very proud of your eating disorder, very open with your weird food habits and with your aghast questions about how people could eat the ordinary things they did eat—for instance, cheese. I remember a long, revolted riff over lunch about that—how horrid the process for making cheese was! How could people stand to eat a substance so produced? I did not put cheese on my sandwiches in front of you. I watched and even tried to emulate your grim dining habits, those hamburgers with nothing on them but salt. I did not say, "Come on! Everything's made out of something. All food has ingredients. So cheese takes milk and salt and rennet, so what?" Eating disorders were fresh news then and all too often elicited sick admiration. No one said, "Oh, hell, shut up with that at the table! Get the fuck over it!" Though I remember guys whose expressions suggested that they'd have liked to say it.

I have kept one other secret of yours, one I didn't look for, one that forced itself on me during a crisis of yours. Something had happened to your eyes. I cannot remember whether it was an infection or a toxic exposure, but it struck you down with no warning. The student health service had sent you back to the dorm with your eyes bandaged, under orders to stay in bed and be still for the next twenty-four hours. I brought you your meals and read your reading assignments aloud to you and tried to ease your anxiety over falling behind with schoolwork. In the familiar mess of your room, the air smelled the usual way, sourly sweet. Part baby powder, part baby aspirin, though I never saw either there. I did see what you'd left in plain view. I closed the cover of a notebook that detailed an elaborate fabrication I'd accepted as true up to that minute. This personal myth was as precious to you as a blood tie to T. S. Eliot would have been to me; it was a tender vanity. If our classmates had learned that your platinum fact was a fiction and laughed you to scorn, it might have slain you outright. I wonder now if nothing at all happened to your eyes and you were doing an experiment. How would a disillusioning truth affect me? What would I do if I learned it? What I did: I said nothing about it to you and nothing ever to anyone except a kind therapist, and that was a decade after the event. She solemnly affirmed that you had lied. I agreed, though I thought, *No, he was making the truth he needed.*

There is the plain truth and the truth-that-should-be, the truth that would be a good fit, the poetic truth. The poetic truth is rarely the plain truth. Your lie and your truth both went with you into the dark where we all go.

When I think of that lie, I am not angry that you were actually not as cold as Cosette at the Thenardiers'. I am glad for every second of suffering that bypassed you. Your desire that I should accept your scenario, half *Les Misérables* and half *Ethan Frome*, was nothing personal. You had everyone at college believing it too: *I am hungry, I am ragged, I am in despair. Feed me, love me, hang on my words, tell me I'm beautiful, say I'm brilliant and I'll be famous someday. Say it again, again, again.*

The couple in Whole Foods had lived to grow up. They had lived to learn what is more valuable than being beautiful and brilliant, perishingly rare, famous. Perhaps they might have said, *We were hungry and cold and in despair when we were young, but now we are all right. We love each other. We know what comes before the rest.*

*

I was not all right when I saw them; I was in Whole Foods to eat free samples and swallow as much free protein as I could. Not that I was starved; I was, though, eating the cheapest food I could buy and still stay healthy. A lot of eggs and raisins figured in this diet, a lot of tea and cheese and store-brand English muffins. The kind of repetitious fuel that people chew and swallow out of earnest hunger. At Whole Foods and Harris Teeter, on sample days, I could get a few mouthfuls that actually tasted good. I remember the tongue-thrills of smoked gouda, spiced avocado, fiery grilled meats. And I remember wondering if you'd have felt contempt for those tiny sensual flares.

In front of the produce section, that day, was a table for some fund drive. A glossy girl was minding the table, giving out leaflets and soliciting funds. There was a big glass jar about half full of money on the table. My couple put a fiver in, and the girl thanked them and tossed her hair. They all were members of the world in which people had money they could give away and could actually shop at Whole Foods, not scarf free samples and/or steal there.

Yes, your old flame knows how to steal vitamins in stores: Open one bottle, take one or two, swallow immediately. Put the bottle behind all the other bottles on the shelf. Leave at an unconcerned, measured pace. Return and repeat as needed. Never risk carrying something with a barcode past the checkout, but take every free thing the world offers. When I walked through a grocery store parking lot, I took all the abandoned, fluttering plastic sacks for my household trash. I was serious about microeconomics and the tiniest economic units: free Splenda packets, paper napkins, paper towels. Every paper towel I used in a public restroom got crammed into my pack and dried out at home to use again.

For a moment, I seriously considered snatching that jar of currency from the glossy girl's table and running. That's how bad off I was at the time. I could have outrun the cop monitoring security from a canopied seat in the parking lot. Typically he was either dozing or ogling women from behind his sunshades, a big latte clutched between his blubber thighs. But he also had a gun; I decided not. I should have thought of Young You: Even in the summers, when Harvard was not feeding us, you were never hungry enough to forage for free samples, attend parties for the food or church for the snacks and coffee after the service, or figure out how to steal. I never saw you gaze at anything with the calculating eyes of an aspiring thief, and not because I didn't watch you. I watched you with the fervor of obsession, to memorize you in case you discarded me or died young. You made up a story; I believed it. If you were alive, I wonder, would you have fought with your brother about his website? I can't imagine you admitting, "John Henry, I told everybody at college that we were dirt-poor! I made a big deal of it! It was part of my persona. Don't rat me out!" I have to admire your work: A lie that lasts this long is a very successful, well-wrought lie, almost fiction. You lived most of your short life as your own invention.

And none of this matters now, so I am not going to worry about it. I have one accomplishment like yours, being thin enough now that my clothes flutter on me in a high wind. That was one free pleasure I could have every time the wind blew, even while poor enough to steal. I love the silky sensation. I imagine you did too.

Election

Most people were impressed by Sigrid's daughter and son-in-law—Professor Kirsten Sigridsdottir, the Devereaux professor of Scandinavian Studies at Ferrier University, and Professor Alexis Klimov, the holder of the coveted Reynolds Price Chair in Poetry and Poetics. "You must be so proud ..." was the typical opener when the topic of Kirstie and Alexei arose. However, in Sigrid's private opinion, Ferrier was a fool factory and Kirstie and Alexei were two of the worst fools it had produced. Furthermore, as the Colville-Simonetti presidential race entered its home stretch, Kirstie and her husband worked hard to validate that notion.

Earlier that warm and wearing autumn, Kirstie and Alexei had approached Sigrid to suggest that she change the deed of her house, which they and their children inhabited with her, by putting it in their names. To lower her taxes, they maintained. Fiscal responsibility was as foreign to them as Fiji, real estate was a novel topic for either of them to broach, and their eyes were open too wide as they broached it, so Sigrid had made some targeted inquiries and learned that they were scalp-high in debt. Most of it was for bail after annoying the government with yet more futile demonstrations at the university, and fines for public-nuisance, inciting-to-riot, and corrupting-the-young charges. They had maxed all their credit cards out on bail and fines. They'd thought to sell her house to pay it all off. "Dream on, kids," thought Sigrid.

After their most recent ruckus, Kirstie and Alexei had barely had time to make bail, get home, and shower before they were due back in class. They had rolled in while Sigrid had her attention divided between spooning Cream of Wheat into their baby and braiding their eight-year-old's hair. They'd been grubby and bruised and reeking of tear gas and jail, but alight with the adolescent triumph they brought home from all their encounters with the law.

While they taught, that very day, Sigrid had ridden the bus downtown to her lawyer's—they'd driven her car—and put her house in trust. Not for them, but for her granddaughter, Katrin. Coming home, Sigrid picked up a rumpled copy of the local "independent" newspaper and saw Kirstie and Alexei's impassioned forty-five-year-old faces amidst the student crowd at the last protest. "What you two don't understand is that the last time that kind of thing did any good was about twenty years ago," she thought. "That was about the last time anyone was seriously listening to any voice except this regime's. To this regime, you're insects. Not even wasps in the window, houseflies. But someday they'll go after you with the Bug-B-Gone, not just the swatter. You don't grasp that and won't grasp it, but there's not going to be a little girl with her behind bare in the wind after you bring the world crashing down on your two brick-thick overeducated heads." So thought Sigrid, and left the paper in the bus.

Sigrid had seen this future that had come—the shimmer of something dreadful, flickering at the edges of her vision or peering like some baleful face from reflective surfaces, as far back as she could remember. Now that threat was realized in the defunct civil liberties and what used to be freedom of speech and the press, each hanging limp in its noose... in the shortages and rationing, in the demands and deprivations and uncertainties now accepted by any American whose surname wasn't Hilton, Gates, Walton, Jolie-Pitt, or the like. Further down the line, Sigrid knew, Katrin would fall asleep one night in a foundering democracy and wake in a brisk, bright military dictatorship that minced no words about what it was and what it intended. In the volatile, destabilized years that would follow, Sigrid intended to give Katrin every advantage within her power.

In the meantime, Sigrid planned to indulge Kirstie and Alexei as she would a child with a brain tumor, letting the good times roll between the present and certain doom. For their parts, Kirstie and Alexei were very pleasant indeed with Sigrid, since they thought she was considering their request. And Sigrid allowed Kirstie to badger her into sewing a half-dozen little stuffed mannikins for, of all things, a voodoo doll party to mark this election-year Halloween. Now, on the morning before the fête, Kirstie and Alexei were doing their scattered best to make the refreshments.

Alexei, sidetracked already, had gone to work on a big sweet potato with a knife and one of his red paper-grading pens. The yam's trailing root had become an evil little nose with a lipsticked slit of a mouth below it. Two dots of whiteout had given it squinchy little eyes. A flourish or two more, and it had become the yam version of Alexei's departmental chairwoman, Courtney Kalinowski, who often declared in front of large captive audiences that, in spirit, she was a handsome and virile gay man. To give Courtney credit where credit was due, that statement took nerve in these reactionary times. To give the literal truth its due also, Courtney in the flesh was a termagant with unequivocal droopy dugs and a wide catfish mouth always maroon with thick lipstick, ugly as hammered shit. Having Kirstie and Alexei suck up to her like Shop Vacs, Sigrid thought, was one of Courtney's few pleasures. All this aside, the yam-Courtney certainly captured her in temperament and contour. And it had done what Alexei intended, making Kirstie laugh herself breathless.

"That's Courtney, all right," Kirstie said, with the complacency of beauty.

"A solid curveless mass from shoulder to bum, and, see, a winky little butthole," Alexei pointed out. He sounded as if he'd been into the pot already.

"At least Courtney knows she's some kind of grownup," thought Sigrid. "You two are teenagers in soul. You never grew up and don't mean to." Sigrid found it amazing how far those adult-sized kids had come—Kirstie and Alexei kept getting invitations to speak at conferences on subjects that, given the present social conditions, were worse than trivial: Viking costume jewelry dug up on the coast of Newfoundland! Patterns of puns in poems by Pushkin! How they loved getting their conference clothes out, packing their suitcases, and flying off to eat hotel food and exchange their golden lodes of irrelevance for applause—at least one facet of academic life that glittered as promised, if briefly. And parents paid Ferrier University's staggering tuition to have their youngsters taught by Kirstie, Alexei, Courtney, and others with similarly slippery grips on reality.

Sigrid kept one ear open to the pair as they did their level best to devil eggs. "Devil the eggs, and bedevil everybody but the baby," was Sigrid's observation. The voodoo-doll party was Kirsten's idea, a typical piece of Kirstenism; still, everyone but nine-month-old Nils would be roped into the work. Kirstie, flushed, had opened all the kitchen windows wide and her blouse down to her cleavage, then tied up her extravagant mass of hair in a kerchief. She looked harried and hot-flashy; she'd be snappy by midafternoon. Sigrid disapproved—not of her daughter's spiky moods in themselves, but of their general bad static and effect on her grandchildren. A Swedish rose, Sigrid thought, fully blown and thorny.

Never one to overlook the obvious, Kirstie cast a critical eye on the mashed yolks. "Alexei, they're lumpy."

"Well, put it back through another time. Put some mayonnaise in it." The stuff went back into the food processor and whirred about.

"Now it looks too—"

Sigrid raised her voice enough to carry to the kitchen. "Get that hummus that's dried out in the back of the fridge and put a little of that in it and run it through the food processor again. That'll give it body but not lumps."

Apparently this tactic succeeded. "Thanks, Ma," Kirstie called, then yelled up the stairs: "Katrin! I need your little fingers down here!"

In a moment, Sigrid's granddaughter descended; in another, the eight-year-old was perched on the kitchen stool, spooning the yolk mixture into the press that Kirsten kept for decorating cakes, then squeezing the stuff out in tidy spirals.

"Momma," Katrin ventured, "this would work better if it were cold."

"Well, never mind that, Kitty Kat." Kirstie looked on with momentary ease and pleasure. "You can make it work. You've got better hand-eye coordination than your old Momma." But what the little kid really had was patience. Next Kirstie moved into the study, where Sigrid sat sewing in the good morning light, and addressed herself to her mother. "Now, Ma, have you finished them?"

Sigrid showed what she had finished: six mannikins, mini rag dolls about six inches long, their bodies cut from an old pillowcase and stuffed with polyester quilt batting. "I'm not embroidering faces on these," she warned her daughter. "Your friends can draw faces on them in ballpoint."

"Do they work as well that way?"

Sigrid nodded. "They work as well."

"You sewed these on the Singer. They don't even look hand-sewn. Do they work as well that way too?"

"They work as well," Sigrid repeated. *No end,* her mind told her telegraphically, meaning to Kirstie and Alexei's childishness. They might be homeless but for Sigrid's house and hungry but for her insistence on the garden, the harvesting and canning, the rabbits raised for meat. Four years ago, after a few months of tightening supplies and spiking prices, Sigrid had ordered a composter and put them to work fencing and tilling the garden plot and building hutches. For his part, combining his cultural heritage with this forced march through *Foxfire,* Alexei had learned to make vodka out of potatoes; since then he'd always kept a batch brewing down cellar. And they were going to spend this Halloween evening sticking pins into voodoo dolls in the company of four equally practical faculty friends, and Kirstie probably believed, in her heart of hearts, that any arcane presences she might summon would respond better to hand-stitched voodoo dolls. She and Alexei had marijuana, too, for which they 'd spent a week's worth of their piddly salaries. For the life of her, Sigrid couldn't see the use of a stinking, illegal weed that might get one arrested and would certainly make a spiky person spikier and a languid one pie-eyed for days.

Now she heard Kirsten again, in response to a warming-up wail from upstairs: "Kat! There goes the baby!"

"Your baby," thought Sigrid. "Not your daughter's. She didn't ask you to have a baby you can't handle when you were spitting distance from menopause. I didn't either. *Get your broad butt out of that chair and go take care of that child* is what you need to hear."

Katrin spread her fingers meaningly, and Kirsten exclaimed, "Well, then, you can wash them!" The little girl slipped down off the stool and headed upstairs.

Kirstie made an exasperated throat-clearing noise. "It's gummy," she pronounced. "It's October. The end of October. Why does it have to be so hot?"

Imminent menopause made Kirstie hot, but it was true that the climate was deranged. The North Carolina summers were uniformly insufferable, the winters erratic. It seemed that some retaining wall had sprung multiple leaks, letting in blasts from Canada and Gulf Coast warmth in disorienting alternation. The plunging freezes and false springs here caused more flu than the winters of Sigrid's Swedish childhood. Winter in Abeskovvu, all six months of it, had been cold and healthy. Now that Sigrid thought about it, there hadn't been any flu in Abeskovvu except when the university people came to film the village's Saami shamans. Since the universities paid good money, the village welcomed the travelers, and the shamans never failed to put on a hair-raising exhibition. Sigrid paused to recall those shows, a pleasant meander down Memory Lane.

Sigrid and her relatives had contributed their special talents to the shamanizing shows, as everyone but the visiting scholars knew. In Abeskovvu, the paranormal talent in Sigrid's family was a tenderly kept local secret, key to a reliable flow of hard cash. Some of the real shamans had a tickle of the talent, but none of them were capable of the depth charge that Sigrid, her grandmother, and her cousin Annika could muster. The visitors wanted to see authentic Saami shamans performing conjuration rituals to their ancestral reindeer gods. They never actually expected to experience any real, wild event that their books could not explain. While the shamans drummed and danced and whooped their way through their authentic rituals, the three blonde Swedes did the conjuration behind the scenes. Sometimes the action got over-intense, as action involving daemons can. Then the shamanizing show left their visitors blanched and sleepless, startling at harmless little noises—the *slmmmpp* of snow off the roof, the pop and drip of ice in the eaves. They'd stare into shadowy corners like scared children. "Served them right," Sigrid thought, "when they brought their city germs with their money and made us sick."

She grinned, recalling how the linguistics and anthropology students and their teachers would arrive, snug and smug and complacent. They'd be expecting stinking primitives in furs, beating drums and bellowing and hallucinating. "Then we'd scare the polarfleece off them. They deserved it, they were as silly as Kirstie and Alexei. That's how I learned that college professors are stupid." Sigrid remembered how the head shaman, the one who wore the reindeer horns, used to rally the gang before the shamanizing shows. Freely translated: ***All right, people, they've paid out the ass, now don't let's stop till they've shat themselves.*** "Since we spoke, what'd they call it, an imperiled minority language, we could say anything we wanted to, and that was pretty much what we chanted to those drums after the conjuration," Sigrid remembered—***Scare them till they shit, till they shit, till they shit!*** The entities she and her kin had summoned to their shaman neighbors' aid did their best to deliver. It had all been great fun.

Sigrid came back to the muggy here-and-now when Katrin put a hand on her arm. The kid whispered, hoping not to rouse her mother. "Grandma Sigrid, I changed Nils, but he's working himself up, and then he'll make Momma mad. Can you settle him?"

Sigrid got her wrapped and linimented old legs under her and followed the child upstairs. Nils, cushiony and blond like his mother, was standing up in the crib and tuning up for a crying bout. He'd thrown the little plastic thingies from his Busy Box and all his fuzzy animals on the floor. Could babies have ADHD? He acted like it, Sigrid thought. He could squall and fuss and whine for hours on end. He didn't sleep properly and could not seem to keep his attention on anything long enough for it to amuse him. Kirstie had been a poor feeder and a touchy sleeper in infancy, but even as a baby, Kirstie had possessed an attention span. Sigrid had stopped trying to identify or explain Nils's troubles and freely applied techniques of her own to settle him. She was about to settle him now, but an idea came to her. "Let's see you settle him, Kitty Kat. I bet you can do what Grandma does. Then if he starts up with one of those bawling tantrums when I'm not here, you can quiet him down for Kirstie."

"Do I say the same words?" asked Katrin.

"And put a couple of drops of water on your palm, and lay your hand on his head the way I do."

"Water conducts it, like electricity?" Katrin asked, and Sigrid nodded.

"And say my words," Sigrid added casually.

"Are they Swedish, your words?" Funny little kid, interested in languages. She had picked up her dad's second-generation Russian with the ease of breath, and a good bit of Swedish from Sigrid, and Sigrid had taught Katrin her special words as well.

"My special words come from the ***nattspråkat.*** And that's a Swedish word, but my special words aren't Swedish." The nearest terms in English were ***night speech,*** or perhaps ***necromantic language,*** both meaning too little and too much. Neither suggested the strength and antiquity of that handful of power-words, and they came nowhere near being a language. No more than a handful of diamonds mined from a mountain were the mountain, Sigrid thought, and decided not to get into this complicated explanation with Katrin right now. There was something she wanted to see. "Now, have a go at settling your brother."

Sigrid had done this in front of Katrin often enough. When Sigrid "settled" Nils, the effects were fast but not instant; his howl would subside to a whine, his whine to a little mouth-drool; he'd relax and let himself sit if he'd been standing, go meditative, and within a couple of minutes be drowsing sweetly and silently, an effect that was generally good for a couple of hours.

Now Katrin dampened her hand at the bathroom tap, spread her little fingers on the baby's forehead, and said Sigrid's words. She added, "Shut up, Nils, don't get Momma started." The baby's blue eyes opened wide like they did when he got an electrostatic shock from a blanket, then glazed over; he went down on his freshly diapered bottom, then slid down onto his side, a flushed limp lump.

"My goodness, I think you're even better at this than Grandma," Sigrid said, impressed.

"I didn't damage him, did I?" Funny little kid with that vocabulary: *damage.*

"No, but maybe the next time you settle him, you need to go easy on him. He's little, and you have my talent very strong," Sigrid said, keeping her voice even, not wanting to alarm the child or anchor her attention unduly. "You go on down and finish with those eggs. I'll watch him a while." With a backward glance, Katrin did, and Sigrid actually did watch the baby for half an hour in case he had taken any damage. But he was just asleep, though deeply, sweatily, conveniently asleep. In fact, he slept all afternoon. He slept and peed through his fresh diaper, and he slept while

Sigrid wiped and re-diapered him. While he slept, the party treats were assembled on their platters, the punch was mixed, and a convalescent quiet descended as the household subsided into its various indulgences. Kirstie had her cool bath and her black-market Valium and her nap; Alexei sank into a characteristic reverie that Kirstie called *a Russian silence* and Sigrid described as *a pre-party high*. He sprawled in the shallow shade of the backyard oak, staring happily at nothing, some book face-down on his lap, and he might have looked romantic doing except that his poetic long hair was greasy and he had egg on his pants. Sigrid gave Katrin her allowance, and the kid returned from the corner store with a Heath bar and a liter bottle of Coke. Sigrid accepted half of the sweet-salty candy from her, but declined the fizzy drink—an American abomination, bad for Katrin's teeth. Sigrid didn't nag the kid about her little pleasures, though; Kirstie handled that all too well. Katrin perched at the kitchen counter and downed the brown bilge while doing homework. She sat concentrated and still, her bare feet on the rungs of the high stool, and Sigrid contemplated her.

Sigrid thought how Kirsten was just a normal American, that stupid kind of smart that was no good for anything but showing off and making grades. "And Katrin came out of my daughter's fat belly, but Katrin's like me. We come from somewhere else. We *are* something else. I have to teach her." Sigrid thought northward and east, across the chilling ocean to the glacier-hammered northern wastes where Sweden becomes Lapland and where she'd been born. She thought of her family far and far and far back, pre-Christian, pre-pagan, bred and born with their faces toward the boreal pole. Maybe the talent was that old, carried all the way from uncounted years of animistic innocence to these terrible times, along with a few words of what Sigrid's grandmother had known to call *nattspråkat*. Perhaps from that spring of ancient genes, Katrin had that straight hair that was not brown, not even dark brown, but black, with a blueblack flash in sunlight like the wing of a crow. Many of the Saami, the wild wandering Laplanders, had such hair. Katrin's skin was milky, her eyes a dark blue rare among either Swedes or Russians. The only way she was at all accountable was the slender build she had from her father and the talent itself. That talent had hopped down the line of her maternal ancestors, sometimes weak, often strong, skipping some generations entirely and blooming like a flame tree in others. Sigrid had first guessed that Katrin had it during the walks they'd taken together until last winter, when Sigrid's legs had gotten really bad. Sigrid had held Kat's hand but usually let the child choose their direction; she had noticed that there were a few streets where Kat never wanted to go. Once, as they neared Hirondelle Lane, she'd asked Kat, "Shall we turn here?" The kid had paused, with a listening look: "No." That expression had taken Sigrid's eye utterly; it was attention focused wholly inward, listening to one's own brain. Sigrid had watched Kirsten for that look throughout her daughter's childhood and never seen it once.

"Why not?" Sigrid asked casually, and Kat promptly said, "Not friendly." Later, safe in the car, Sigrid cruised slowly down Hirondelle. Far from that street corner, well beyond the sharpest sight from that point, was a tattered house with three pit bulls tethered with clothesline to a spindly tree, and a sign bearing the name of a neo-Fascist politician.

From the time Katrin developed a recognizable personality, Sigrid had loved her the way she wished she could love Kirsten. With intimations of Katrin's talent, the affection took on a new focus: Sigrid's motherhood had finally worked out. And Sigrid's rancor toward the child's feckless parents achieved a new heat. Even Katrin's looks did not work in her favor as they should, for Kirstie never bothered with her daughter's clothes, and Katrin ran ragged because that was what people did in this house. Kirstie and Alexei both slopped around home and garden in jeans and teeshirts, barefoot as beggars, and that was not the only way they were careless. One time during a summer power outage, they'd gotten busy and left their bedroom door open when they should've closed it, and Sigrid had passed and glimpsed them, Swedish-American slattern and Russian-American sloven, in postfuck huddle. Their grubby clothes lay guilty on the floor at their bedside, and facing her were their two pairs of candid filthy soles. Sigrid had closed their door—let them sweat! And she'd crept downstairs thinking that these two couldn't housebreak a puppy, much less train a child in the subtlety and guile these times required. Even now Sigrid couldn't get over the gall of a woman of forty-five, demonstrably uninterested in tending one child, having a second and shoving his care onto his eighty-year-old grandmother and eight-year-old sister.

Weirdly enough, Nils was still an afterthought to Kirstie, who paused in the midst of their desultory supper and said, "Nils. He's still napping?"

"Yes," said Sigrid. Before Kirstie could suggest that someone else do it, Sigrid added, "You better go get that child."

Kirstie brought the groggy baby downstairs, stuck him into his highchair, and made a pass at feeding him. He spat applesauce dispassionately and said, "Ma foo foop," which might have meant, "No thank you, Mother." Lulled by her nap, Kirstie just wiped the applesauce off her bathrobe, tucked him under one arm, and headed upstairs to dress. A sulky, summery autumn night came down. In time, Kirstie descended in a voluminous silk dress nearly the same color as the night sky: a gothic bruised plum. Dressed up, Kirstie looked astounding, fifty extra pounds or not—Sigrid wished she admired her daughter more. Kirstie had her silver Swedish jewelry and her hairbrush in hand, and she stood in her stocking feet, putting the jewelry on before the mirror above the fireplace. Then she took her position, kneeling before the armchair while Alexei brushed and brushed her hair—she had enough of it for two or three women. He wove it into a cabled crown of heavy flaxen braids, and when he finished and Kirsten turned toward him, he cupped her face with both long hands.

"Beautiful," he said, as always, with the same touch of wonder. He slid down on his knees and went eye-to-eye with her. *Teenage love,* old Sigrid thought, wondering how they'd carried that that sweet soap bubble so far.

Then the little moment broke, and Alexei began fiddling with the fireplace, stacking the wood in the grate. "Oh, sugar, don't light it now," said Kirstie. "It'll be so hot."

"I'll run the fans, then. Make it chilly inside. We need the fire for atmosphere."

"You'll need your power ration later," Sigrid contributed. "When the first freeze comes, you'll wish you hadn't wasted electricity and wood for atmosphere on a night like August."

"I'll make up for it," said Alexei. "I'll scavenge some blowdowns for the woodpile." He smiled sweetly, earnestly.

"No," thought Sigrid. "You'll laze around under your down quilt, reading Pasternak and drinking basement vodka, until the next power allotment comes in. Kirstie won't mind; she'll put on a couple of extra sweaters and be fine. Katrin and I and your son will be cold."

Under the late defunct Republic, every drop of crude oil had been vampirized from vassalized Iraq and Iran, from Romania and Alaska. Under the current regime, every household got a power ration: *x* number of kilowatts according to family size and geographic location. You could use it on the first day of the quarter or the last, but once you'd used it, you got no more till next quarter. If you used it the first week, you'd be reading by kerosene lamps and washing clothes in your bathtub and heating your house with wood, if you could find any. Or sweating during the sodden summer as your air conditioner stood idle and your food spoiled.

Alexei opened every window wide and turned the four fans on. Air rushed in, tepidly cool. As Sigrid shook her head, Kirstie said, "You know, Ma, you could do the wind."

"I could, or I could save my strength," Sigrid told her. She had chosen a purpose after Katrin's slam-dunk with the baby, though she had no intention of discussing that purpose with her daughter. As much as she deplored the voodoo doll party, it offered a camouflage that Sigrid did not intend to waste. Tonight she could teach Katrin a thing or two.

Balked, Kirsten studied her mother. Kirsten wanted cost-free ventilation, but she wanted something else more. "Ma, are you thinking about the house?"

"I am." Sigrid got up and started clearing the supper dishes.

*

Antique bands that the American political regime disapproved of but had not outrightly proscribed, not-yet-banned bands, sounded from the living room as the party got underway: Black Sabbath, Blue Öyster Cult, Aerosmith, Guns & Roses. The Courtney Kalinowski yam had been concealed under twenty pounds of undespoiled root vegetables well before Courtney walked in the door and air-kissed Kirsten's fair cheek.

Sigrid set a big bowl full of Tootsie Pops on the porch for the few trick-or-treaters who'd come by; let them help themselves. She put Nils to bed, took a laborious bath, then coaxed Katrin into the bathtub. The old, fragmented traditions Sigrid knew included lustration, purification by bathing, before rituals such as that she meant to try this evening with Katrin's aid. Now the little girl was clean and dressed in fresh jeans and shirt. Sigrid was just waiting until the child's parents reached the identifiable point of oblivion before getting to work. By flickering candles and atmospheric firelight, Kirstie and Alexei and their guests were shrieking over the voodoo dolls, doing unpleasant little things to them with pins and cigarette lighters and matches. "Eeek! Eeeueww! His balls!" Sigrid heard, as she did a walk-through in spurious search of a snack and checked the progress of the party. *Pretty well baked* was her assessment, so she expected to hear no more from them until she hobbled downstairs at seven to start the Mr. Coffee and most likely encounter a few holdover groaning bodies on the couch and floor. Thus it was a surprise when Kirstie, hectic, flounced upstairs to her mother's room.

"Katrin! Where is that child? Kat, you give that doll to me, that's Momma's, it's not a plaything!"

"What doll, Momma?" asked Katrin, puzzled and already apprehensive.

"You know very well. My Colville doll."

"I don't have it, Momma."

"We haven't got any Colville doll," Sigrid said levelly. "After I made you all those little stuffed thingies, what do you want with any Colville doll?"

"We're going to jinx the election, damn all!"

"You can do that just as well with one of those little stuffed people as you could with a Colville doll." That is to say, not at all. "I've told you how this stuff works," Sigrid said, looking as patient as she could. "It's the talent itself that accomplishes anything people ever manage with these rituals. And you don't have it."

"It's a game, Ma, damn it, but I want it to feel real!" Kirstie splutted. "And I got the Colville doll for my party, and I just know she took it to play with it. Kat, get up and give it to me right now, and maybe the consequences won't be as bad as if you keep stalling."

"She doesn't have it," said Sigrid, as Katrin's lip quivered. She put a calming hand on the child's arm. "Why don't you go through her room and see for yourself?"

And Kirstie did. They both held still while she ransacked her daughter's closet, drawers, and toy chest, rubbishing the kid's neat room before finding that, indeed, no Colville doll was there.

Then Kirstie returned, pink with pique. "I can't find it, but that just means she's hidden it. Kat, I'll fan your pants rosy red if I don't have that doll in my hand in the next sixty seconds."

"You'll do no such thing. Go take care of your guests," Sigrid told her. But her daughter bristled and stuck out her full pink underlip, even took a step forward. "I said, go take care of your guests, Kirsten. Get one of Kat's Barbie dolls if you need some plastic person to maim. Those people are so drunk and high that they won't know that Ken doll from Colville." As

Kirstie hesitated, Sigrid added in her seriously-annoyed voice: "I mean *right now*, Kirsten. And that was the second time I said it, and you don't want to make me say it again."

This brought the response that Sigrid expected, a flash of fear and quickly, quickly tamped rage. The split-second glance between them was an acknowledgment of long-known facts: that Kirsten was perfectly aware of Sigrid's coolness toward her and of the old woman's calm, fierce preference for her granddaughter. That Kirsten knew what Sigrid could do. That Kirsten had never had that power turned upon her but could imagine what it might feel like. That she never meant to push her mother far enough to find out. "Dammit, Ma," she said, a bit shakily.

"Close that door, and don't call me *Ma*. *Ma* is the noise a sheep makes."

When Kirstie had flounced downstairs, Sigrid said, "Kat, lock it." Katrin did, then turned nervous wide eyes on Sigrid.

"How do you know I don't have it?"

"Because I do," said Sigrid, trying not to grin evilly, like some Disney witch. She reached into her sewing basket and brought out the Colville-for-President doll that the Colville campaign was selling. It was made of hard plastic like the Barbie doll and her consort. It wore a well-tailored miniature suit with blue oxford cloth shirt, red silk tie, dark socks, and little black vinyl lace-up shoes. On its box, fine print said that its outfit was designed and created by Brooks Brothers and that its small parts constituted a choking hazard. With its full ash-blond hair and soldierly jaw, it did resemble Jeffrey Colville. The politician had started out in public life as the host of a conservative talk show that had attained meteoric popularity. During his stint with the talk show, Colville had gotten (if he indeed needed it) a thorough education in American avarice. Bluff, handsome, unflappable under the hot lights, Colville had quickly accrued more influence than he should have. His political philosophies made the second President Littletree look like a bleeding-heart liberal. Indeed, Colville's charisma made Sigrid think he might have some of the same abilities she herself had. A good politician (was that an immediate contradiction?) with the talent very strong might roll back years or decades of harm. But Colville was not a good politician. He sympathized openly with the White Power movement, yet reconciled that aspect of his belief system nicely with fundamentalist Christianity. He knew how to play on fear; he knew how to inflame that frantic greed that people have about what they've got left after they've lost everything important. *America for Americans*, he had repeated, meaning America for white people who agreed with him—their numbers were legion. And he looked like a cigarette ad cowboy and sounded like the father every sad American wished he'd had. "Daddy, Daddy, we do!" was what the voters would all too likely say to Colville on Election Day. Sigrid felt that once this man took the oath of office, no voice would be strong enough to refuse him. Sigrid's time on earth was a rapidly emptying glass, she already knew that, but this man might hold power over her grandchild. *My grandchildren*, Sigrid reminded herself; she certainly didn't wish Colville on poor nervy

Nils either. And for this reason, Sigrid had appropriated the Colville doll upon which Kirstie had spent half this week's grocery money, intending to do in serious what Kirstie planned to do "to make a statement" or "to help people vent."

*

"When the Second President Littletree was going for his third term, getting the Constitution changed so he could run again," Sigrid told Katrin, "my cousin Annika did the thing I'm going to show you."

"But how could he?" interrupted Katrin. "I mean, get the Constitution changed?"

"Well, he was one of the oil-and-munitions Littletrees, you know. They had more money than we can even imagine. In America there's no law for people with that much money."

"How'd they get it?" asked the curious Kat, who'd become very aware of money and their lack of it. Unlike Sigrid, she didn't know how Kirstie and Alexei pissed it away, but her clever brain told her that lack of money equaled lack of safety, even such safety as still existed for some other children.

Sigrid tried to sum it up; it was simple. So simple that few Americans saw it, in fact. "War. The political Littletrees did what they could to keep this country at war, then the manufacturing Littletrees sold our government the guns and bullets and bombs to fight the wars with. That name, Littletree, made them sound like they should be just folks, good country people who happened to own gun factories and bomb factories and run for office, and they made people believe that about them. I think they believed their own lies almost as much as those people they foozled. They were an awful family. But I'm talking about our family now, not theirs. Even as far away as we were, we knew what that man was. Annika's the other person in my generation who's got talent like mine... like yours. There were these joke dolls being sold, like your Barbies but they looked like Littletree #2. They were talking dolls like this one. They said the things that the Second Littletree said, about abortions and family values and stem cells and terrorist cells, all the things he either loved or hated. He was a man for punchy short phrases that went nice and slick into punchy little minds. Annika bought a talking President Littletree doll and did the thing we're going to do, and what do you know... the Second Littletree came down with a growth in his vocal cords... his brain wasn't the part of him Annika decided to attack. The Washington surgeons cut the growth out, but it came back, and came back, and came back yet again... and ate off most of the Second Littletree's face."

"Did he die?"

Sigrid tried to resist a smile, which wouldn't have been at all a nice one. She remembered her late husband viewing one of the Second Littletree's floundering attempts at political reinstatement and her husband's remark about what a handy thing instinctive horror of damaged faces was. A missing hand or leg just startled the eye, but a missing jaw or chin or an obvious facial prosthesis covering up some horror of absence shocked some primitive place in the brain. You might train yourself not to flinch when you knew that incomplete face was coming your way, but horror was what you'd feel seeing such a wreckage, every single time. It was uncool to call that limbic flare of feeling *horror*, but that's what it was. Because such a sight was so intolerable, cancer-via-necromancy had unmanned, ungunned, and unseated the Republicans, at least for a breathing spell. The mass madness in the United States had lost its raging energy almost overnight. Sigrid remembered how she'd gotten out the aquavit, and everybody at her table drank a toast to Annika that night. The shimmer of something dreadful, which had been with Sigrid very strongly, had receded; for a while she'd felt free to live an almost-comfortable life.

"Did he die?" asked Katrin again, as Sigrid's stroll down Memory Lane lengthened out.

"No, but he was an upsetting thing to look at," she told Katrin, "and ugly is the same as dead in American politics. Just like with the movies. And this movie-star-looking Colville man is a worst threat than the Second Littletree was on his meanest day."

"You know?"

"I've seen it," Sigrid said. Last year, while driving her wheezy Chevy, she had had one of those experiences that witches sometimes have with mirrors. The car's mirror had filmed over, divorced itself neatly from the task of reflecting the physical world, and shown her something that had kept her from sleeping that night and the next. To some extent or other, what she saw in that mirror had troubled all her nights thereafter. "So we're going to do for real what your Momma's doing as a party game and a way for people to blow off steam and express their feelings," Sigrid said evenly, tucking the kid's crow-dark hair behind her ears while thinking: *necromancy*. Black magic, the kind that could rebound fiercely on the practitioner.

"Will that work?" asked Katrin, her hands wringing the tough cloth of her jeans. She was unnerved by Kirstie's recent snit, Sigrid knew, but also... *how tense she is, all the time,* Sigrid thought, with anger against Kirstie and Alexei for leading lives that poured kerosene on this child's anxieties about the larger world and gave her nowhere to hide from them but Grandma Sigrid's room.

"We can try, and we can see. You're very strong and not tired, and I've been saving my energy," Sigrid told her, trying for a reassuring expression. Saved energy mattered; black magic was not one of these arts where practice made perfect. The rituals were simple, dire things. Without talent like Sigrid's, practice was meaningless. And you needed a great store of accrued force to deploy when you'd made up your mind to work black magic, not practice. You didn't want to piddle away this kind of dangerous strength.

Kat nodded. "That's why you wouldn't do the wind for Momma." That was the first witch-thing Sigrid had let Katrin see her do: making the wind blow hard for as long as an hour at a time, sweeping the summer fug and humidity out of Old Westmount, their neighborhood. And she and Katrin would swing in the porch swing, bathed in the sweet flow of the air.

"That's right." Sigrid forbore to say the rest. *Your mother is a grown-up child playing little head games, and so's your father. You and I are all the strength there is in this house, and pretty soon you'll be all there is.*

*

"Isn't it wrong?—Shouldn't we turn the lamp out and get a candle?" whispered Katrin as Sigrid set out the Colville doll and the other objects she had gathered.

"Oh, foo, that's just Kirstie and her notions. Electric light's fine." Sigrid strained to recall the sequence of Annika's ritual and the words. The *nattspråkat* was unrelated to Sigrid's other languages, and its words were not reinforced by frequent use. Sigrid sequenced and aligned the syllables in her mind. Then she arranged the articles she would need. These, if stereotypically predictable, would have included weeds picked in the nearby cemetery at moondark, fingernail clippings, a black cat's blood, maybe some fungus smut; what she had was the kitchen shears, a length of thick nylon clothesline cord, and a tube of acrylonitrile glue.

"Take his little clothes off," she told Katrin. When the Colville doll lay before them naked, his plastic body innocent of nipples or genitals, his brilliant smile incompatible with nudity, Sigrid said the first words. *You who lie,* they meant, *now you will be silent.* Katrin, arms goosepimpling, watched as Sigrid squeezed the glue out onto the politician's smile. She covered them over well, those big white Hollywood teeth. "Say it after me, Kat," Sigrid said gently, calmly, trying to pull the child into the purest, most single focus. She waited while Katrin repeated the words. Then she set her fingertip in the middle of Katrin's forehead, right above the browline. "Think from *here*. Push. Take aim."

"At that doll?"

"That's right. Think of the doll like an electric wire that'll take your thought to the real man." Sigrid gripped the child's little fingers and pushed from that strong spot in her own head. Sigrid's strong place always felt as if it were only about an inch and a half in—that would be in the corpus callosum, that part of the brain that carried electrochemical messages back and forth between the two halves.

She and Katrin both jumped when the digitized voice... or perhaps not digitized at all... came out of the doll. The Colville voice, which was Louisiana slicked and sharpened by an Ivy League college and some California elocution training, said: "We will not be deterred, we will not be silenced."

"That's not supposed to talk unless you press its button," said Katrin. Neither of them had a hand anywhere around the doll.

You will be silent, said Sigrid in the *nattspråkat—you will be bound.* This time she used the cord to tie and bind the mannikin from shoulders to ankles, and she enlisted Katrin's nimble aid to make tight, tight knots. She squeezed the reeking glue onto them for good measure. The fumes gave her a dizzy, shimmery feeling in her head. *"Ave, ave, ave.* Come, Nebiros, fair and reasonable servant, may it be."

"Who's Nebiros?" Katrin wanted to know.

"A daemon. One who's supposed to protect the interests of Americans, and that's what you are. Now say it yourself," said Sigrid, hoping the child got her tongue around it right. Katrin did. After the glue had dried, Sigrid put the trussed doll in the sewing basket, where she'd also stowed a trowel, and Katrin followed her down the fire escape—the party shrieks less frequent, less hysterical now that the guests were all higher than a buzzard circling over Mount Mitchell. Sigrid had Katrin dig a hole in the soft earth near the garden shed, and they buried the little image head down, an ancient gesture of negation in spellcraft. Then Sigrid got to her knees with the child to tamp down the loose soil over it and said the final words. *I bind you,* they meant. *I silence you. I bury you. You shall not be heard.* To her granddaughter she said, "Push, try, let it hurt, don't hold back." And she did the same. *I bind you, I silence you, I bury you, you shall not be heard.*

When she had spoken till she was breathless, Sigrid signaled to Katrin to be silent. They knelt, panting, on the moist earth. Sigrid's knees throbbed. Under the dirty purple of the sky, any natural sounds were all but stilled. All Sigrid could hear was the window fans, humming to dispel the heat of those atmospheric flickering flames. The smoke rose straight up from their chimney; there was no wind at all. Indeed, the trees seemed to be pulling in on themselves, as if trying not to move. Sigrid had pushed very hard from the strong place in her head, and that place pulsed hotly back at her. Katrin had her grubby little hand to her forehead.

"Does it hurt, baby?"

"Unh-hunh. It does. It hurts."

"Sometimes it hurts when a person pushes very hard. It's okay. It's just work." *It'll stop,* Sigrid was about to say, when they both felt something, as if the dirt they'd disturbed had moved. Katrin scrambled to her feet.

"Fuck you, you old bitch!" snarled the thing they had put in the earth.

Something rolled through Sigrid from her old calves and knees upward, some leaden inevitable pain. It lodged itself under her heart and jabbed it, then wrung the old muscle like a brutal hand.

As the pain slacked off and her breath came back, Sigrid's mind riffled dizzily through its English thesaurus. *Couth,* she thought first. *Uncouth, stripped. Veneer,* that was the word, stripped of its veneer of education and gentlemanliness and good intentions. "Colville's real voice," she thought. The one that you would hear if you dosed him with one of those drugs that make people tell the truth in interrogations, or if you were someone he trusted with his life and the two of you were very drunk together. Or if you were the woman who slept beside him and woke when he talked in his sleep.

"And you, you meddling little cunt!" added the voice from... *not* from...a chip in the chest of a mass-produced novelty doll. It sounded like a very angry man, a dangerous angry man, speaking from a few feet away, but no one was there. "I see you! I'll get you!"

Katrin all but levitated. She would have bolted, but Sigrid grabbed her wrist and pulled the struggling child down. "Help Grandma!" she hissed. "Hands down and push."

The two of them pressed both palms to the loosened earth, which roiled horridly beneath their hands. They leaned all their weight and will on it. And Sigrid said some even blacker, even more dangerous words, some words she had heard only once. Annika had whispered them to Sigrid only after making a charm that was supposed to forestall the effects of that rhyme of annihilation, and had repeated the charm after it for good measure so that no cosmic **SEND** key released those words on the world.

The fans hummed, the party guests spilled red candle wax and red ink on their martyred rag dolls and finished off the deviled eggs and smoked ham and goat cheese and rosemary crackers. They guzzled orange juice spiked with Alexei's basement vodka, which would drive blunt spikes between their eyes by morning.

And the thing Sigrid and Katrin had put in the earth cursed them both fluently in Colville's real voice, in terms that would have made a serial rapist hide his face. Finally whatever energy had driven that voice fizzled out, and under the patch of ground by the garden shed, the rest was silence.

Sigrid took her shock-groggy granddaughter upstairs, washed Katrin's hands, and led the child into the hot liniment-smelling haven of her room. She looked in on her sleeping grandson. She then went downstairs and microwaved the last of the milk for hot chocolate, ignoring the sleepy, druggy laughter of the subsiding party; it had served its purpose. She got the child to swallow half an aspirin and drink the chocolate and brush her teeth, then put her nightgown on her and watched her curl up on one side of the bed. She dampened her hand at the bathroom tap and felt Katrin lean eagerly to it when Sigrid laid it on her brow, as if to say: *Yes, make me sleep. Yes, help me forget.*

Then Sigrid withdrew a bottle of cherry brandy from her underwear drawer and washed down the leftover half-aspirin and a second one, for whatever good they'd do. If tonight's work took, she thought, the possibilities of this election were perhaps aborted. At the least, they'd be diluted or postponed.

The glass runs out soon, Sigrid thought, as the blunt ache under her breastbone pressed upward. It was worse when she lay down, but she did, drawing a light quilt over both of them. On the edge of sleep, she felt some pressure shift within her. The strong thing in her head broke painlessly from overuse, and the heart-pain dissolved. She felt herself leave her body. It didn't hurt; why should it? It was natural. And the hand that had held the winds so tightly let go. The last thing Sigrid heard was Katrin, in her sleep, saying: "The wind—!"

The wind picked up. It blew fiercely: twenty miles per hour, thirty, forty, gale force. It picked up the Klimovs' rabbit hutches and smashed them against the shed and let their rabbits loose for the neighborhood dogs to savage. It hurled broken tree limbs into their greenhouse and pitched their solar panels into the Cunninghams' yard next door. It blew the Cunninghams' life-sized Dracula dummy into the Harrells' wisteria trellis. The temperature fell thirty-five degrees in two hours, and Sigrid went as stiff as a woman of wood and quite cold. The chill of her, blooming under the quilt as her body heat had done in life, was what woke Katrin up in the downdrafts of dawn.

Grandma Sigrid was waked and cremated before the election, which Colville lost. He demanded a recount. Hollow-eyed, Katrin followed the recount on television with a concentration Kirstie found very odd in an eight-year-old who had just lost the person she loved most. Katrin kept her vigil until Colville had definitively lost the election. Through no coincidence at all, he developed a case of laryngitis that laid him low for a fortnight after his defeat, and hoarseness plagued his honeyed cobra throat at intervals thereafter.

Whenever she could do it unobserved, Katrin crept out to the patch of earth by the garden shed and spoke the *nattspråkat* words that meant *stay down.*

Laura Argiri

Water and Mosses

Erstwhile Friend, you don't say why our government's gunning for you when you make contact. I am notified of your current predicament not by letter either handwritten or word-processed, not by phone or email. No, it's a mutual acquaintance who assails me. A woman in snowboots, puffer coat, and an overpriced colorful hat knitted from itchy wool in some third-world country. In short, a woman dressed like nearly every woman on this street today. She grabs my arm with a chummy urgency that makes no sense—she is not a friend. I met her at a party or two, one of them at your place.

"I need to talk to you," this woman hisses into my ear in the new Asia Joy Bubble Tea Shoppe. It's a gray day of late winter and wet wool; the floor is brown with melty mud, and I smell people's coats. The current political regime casts a penumbra of authentic fear over us all. There have been disappearances; there are frightful rumors about those who have dropped from sight. Because I do not want to attract notice, I have not yanked my sleeve from this near-stranger's clasp. I think about how even the most repetitious scenarios have the sheen of hyperfocus and adrenaline on them, how the need to guard one's public behavior thrusts me into cooperation/collusion with this person—her name is Kylie Something.

"Erstwhile says she had a bad... she said something she didn't mean to you once," Kylie Something tells me.

"It isn't important now," I say, though I'd felt like I'd been knifed, and Erstwhile's cold and superior fervor had sounded sincere enough.

I meant to get a Honeydew Creme here and spend a pleasant half-hour chewing the tapioca balls. I still mean to get my bubble tea, even if I must drink it on the run to escape this woman and a possible postmortem of Erstwhile and me. "Excuse me," I say, and slip free, and put in my order. I am heading out with the tall plastic cup and its special thick straw when she sidles up to me again, a skitty determination on her face.

"Wait, I really have do to talk to you," Kylie Something perseveres, her eyes too wide, intent and insistent—what's it to her? She continues: "Erstwhile, well, she's in trouble, and she says you'll understand."

"No, I wouldn't."

"Please. I mean bad trouble—in hiding. I was taking stuff to her, but I can't go back, I think someone saw me last time."

"What, are we in *The Handmaid's Tale* or something?" I try to keep this exchange light and disposable. To make us two bantering friends, no more, on the place's surveillance video.

"Well, it's sort of like that. I told her I'd find you. This is the address." She presses it into my palm. "I've been up there one time too many. Foodstuffs, she needs food. Nonperishables, she's got no fridge, no electricity. And fuel. She's got a camp stove, she can burn propane or kerosene."

"What about Alice Anne?" I say, naming her child.

"In a foster home. The state took her."

"And what about Selby?" I name Erstwhile's husband.

"He left her when all this started, the rat bastard."

*

From Kylie Something, I have an address in ballpoint on a paper napkin, written small. I find the place on the map. Erstwhile must be in trouble to go so far north alone in winter! Why not twenty miles more, all the way to Canada? Is it possible she'd be stopped at the border, just like in *The Handmaid's Tale*? Is her situation that desperate, or is this bid for rescue a flight of the same paranoia that wrote my dangerousness so large in Erstwhile's mind?

Friday evening, I buy crackers and canned stew and matches, dish soap, and apples. Powdered milk. Juice concentrates. Cheese. A big bucket of Teddie's peanut butter. Teddie's is cheap, but Teddie's is good, the best! Teddie's is nicer than she deserves, I think. Aspirin and vitamins. I avoid high-end treats suggestive of a seduction effort. I don't even include Coke, which she loved. I buy one of those scary white cylinders of propane meant for grills and barbecues.

Saturday morning, loathing myself for ever having craved her approval, I drive north. Driving, I recall watching people and wondering how many of them were like I'd been after she'd finished with me: stabbed with a glass dagger and working hard to smile, even with someone's broken-off blade lodged between ribs or vertebrae. I was not too young to know that looking grieved would attract derision and further damage. Not knowing whom to pity, I felt sorry for clothes in thrift stores, those repositories of the discarded. I've rarely found utilitarian black turtlenecks or white shirts in thrifts. Rather, one finds designers' overreaches: whimsical sleeves, asymmetrical hems, clever prints that match nothing, edgy colors like ashes-of-roses and neon lime. I felt fellowship with them. Even if they are pristine silk or cashmere, their bolder attributes send them to their exile in those sad, stale stores.

By evening, every nerve in my head feels fried. I've learned to keep still in such a mood, so I stay the night in a threadbare motel in a northern Vermont town, then press forward in the bright thawing weather. An ill-kept secondary road takes me out of pretty Vermont, ski-resort-and-maple-sugar Vermont, into a landscape where the glaciers have ground the picturesque broken terrain down and the human population is negligible. Far past the last tattered town, the last leg of my journey is on a scary little snake of road through the woods. It comes to an end at a bridge and a sign: Chillicott Cabins.

I will not drive over this bridge. Given my druthers, I wouldn't attempt it on foot either. It is an ancient-looking timber structure over a small roaring river, pouring down hectic with snowmelt from higher ground. It churns with chunks of broken ice. The water looks delicious; it would taste of snow and pure oxygen. It makes me thirsty to see it. Through the ice on the bridge timbers, I see green veins of moss, that brilliant velvety kind that always looked good enough to eat. Don't they eat this kind of moss in Finland or somewhere? Hasn't it got vitamin C?

When she's out of people to fetch groceries, I think, there's always water and mosses. I have lived on ghost-rations. Let her try.

Clutching the grocery box with my left arm, cradling the propane cylinder with my right, I venture over the bridge. I listen for rotting-timber, giving-way sounds, but there's only the underfoot crunch of melty ice. It hits me that this is a fairy-tale scenario, one of these places that a heroine with any sense would never go in the first place, thus shooting the plot completely to shit. The path disappears swiftly on the other side, and in the shade of the thick evergreens, there is no melt and no thaw. Get away from the amplified solar radiation from asphalt and concrete and uninterrupted light, and you are back in deep winter. I straggle through the snow to the row of dismal camps. They are woodframe cottages, inconceivably difficult to heat in winter. They probably have toy fireplaces for summer nights when the temperature goes down to forty-five, and tenants young enough not to be depressed in these poor little frail shells fuck by the flickering flames.

I wonder what'll be the first thing she says. I have the box between her and me in case of impulsive hugging attempts.

She has a scarf pulled up to her nose when she opens the rickety door of #4, and the first thing she says is "Apples!"

I pull back. She lets the scarf fall. "I'm not supposed to be here," she says. "Nobody knows I am."

So she's broken into this camp. "Kylie knows you are," I say.

"Oh, yes, Kylie does. Kylie brought me food and stuff, and now you—" Again a reach for an apple. I set the propane down, put the box on a spindly chair, and stand between it and her.

"Yes, I've brought you some stuff, but it's got a price on it. The price is that you explain yourself. Then I go away again, and you can eat this stuff. In one big sweet binge if you feel like it."

I can say that; resentment is a luxury she can't afford unless she just wants to eat snow instead of Teddie's peanut butter. Instead of a glare, she gives me a coy look from beneath her lashes. It's no mistake, the notion that she used those eyes on me the same way she used them on men. I shudder, half with nerves. It's deathly cold in here.

"Yes, it's cold," she suggests, with a gesture toward the toy hearth. "I ran out of kerosene and propane. I've been going into the woods for blowdowns and trashwood and burning that. I have to forage during the day, it's risky. I'd do it at night except that there are wild animals up here. Bears."

"I don't know how long propane lasts. I don't use it myself. I'm terrified of stuff that explodes. This probably won't last long," I say, surprised at my reasonable voice. "I'd ration it if I were you. Burn wood when it isn't so cold, propane when it's bad."

"Maybe you can bring me some more later."

"No, there's no *later*, and like I said, I'm actually not giving you this propane and other stuff unless you explain." If I did what you deserve, I think, I'd promise to return next weekend and have you write up a shopping list for me. And then I wouldn't come back. That's just the kind of gesture you understand. I pause, then drive my point in like a tack since she's still being kittenish. "I mean it, I'll pick this stuff up and throw it in the water from the middle of the bridge, in the deep part, and drive straight home unless I hear something that makes sense. If you don't explain yourself, I'm out of here, and so's this food. Everyone's got her price, that's mine."

"You're the same," she sighs. "Relentless."

"I'm not the same."

And here's how. Love is a delightful, unacceptably dangerous drug I will not put into my body now; need is an allergen. No longer a fond, reliable friend, I say, "I can't," and "No thanks," and just plain "No." When someone gets desperate and repetitious, I evaporate; I have spells of turning off the phone and erasing the messages unheard, relaxing into the abounding silence. The world feels suddenly big enough and cool enough and like there really is plenty of oxygen. I resurface when I feel like it, smiling: I *needed space*. I make no pretense of being reliable, resourceful, or accessible, and I still feel a certain sour surprise at the devotion and attention that this chilly, mercurial version of myself elicits. My tender default self, the first version of me, would have reveled in such tendresse. Some people call and email to ask over and over, "But do you need anything?"

I need to make sure that love's hold over me is never the final hold. I would rather drink river water and eat moss from the crevices of rocks than be destabilized by malice or love.

*

This is a nasty little camp. It has a scary little camp stove, thin wood paneling on the walls, and furniture I could demolish with a few good kicks. It has a bed with a heap of quilts and comforters to cocoon her heat through these terrible nights, when hers is probably the only human heart beating in twenty square miles. She must be terrified; I would be. Ancient pictures on the walls: Lassie and Jesus. The fire helps a little. Perhaps it brings the air temperature in here up to forty-five. Erstwhile loosens her scarf and undoes the top button of her coat. It is too cold for me to smell much of anything, but otherwise she'd probably smell of very stale wool and unwashedness. I get intimations that her outlines are expanded and softened but not spoiled. At nineteen, she looked almost holy in some lights, a woman whom construction workers somehow didn't dare to hoot after, and literary types tended to bestow her face on their dearest book-heroines, whether Tatiana Larin, Anne Shirley, Arwen Evenstar, or Heidi. She got accustomed to that. Now she's middle-aged, she's stale and skanky, but she's not ruined. A bath and a hair wash, clean underwear and a spiff new outfit, and she would be as hazardous as ever, or nearly.

"Now people shy away from others who're politically inflammatory," I say. "Now there are people going underground with some of their friendships. That's how they put it. People organize chance meetings. They meet up in greaseball restaurants in country towns and pretend they all just wound up there by chance, and then they eat together and drive back home by different routes. That kind of thing. Rather than discard each other summarily. Now there really is a reason to take certain friendships underground. Back then, though, no one gave a rat's ass. Certainly not about you and not about me. I wrote poems, for Christ's sweet sake! And you designed toys."

"It was the church elders at the pre-Cana seminar that Selby and I had to go to before we got married," she says. "They told me I was inviting a pernicious influence into my marriage by having friends like I had." A pause and snuffle. "I mean, they didn't mention you by name, but I knew what they meant."

"And you didn't tell them where they could go?"

A sigh. "No. I didn't tell them that. I don't tell people where they can go, or flip them off when they act like jerks in traffic." She means me: I do.

"And where are the church elders now that you need groceries and fuel and a place to hide?" I hope they're at least as uncomfortable as either of us.

She seems to think so. "In the same situation, most of them. Or in Canada, if they left in time. But you're not paying attention to something here, and that is that I didn't do what they said. Not for four years."

I try not to count off four on my fingers and ask if this means she gets a gold star. I just say, "And I'm to give credit where credit's due?"

"I liked you," says Erstwhile, her helpless pretty hands linked before her. "They kept pressuring me, but I resisted all that pressure up until a point."

"And what was the point?"

She weighs that one carefully. "Until," she finally says, "I began to feel you were dangerous myself. Dangerous ideas. And I worried ... that you were erotically interested in me."

"Worse than that could happen to you. Apparently it has."

"I didn't know what I'd do if you ever made a pass at me."

"Say 'No thank you,' if you weren't interested, I'd think. That's what I do when someone makes a pass and I'm not interested."

"I didn't know if you ever had. Made a pass at me, that is."

"If I ever had, you wouldn't be wondering," I say. I try not to sound astounded, but that notion is astounding, even from someone brought up in a cult. "I'm not the subtle type. Any pass I make is hard to mistake for something else. But the fact is, I didn't, because I thought it might scare you."

"I was scared. I had thoughts about a different life. Without Selby, maybe with someone ... wild and different. Outside the boxes. And how empty and brilliant it might be."

"How could it be empty *and* brilliant?" I ask.

"I mean, doing what I wanted and not worrying about being a good example, like you have to be for kids. No child, no church, no God. It would be like ... freefall. Falling slowly, like a kite on a bright windy day. This dreamlike, brilliant, dangerous life that I imagined." She smiles.

"You nearly bled to death on the delivery table. What you got was dangerous." The soft, unrelenting abrasion of domesticity, too—wear and fatigue that would probably turn me into an axe murderer if it went on for twenty years. Or ten, or five.

"That's a natural danger," she says, shrugging. "I mean, I don't even know what would happen if I threw over the rules. I think I probably couldn't stand it. People have to pick the sins and hazards they can live with, not the ones they can't. Does that make any sense?" she asks, with a touch of, yes, grief.

It does. I admit as much. It makes the kind of sense that makes me weary enough to lie down in the snow and try not to breathe. The kind of sense that grinds people down until they are as sad and insignificant as that gummy grit that air pollution deposits on city stone.

"And you have such extravagant emotions," she says.

"Not anymore," I say. I set the box on the table. "Here. That was an explanation. Take your apple."

She approaches it and takes a red fruit. "I figured that if anyone's smart enough to get around the regime, it's you. For someone with extravagant emotions, you could also be ice-cold logical. It was kind of hard to take both things at once. But I figured you'd be a survivor now, I figured you'd know what to do—"

I've kept this exchange civilized. I'll keep it that way sixty seconds more. And I intend to roadblock any information on exactly why she's in hiding. "I don't have the first inkling of what to do. I'm just bringing this stuff," I say. "Don't tell me anything more, I don't want to know it. For practical reasons, I don't want to know it. No one can make me tell what I don't know in the first place."

"You really mean it, you won't come back? You won't do anything?"

I say, "I have done something, I've come here once. If I came back, that would end badly. You can take credit where it's due, I don't roll the dice on a situation like this anymore, I do what'll keep me in one piece and leave. Which is what I'm doing this minute." *Having mercy on myself,* I add to myself alone. Will whoever or whatever hunts you down find you, then, I wonder—here by the treacherous bridge, the galloping waters?

"But I will tell Kylie that she'll have to get someone else to do this," I add. My mouth is papery and sticky; the cold has left me as dry as heat. I take an ancient jelly glass out of the kitchenette cabinet. "I'll leave this on the rocks by the river," I say, and I go out even as she says, "But this place does have water—"

She watches me. I put my bag in the car and go down to the water's edge, crouch and dip the glass in the torrent. It must have pollution, but I can't taste that, only that faint taste of minerals and metals that Vermont water has. The rocks are veined and furred with the green of that same moss under the ice. I use my car keys to break the ice shell on one rock and scrape up the moss like cheese. I taste a bit: green and insubstantial, a ghost-snack. I drink the glass empty. Water and mosses.

Again

No success, I somehow have a chance to do my half-wrong life right. I have woken into that possibility, and you, sensible dear friend, are the messenger bearing this chance, this news. That is how we two are on the Cambridge Common this windy white day in late March or early April, a place on the calendar that I surmise because there is almost no snow left, only the filthy packed piles in the shaded places.

So what we time-travelers from 2016 experience now is just-spring in the days before global warming, the sweet, wild 1970s, and we two are reprieved from female adult midlife. There's a clear sense of being in two timeframes at once, disturbing but exhilarating. By this miracle we are girls today, and in the winter coats our parents bought us for college. Mine is jade green, yours a sober, severe midnight blue. Your coat accentuates the Garbo line of your broad, thin shoulders, the gilt of your hair. True creatures of the seventies, we both have long hair that is washed every day with horse shampoo, which is supposed to thicken it and make it shine. Mine is ordinary brown, but I have a lot of it. I can feel it move with the gusts. Yours, straight and gold, is the cleanest and brightest thing in sight. Somehow, without being vain, you are used to people looking at you first in any group. Or perhaps you are a little vain; you won't wear a hat over that hair except in the very coldest weather, and today's doesn't qualify.

We have not been girls for thirty years. Those thirty years are occupied by my sputtering, flailing career and its occasional flares of success. By your straight-arrow, stellar career and your dreadful marriage, a disaster that is not your fault unless you are to blame for failing to recognize pathology or run from evil—Beauty, bleeding compassion for a Beast who proved bestial to the bone. We are somehow before the time when the success score started to be counted—twenty-one again. A blustering breeze makes the loose paper trash frolic and blows our long hair. Here you are, Selena, with Saskia. What are we doing out so early, though? Most people are still asleep.

When we talk in the true present, these days, one of our topics is sleep and how we get it. In midlife, good sleep is an accomplishment, and I'm lucky if I can sleep until seven AM. Fiftysomethings turn themselves off with benzodiazepines if they can get them, Benadryl if they can't; they kiss the fingers of doctors who write scripts for real sleeping pills. Young people, real young people at least, fall into sodden trances of fatigue. They sleep in, sleep ponderously, suck fiercely on the fat tit of sleep. They can't get enough. Cambridge is full of students sleeping now. I can imagine their legions sprawled in messy little rooms, couples tangled in the cramped twin beds of dorms. Many of the rooms would smell of stale sex, but most would smell mainly of winter sleep: down quilts and breath and the salt sea of dreams, the scrim of sweat between skin and nightclothes when a person sleeps under an arctic-weight comforter in a cold room. Among my keenest memories of college, along with numbing boredom and the inexhaustible snark of the conversation classes called "seminars," are my crying need for sleep and the misery of morning. What gives us, those fiftysomething souls who woke up in young bodies today, such razored clarity at this catatonic hour?

You have always had your stern side. You get out of bed on schedule. Perhaps now I am like you, whose judgment I have always felt like a small cold breeze at the warmest of times, and my schoolwork is caught up like yours probably was. Mine never used to be caught up. I hit the end of every college term like a speeding sports car hits a stone wall. In the convalescent aftermath, I'd think how glad I was that you didn't attend college here. I missed you, but if you'd been here, you'd have known for sure what intuition probably suggested. You'd have seen how I never took care of business as fast as I should. (What would you have thought of all my preliminary rituals to calm myself down or jack myself up to those interminable assignments? Coatless walks in the cold, sweets, Cokes, music, all to find some level midpoint where concentration was possible? If I try to imagine you at the same frantic foolishness, I can't; it doesn't work. I *can* imagine you making yourself venomous instant coffee with hot water from the tap and getting down to business, however much it hurt.)

What is my business here and now?

I am not sure. I have not always known my business and have not always done it when I knew it perfectly well. I was never a huge sinner, but I wasted a lot of time that other people did not waste. While wasting it, I learned innumerable useless things, such as that the overcast white light of today was one of Wyeth's favorite kinds of light, and apparently it is as common in the transitional seasons in Pennsylvania, where he painted, as here. It is a grubby white, not the clean, swan's-down white sky of overcast winter. With my new chance, will my brain still fill up with all this culture that achieves exactly nothing except making a person cultured? Will I still read myself to sleep with stacks of fiction on thousands of nights and get to know so many invented people so intimately, and drink all those glasses of milk to soothe me to sleep? Do I know how much time I could waste that way? How much of my life has disappeared down such warm and welcoming wormholes?

Do I fear? Do I think that today brings judgment?

*

You are thoughtful; you say that the coffee shop will be open and we should get coffee and muffins. Your mien and tone do not indicate judgment, which I have spent/wasted a lot of time dreading. When I was young, though, the fear tipped over into defiance or indifference as often as not; I reached the point of ***don't-care-whatever-the-cost.*** There are some outrageous don't-care things I've done.

What will I do right in my new youth? Will I refuse to invest energy and tears in relationships that will stop mattering within a few years? Will I close one door to damage and *not* leave a note for the unsuitable, unlovable man I loved? Will I be kind and responsive to the suitable one whose timid touch I dreaded? Learn to tolerate him as a horse learns to accept a saddle? Will I dismiss the passionate notion of demonstrating originality in my college papers and spit back the dust of historical criticism docilely, damp with the due amount of saliva? Will I avoid the scalding scorn and professorial curled lips that I earned by opening my arms to risk and trying to think and write new ideas in new words? What is today's opportunity? What misery or sin can I avoid?

Little sins! I think. I have the same skittery mind that I had at five; it keeps seventeen channels open at once and can skitter off down any of any of them at any time. ADHD, they call it now. Adults can have it. I used to think of myself as someone who grew easily bored, who found boredom more painful than most people seemed to find it.

Now my ADHD mind scampers down the tinted tunnel of sin as our boots grind grit on filthy ice. I have knowingly done something wicked very few times, maybe two or three, and about the same number of times, I've done things I knew were wicked only after the fact. My sins, the ones that are legion, are fatigue and the-hell-with-it. Mulish perseverance that felt like determination at the time, which has surely bored the piss out of multitudes. Failure to learn about finances that felt like high-mindedness. But most of my sins? They're croissants. They're chocolate. They're favorite films watched over and over and books read likewise, wasting time. They are the cushiony, easy pleasures that keep people, or at least people like me, from swallowing the whole bottle of sleeping pills at once or taking the sharp new knife to the carotid. Or the way I'd favor, going out on some lethally cold night, buying a liter bottle of Coke Zero at a convenience store, and making my way to some private place with high drifts. Then lying down in the snow, in the snowlight, swallowing the pills in one gulp and waiting for the dozy warmth that people are supposed to feel when freezing. Believe me, I've wanted to so often that suicidality has gotten tiresome and routine, like allergies. I don't owe the fact of not having extincted myself to therapists, but to Stephen King. To Philippa Gregory and Tanith Lee and Nabokov. To milk and croissants and chocolate and Coke. Even the worst day ends, and at its end are my shabby luxuries: my books, my cats, my bed, the acrylic fleece blankets that feel almost like the cats' fur, and that late snack that eases me into sleep. What have I failed to achieve while between my blankets with my fiction, my cat, my milk and carbs? Are those indulgences sins, and does it matter?

And are all such thoughts, I wonder, predicated on the notion that we matter beyond the limits of our lives and the people we love, those who love us back? Happiness is probably easier if you have a lightweight ego and few expectations, if you ride lightly on the tide of time. Why do we think about ourselves as if we had proof that we mattered? And waste so much time and thought on the unknowable!

I hate suspense. I hate conundrums and mysticism and through-a-glass-darkly horseshit and doubletalk. I want to know whatever our presence here in nineteen-seventy-fuckever is meant to tell me. And what is the pivot to that knowledge?

If I were a king in a myth, it might be a still, glassy sea that stalled my army on a blazing beach; it might be mad gods raving for my beloved child's blood. Through such stark choices, everyone learns what a person will and will not do. For me, the pivot is the terrified small dog running loose on the Common. This dog is plainly not used to running loose, not used to even the mild city noise of the catatonia hour. I don't care for dogs. But I call and coax him to me. A neutered male, someone's pet, wearing a collar and tags with a name and address engraved.

If I have been scattered thus far, now I'm not. "Jake," I say to him, since that's his name. He lets me touch him; I can feel scabs under his dark, wiry terrier coat. I can feel his trembling and hunger.

In tones kind and neutral, you speak. "We should call Animal Control."

"His address is near," I say. "Humboldt Street. I'm going to take him home. After all, what am I going to achieve today?"

"Less than you might if you don't get involved with this dog." Not so kind and neutral now; quite disapproving. Rightly so: I have very often allowed my plans to be interrupted by other people's emergencies that, as you have noted, did not pertain to me.

I carry the shaking, squirming dog, and you follow me to Humboldt Street. Your expression is exactly the same as when our barking-mad geometry teacher demanded that the whole class, in unison, tell her that they loved her. You sat cool and silent and got sent to the principal's office, to the principal's baffled shock. You sat in the chair normally occupied by squirming young thugs, and the old wuss quailed before the raised shield of your undaunted slate-blue gaze. When he learned why you were there, he stammered out something about his inability to curtail the lady's whims because she had tenure.

"You've been here before, Sass?" you ask as we approach.

"I had a job here." When I was this young, the *first* time I was this young, I baby-sat for a family on Humboldt Street, not far from my dorm. They had a tiresome child. I can remember a sin: not my indifference to the kid, but the three yellow apples from the big sack of apples in their pantry. One apple would have been quite enough for me to eat after the boring kid had nodded off. The other two were my tedium toll. God, how young people eat!

When we get to #19-A Humboldt Street, you say, "Sass, this is trouble." I would ask how you know already except that I can feel that it's true, and the door's slightly open. You say, "We really ought to call the police. Something's not right. Who lets their door hang open here? You're not going to go in there?"

Of course I am.

Inside, I call out a very cautious, "Excuse me? Hello?" because it is not the Cambridge way to open even a close, friendly neighbor's unlocked door, much less some total stranger's. It is completely against the Cambridge way to do this, just as it is against the Cambridge way to leave any exterior door unlocked and unguarded. We are defensive here. An unsecured exterior door suggests nothing good. There might be someone dead inside, the victim of violent crime—or at best, someone who has slumped down, unconscious with blood sugar either too low or too high, or from a seizure or allergic reaction, just before clipping Jake's lead to his collar to take him out for his walk. One Sunday evening I found a woman sleeping on the ground in a park, getting vampirized by ecstatic mosquitoes while a toddler ran loose in the jewel-blue dusk. No one else was there. A stroller, loaded with her purse and his kiddie stuff, stood near the slide. I tried to wake her; she slurred, "I don't know you," and slept again. When I called 911 for her, the EMTs found that she was a diabetic having a blood sugar crash: sugar level down to 30, a notch or two up from coma. I stayed until they had stabilized her, contacted her daughter in New Jersey, and loaded her and her grandson into the ambulance. Not a story with a bad ending, though it could have been if no one had found her, or if someone else had, someone different from you and me. Now that I think of it, the bad ending was likelier: someone who'd have taken her wallet and left her to die and left the baby to run into the street, or perhaps taken the wallet *and* the baby. The neighborhood had had its supper and was socked in solidly before its screens, watching *Game of Thrones*. I could tell that from the windows.

Now I put Jake down, and he runs to his nearly-empty dish (personalized *JAKE*) to lap out the remaining kibble.

No human, though, is inside. We open every interior door, and the absence of any human is clearly established. There is not enough furniture to conceal an unconscious human. In the closet are shoes and clothes. Behind the unlocked front door, no one is home.

I move around, finding dog food and filling his bowl, rinsing the empty water bowl and refilling it.

There is nothing here I don't recognize. Everything here is a version of something I've either loved or suffered.

The walls of this overpriced dump, probably insulated with nothing more than tarpaper, are painted in a sweet pale pink, the blanched blood of winter sunset. There are a few sticks of furniture, a foam mattress on the floor, some art glass, and a framed print, Man Ray's "Peach." The space between all these objects is eloquent, and they are too. There is a platinum-blonde baby doll in an antique dress made for a real baby, and the dress has been lovingly ironed with starch. There is a metal pencil holder with a print of ballet dancers on it—the type that used to come with candy in it, someone's kind present to a little girl with cultured interests, a little girl who appealed to cultured adults. I know because I have such items and still value them, remembering the generosity of the giver. Such gifts travel with us from middle-class childhood into the shockland of young adult life in mean cities. Mine are still with me, back where I belong.

This place is not a home, but it cries aloud the need of a home. This is the domicile of a very young woman who dearly wants a home. Chemistry is to blame: A young woman's veins are hot with estrogen at that age, that same estrogen that makes us overflow with tears then and find babies adorable. She can't help wanting a home; chemistry makes her want a nest, even if she doesn't yet want a husband and children to put into it. She has made a beginning by getting a dog. She is a cultured young woman, probably with a worthless humanities degree like mine. In here it's cold but not freezing; the thermostat's set to 60°. She doesn't know how to live in the slum she might actually be able to afford; she would be terrified. So she lives in Cambridge and cuts every corner she knows how to cut, though she doesn't know all those corners yet. If I examined her closet, I'd find holdover clothes from college and a few new items, clever adult clothes, chosen with painful care because clever clothes cost so much. She lives in this expensive dump and tries to make it charming, she yearns for a safe, warm place gleaming with light and art glass, she knows enough to lock a door, and someone has forced her out of her place.

"It's someone our age, and something's happened to her," I say.

"Right, and we need to find a phone and call the police," you say. *And that,* adds your tone, *is the long and the short of it and all we should do.*

I have the fleeting notion that I should have a phone in my pocket or purse, a flash of time-present that does not fit into my new youth, my second chance. Back where/when we are, to make a call away from home, one must look for the nearest pay phone, put a dime in, and pick up the heavy receiver, sticky from countless anxious hands. The receiver will smell of breath, even in the coldest weather. Or, in a residence, one must use what we don't yet call a *landline.* I look for the landline.

"And we need to leave, Sass. We need to leave and call the police and turn this whole mess over to them." Oh, this is an episode from *The Selena and Saskia Show,* one that should have happened when we were barely old enough to buy alcohol, and the dialogue is predictable. It isn't, though, the repartee between daredevil and steady-head; we are both very careful people capable of wide-spaced, sweeping acts of impulse—just not the same acts. We have both gone airborne over different abysses. I can tell that you are truly frightened; your pitch lowers, and your breath goes a bit tight. Fear could make you sound like thirty when you were fifteen. "This isn't safe," you say.

"Nothing's safe," I say. And I don't act as you suggest because of what I see next—the white cat who edges out of hiding and comes to rub her face against my boot.

I pick her up at once. My head hums with tears. Where I really dwell on the timeline, in the twenty-first century, in the decade of fast global warming and no snow in March, my cat has died and I have not gotten another. Her name was Chris, and she was a flamepoint Siamese, a variant that didn't exist when I was a girl, and she was kind, smart, affectionate, and gifted with delight in all her world, including me—truly a counter-depressive cat! She slept in my arms. I don't think I've ever felt so loved. I feel my grief for her the same disorienting way I think I should have my mobile in my pocket, except that grief hurts. Grief rises like those waves of nausea I've occasionally had when I thought I was perfectly well, seasickness on dry land. I loved my cat as much as any human I've ever loved, but there will be no cat like her, and I have decided not to have another.

One reason for not having another cat is the lunatic who is the Republican nominee in 2016, and the need for max mobility and liquidity in case the lunatic wins and I need to cross the Canadian border and stay there. Cats settle us; they cast the illusion of permanency over the most fragile and temporary domiciles. If you have a roof, a cat, and a lamp, you have shelter, company, a pool of light to read by, and at least the illusion of safety and home. Cats are antithetical to flight. Who can sneak over a border dragging a carrier and a yowling beast? Or abandon her cat?

Another reason is all the money and time I have spent on cat food, cat litter, and vets, and all that time cleaning up after cats. How many dollars, how many hours have I expended on creatures who could offer nothing but love? And the bliss of touching them, their fur that is somehow at once cool and warm, and their bliss when caressed. There is no justification for cats but love. Or perhaps there is if I add cats to the list of comforts that have kept me from making some bad day my last—though that notion is predicated on the idea that my ongoing breath matters in the first place. And if it does, I should not waste time.

"Sass, you're *not*. This is the first time since you were a kid that you haven't had some damn cat to drag you down. And you don't even like dogs."

All true. I particularly dislike terriers, brainless barking beasts.

"You're *not* going to take these two home," you say. "You're going to call the police and let the police call Animal Control."

"They'll put them in the pound. Do you think either of them would stand a chance?" I want to cry. I feel a hot hum in my head—grief for the woman who is not here, who has come to harm, and for her animals. She wanted a nest and pets and did not consider how those desires could drag her down. She started wasting her time early on. She lived here in hope, cold and probably hungry, and bought cat food and cat litter and dog food. She could be me. I could be her. My grief is for her and me, my consumed self. Her ongoing breath matters, and if hers does, so does mine. Whatever I do about this, I will be doing it for her and for me.

Long story short: I find the phone and call the police; they come and make their notes on clipboards. The landlord is nowhere around and doesn't answer their calls. I find the cat carrier and the dog's leash, planning to take Jake to a vet for his skin. One cop takes my phone number so that the owner of these animals, if she turns up, can call me and retrieve them. He doesn't say that outcome would surprise him, but his expression suggests pessimism.

You are midway between despair and disgust. "This is going to cost you a pack of cash, Sass. You're doing what you've always done. Isn't that the point of being here—not to keep doing what you've always done? Is that what you want? Who was it that said hell was repetition? Camus?"

"This is not something I *do*," I say. "Not something I *want*. It's me being who I *am*. How do I stop that?" And you supposedly *like* me, I think crossly, like a real, petulant post-adolescent.

"It isn't always sin that drags people down," you say, and how tired you sound! "I wasted twenty-five years with Sherman because I was raised to be broadminded! Because I thought he was just different! And I didn't get that he was crazy! I was raised to be kind!" ***Broadminded, different, crazy:*** All those words get a steely lick of fury, like a whack on the knuckles with a ruler. ***Kind*** gets spat out like a worm in a sweet peach.

"You are kind," I murmur, "and Sherman is crazy." Sherman is a manic brute, and everybody who loves you has shuddered at the thought of his hands on you ever since the wedding.

Perhaps it is not what Plath called the "isolate, slow faults" that eat us up and erode our hopes and dissolve our most urgent dreams at the horizon. Perhaps it is our kindness, our broadmindedness, our true loves, the ones that make us feel most wholly alive and worthwhile.

"Do you remember those people in Stephen King's books, who ask, 'Do you love?'" I ask you. "Sometimes it'll be a character, or maybe it's the narrator of a story who just turns to the reader and asks, 'Do you love?'" I speak now from 2016; in 1970-whatever, those books weren't written yet.

"No." You are kind; you don't say that you don't read rubbish. "Why?"

"He doesn't come out and say so, but *no* is a bad answer to 'Do you love?' If you say *no*, you're doomed."

"If you say *yes*, I bet you're doomed too, just in a different way. Sometimes they bait the trap with cheese, not poison."

Today is probably such a time, such a trap. I walk into it like home. I take the cat with me from love, the dog from duty. It's repetition. Camus didn't say that hell was repetition, I remember; it was Andre Linoge, the demon in *The Storm of the Century*. He said it to Robbie Beals during a fraught conversation about—surprise!—sin.

When I wake up tomorrow, I might not find these two animals because I'll probably wake where I belong. There/then you'll be waking up a thousand miles away, Selena, and getting right out of your bed, and Chris will not be with me in mine. Perhaps you'll wake reaching for the trailing ends of a long, disquieting narrative dream involving me. Whatever this is, it'll be over. But what I am doing now is the first certain thing I've done today.

The Fourth of Six

Josef has the Praetorius Christmas album playing on the phonograph that Deutsche Grammophon sent him; the sound quality is superb. He has a cognac at his elbow and his children in their crimson velvet Christmas outfits, playing around the candled and bedecked tree. All of them but Holde, who is in his lap, content just to look at the tree and be cradled by someone, even by him. Especially by him. If he asks her why she doesn't want to play around the tree like her siblings, to pick at the ornaments and rattle the packages as they're doing, she'll say, "I just like the colors, Vati. I like to relax my eyes and let the colors blur. The colors are enough."

It is a mystery, how one responds to children. Children's strengths and weaknesses have surprisingly little to do with the love one bears them. Among his children, Helga is the smartest, Hilde the most droll; Helmut is the dull one, living proof that the purest Aryan genes perform vicious recessive flips. Hedda is charm personified; Heide is a pretty baby who hardly ever cries. But Holde is the one who elicits from Josef a parental love that surprises him with its focus, force, and purity. "When I'm thinking about her," he thinks, "I'm a good man. With her face in my mind's eye, I'm as good as any man who ever lived. Why not love someone who makes at least a part of me so good?"

She's five this year, the beautiful one among the pretty six. So lovely he wonders how he and his hard-jawed wife had anything to do with her making. They named her Holde after the Germano-pagan goddess of spring. Perfect Aryan blonde hair looks like lank straw next to her lush dark locks. She has the biggest eyes of all Josef's children, and hers are not plain blue but almost lavender. All his children have pleasant features, which no one has ever said about him, but Holde's features have a clarity that lets her bypass pleasantness and prettiness and attain beauty, even at five. She's also the weakest of the six, born almost two months premature, who survived only through the Reich's cutting-edge medical technologies. She's not a sickly child, but she's sensitive. She hates roughness and noise. Too often, her fine eyes express apprehension, a kind of generalized pain in a world not gentle enough for her—although this household is as gentle as the Third Reich gets. She hides and cries by herself over her siblings' casual mean remarks—Josef puts paid to nasty talk from his children right swiftly if he catches them at it, but he isn't always here to catch them—and sometimes her eyes tear up simply because someone startles her. She goes very still when trying not to cry. She's so reserved that Josef can't tell whether she's really just terribly timid or a touch slow. Sometimes he thinks that maybe no one will ever know. A silent woman with such beauty appears mysterious, not tongue-tied. Her homecoming husband could heal himself from the day's hurts in the cool pool of her beauty and her silence.

In the Christmas pageant, Holde was chosen as Maria the Virgin, just like last year, and their Catholic grandmother in Rheydt was ecstatic with the photos. "Ach, the blessed little one!" she'd crooned over the phone after the pictures arrived in the mail. And Holde had looked beatific, perhaps because as Maria she didn't have to speak or sing—just wear that blue satin tunic and headdress and hold last year's Christmas doll. But beyond that, thinks Josef, she's weirdly suitable to the role. Josef can imagine her at thirteen or fourteen, that barely-ripe stage in girls, as some Renaissance painter's model for the Virgin in the Annunciation. He can imagine her as God's Chosen: kneeling on that arid hardpan, arms open, blue-purple eyes wide with awe, saying *Be it unto me according to Thy will.* Absorbing the body-blow of holy lust with a sort of shrinking willingness. Such submission would be natural as breath to her, and at even at fourteen, her father thinks, she'll be innocent enough to attract an angel.

Oh, but she has none of those steel virtues that the Reich prizes! Josef has all his children taught at home, and that's mainly for Holde's sake, though her slow brother Helmut profits by it too. Josef also intends to keep her out of the Bund Deutscher Mädel, for she'd be paralyzed by the crowds and the screaming competitive games. Nor will Josef ever allow Holde to go away at sixteen and work for a year on a farm as many girls do, for a farmhand could rape her a great deal more brutally, and just as easily, as pragmatic and opportunistic Jahweh did the little Jewess in the wilderness. Holde has no fight in her, no ego at all. He can imagine her, grown into a lush Tess d'Urberville-like young womanhood and passivity, shrinking from some young man's hard hands. It wouldn't occur to her to tell the pawing lummox, "My father is *the* Dr. Goebbels, take your hands off me, he'll throw you in a camp!" Josef can just imagine her, silent tears sliding from her eyes as some farmhand raped her raw in the shelter of the waving grain.

"Why are you sad?" Holde asks, *sotto voce* into Josef's ear, as if sadness is a secret. Every time he seriously wonders if she's slow, she gives some powerful evidence that she can see straight to the center of him. Mother, wife, lover, casual single-shot slut or enterprising starlet spreading herself for him like honey, no one else has looked to his center like that. He hopes Holde can't see everything inside him. Now he smiles and says, "Because some day my daughter will leave me."

"I don't want to," she says, with no coyness. Indeed, he can imagine her living in her childhood bedroom until the day of her marriage, the décor getting more grown-up by degrees. Perfume and rouge appearing on the dressing table, which at some point would acquire a lacy satin skirt, an illuminated mirror. Now he kisses the brow under the dark hair. All children have lovely skin, but he fancies that hers is positively flowerlike. No grown woman's silk-shielded belly is as soft as her cheek, her arm.

"What's the other reason you're sad?" she perseveres.

"I have another reason?"

"Lots," she says, telegraphic: *You have many reasons to be sad.*

Because, Josef thinks, *your Vati is under no illusion that he's a good man.* Christmas makes him especially aware of his faithless graft and grasping. Vati is having the best political run that he can, being a concupiscent cockroach of a man with a gimpy leg. It's a bitter fact: Vati's good run as Reich Propaganda Minister and Arch-Liar is by no means as good as it should be. Vati is smart enough to know the truth if not brave enough to tell it, and Vati sold his personal mess of pottage for a pot of message and Nazi claptrap long ago.

Actually, the idea of selling his soul amuses Josef, for it had been ripe as carrion from his earliest youth. A botched soul sewn into a botched body... *even if your Vati had had just the average good looks that his stupid little son might have in manhood, our whole life might have been different...* but Josef isn't as sad about that as about some other matters. All these children are too young to know that Vati's power is all poised on the broken glass and wet ice of murderous, manipulative lies. But in the privacy of his own conscience, he knows that he might be able to live with that quite well but for this child who deserves a good man's love. If all of him were as bad as most of him, he'd resent her for reminding him of this. Instead, in the intimate ear of his conscience, he hears the single tone of an immaculate sadness, an angelic lone oboe. A *Weheklage,* one note expressing the whole of a lament, evocative as lilac in rain.

The self-consciously bad man is really sad, though, because of his fey certainty about what will *not* happen. Lies build a fragile house, and that house will fall before his favorite child is old enough to judge him. Often he used to imagine a wedding: himself hanging Japanese pearls around Holde's neck, then turning her bridal veil down and giving her into some golden SS warrior's keeping in a National Socialist hand-fasting ceremony according to the reformed pagan rite Dr. Rosenberg had reinvented for the marriages of the elite military caste. Recently, though, he has the clearest sense that he will never choose those jewels for her or veil her in that mobile sacristy of silk tulle. He will not be doing these things because the fourth of six, the weakest, the most beautiful, the gentlest and most loved, will die with the other five when the good run is over. *Yes,* he thinks fiercely, *spoil these children silly, buy out the doll shops, see that their little clothes fit perfectly and haul them around in their pony cart, this is their good run and the only one they'll have.* For Josef is feeling a clairvoyant despair: his clever eldest, his spirited second, his dense, plodding, well-meaning son, his flirting fifth, and the pretty dark baby still too young to have much of an identity yet will all die. Holde also, too frail for the Thousand Year Reich that will barely reach twelve. He really needn't worry about the Reich chewing Holde up like a violet under a mower. He thinks: *You won't reach ten. My weakest, my best.*

There

Eager for the full, hot English summer that ozone depletion had provided the last couple of years, Elunn opened her armoire for T-shirt and skort and sandals the morning after coming home from Roedean. Then, with toast and milky tea in hand, she scurried for the sitting room and the electric fire. There her ancient grandmother, Kachia, was avidly intent on *The Two Towers*. Kachia had her left hand up, forefinger to cheekbone, as she tended to do when interested or amused. Her wrist seemed a mere bone-twig under a thin scrim of skin. It seemed to Elunn that Kachia was thinner all over, more angular than ever in her thrawn frailty... there seemed even something insectile about her grandmother's big eyes and the sharp old bones of her ancient face. Elunn thought, "If this is the way women in this family age, I can forget about being a pretty old lady."

Kachia noticed Elunn's goose-pimpled legs and took time out to say, "Put some clothes on, girl. It may be June, but it's still England." So Elunn dug into her suitcases for jeans and wool socks. As she retraced her path, her mother, Marim, called her: "Here, take Gran's breakfast." So Elunn bore the loaded tray back into the warmth of Gran's den.

"I wish you could've come, Gran." Elunn meant the fête at the glorious end of her boarding school career, final showcase of her maths and language prizes, her fine A-levels.

"I wish so too, girl, but the Mayoress can't leave Shining Stone. Even if the Mayoress hasn't just turned a hundred and four." Kachia had just turned a hundred and four and was still the Mayoress of Shining Stone, their town. She insisted on the old-style title: "If I wrote verse, I'd be a poetess. Like Sappho, or Millay." Kachia's birthday was June 10, when Elunn was revising for her final examination in Latin. In no uncertain fashion, Kachia had vetoed the idea of Elunn interrupting her studies and coming home for the party. She insisted that her granddaughter finish her last year of boarding school out to its last official minute. On the tenth, the school kitchen had served heaps of big, perfect California strawberries, tastelessly tart, at elevenses. Elunn had thought of the strawberries people were probably eating in Shining Stone at Kachia's birthday tea. The Shining Stone strawberries would be tiny, intensely sweet and sour, with a wild tangy fragrance. Because they ripened slowly and were not prolific, there would not be piles of them. But after you'd had a handful, you'd know you'd eaten strawberries. Shining Stone was a very small place with very high standards.

Shining Stone was in many ways unusual, as Elunn had learned from time elsewhere, and Kachia's tenure as Mayoress was just one of those ways.

"Happy to be back, are you?" was Kachia's next query, and when Elunn agreed that she was, Kachia added, "Going away helps a person appreciate Shining Stone." But the film absorbed her mightily, and presently she returned her attention to Liv Tyler. Kachia smacked her old lips: "Now that's a healthy girl with a nice big bosom and backside. Too good for those peroxide-blond nancing elves."

"She doesn't marry any of the elves, she marries the hunk with the big sword and greasy hair," Elunn said. "The human who's going to be a king. Aragorn. Viggo Mortensen. We had a fan club for him at school."

"Huh? Good. Fine chap. Good bones." When admiring men, Kachia often sounded like some old farmer on livestock. Her emphases were strength, structure, favorable genetic propensities.

"I thought elves were supposed to be ethereal, though," Elunn ventured, with the merest teasing edge. She put the tray within convenient reach.

"Fantasy-writer crap," Kachia snorted. "Sod those writers. Dreamers and diddlers, whomping up crap to amuse the stupider kind of teenager."

"Well, so much for all you Tolkien fans out there," Elunn thought as the old lady attacked drop scones with butter, eggs, lean ham, and cantaloupe, stopping often to snort with hilarity and contempt at scenes that were not supposed to be funny. Senility, if that was her problem, hadn't put a dent in her appetite. Her ancient teeth looked hard and strong.

"If it's elves they're writing about, I reckon they have to make it up, Gran. Being as there really aren't any," Elunn ventured. "I doubt if Orlando Bloom has any problem with it."

Kachia harrumphed and gestured toward the orange marmalade. "I keep telling your mother not to buy this stuff. It's cloying. Go see if she's got any grapefruit marmalade in there. And more toast."

"Ma," Elunn asked Marim in the kitchen, "is Gran, like, slipping any?"

"Slipping?"

"You know. Senility."

"No, not that I know of," said Marim. Her grave eyes widened. "What makes you think that?"

Elunn shrugged. "She's laughing at *The Two Towers*."

"She's amused," Marim said. "I don't think having a sense of humor means Gran's senile." She located a jar of grapefruit marmalade. "Here. This stuff is horrid and bitter, but she likes it. The main way I think she's changed is she doesn't taste anything subtle. She wants hot green curry and dark chocolate and broccoli rabe. Chili with Scotch bonnet peppers. Nasty bitter grapefruit marmalade."

"The *Lord of the Rings* films aren't funny, though," Elunn persisted. "There's not too much in them that's supposed to be funny. A few scenes with those two ADHD hobbits kifing fireworks and dancing jigs on tavern tables, and that's not what she's chuckling about. Gran's really getting up there, too."

Marim looked offended by her sixteen-year-old's speculations on age. She just said, "We live a long time in Shining Stone. Have you hung your prism back in your window yet?"

"Not yet."

"Well, take this to Gran and go hang your prism back where it belongs, then. So the town knows you're home."

Perhaps Shining Stone had been named for its prisms, one per citizen, hung in each person's bedroom window. Elunn's prism had accompanied her to boarding school and now had come home for this memorial summer between Roedean and the American university she planned to enter in September. Elunn looped its string around its accustomed hook. And the returned prism served as a signal. Over the next two days, people called to welcome the Mayoress's granddaughter back and congratulate her on her university admission, her stunning scores. Their next-door neighbor Eveide appeared with her infant girl, bringing homemade chocolate truffles, each crowned with a candied violet, for Elunn. A welcome-home present. Elunn was touched that someone contending with first-motherhood would have time, or take time, to make her a gift.

Eveide was twenty-eight to Elunn's sixteen, but both had a tacit status as Shining Stone's youngsters, due recipients of guidance and support. The news of Eveide's expectations, in one of Kachia's emails, had surprised Elunn. By Shining Stone's standards, Eveide had taken a husband and had a first child shockingly early. The townspeople had acted as if she'd been twelve.

Elunn was surprised to see such a young infant, and its mother up and about. "I never can tell with babies, but she looks really new," Elunn ventured, touching lightly the floss on the baby's pulsing little head.

"Last week," said Eveide. "June 15. Kachia and Marim helped me." No residual shudder, no "Between the two of us, it hurt like hell," nothing of the kind. Just brimming pride, bright and bubbly as running water; Eveide couldn't seem to stop smiling. "We're having her naming Saturday, I'm so glad you're back with us for it. Her name's going to be Hulimay."

"Why not *Katherine*?" Elunn thought. "Or *Jessica*, or *Danielle*?" Some minor surgery to her own weird name was almost the first thing she'd done after arriving at boarding school: *Hallo, I'm Ellen.* And *Hulimay* was harder to work with.

Out of nowhere, Eveide looked at Elunn with compassion and said, "You feel stunned, don't you, being back? It's like getting warm after you've been terribly cold. When I had to go away to school, the prefect told us that we'd get over being homesick, but I didn't. I got there and I hated the place, everything about it. And the last night I spent there, I remember staring up at the ceiling and thinking how I still hated it. I felt terribly punished, I haven't yet figured out what for. There was no use in me going." Eveide shrugged. "Let's face it, I'm not academic like you. I don't have those interests, and being exiled to that place didn't make me develop any. When I got home to stay, I felt positively numb the first few days after three years of trying not to feel and look as unhappy as I was there. It's so deadly to look unhappy at school. People try to make you unhappier if they can."

"I certainly do feel ready for something else," Elunn admitted. "How's Kevin?" she asked next, meaning Eveide's young husband.

Eveide shrugged and said, "Oh, he's gone," as if Kevin's well-being was irrelevant. Marim shot Elunn a warning glance, so Elunn dropped the subject and did not say anything about Hulimay's exclusive resemblance to Eveide; the baby's looks gave no indication that red-haired Kevin might have fathered her. And Marim flashed Elunn another warning look when Elunn was midstream in an innocent conversation with their scholarly other-side neighbor, Larnavint, about her studies.

"I had four years of French and German," Elunn was saying, "and a survey course on languages in my last year. I wanted to learn the source of our names here, and I didn't get far. Except to be sure that they aren't Welsh, or Manx, or Cornish, or Brythonic, or Goidelic, or Norse." As if the girl had been saying something suggestive or improper, Marim even shook her head slightly: *No!* Elunn fell silent.

Larnavint's glance was tolerant, though. He said, "I expect that before you go to America, Kachia will instruct you about names and similar details." There was a longish silence. Uncomfortable about saying the wrong thing and not knowing what that might be, Elunn felt chilled with the visitors and waxed monosyllabic, which Kachia didn't fail to notice aloud once the company had gone home: "Cat got your tongue? You starting to feel shy with your own?"

"No, Ma's giving me dirty looks when I ask questions."

"So don't ask them over tea with the neighbors."

Irritated by now, Elunn asked her, "How should I ask them?" Being away from Shining Stone had pointed up for her its lodes of weirdness, like caches of cigarettes or drugs hidden around a house by someone who was supposed to quit those things. Hidden in plain sight, where you'd find them if you were looking for stamps or sugar.

Kachia gave Elunn her complete attention for a moment. "How about doing what they were supposed to be teaching you at that fancy school, thinking out your questions exactly? Then write them down, and when you think you've got them as clear as you can get them, bring them to your old Gran." Then, quite kindly: "Gran's not barmy, sweet pie, I was just tickled by that foolish film and its foolish elves. I've been giggling under my breath at all three of those films ever since they came out. For sensible questions, I give sensible answers. Make a list."

That did not take long.

*

One wasn't really a question: *I was supposed to get used to boarding school and stop being homesick, but I didn't. There wasn't a day I didn't want to be back in Shining Stone.*

Two *Why did you and Ma exile me? Why couldn't I have been a day pupil at Bradleigh Hall?*

Three wasn't a question either. *People live to a very great age in Shining Stone.*

Four *Why don't we have more children? It's very weird to grow up as the only kid in your town, even if it's a little town like Shining Stone. And I've been the youngest in town, and the next baby, Evie's little Hallo-I'm-May, comes along nearly seventeen years after me.*

Five *Why do we have our children so late? And take so long to look old?* Kachia had produced Marim at an age when most women are well into menopause, and Marim had birthed Elunn likewise. And while age had had its way with Kachia, Marim could pass for thirty any day.

Six *Why do most people's husbands take off, and the women don't seem upset about it?* Elunn's father had not stayed with Marim even until Elunn was born, a scenario which seemed to happen often—no, let's be exact, nearly every single time a woman took a husband in Shining Stone. Unlike the women in the outer world, the Shining Stone women never blamed the departed men; if they missed their absent husbands, they did a splendid job of concealing their emotions. Elunn could not remember a wedding ceremony in the village, or any whisper of the bitter dance of divorce. The men just left.

Marim had always been talented at not talking about anything she didn't want to discuss; to Elunn's questions about her father, Marim would just say, "He didn't stay here. Men don't really like being married, it's their psychology. And I'd have hated to hold him prisoner when he really wanted to go." But what possible reason was there to want to go? When Elunn asked Kachia about her departed dad, Kachia would say nothing about where he'd come from or why he'd left, just smile reminiscently and give one of her livestock responses: "He was a looker, that one, a true flaxen Saxon. Just like you, girl."

Seven *Why do we all have prisms, and what makes the prisms different from ordinary prisms? I know they are.*

Eight *Where do these names we carry come from?*

Seven and **Eight** had gone onto the list the evening after the village convened under the plane trees on its green common to name Eveide's newborn. The baby's long white dress, with Marim's handmade lace foaming from its hem and cuffs and collar, was the sole particular in which this celebration resembled a christening. According to the custom in Shining Stone, functional baby gifts—nappies and sleepsuits, socks and bibs and bedding—had been given before the child was born. The gifts that appeared at the naming festival were gifts dedicated to pleasure, to beauty, to the future. All of Shining Stone—a hundred and thirty-six souls, each bearing a name borne by no one else in England—convened to name Hulimay. The townspeople brought dresses with lace and tatting, playthings of every description, books, and contributions to a feast eaten on the new-mown grass. They brought cakes and sweets made by hand for the start of a sweet life, and together they enjoyed these sweets, and prawns and lobster salad and tart tender greens and watercress sandwiches, and the flavorful Shining Stone strawberries that Elunn had craved at Roedean. They toasted Eveide and her newborn in the best champagnes, both sweet and dry. The town's string quartet serenaded the company. After the meal, ancient Kachia had taken a prism out of a stone casket that looked older than sin, making Elunn wonder if prisms went into that box when their people died, to be rededicated to the occasional new citizen. Kachia made the ceremonial presentation of the jewel—"to Hulimay, daughter of Eveide, daughter of Nassivra, daughter of Gaverille, this stone that was Gaverille's in life—now yours, Hulimay of Shining Stone." Then Kachia, Larnavint, and a couple of the other elders filled a basket with food and wine and borrowed the baby. Kachia carried the infant and Larnavint the food basket; the elders proceeded to The Croft.

The Croft, a walled and thatched manse that was supposed to be eight centuries old, was the residence of the town's oldest citizens. There Shining Stone's young people, even the baby's mother on this ceremonial occasion, were not allowed to go. The aged Mayoress and her retinue went behind The Croft's wisteria-grown walls and presented the town's newest citizen to the town's oldest citizens and left them their feast. Elunn had never really thought before about those people older than Kachia, living their customary hermetic lives. The house was set far back within its garden walls so she couldn't see through the windows and into the rooms, but in the three upper casements, prisms glittered in the westering sun.

Apparently the powers-that-were in Shining Stone did not subscribe to the popular idea that Winter enjoyed the company of Spring, as in the outer world. Elunn's school had had a community service requirement, which she'd fulfilled by visiting the people in a nearby eldercare home. She usually read to them; there'd been a little fracas involving a gent almost as old and sharp as Kachia. His eyes had roved relishingly over Elunn's school-uniformed body, and he'd wanted her to read from a rather racy volume called *Young Lady Chatterley*. The school program coordinator had called a halt to that and substituted a volume by Hilary Mantel. "Take that shite away!" said the pensioner after a few pages. "It's a farking yawner!" Elunn wondered if the Shining Stone elders were allowed to enjoy the porn of their choice.

And after the naming party, under a chill sky of twilight, Elunn watched the townspeople disperse and retold herself all their names, their alien names. The church bells dimly chimed in Durberville, two towns over.

Nine *Why aren't we Christian? I found out at school that most Brits are some kind of Christian. And here we're not. Not just not Christian, but far from Christianity, any kind. We call the Christ "the Christians' dying-god" much as you might say "the Hindus' suttee.*

*

"You haven't asked the real question, the shore I push off from to answer the rest," said the Mayoress, once presented with the list on the first evening of July. As the girl didn't say anything, just hunkered down by Kachia's chair with the usual docile, dogged look on her fair face, the old woman continued: "The important question, girl, is *Where?* Where do we come from?"

"All right, Gran, where do we come from?"

Kachia looked out the window and up, into the twilight just pierced by the silverpoints of that night's first stars. "What d'you see?"

"Stars. They don't just look like burning balls of gas," Elunn faltered.

"Like what, then?"

"Like doors, like windows. Portals to somewhere else." Where?

"There," said Kachia, pointing.

*

Shining Stone, said Kachia, had been an inhabited place for thirty thousand years. Their people journeyed here from a dying star and purchased their place in the midst of the natives here with other shining stones, and with knowledge. Those natives they'd tamed first were Saxons. "Well, pre-Saxons. They were of the stock that became Saxon in time."

"Saxons settled around Oxfordshire," Elunn argued. "So what were Saxons doing in the far north, near the Scotch border?"

"We preferred it here," Kachia forged on. "We picked the best of them, the strongest and soundest, and we moved them here. Some remoteness was to our advantage. We settled them here and taught them about iron, about fire," she told Elunn. "About using fire to make glass, and glass to make fire. Then about metals and machines, about reading and writing. And germ-killing medicines from molds and cancer-killing medicines from flowers and tree bark. Their science has begun to catch up with that we brought, of course. Oh, yes, when we found them, they were filthy and lousy and undergrown, but we could appreciate their potential. They were fine breeding stock, with a compatible genome and a pleasing phenotype. Give them a good diet, all the proper amino acids, and their comeliness made itself apparent. We domesticated them, healed them, and instructed them. Like Tolkien's Eldar schooling the long-lived humans of Numenor. Now that's on target. An imagined legend about a true thing. Our first humans called us *alfyr.* And we let them call us that, and you know the word's been corrupted to mean these pointy-eared, tree-hugging New Age cultists in those Tolkien films." To Elunn's quick question: "Yes, we married some of our pre-Saxon tribe's men. Males are few among us, and our men have never survived here as long as the women. Not as strong."

"And those Saxons accepted, well, *space aliens* among them?"

"That would have been the dicey part, only we have some shape-changing ability, and we learned to assume the fair shape they should have had, the beauty that was in their genes and would have shone in all of them but for their filth and worms and barley-porridge diet. They accepted us once we assumed their form and semblance, and we made them strong as they could not make themselves. We'd known their genes were serviceable, too, but it was even better than we'd projected: We learned that the children of marriages between ourselves and the locals were entirely our own on the inside, but inherited the gift of assuming the human form from birth. So we kept it up, we married the humans and bred from them. They didn't become us, but we became them. At least as much as we needed to be."

"Gran, I don't believe that," said Elunn, though it made her teeth chatter and her new-tanned skin crawl.

Kachia regarded her grandchild with annoyance. She must've been anticipating this conversation, Elunn thought. Maybe dreading it if it didn't go well. That aggravation certainly sharpened Kachia's edge and made her forthcoming in a way ordinary bothers did not.

"You're not so tractable as you look, are you? Underneath that docile expression there's something else, isn't there? Well, I don't give two straws what you believe. The truth is the truth. And you're less than I've hoped if you push truth away like bad potatoes. As to why you missed Shining Stone, that's because your species, your family, is here. Part of why we send our children away for a few years is to show them loneliness, to make their love for this place heart-deep. So that they can go away again, but they'll always come back. We live a long time, and there's a long span of our lives in which we can have children. As to why the men leave, they leave when we're through with them. As to why they don't give trouble about it, it's because people in this area know who we are and what we give. They consider it well worth their while to serve us. In all the ways we need to be served."

"So what do we give?" Elunn asked, though her mind's eye knew the answer, or part of it. That inner vision encompassed the ancient but immaculately maintained buildings of Shining Stone, the civic order, the absence of crime, the health and good looks and staggering longevity of the townspeople. Also the differences between the people in Shining Stone and those in the nearby villages of Bradleigh, Wendover, and Durberville… and the differences between the residents of those villages and people in the natural, outer world. Elunn hadn't known until she traveled into that outer world and returned, but there seemed to be a sacred circle drawn around Shining Stone and its satellite villages of pampered vassal humans. The vassal villages had experienced time without many of its scars, the ravaging gouges of history.

"What do we give? Well, here are just two things we've given," Kachia said, with an emphasis that wasn't anger, exactly… just absolute seriousness. "Two of many. The rat-plague that killed off half England in 1348 never came here. And the Inquisition tried to come here, but came to grief on the way… time after time, Bloody Mary's inquisitors lost their way and fell into that bog outside Talton. That bog is full of inquisitors' bones. During times of threat, it might have seemed that Shining Stone and our humans' towns disappeared from the maps and paths of the known world and from memory, and so did that circle around us. Science... magic. Call it either one you like. Some of the villages' men have experienced a singular honor, and none of them have been bled on the altar of war. Where else in England has every single sound man born since Stonehenge lived to be old? The upshot is, the humans have benefited from us, and we've benefited from them. Their bloodline is uninterrupted and pure. And when Eveide was ready to conceive, she had the pick of our villages, and she chose young Kevin. He knew that he would spend a season with the most beautiful woman who'll strip off for him in this life. He knew he'd stay with her until she conceived and then go back home. There was no nonsense about marriage and lingering. For that we didn't need him."

Elunn felt trite and childish, cringing at hearing Kachia go on about stripping off, but she cringed anyway. The whole business sounded more like racehorses and stud service than romance in novels, even the unhappy ones like *Wuthering Heights*. "Gran, that's horrid."

"Girl, that's history." Kachia pointed again, at the glinting jewel in her window. "The prisms are different because they came with us... from there. They aren't glass or even diamond. They're harder than diamond, they're made of a metal that doesn't occur on Earth, and that conducts light and energy. And plays a special little head trick, too. Looking at your prism makes you happy, doesn't it? Lifts your mood if you're sad or tired? So you don't have to go out like your schoolmates at Roedean and get Prozac or buy something illegal?"

This was true, though Elunn hated to admit it. Those faceted refractions through sunlight or tears might not have fixed anything that made her cry, but somehow looking at their shifting tints had comforted her, left her calmed and warmed.

"*Alfyr* is the name our humans gave us," reiterated Kachia. "We're their elves. As to our names that seem to come from no known language, they don't come from any language known here. And I hope I've already covered why we're not Christians."

Because, thought Elunn, some of us already think we're gods.

*

When Elunn went to her mother about getting Gran "help," Marim was livid. "I'm not listening to such rot. I'm not going to argue with you. And I'd better not hear of you discussing those matters with outsiders, or with anyone here until you get your mind right."

Elunn sulked, affronted at Marim's stern tone and Marim's dismissal of what was probably Alzheimer's disease or worse. That river was called De Nial, as Elunn had learned in her advanced psychology course. Elunn took her prism down and lounged on her bed, tilting and shifting the jewel in the sun.

She woke up the next day, feverish to repack her suitcases and go—where? Back to the school that she hated, to beg the dorm mistress to let her stay the summer and earn her keep with work, saying that at home she was in danger because—why? Her mother and grandmother claimed to be space aliens, and had as good as told her that she was one too? Elunn stayed in Shining Stone, though. Had she not been gasping for its air these three years past? And, however mad Kachia and Marim might be, most likely they'd always been that way, yet never had they offered her anything resembling harm. So Elunn settled in, pretended with all her strength that that conversation hadn't occurred, and tried to unremember it.

"I'm not doing anything wrong," she told herself. "I'm just doing what they taught me in Philosophy & Logic. I'm looking actively... critically... at everything I've always accepted." In this spirit, she investigated Shining Stone's solar electric utility, which occupied the southern slope of the town's highest hill and was by no means a huge, sprawling, and awkward apparatus like the cutting-edge home solar electric systems she'd seen. Their neighbors often sued the people who installed these eco-friendly monstrosities because they were so big and ugly, and bits of them flew off during windstorms and went crashing into the neighbors' landscaping. The fence around Shining Stone's solar-generator system was gated but not locked; anyone could go in and look at it. Though it powered four little towns, it filled a plot only as large as an ordinary kitchen garden. It was constructed of... prisms. Made, presumably, of metal as transparent as glass. Pretty, like some interactive sculptural installation. Watching them turn and throw their brilliant dapples on her white clothing, Elunn made another connection: lack of dirt. She pictured the grime on ceilings and walls that had shocked her when she visited her schoolmates, even the wealthy ones with stately homes. That was carbon, the uncleanable dreck from centuries of peat and wood and coal fires. Seven-hundred-year-old plaster in Shining Stone was as clean as the gleaming white shelves of the Wendover Tesco. As if, for ages here, they'd flicked a switch and strong, clean heat and light came on, and their taps gushed hot pure water to wash both themselves and anything else that got dirty.

Elunn investigated further by cycling into the satellite villages of Wendover, Bradleigh, and Durberville. From the age of nine forward, she'd been allowed to go on her own to all three places. They were not great distances—four miles, two miles, six. But the roads went through sparsely settled, hilly country. She had always accepted that she could make these journeys and no one would abduct her, molest her, or even step out from a thicket and open his coat to flash his naked parts. She'd accepted that safety so well that she'd never even thought of it... until she spent weekends with schoolmates whose mothers insisted on driving them any little distance and were horrified that Elunn's mother let her cycle all around Shining Stone.

In Bradleigh she met up with Kevin, who was back working at the computer store there. She fiddled with the optical mice, and when Kevin asked if he could help her, she shrugged and chatted. "Your daughter's gorgeous," she said. "She's doing well."

"Uh, good," Kevin faltered, as if he shouldn't be discussing such a matter.

"Eveide's fine too." Elunn watched Kevin turn violently red.

In the villages, Elunn lingered and shopped. She bought paperbacks or jerseys or pastries, or toys for the flourishing Hulimay. She ordered ice cream in warm weather, tea on cool days, and watched the other customers as if they were another species. She didn't like to think about it, but she began to see how they were different. On her own, she was still the recipient of elaborate courtesy and assiduous service. As a little girl, coming here with Kachia, she'd thought people in the shops rushed to serve them due to Kachia's status as Mayoress of Shining Stone. In the shops, trolling for necessary knowledge, Elunn spent money on unnecessary things.

She didn't need to buy groceries or other basics for her household because someone from the villages drove up and collected the order Monday morning, then delivered the shopping from Tesco or Sainsbury Monday afternoon—an arrangement Elunn had never questioned until after boarding school. She'd never seen money change hands in this transaction as a child, and after watching it every Monday that summer, she knew that money never did change hands. The grocery-fetching was but one human homage to the alfyr.

In questions and observation, Elunn passed the summer between childhood and university until time came to pack for her flight to the States. All the idle summer shopping had produced an excess of possessions, and Elunn was struggling with her jumpers, cramming them into those vacuum bags that roll up and extrude air through one-way valves and flatten the clothes to about a fifth of their original volume, in hopes of getting them all into her wheeled Pullman case.

"Gran, I'd really like to stay away from that, if you don't mind," was what she said when Kachia crabbed her way up the stairs and opened her door, then the subject that had stayed closed all July, all August, and these first twenty days of September. The term at Harvard did not begin until September 24.

Kachia eased herself down on Elunn's chaste bed. "We botched it, your mama and your old Gran. Abrasive, both of us. The way we told you, we managed to set you against the truth and yourself."

Elunn's throat felt tight. "If you don't mind, Gran, my cup of stress is full right now. If you start up again with that, I won't listen."

"You don't have to listen long. Just three minutes. Your schoolmistresses probably told you how not to fall pregnant, didn't they? That's part of the curriculum these days even in England, not falling pregnant?"

"Yes, we had a unit called 'Families and Society.' It covered that." The unit had not covered why anyone would want to do the thing that got people pregnant. To Elunn, it sounded as nasty and a great deal riskier than drinking a glassful of Talton Bog water, green with slime and dissolved inquisitors. She supposed she was backward to think of it this way; most of the girls at Roedean had wanted to do it, preferably with that actor who'd played Aragorn. Maybe her lack of lust was part of being a late bloomer, one of these ever-more-rare females who are just edging gently into puberty at fifteen. Elunn shuddered, remembering how she finally got the curse this past September, having pretended to have it at appropriate intervals ever since she got to boarding school.

Digging in to deliver the truth, Kachia elaborated. "You can discount whatever they said in this "unit." You don't need birth control pills or patches, so don't be putting useless chemicals into your body. In the pregnancy area, alfyr are both angel and animal. You won't fall pregnant unless you want to, that's the angel part, and you won't want to unless it's time, physiological time. That's the animal part. You'll feel that in your body. Your body will let you know if a male is right to do that duty by you."

"Like a cat going into heat?"

"Well, yes, a little like that."

Charming. "Any other great news, Gran?" Elunn asked, going down on her knees on the vacuum bag. *S...s...s...s* went the air going out of it, smelling of sizing and lanolin. She supposed she must have an insolent look on her face, sound insolent, or both. Certainly Kachia's expression was of forbearance, grudging, for insolence or worse.

"This is important, girl, and I don't say ***drop that tone*** as I would about something not so important. So be as sarcastic and ironic as you want, but listen. When you fall pregnant, the pregnancy will take a full Earth year, not nine months. When you know you're pregnant, it's best you come back here. Marim and I will look after you when it's your time. You won't be sick, you'll have no use for human doctors, and you must, absolutely must, stay away from them." She pointed to the sky beyond the window. "When your child is born, it'll look like we looked when we lived there."

"And I guess that was different from how we look here and now?"

"Your eyes think they're human, and you'll shriek... you'll want to do it in when you see what you've birthed. But you have to fight that urge down. Remember you were the same once, and the same thing happened with you that'll happen with your newborn. You'll need to hold that child to your human-looking skin, and its skin will learn to be the same. It'll change. It'll achieve... what's the science word for changing to look like something else?"

"Mimesis," Elunn managed. "This is all very sci-fi, Gran." Get some humor into this muddle, might as well. "Yet another way Professor Tolkien got it wrong?"

"Only this isn't fiction, and you need to take this seriously, so that when that time comes, you're with those who understand. I'd been told, but when I got my first look at Marim, it was like... a baby-sized cockroach, and I responded just like that was what had just come out of me, my familiar body. I wanted to catch it by the feet and slam its head into the floor. To kill it. My Gran caught my wrists and put the baby to my skin, and in a moment there she was, my Marim we all know. I know from the look on your face that you're thinking you can't get away from this lunacy fast enough... but don't ignore any of this, sweet pie."

I'll ignore anydamnthing I please. Just see, thought Elunn, *how fast and how far and how long I can remove myself from this madness.*

*

It was true that you couldn't really appreciate a place until you'd left it and known others, known them well. Elunn learned that way about Shining Stone and its cult of itself. Later, Germany drew Elunn in because so many Germans, like her townspeople, also believed that something better than blood flowed through their veins with the cholesterol. Studying in America, then in Germany, she learned about human languages and human history and how the iron of violence had enriched almost every inch of soil through human blood, unlike in Shining Stone and its vassalages. She studied the music of many nations and surmised that the tunes played on the village green in Shining Stone also came from *there.*

Growing up in Shining Stone, you thought it was 90% like other places; living somewhere else, you realized that Shining Stone was actually 90% different, but for the most part in ways so evanescent or so natural that it was hard to describe them.

The part about heat was true.

Elunn was living in Berlin and teaching linguistics at a German university when she first saw Klaus, the actor. Having written a book, Klaus was doing a book tour and signing copies. He was known as a lustful man, one who seduced many women—though, from his style of achieving this goal, *seduce* might not have been the right word. Klaus's hand brushed Elunn's as he signed her book, and his ultramarine eyes roved speculatively over her. Mimesis was her body's natural talent; among Saxons, she had appeared the healthiest, the prettiest, the most glowingly fit representative of their type. Over twenty years among the Germans, she'd changed slowly and subtly until her classic blonde Saxon looks had become classic blonde German. Heftier than she'd been as a girl, she was athletically lithe as so many German women were, whether or not they actually played sports, and her features were a tad softer and more feminine. Almost unbelievable that a body could change to make itself appeal to the eyes of those surrounding it and inspire them to offer the person in that body resources, friendship, sex, love, or whatever they had. Klaus was no exception.

The actor felt up this archetype of Aryan womanhood with his eyes. His expression was much the same as it would have been if they'd been alone, as if he were already groping her under her clothes, his small, crude, expert hands working the nerves in her skin. Elunn felt something between her hipbones open like a mouth and throb like famine. At first, she thought this might be because the man was so weirdly beautiful with his aquiline profile, his hard cruel white teeth, and the shining gold of his long hair. A Norse god, she thought. Loki. Wickedness and flame.

I'm Ellen, she was about to say, but decided to leave that part out. "I could meet you somewhere afterward," her mouth said, without her permission. Her eyes sampled his levelly, brazenly.

Klaus smiled, nodded, and scrawled something filthy, something no decent man would have written or said or thought, on the flyleaf of her book. *It doesn't matter,* her mind said to her, before she could feel horror at it. And she could believe that her body had somehow identified his as a good match, a favorable and harmonious genome. His character had nothing to do with that. She read his filthy scrawl.

His expression said he'd hoped to shock her. It was somewhere right between leer and sneer. She met his gaze levelly and said, "I'll hold you to that." She saw that she'd shocked him, which was the nearest he probably ever came to respecting anyone.

A frantic new heart beat in her pelvis throughout the time she waited for the book-signing to be over. The actor, resplendent in his white linen suit and tan, bared his teeth in smile after smile, to woman after woman. Elunn waited them out. Klaus took her back to his suite in the Vier Jahrezeiten and broke into her, made her scream. Though not with pain.

Klaus was fifty or more, and she had to talk filth to him to keep him going as long as she needed him, she had to let him dig his teeth into her shoulder and use his hands painfully upon her. Finally he had given all he had to give and she could let him fall heavily asleep, still half on and half in her. He was ideal in more ways than one, she thought; he was a perfect fit. Hundreds of women had thought so, too, *though not in quite the same way I did,* she mused. And he would forget her.

*

To her friends and colleagues in Berlin, Elunn pretended to be visiting the prenatal clinic throughout those months they watched her grow blooming and huge. To anyone who asked her how far along she was, she underrepresented by three months. Since she did not put on much weight or change conspicuously in girth for the first five or six months, no one questioned the count. In her leisure, she watched Klaus's movies. Having avoided sonograms as well as other prenatal attentions, Elunn didn't know the sex of her child. He or she would be beautiful, though, and not knowing the sex created latitude for fantasies about this passenger she carried, the grown child who'd eventually be her friend—her eagle-browed, ferally handsome son? Her lush lavender-eyed daughter?

She had not announced her expectations to those in Shining Stone. What she wanted or intended to do about that, she didn't know. Her pregnancy, begun in January, went smoothly through mid-December, when she happened to board an S-Bahn trolley that derailed. The lurch pitched her hard onto her hands and knees. Her condition prompted strangers to help her up and offer to take her to a clinic, but she slipped from their kind hands and took the next trolley back to the flat where she'd lived the past five years. Nothing seemed to be wrong—only the beginnings of bruises on the knees banged on the tram floor. She had started a film and settled in with cushions at her back, eating ham and smoked Gouda and black bread with cherry cider. That had been her favored combination for the duration of the pregnancy, which had made her whimsical about food, though never nauseated. Nor was she nauseated then, eating and watching Klaus in the green, germy surf of an African ocean. But while straining over her domed belly to rub her bruises, she had a pain in the small of her back, definitive and somehow clean. It felt as if something had ripped and peeled. And a spill and spatter of brilliant blood confirmed this notion.

Weary, her first emotion was annoyance: "Oh, not now!" Then: "How Victorian, how trite. A fall. A miscarriage!"

That thought got her up to call a taxi and look up the address of a nearby hospital. There she gave a false name and told them it wasn't time, that she had two weeks to a month to go. They put her in a dim, warm room, propped her feet up, and ran an IV into her arm. She received that extra solicitude that Germans give, in spite of themselves, to extra-beautiful Germans, or people who pass as such. The large, warm-handed nurse stroked Elunn's hair off her brow, unbraided it, and put a minty compress on the young woman's head. Elunn wondered what Marim would do if she were here. She thought she'd rather have Gran, who was steadier.

"First child?" asked the nurse, smiling. "You're doing very well, don't you worry. This'll take a while to hit its stride. Sleep if you can, rest up for the real work." She gave Elunn a shot of a narcotic and something that stopped the bleeding. When things had calmed down, they sent the sonographer in. Without the narcotic dragging her under, Elunn might have refused the sonogram, but she barely roused at the cool gel on her belly. About forty minutes later, someone pulled the curtain around her bed, and she heard hushed voices in the hall. Some part of her brain came wide awake to perceive the emotions behind those voices: shock, worry, consternation. She couldn't hear the words, but the affect was plain enough. Turn it up one more notch, and it would be horror. Patently something had spooked them—the sonogram, or something in that vial of blood they'd coaxed from her forearm.

A very gentle doctor came in and asked her if there was any history of genetic disease in her family. Elunn told him she didn't know. When he left, she forced herself to sit up, think past the blur of the drug, pluck the IV from her arm, and find her clothes. Feeling that she mustn't leave any part of herself behind, she stuffed her bloodied tights into her coat pocket. As if she were leaving the obstetrics wing after visiting a friend, not escaping doctors who thought she bore some mutant in her belly, she made herself walk straight, undrunkenly, to the visitors' elevator. In thirty minutes, she'd managed to get a taxi back to her flat and was easing out of her coat on the sofa she'd bled all over, which wasn't even dry. *So I go it alone,* she thought. At least she could relax her face and stop trying to look not-in-pain.

She called her family's number in Shining Stone for the first time in many months and got Marim, then Kachia, on the phone. Actually, Kachia had taken the mobile from Marim and appraised the situation after very few words.

"It may wait, but it may happen before I can get there, girl. You may have to go it alone, but it'll be all right, I promise. The main thing is, you mustn't hurt it. You have to hold it, and you have to look at it. Then you can look away, the rest'll happen. You just have to resist the impulse to hurt it, do you understand your old Gran?"

Gasping, Elunn said she did.

"I'm coming, girl," said Kachia. She must have said something else before she rang off, but that was what Elunn remembered. Elunn got through the next few hours by visualizing Kachia on a plane, a direct flight. Her mind distracted itself with the idea of flights. Edinburgh, just over the Scotch border, was the airport nearest to Shining Stone. Edinburgh-Tegel would be the fastest. The painkiller wore off. Soon enough, she had all she could do not to groan or yell and rouse her neighbors. A medicine cabinet belonging to someone with a human body might have held something that would help, even just a little—stale codeine left over after dentistry, muscle relaxants or tranquilizers. Hers held a tube of toothpaste and stick of sunblock. And Klaus's child had sharp edges that gouged her; she shivered and bled. She slid into a delirious dream of childbirth among veiled nurses whose hands were mere bones covered with a thin, dry, metal-black integument. The light in the dream was orange; it was horrible, it was wrong, the light. A sun set in the east, but the parched heat lingered in the darkened desert air. Her mouth was a dry gulch after years without rain. In the dream, they made her walk and did not let her lie down, and she found that pushing was a little easier when she sat up on the edge of the bloodied sofa. *Gravity,* she thought, and as if obedient to the suggestion, Klaus's child and hers slipped out with a final gouge and a splash of fluid. She caught it by the legs. *Stick insect* was what she thought, *not a baby,* and all the wrong angles. It was in her mind to fling the thing from her, to hit its head on something hard. Blood loss was the kid's salvation, for Elunn fainted and slid down on the creamy carpet, and her arm fell over the little alien body. Being horizontal brought her around in short order. As her eyes blinked open, through the screen of her golden lashes, she was able to witness the change.

Mimesis!

Alfyr.

*

It seemed to take them a very long time to come. Stunned and shaky, needing liquid and sugar, Elunn managed to get up and drag a jug of cherry cider back to bed with her. She wrapped the baby in a fleece throw and cranked the heat up and got her shivering self into bed. She tried to get the baby, who was a boy, to suck. Less tired, she might have wept from the frantic sense of severance she had, having proved with her body the truth she'd thrust back when it came in mere words. Alfyr in the midst of another species, she was lonelier than any Englishwoman could be in a city and country of Germans. Less tired, she might have worried about the hospital people finding her, but her German was perfect and she'd given them a credible name—Dagmar Herzog—and a credible address, just not this one. So she was undisturbed in her long drained sleep, and the lashing sleet woke her as the December dawn blued her windows. And the door she'd failed to lock opened, and Marim and Kachia, who'd never been in this apartment, found their way to her bed.

"Now, I'd say that's a very fine child," said Kachia. "Let's see her."

"He's a boy," Elunn managed. She hadn't put clothes on him, just a nappie improvised from paper towels, and this made her ashamed. She sat herself up, though, and unwrapped him. Her mother and grandmother fingered his cushiony arms and legs, stroked his brow to make him open his eyes. He was all that came to mind at the phrase ***beautiful baby.*** His unfocused eyes were slate-blue.

"So he is. Down the road a bit, someone can have a husband who stays in Shining Stone," said Marim. "Men born of our women don't leave, you know. Some lucky woman can have a husband who's truly one of us. Like Larnavint. He's an alfyr-born male."

"I didn't know. I left before you could tell me that," said Elunn. "I didn't believe you." No need to say *Now I do.*

The two of them got busy with her at that point: helped her bathe, gave her some powerful, pleasurable, head-dizzying painkiller they'd brought for her. It made her drunk and complacent while they proceeded with some midwifery activities which otherwise would have hurt plenty, since they involved sutures and surgical needles. Her fall had made the birth too-fast and traumatic; they sewed her damage up. Then they got fresh clothes for her, cleaned up, burned the ruined sofa cushions, set the bloodied clothes and sheets and towels sloshing in the washer, and made dinner, which she wanted by then. At that point, Elunn noted the thin knit scarf around Kachia's throat and swathed around her face from the cheekbones down. Too chilly in here for her, perhaps. Other things had taken up Elunn's attention until then, when she noticed that Gran seemed reluctant to unswath, even to eat lunch.

"Gran, are you cold? The heat dial's right over there. You don't have to huddle in your wraps in here."

"It's not that," Marim cut in. "And we weren't as fast as we'd have liked, see, because Gran can't travel by plane. We drove and took the Chunnel. Then overland."

"Through France? But why not by plane?" The drive couldn't have been pleasant, not this time of year, in this kind of weather. Rough on Gran, though she still seemed tough as a bag of rocks. Rougher on Elunn, going it alone! "There are plenty of cheap flights."

"You've seen it by now," said Kachia, in perhaps the first diffident tone Elunn had ever heard from her. "The mimesis? Your boy there?"

"Yes, I saw. And it seems... well, the first change made him look like, well, a proper baby, and now he seems... he keeps looking more like me." He did. The enviable skin, the blonde Saxon hair with its blonder streaks. The July-in-England blue eyes.

"And before that started to happen, you probably wanted to throw him across the room, but we know you didn't. If you'd not held him to you, he'd still be the same little horror he was, coming out."

"It was like a stick insect," said Elunn, queasy. The thought made her throat tighten, and not with pity. Rather, with human revulsion as strong as an allergy. She remembered making a weak move to bash the creature's head in; she had meant to. If she'd had the strength, she'd have done it.

She started to shiver, and Marim tucked a throw around her shoulders. *Mother being motherly,* Elunn thought: the exception to the rule. "Like a praying mantis, only a praying mantis is, I don't know, droll, not frightening, and not the size of a baby," she continued, as if talking about what she'd seen might neutralize it. "And a praying mantis is a pretty leaf-green, and it, it was this... horrid... burnt color."

Kachia nodded. "Yes, and you can't help it, you say *it*. Well... there's that change, and there's another. Another non-Tolkien detail. When we're very old, we revert to type. I'm reverting. When Kevin delivers our groceries, he has to brace himself not to flinch at the sight of me. He's a good lad, he feels badly about it, but he can't help what his human eyes see. If I book a plane ticket and fly on a plane, I'll attract too much attention," said Kachia. "Though I suppose I could wear a burqah and claim to be a Muslim fundamentalist... then they might think I'm an Islamic terrorist, though. I don't know which would be worse."

"Well, you don't have to cover your face in here, with me," Elunn said.

"Don't want to give you a shock, girl. This chap already gave you a hard time."

Elunn looked hard at Gran. Above the scarf, the eyes seemed vast—cat eyes, lemur eyes, more lambent, more green. Kachia put her sere hand to her swathed jaw. "We shrink, rather," she said, rueful. "Our skin gets tighter and darker and closer to the bone. It and the bone finally become the same tissue. It's not a pathology, it doesn't hurt. It's just a shock to the human-adjusted eye."

"That's why the elders have their own house and people don't visit."

"Oh, people do, just not those who're so young they can't take it. When I get entirely grotesque, I'll move into The Croft, and you can visit me. That won't be for a while. And if I change under your eyes, you'll get used to me. I'll be ordinary to you." As allergic as ever to whining and repining, Kachia added: "They have everything in The Croft. Better computers than at Oxford. Gardens and a library and any new book or film they want, a heated pool, fish tanks and cats and... what d'you call them, one of those big daft yellow dogs that love everyone... a Labrador retriever. When their dog died, we went to replace him and got them a standard poodle first, but that dog was too bright, she was spooked of them and wouldn't let them touch her, we had to give her to someone in one of the villages and get the Lab. And our elders are the ultimate authority in Shining Stone, they can veto any decision of the Mayoress or the town council. Every week I go to The Croft with any orders I intend to give to someone else, and I have those orders ratified by the elders. They're the only ones I have to answer to."

"And how ancient they must be if you're not considered one of them," Elunn reflected. They must have some way of getting themselves out of the public records when they lived that long. Perhaps, when they went into seclusion, the undertaker in Durberville filed the death certificate. And the greatly-aged alfyr, dead to the official human world, lived on. It would have been a horrible thing if she'd kept to a birthday-present-and-greeting-card level of contact when Gran had to step aside, living, from the younger living ones. How vile it would have been to leave Gran unvisited behind those vine-draped walls.

"And you're, what? A hundred and twenty-four?" Elunn asked Kachia.

"Actually much older than that, sweet pie. And your Ma, she's older than you've been thinking too. We live long. You and this boy will see the waters rise on Earth, and the next ice age after that. And we two may see it with you. And this may be our planet after that. Or not. That'll be the litmus test for our human fosterlings. We'll find out how strong they are."

Elunn shut her eyes to absorb that idea. As she focused on it, she had a brief but very keen flash of inquisitors on horseback, dressed in robes the color of char. The fifteenth century, the days of Queen Mary Tudor's insanity, and these were Queen Mary's minions who tortured and burned people because of the way they interpreted the myth of the humans' dying-god. Talton was the borderland, the town on the road between the outer world and Durberville, Wendover, Bradleigh, and Shining Stone. Elunn saw the bog shimmer and take on the appearance of the sandy road. Then it reverted to green water and gulped the travelers down, men and horses alike. More men and horses came, and the bog ate them too. Winter ice or summer slime, it knew them and ate them. Their bones sunk into the silt beneath the green water, rich and foul with rotted encroachers. She saw the smokes of martyrdom rise in every town in England except Durberville, Wendover, Bradleigh, and Shining Stone. In those four places, the manias of princes, those of both church and state, counted for naught. In this little vision, Elunn did not see Kachia, but she had the clear sense that it was Kachia's mind, Kachia's science, drawing that circle of salvation around that small and removed part of the world. And perhaps this had been the young Kachia, goddess-magus to Wendover, Durberville, and Bradleigh as well as Mayoress of Shining Stone.

"Yes," Kachia answered the thought. "And your Germans, their Luftwaffe flew over us a thousand times and never saw us. But do you want to know the part that's really hard to accept? I don't mean this," she said, gesturing toward her swathed jaws. "I mean, we've always been few. We live long, but we don't increase, we just barely manage to replace ourselves. There's no place on this Earth that doesn't need the science and magecraft we have. But there are just enough of us to do what we do. To hold three villages in a motherly hand and turn aside harm from them. Like a good parent or a good god. To keep ourselves secret and our humans safe. That's as much as we can manage. I tell myself it's more than any creature who's ever called himself a god did here, though. And the leaving... maybe that's one Tolkien detail that's correct. Those Tolkien elves leaving for Aman, or Valinor, or whatever it's called. We don't get on a swan boat and sail over a sea of glass to some eternal resort town, but we leave... even if it's just half a block to The Croft, it's leaving. It's going apart. It's a sorrowful hill to climb, level ground or not."

"Gran," said Elunn, her throat aching with impermissible pity, and pulled the scarf down slowly, gently. "Come on, you've seen everything I've got to show, and darned me like a sock down there. Let's not have secrets." And Kachia let her pull the scarf down. Elunn could see, first with horror, the dark, thrawn look of the skin. Her child had come out all tearing angles, and the color of motor oil. Her grandmother's cheeks had darkened toward that color and somehow tightened, so you could all but see the outlines of her jaw hinge, her ancient teeth. Her neck seemed a mere notched stem.

Kachia's great eyes seemed to steel themselves against Elunn's horror. Elunn swallowed it back.

"Well, now you see. Not Galadriel, but Gollum," said Kachia, rueful. "Or maybe E. T. It's the neck that really gives me away. Hard to believe I used to look like you."

"Further back than I thought," Elunn reflected. "You're not so bad, maybe you just need Oil of Olay," she said. "Curél or something. You're still my Gran." She reached for one of the small leathery hands. "Space aliens," she said. "That was what I kept thinking when you first told me. I don't know why it didn't occur to me that... well, *they* weren't exactly the kind of human that they are now thirty thousand years ago. They were *homo sapiens*, but there's a lot of evolution between then and now. Practically all of the learning curve that made people civilized happened between then and now. And so, in a real way, we're almost as old on the planet as they are."

Kachia's sigh of relief seemed to involve her whole tough old body. She smiled and didn't draw the scarf over the smile. "Yes, that works for me. We're all fellow travelers. We just get born and die a bit differently," she concluded. Count on her to wrap even difficult ideas into neat, businesslike packages. And to look to the future. "Now we have to get you and your chap home. Not forever," Kachia added quickly. "Not unless you want. Only as long as you want. You can meet young Hulimay, she's back from university. She got a second. No surprise, her mother's always been a dreamy dunce, it's no shock that she's half one. They're both disappointed with her second, can you imagine the conceit? It's only because the girl's such a tearing beauty that the dons didn't turn her out with a third. She's a minx, that one. And of course we'll have to organize a naming ceremony, and you'll have to choose your chap a name." Pausing, Kachia swallowed hard. "I had a husband who was alfyr and stayed with me, but our men die before their wives. If you marry one, you get to keep the man and raise a child with a father, but then you have to survive and grieve him and learn to do without. My man's name was Claïs."

"Did you love him?"

"He was a sweet chap," sighed Kachia. "And a fine helpmate, and a looker too, before the change took hold of him. I see bits of him in you. He had a sensitive temperament, not like me, and I bruised it sometimes. Usually not meaning to. My mouth—I've never learned to control it. I doubt I ever will. And now you should get some rest while Marim and I pack the car."

Elunn did, and then stretched out on the cushions Marim had placed in the backseat. Warm under her feather quilts, baby breathing his feather breaths on her shoulder, she fell asleep in Prussia and woke up in Alsace-Lorraine as the stars rose in the blue evening. Kachia obviously appreciated the no-speed-limits aspect of the Autobahn: Once out of Berlin, the old lady had put pedal to metal in no equivocal fashion. By tea-time tomorrow, she'd have them home in Shining Stone.

"What does *Elunn* mean, Gran? And *Claïs*. You have to teach me this language, you know. And all the rest."

"You're awake! And that fast, back to asking your questions. There's no end of it, girl!"

"I teach linguistics, Gran. Or used to. That's what fascinates me. And our names are why it fascinates me, after all. That's where it began, me and languages. Our words. Our names."

Kachia's silence then was very long. Elunn heard Marim sigh.

"Gran?"

"I was just thinking." (Here a long exhale.) "That an estrangement longer than twenty years started when Marim and I stalled about answering your questions about names. Well, let me answer you properly now. In our old language, every adjective has a name form. *Kachia* is the name form of *kachæn*, which means *scientist*. Or *magus*, or *priestess*. The old tongue has no humanlike division of those roles. And Elunn... your name is a high compliment, sweet pie. *Elunn* means *prism*. It means *Shining Stone*. We gave you that name in, I don't know, gratitude... because we'd had no child in so long. You might have been the last, for all we knew, and I guess we thought to preserve at least our name in you if you were the last." Then, with that forefinger pointing beyond the window in the familiar way: "And *Claïs* is a name form that means *there*. It also means *eternity* and *home*. And every culture on this circling rock has a myth of heaven, so why shouldn't I have one for myself? I like to tell myself that when we finally die, we go back to our first home and find it and those we love in all their undecayed fineness. *There*."

"I think that *Claïs* would be a lovely name for your grandson," Elunn told Kachia, who nodded her swaddled head gruffly—too pleased, too touched to speak.

Head tilted back, looking up *there*, Elunn recalled words from an Easter sermon at school. Presumably they had to do with the humans' dying-god: *In my end is my beginning.* The being who began as a creature from *there*, some silverpoint beyond this world's windows, would end as one. Alfyr and omega.

Attributions

"Cottage Industry" appeared in *Mindscapes and Dreams, Gnu Journal,* Winter 2017 Issue

"Want" appeared in *Chelsea Station,* May 1016.

About the Author

Laura Argiri wrote *The God in Flight,* Random House 1995, published in paperback by Viking Penguin, May 1996, and in its second edition by Lethe Press in 2016. *The God* is about love, and *Guilty Parties* is about guilt, from the perspectives of perpetrators, their targets, and an occasional innocent witness or two. She does not encourage people to tell her the worst things they've ever done, but many do, as if they expected her to make use of them. And so she has.

CPSIA information can be obtained
at www.ICGtesting.com
Printed in the USA
BVHW030229181120
593615BV00008B/271

9 781590 217184